THE GREATEST WORKS OF

JOHN
MILTON

PARADISE LOST
PARADISE REGAINED

CLASSICS

Published 2024

FiNGERPRINT! CLASSICS
An imprint of Prakash Books India Pvt. Ltd

113/A, Darya Ganj,
New Delhi-110 002
Email: info@prakashbooks.com/sales@prakashbooks.com

 Fingerprint Publishing
 @FingerprintP
 @fingerprintpublishingbooks
www.fingerprintpublishing.com

This version was originally created in 1964-1965
by Dr. Joseph Raben

ISBN: 978 93 5856 501 0

"Say, heavenly Powers, where shall we find such love?
Which of you will be mortal, to redeem
Man's mortal crime, and just the unjust to save?
Dwells in all Heaven charity so dear?
He ask'd, but all the heavenly quire stood mute,
And silence was in Heaven: on Man's behalf
Patron or intercessour none appear'd . . ."

Born in London in 1608, John Milton was an English poet, polemicist, man of letters, and a civil servant for the Commonwealth of England under Oliver Cromwell. Educated under a strong Protestant influence, he attended Christ's College, Cambridge, with the intention of pursuing a career as a minister. His poems *L'Allegro* and *Il Penseroso* were produced during his college years. He spent time composing poetry after leaving Cambridge, changing his mind about his future. The dramatic verses of *Arcades* and *Comus* were written during this time.

In 1632, Milton received his MA and retired to Hammersmith, his father's new home. From 1635, he lived at Horton, Berkshire and undertook six years of self-directed private study. In preparation for a prospective poetical career, he read both ancient and modern works of theology, philosophy, history, politics, literature, and science. He had a command over Latin, Greek, Hebrew, French, Spanish, and Italian from his school and undergraduate days, in addition to his years of private study.

Milton wrote in the seventeenth century. It was the century of transition into our modern world, when the Civil Wars separated men from the older ways of living, and much that remained lively in the national imagination since the Middle Ages, was killed by the religious controversies.

His career spanned three distinct eras: Stuart England; the Civil War (1642–1648) and Interregnum, including the Commonwealth (1649–1653) and Protectorate (1654–1660); and the Restoration. His poetry was slow to see the light of day. *On Shakespeare* (1630), was his first published poem. It was anonymously included in the Second Folio edition of the works of William Shakespeare. His early work, written before the Civil Wars, was first collected in *1645 Poems*.

Milton is best known for his epic poem *Paradise Lost*, a magnum opus written in blank verse. It was composed by the blind and impoverished Milton from 1658 to 1664 with small but significant revisions published in 1674 (second edition). Milton is supposed to have dictated his verse to a series of aides in his employ. It has been argued that the poem reflects his personal despair at the failure of the Revolution, yet affirms an ultimate optimism in human potential. Milton sold the publication rights of *Paradise Lost* in 1667 to the publisher Samuel Simmons.

A great stylist and an experimentalist, Milton employed a language in this poem which is remarkable for sustained dignity. He created a special and elaborate type of language for his poetry called the 'grand style.' He also created diction appropriate for his theme. Milton did not use simple and everyday language, even for describing simple and natural objects. He revived the Elizabethan values as a traditionalist. The par excellence poet of the academic world, his verses flowed melodiously, and its classical allusions never failed to delight its readers. Matthew Arnold, the nineteenth-century English poet, praised Milton for his lofty, neoclassical style. Milton banished, from his own and from much of the most admired English poetry after his time, the natural rhythm of common speech.

Paradise Regained followed *Paradise Lost*. It was published alongside the tragedy, *Samson Agonistes*. Milton saw life as a struggle, the Puritan struggle, for the survival of the good and the virtuous. So in *Paradise Lost* Adam and Eve were told to contend; Christ struggles against Satan in *Paradise Regained*; and Samson struggles against false counsels in *Samson Agonistes*.

Milton died of kidney failure in 1674, aged sixty-five, in Bunhill, London, England. He was buried in the church of St. Giles Cripplegate, Fore Street, London. He achieved international renown within his lifetime. His celebrated *Areopagitica* (1644), written in condemnation of pre-publication censorship, is among history's most influential and impassioned defences of free speech and freedom of the press. Milton's poetry and prose reflect deep personal convictions, a passion for freedom and self-determination, and the urgent issues and political turbulence of his day.

THE VERSE

The measure is English heroic verse without rhyme, as that of Homer in Greek, and of Virgil in Latin; rhyme being no necessary adjunct or true ornament of poem or good verse, in longer works especially, but the invention of a barbarous age, to set off wretched matter and lame metre; graced indeed since by the use of some famous modern poets, carried away by custom, but much to their own vexation, hindrance, and constraint to express many things otherwise, and for the most part worse than else they would have expressed them. Not without cause therefore some both Italian and Spanish poets of prime note have rejected rhyme both in longer and shorter works, as have also long since our best English tragedies, as a thing of itself, to all judicious ears, trivial and of no true musical delight; which consists only in apt numbers, fit quantity of syllables, and the sense variously drawn out from one verse into another, not in the jingling sound of like endings, a fault avoided by the learned ancients both in poetry and all good oratory. This neglect then of rhyme so little is to be taken for a defect, though it may seem so perhaps to vulgar readers, that it rather is to be esteemed an example set, the first in English, of ancient liberty recovered to heroic poem from the troublesome and modern bondage of rhyming.

CONTENTS

PARADISE
LOST

BOOK I

THE ARGUMENT

This first book proposes, first in brief, the whole subject, man's disobedience, and the loss thereupon of Paradise wherein he was placed: then touches the prime cause of his fall, the serpent, or rather Satan in the serpent; who revolting
5   from God, and drawing to his side many legions of angels, was by the command of God driven out of Heav'n with all his crew into the midst of things, presenting Satan with his angels now fallen into Hell, described here, not in the centre (for heav'n and earth may be supposed as yet not made,
10   certainly not yet accursed) but in a place of utter darkness, fitliest called Chaos: here Satan with his angels lying on the burning lake, thunder struck and astonished, after a certain space recovers, as from confusion, calls up him who next in order and dignity lay by him; they confer of their miserable
15   fall, Satan awakens all his legions, who lay till then in the same manner confounded; they rise, their numbers, array of battle, their chief leaders named, according to the idols known afterwards in Canaan and the countries adjoining. To these Satan directs his speech, comforts them with hope
20   yet of regaining Heav'n, but tells them lastly of a new world and new kind of creature to be created, according to an

ancient prophecy or report in Heav'n; for that angels were long before this visible Creation, was the opinion of many ancient Fathers. To find out the truth of this prophecy,

25 and what to determine thereon he refers to a full council. What his associates thence attempt. Pandaemonium the palace of Satan rises, suddenly built out of the deep: the infernal Peers there sit in council.

Of Man's first disobedience, and the fruit
Of that forbidden tree whose mortal taste
Brought death into the World, and all our woe,
With loss of Eden, till one greater Man
5 Restore us, and regain the blissful seat,
Sing, Heav'nly Muse, that, on the secret top
Of Oreb, or of Sinai, didst inspire
That shepherd who first taught the chosen seed
In the beginning how the heav'ns and earth
10 Rose out of Chaos: or, if Sion hill
Delight thee more, and Siloa's brook that flowed
Fast by the oracle of God, I thence
Invoke thy aid to my adventurous song,
That with no middle flight intends to soar
15 Above th' Aonian mount, while it pursues
Things unattempted yet in prose or rhyme.
And chiefly thou, O Spirit, that dost prefer
Before all temples th' upright heart and pure,
Instruct me, for thou know'st; thou from the first
20 Wast present, and, with mighty wings outspread,
Dove-like sat'st brooding on the vast Abyss,
And mad'st it pregnant: what in me is dark
Illumine, what is low raise and support;
That, to the height of this great argument,
25 I may assert Eternal Providence,
And justify the ways of God to men.

Say first—for Heav'n hides nothing from thy view,
Nor the deep tract of Hell—say first what cause
Moved our grand parents, in that happy state,
30   Favoured of Heav'n so highly, to fall off
From their Creator, and transgress his will
For one restraint, lords of the World besides.
Who first seduced them to that foul revolt?
Th' infernal Serpent; he it was whose guile,
35   Stirred up with envy and revenge, deceived
The mother of mankind, what time his pride
Had cast him out from Heav'n, with all his host
Of rebel Angels, by whose aid, aspiring
To set himself in glory above his peers,
40   He trusted to have equalled the Most High,
If he opposed, and with ambitious aim
Against the throne and monarchy of God,
Raised impious war in Heav'n and battle proud,
With vain attempt. Him the Almighty Power
45   Hurled headlong flaming from th' ethereal sky,
With hideous ruin and combustion, down
To bottomless perdition, there to dwell
In adamantine chains and penal fire,
Who durst defy th' Omnipotent to arms.
50   Nine times the space that measures day and night
To mortal men, he, with his horrid crew,
Lay vanquished, rolling in the fiery gulf,
Confounded, though immortal. But his doom
Reserved him to more wrath; for now the thought
55   Both of lost happiness and lasting pain
Torments him: round he throws his baleful eyes,
That witnessed huge affliction and dismay,
Mixed with obdurate pride and steadfast hate.
At once, as far as Angels ken, he views

60　　The dismal situation waste and wild.
　　　A dungeon horrible, on all sides round,
　　　As one great furnace flamed; yet from those flames
　　　No light; but rather darkness visible
　　　Served only to discover sights of woe,
65　　Regions of sorrow, doleful shades, where peace
　　　And rest can never dwell, hope never comes
　　　That comes to all, but torture without end
　　　Still urges, and a fiery deluge, fed
　　　With ever-burning sulphur unconsumed.
70　　Such place Eternal Justice has prepared
　　　For those rebellious; here their prison ordained
　　　In utter darkness, and their portion set,
　　　As far removed from God and light of Heav'n
　　　As from the centre thrice to th' utmost pole.
75　　Oh how unlike the place from whence they fell!
　　　There the companions of his fall, o'erwhelmed
　　　With floods and whirlwinds of tempestuous fire,
　　　He soon discerns; and, weltering by his side,
　　　One next himself in power, and next in crime,
80　　Long after known in Palestine, and named
　　　Beelzebub. To whom th' Arch-Enemy,
　　　And thence in Heav'n called Satan, with bold words
　　　Breaking the horrid silence, thus began:—
　　　"If thou beest he—but O how fallen! how changed
85　　From him, who in the happy realms of light
　　　Clothed with transcendent brightness, didst outshine
　　　Myriads, though bright!—if he whom mutual league,
　　　United thoughts and counsels, equal hope
　　　And hazard in the glorious enterprise
90　　Joined with me once, now misery hath joined
　　　In equal ruin; into what pit thou seest
　　　From what height fallen: so much the stronger proved

He with his thunder; and till then who knew
The force of those dire arms? Yet not for those,
95   Nor what the potent Victor in his rage
Can else inflict, do I repent, or change,
Though changed in outward lustre, that fixed mind,
And high disdain from sense of injured merit,
That with the Mightiest raised me to contend,
100   And to the fierce contentions brought along
Innumerable force of Spirits armed,
That durst dislike his reign, and, me preferring,
His utmost power with adverse power opposed
In dubious battle on the plains of Heav'n,
105   And shook his throne. What though the field be lost?
All is not lost—the unconquerable will,
And study of revenge, immortal hate,
And courage never to submit or yield:
And what is else not to be overcome?
110   That glory never shall his wrath or might
Extort from me. To bow and sue for grace
With suppliant knee, and deify his power
Who, from the terror of this arm, so late
Doubted his empire—that were low indeed;
115   That were an ignominy and shame beneath
This downfall; since, by fate, the strength of Gods,
And this empyreal substance, cannot fail;
Since, through experience of this great event,
In arms not worse, in foresight much advanced,
120   We may with more successful hope resolve
To wage by force or guile eternal war,
Irreconcilable to our grand Foe,
Who now triumphs, and in th' excess of joy
Sole reigning holds the tyranny of Heav'n."
125   So spake th' apostate Angel, though in pain,
Vaunting aloud, but racked with deep despair;

And him thus answered soon his bold compeer:—
"O Prince, O Chief of many throned Powers
That led th' embattled Seraphim to war
130 Under thy conduct, and, in dreadful deeds
Fearless, endangered Heav'n's perpetual King,
And put to proof his high supremacy,
Whether upheld by strength, or chance, or fate,
Too well I see and rue the dire event
135 That with sad overthrow and foul defeat,
Hath lost us Heav'n, and all this mighty host
In horrible destruction laid thus low,
As far as Gods and heav'nly Essences
Can perish: for the mind and spirit remains
140 Invincible, and vigour soon returns,
Though all our glory extinct, and happy state
Here swallowed up in endless misery.
But what if he our Conqueror (whom I now
Of force believe almighty, since no less
145 Than such could have o'erpowered such force as ours)
Have left us this our spirit and strength entire,
Strongly to suffer and support our pains,
That we may so suffice his vengeful ire,
Or do him mightier service as his thralls
150 By right of war, whate'er his business be,
Here in the heart of Hell to work in fire,
Or do his errands in the gloomy Deep?
What can it the avail though yet we feel
Strength undiminished, or eternal being
155 To undergo eternal punishment?"
Whereto with speedy words th' Arch-Fiend replied:—
"Fallen Cherub, to be weak is miserable,
Doing or suffering: but of this be sure—
To do aught good never will be our task,
160 But ever to do ill our sole delight,

As being the contrary to his high will
Whom we resist. If then his providence
Out of our evil seek to bring forth good,
Our labour must be to pervert that end,
165 And out of good still to find means of evil;
Which ofttimes may succeed so as perhaps
Shall grieve him, if I fail not, and disturb
His inmost counsels from their destined aim.
But see! the angry Victor hath recalled
170 His ministers of vengeance and pursuit
Back to the gates of Heav'n: the sulphurous hail,
Shot after us in storm, o'erblown hath laid
The fiery surge that from the precipice
Of Heav'n received us falling; and the thunder,
175 Winged with red lightning and impetuous rage,
Perhaps hath spent his shafts, and ceases now
To bellow through the vast and boundless Deep.
Let us not slip th' occasion, whether scorn
Or satiate fury yield it from our Foe.
180 Seest thou yon dreary plain, forlorn and wild,
The seat of desolation, void of light,
Save what the glimmering of these livid flames
Casts pale and dreadful? Thither let us tend
From off the tossing of these fiery waves;
185 There rest, if any rest can harbour there;
And, re-assembling our afflicted powers,
Consult how we may henceforth most offend
Our enemy, our own loss how repair,
How overcome this dire calamity,
190 What reinforcement we may gain from hope,
If not, what resolution from despair."
Thus Satan, talking to his nearest mate,
With head uplift above the wave, and eyes
That sparkling blazed; his other parts besides

195   Prone on the flood, extended long and large,
        Lay floating many a rood, in bulk as huge
        As whom the fables name of monstrous size,
        Titanian or Earth-born, that warred on Jove,
        Briareos or Typhon, whom the den
200   By ancient Tarsus held, or that sea-beast
        Leviathan, which God of all his works
        Created hugest that swim th' ocean-stream.
        Him, haply slumbering on the Norway foam,
        The pilot of some small night-foundered skiff,
205   Deeming some island, oft, as seamen tell,
        With fixed anchor in his scaly rind,
        Moors by his side under the lee, while night
        Invests the sea, and wished morn delays.
        So stretched out huge in length the Arch-fiend lay,
210   Chained on the burning lake; nor ever thence
        Had risen, or heaved his head, but that the will
        And high permission of all-ruling Heav'n
        Left him at large to his own dark designs,
        That with reiterated crimes he might
215   Heap on himself damnation, while he sought
        Evil to others, and enraged might see
        How all his malice served but to bring forth
        Infinite goodness, grace, and mercy, shewn
        On Man by him seduced, but on himself
220   Treble confusion, wrath, and vengeance poured.
        Forthwith upright he rears from off the pool
        His mighty stature; on each hand the flames
        Driven backward slope their pointing spires, and rolled
        In billows, leave i' th' midst a horrid vale.
225   Then with expanded wings he steers his flight
        Aloft, incumbent on the dusky air,
        That felt unusual weight; till on dry land

He lights—if it were land that ever burned
With solid, as the lake with liquid fire,
230 And such appeared in hue as when the force
Of subterranean wind transports a hill
Torn from Pelorus, or the shattered side
Of thundering Etna, whose combustible
And fuelled entrails, thence conceiving fire,
235 Sublimed with mineral fury, aid the winds,
And leave a singed bottom all involved
With stench and smoke. Such resting found the sole
Of unblest feet. Him followed his next mate;
Both glorying to have scaped the Stygian flood
240 As gods, and by their own recovered strength,
Not by the sufferance of supernal Power.
"Is this the region, this the soil, the clime,"
Said then the lost Archangel, "this the seat
That we must change for Heav'n?—this mournful gloom
245 For that celestial light? Be it so, since he
Who now is sovereign can dispose and bid
What shall be right: farthest from him is best
Whom reason hath equalled, force hath made supreme
Above his equals. Farewell, happy fields,
250 Where joy for ever dwells! Hail, horrors! hail,
Infernal world! and thou, profoundest Hell,
Receive thy new possessor—one who brings
A mind not to be changed by place or time.
The mind is its own place, and in itself
255 Can make a Heav'n of Hell, a Hell of Heav'n.
What matter where, if I be still the same,
And what I should be, all but less than he
Whom thunder hath made greater? Here at least
We shall be free; th' Almighty hath not built
260 Here for his envy, will not drive us hence:
Here we may reign secure; and, in my choice,

To reign is worth ambition, though in Hell:
Better to reign in Hell than serve in Heav'n.
But wherefore let we then our faithful friends,
265 Th' associates and co-partners of our loss,
Lie thus astonished on th' oblivious pool,
And call them not to share with us their part
In this unhappy mansion, or once more
With rallied arms to try what may be yet
270 Regained in Heav'n, or what more lost in Hell?"
So Satan spake; and him Beelzebub
Thus answered:—"Leader of those armies bright
Which, but th' Omnipotent, none could have foiled!
If once they hear that voice, their liveliest pledge
275 Of hope in fears and dangers—heard so oft
In worst extremes, and on the perilous edge
Of battle, when it raged, in all assaults
Their surest signal—they will soon resume
New courage and revive, though now they lie
280 Grovelling and prostrate on yon lake of fire,
As we erewhile, astounded and amazed;
No wonder, fallen such a pernicious height!"
He scarce had ceased when the superior Fiend
Was moving toward the shore; his ponderous shield,
285 Ethereal temper, massy, large, and round,
Behind him cast. The broad circumference
Hung on his shoulders like the moon, whose orb
Through optic glass the Tuscan artist views
At evening, from the top of Fesole,
290 Or in Valdarno, to descry new lands,
Rivers, or mountains, in her spotty globe.
His spear—to equal which the tallest pine
Hewn on Norwegian hills, to be the mast
Of some great ammiral, were but a wand—
295 He walked with, to support uneasy steps

Over the burning marl, not like those steps
On Heav'n's azure; and the torrid clime
Smote on him sore besides, vaulted with fire.
Nathless he so endured, till on the beach
300   Of that inflamed sea he stood, and called
His legions—Angel Forms, who lay entranced
Thick as autumnal leaves that strow the brooks
In Vallombrosa, where th' Etrurian shades
High over-arched embower; or scattered sedge
305   Afloat, when with fierce winds Orion armed
Hath vexed the Red-Sea coast, whose waves o'erthrew
Busiris and his Memphian chivalry,
While with perfidious hatred they pursued
The sojourners of Goshen, who beheld
310   From the safe shore their floating carcases
And broken chariot-wheels. So thick bestrown,
Abject and lost, lay these, covering the flood,
Under amazement of their hideous change.
He called so loud that all the hollow deep
315   Of Hell resounded:—"Princes, Potentates,
Warriors, the Flower of Heav'n—once yours; now lost,
If such astonishment as this can seize
Eternal Spirits! Or have ye chosen this place
After the toil of battle to repose
320   Your wearied virtue, for the ease you find
To slumber here, as in the vales of Heav'n?
Or in this abject posture have ye sworn
To adore the Conqueror, who now beholds
Cherub and Seraph rolling in the flood
325   With scattered arms and ensigns, till anon
His swift pursuers from Heav'n-gates discern
Th' advantage, and, descending, tread us down
Thus drooping, or with linked thunderbolts
Transfix us to the bottom of this gulf?

330   Awake, arise, or be for ever fallen!"
         They heard, and were abashed, and up they sprung
         Upon the wing, as when men wont to watch
         On duty, sleeping found by whom they dread,
         Rouse and bestir themselves ere well awake.
335   Nor did they not perceive the evil plight
         In which they were, or the fierce pains not feel;
         Yet to their General's voice they soon obeyed
         Innumerable. As when the potent rod
         Of Amram's son, in Egypt's evil day,
340   Waved round the coast, up-called a pitchy cloud
         Of locusts, warping on the eastern wind,
         That o'er the realm of impious Pharaoh hung
         Like Night, and darkened all the land of Nile;
         So numberless were those bad Angels seen
345   Hovering on wing under the cope of Hell,
         'Twixt upper, nether, and surrounding fires;
         Till, as a signal given, th' uplifted spear
         Of their great Sultan waving to direct
         Their course, in even balance down they light
350   On the firm brimstone, and fill all the plain:
         A multitude like which the populous North
         Poured never from her frozen loins to pass
         Rhene or the Danaw, when her barbarous sons
         Came like a deluge on the South, and spread
355   Beneath Gibraltar to the Libyan sands.
         Forthwith, form every squadron and each band,
         The heads and leaders thither haste where stood
         Their great Commander—godlike Shapes, and Forms
         Excelling human; princely Dignities;
360   And Powers that erst in Heav'n sat on thrones,
         Though on their names in Heav'nly records now
         Be no memorial, blotted out and rased

By their rebellion from the Books of Life.
Nor had they yet among the sons of Eve
365   Got them new names, till, wandering o'er the earth,
Through God's high sufferance for the trial of man,
By falsities and lies the greatest part
Of mankind they corrupted to forsake
God their Creator, and th' invisible
370   Glory of him that made them to transform
Oft to the image of a brute, adorned
With gay religions full of pomp and gold,
And devils to adore for deities:
Then were they known to men by various names,
375   And various idols through the heathen world.
Say, Muse, their names then known, who first, who last,
Roused from the slumber on that fiery couch,
At their great Emperor's call, as next in worth
Came singly where he stood on the bare strand,
380   While the promiscuous crowd stood yet aloof?
The chief were those who, from the pit of Hell
Roaming to seek their prey on Earth, durst fix
Their seats, long after, next the seat of God,
Their altars by his altar, gods adored
385   Among the nations round, and durst abide
Jehovah thundering out of Sion, throned
Between the Cherubim; yea, often placed
Within his sanctuary itself their shrines,
Abominations; and with cursed things
390   His holy rites and solemn feasts profaned,
And with their darkness durst affront his light.
First, Moloch, horrid king, besmeared with blood
Of human sacrifice, and parents' tears;
Though, for the noise of drums and timbrels loud,
395   Their children's cries unheard that passed through fire
To his grim idol. Him the Ammonite

Worshiped in Rabba and her watery plain,
In Argob and in Basan, to the stream
Of utmost Arnon. Nor content with such

400 Audacious neighbourhood, the wisest heart
Of Solomon he led by fraud to build
His temple right against the temple of God
On that opprobrious hill, and made his grove
The pleasant valley of Hinnom, Tophet thence

405 And black Gehenna called, the type of Hell.
Next Chemos, th' obscene dread of Moab's sons,
From Aroar to Nebo and the wild
Of southmost Abarim; in Hesebon
And Horonaim, Seon's real, beyond

410 The flowery dale of Sibma clad with vines,
And Eleale to th' Asphaltic Pool:
Peor his other name, when he enticed
Israel in Sittim, on their march from Nile,
To do him wanton rites, which cost them woe.

415 Yet thence his lustful orgies he enlarged
Even to that hill of scandal, by the grove
Of Moloch homicide, lust hard by hate,
Till good Josiah drove them thence to Hell.
With these came they who, from the bordering flood

420 Of old Euphrates to the brook that parts
Egypt from Syrian ground, had general names
Of Baalim and Ashtaroth—those male,
These feminine. For Spirits, when they please,
Can either sex assume, or both; so soft

425 And uncompounded is their essence pure,
Not tried or manacled with joint or limb,
Nor founded on the brittle strength of bones,
Like cumbrous flesh; but, in what shape they choose,
Dilated or condensed, bright or obscure,

430 Can execute their airy purposes,

And works of love or enmity fulfil.
For those the race of Israel oft forsook
Their Living Strength, and unfrequented left
His righteous altar, bowing lowly down
435 To bestial gods; for which their heads as low
Bowed down in battle, sunk before the spear
Of despicable foes. With these in troop
Came Astoreth, whom the Phoenicians called
Astarte, queen of heav'n, with crescent horns;
440 To whose bright image nightly by the moon
Sidonian virgins paid their vows and songs;
In Sion also not unsung, where stood
Her temple on th' offensive mountain, built
By that uxorious king whose heart, though large,
445 Beguiled by fair idolatresses, fell
To idols foul. Thammuz came next behind,
Whose annual wound in Lebanon allured
The Syrian damsels to lament his fate
In amorous ditties all a summer's day,
450 While smooth Adonis from his native rock
Ran purple to the sea, supposed with blood
Of Thammuz yearly wounded: the love-tale
Infected Sion's daughters with like heat,
Whose wanton passions in the sacred porch
455 Ezekiel saw, when, by the vision led,
His eye surveyed the dark idolatries
Of alienated Judah. Next came one
Who mourned in earnest, when the captive ark
Maimed his brute image, head and hands lopt off,
460 In his own temple, on the grunsel-edge,
Where he fell flat and shamed his worshippers:
Dagon his name, sea-monster, upward man
And downward fish; yet had his temple high
Reared in Azotus, dreaded through the coast

465   Of Palestine, in Gath and Ascalon,
        And Accaron and Gaza's frontier bounds.
        Him followed Rimmon, whose delightful seat
        Was fair Damascus, on the fertile banks
        Of Abbana and Pharphar, lucid streams.
470   He also against the house of God was bold:
        A leper once he lost, and gained a king—
        Ahaz, his sottish conqueror, whom he drew
        God's altar to disparage and displace
        For one of Syrian mode, whereon to burn
475   His odious offerings, and adore the gods
        Whom he had vanquished. After these appeared
        A crew who, under names of old renown—
        Osiris, Isis, Orus, and their train—
        With monstrous shapes and sorceries abused
480   Fanatic Egypt and her priests to seek
        Their wandering gods disguised in brutish forms
        Rather than human. Nor did Israel scape
        Th' infection, when their borrowed gold composed
        The calf in Oreb; and the rebel king
485   Doubled that sin in Bethel and in Dan,
        Likening his Maker to the grazed ox—
        Jehovah, who, in one night, when he passed
        From Egypt marching, equalled with one stroke
        Both her first-born and all her bleating gods.
490   Belial came last; than whom a Spirit more lewd
        Fell not from Heav'n, or more gross to love
        Vice for itself. To him no temple stood
        Or altar smoked; yet who more oft than he
        In temples and at altars, when the priest
495   Turns atheist, as did Eli's sons, who filled
        With lust and violence the house of God?
        In courts and palaces he also reigns,

And in luxurious cities, where the noise
Of riot ascends above their loftiest towers,
500   And injury and outrage; and, when night
Darkens the streets, then wander forth the sons
Of Belial, flown with insolence and wine.
Witness the streets of Sodom, and that night
In Gibeah, when the hospitable door
505   Exposed a matron, to avoid worse rape.
These were the prime in order and in might:
The rest were long to tell; though far renowned
Th' Ionian gods—of Javan's issue held
Gods, yet confessed later than Heav'n and Earth,
510   Their boasted parents;—Titan, Heav'n's first-born,
With his enormous brood, and birthright seized
By younger Saturn: he from mightier Jove,
His own and Rhea's son, like measure found;
So Jove usurping reigned. These, first in Crete
515   And Ida known, thence on the snowy top
Of cold Olympus ruled the middle air,
Their highest heav'n; or on the Delphian cliff,
Or in Dodona, and through all the bounds
Of Doric land; or who with Saturn old
520   Fled over Adria to th' Hesperian fields,
And o'er the Celtic roamed the utmost Isles.
All these and more came flocking; but with looks
Downcast and damp; yet such wherein appeared
Obscure some glimpse of joy to have found their Chief
525   Not in despair, to have found themselves not lost
In loss itself; which on his countenance cast
Like doubtful hue. But he, his wonted pride
Soon recollecting, with high words, that bore
Semblance of worth, not substance, gently raised

530   Their fainting courage, and dispelled their fears.
Then straight commands that, at the warlike sound
Of trumpets loud and clarions, be upreared
His mighty standard. That proud honour claimed
Azazel as his right, a Cherub tall:
535   Who forthwith from the glittering staff unfurled
Th' imperial ensign; which, full high advanced,
Shone like a meteor streaming to the wind,
With gems and golden lustre rich emblazed,
Seraphic arms and trophies; all the while
540   Sonorous metal blowing martial sounds:
At which the universal host up-sent
A shout that tore Hell's concave, and beyond
Frighted the reign of Chaos and old Night.
All in a moment through the gloom were seen
545   Ten thousand banners rise into the air,
With orient colours waving: with them rose
A forest huge of spears; and thronging helms
Appeared, and serried shields in thick array
Of depth immeasurable. Anon they move
550   In perfect phalanx to the Dorian mood
Of flutes and soft recorders—such as raised
To height of noblest temper heroes old
Arming to battle, and instead of rage
Deliberate valour breathed, firm, and unmoved
555   With dread of death to flight or foul retreat;
Nor wanting power to mitigate and swage
With solemn touches troubled thoughts, and chase
Anguish and doubt and fear and sorrow and pain
From mortal or immortal minds. Thus they,
560   Breathing united force with fixed thought,
Moved on in silence to soft pipes that charmed
Their painful steps o'er the burnt soil. And now

Advanced in view they stand—a horrid front
Of dreadful length and dazzling arms, in guise
565 Of warriors old, with ordered spear and shield,
Awaiting what command their mighty Chief
Had to impose. He through the armed files
Darts his experienced eye, and soon traverse
The whole battalion views—their order due,
570 Their visages and stature as of gods;
Their number last he sums. And now his heart
Distends with pride, and, hardening in his strength,
Glories: for never, since created Man,
Met such embodied force as, named with these,
575 Could merit more than that small infantry
Warred on by cranes—though all the giant brood
Of Phlegra with th' heroic race were joined
That fought at Thebes and Ilium, on each side
Mixed with auxiliar gods; and what resounds
580 In fable or romance of Uther's son,
Begirt with British and Armoric knights;
And all who since, baptized or infidel,
Jousted in Aspramont, or Montalban,
Damasco, or Marocco, or Trebisond,
585 Or whom Biserta sent from Afric shore
When Charlemain with all his peerage fell
By Fontarabbia. Thus far these beyond
Compare of mortal prowess, yet observed
Their dread Commander. He, above the rest
590 In shape and gesture proudly eminent,
Stood like a tower. His form had yet not lost
All her original brightness, nor appeared
Less than Archangel ruined, and th' excess
Of glory obscured: as when the sun new-risen

595   Looks through the horizontal misty air
Shorn of his beams, or, from behind the moon,
In dim eclipse, disastrous twilight sheds
On half the nations, and with fear of change
Perplexes monarchs. Darkened so, yet shone
600   Above them all th' Archangel: but his face
Deep scars of thunder had intrenched, and care
Sat on his faded cheek, but under brows
Of dauntless courage, and considerate pride
Waiting revenge. Cruel his eye, but cast
605   Signs of remorse and passion, to behold
The fellows of his crime, the followers rather
(Far other once beheld in bliss), condemned
For ever now to have their lot in pain—
Millions of Spirits for his fault amerced
610   Of Heav'n, and from eternal splendours flung
For his revolt—yet faithful how they stood,
Their glory withered; as, when heav'n's fire
Hath scathed the forest oaks or mountain pines,
With singed top their stately growth, though bare,
615   Stands on the blasted heath. He now prepared
To speak; whereat their doubled ranks they bend
From wing to wing, and half enclose him round
With all his peers: attention held them mute.
Thrice he assayed, and thrice, in spite of scorn,
620   Tears, such as Angels weep, burst forth: at last
Words interwove with sighs found out their way:—
"O myriads of immortal Spirits! O Powers
Matchless, but with th' Almighty!—and that strife
Was not inglorious, though th' event was dire,
625   As this place testifies, and this dire change,
Hateful to utter. But what power of mind,
Forseeing or presaging, from the depth

Of knowledge past or present, could have feared
How such united force of gods, how such
630   As stood like these, could ever know repulse?
For who can yet believe, though after loss,
That all these puissant legions, whose exile
Hath emptied Heav'n, shall fail to re-ascend,
Self-raised, and repossess their native seat?
635   For me, be witness all the host of Heav'n,
If counsels different, or danger shunned
By me, have lost our hopes. But he who reigns
Monarch in Heav'n till then as one secure
Sat on his throne, upheld by old repute,
640   Consent or custom, and his regal state
Put forth at full, but still his strength concealed—
Which tempted our attempt, and wrought our fall.
Henceforth his might we know, and know our own,
So as not either to provoke, or dread
645   New war provoked: our better part remains
To work in close design, by fraud or guile,
What force effected not; that he no less
At length from us may find, who overcomes
By force hath overcome but half his foe.
650   Space may produce new Worlds; whereof so rife
There went a fame in Heav'n that he ere long
Intended to create, and therein plant
A generation whom his choice regard
Should favour equal to the Sons of Heav'n.
655   Thither, if but to pry, shall be perhaps
Our first eruption—thither, or elsewhere;
For this infernal pit shall never hold
Celestial Spirits in bondage, nor th' Abyss
Long under darkness cover. But these thoughts

660	Full counsel must mature. Peace is despaired;
	For who can think submission? War, then, war
	Open or understood, must be resolved."
	He spake; and, to confirm his words, outflew
	Millions of flaming swords, drawn from the thighs
665	Of mighty Cherubim; the sudden blaze
	Far round illumined Hell. Highly they raged
	Against the Highest, and fierce with grasped arms
	Clashed on their sounding shields the din of war,
	Hurling defiance toward the vault of Heav'n.
670	There stood a hill not far, whose grisly top
	Belched fire and rolling smoke; the rest entire
	Shone with a glossy scurf—undoubted sign
	That in his womb was hid metallic ore,
	The work of sulphur. Thither, winged with speed,
675	A numerous brigade hastened: as when bands
	Of pioneers, with spade and pickaxe armed,
	Forerun the royal camp, to trench a field,
	Or cast a rampart. Mammon led them on—
	Mammon, the least erected Spirit that fell
680	From Heav'n; for even in Heav'n his looks and thoughts
	Were always downward bent, admiring more
	The riches of Heav'n's pavement, trodden gold,
	Than aught divine or holy else enjoyed
	In vision beatific. By him first
685	Men also, and by his suggestion taught,
	Ransacked the centre, and with impious hands
	Rifled the bowels of their mother Earth
	For treasures better hid. Soon had his crew
	Opened into the hill a spacious wound,
690	And digged out ribs of gold. Let none admire
	That riches grow in Hell; that soil may best
	Deserve the precious bane. And here let those

Who boast in mortal things, and wondering tell
Of Babel, and the works of Memphian kings,
695   Learn how their greatest monuments of fame
And strength, and art, are easily outdone
By Spirits reprobate, and in an hour
What in an age they, with incessant toil
And hands innumerable, scarce perform.
700   Nigh on the plain, in many cells prepared,
That underneath had veins of liquid fire
Sluiced from the lake, a second multitude
With wondrous art founded the massy ore,
Severing each kind, and scummed the bullion-dross.
705   A third as soon had formed within the ground
A various mould, and from the boiling cells
By strange conveyance filled each hollow nook;
As in an organ, from one blast of wind,
To many a row of pipes the sound-board breathes.
710   Anon out of the earth a fabric huge
Rose like an exhalation, with the sound
Of dulcet symphonies and voices sweet—
Built like a temple, where pilasters round
Were set, and Doric pillars overlaid
715   With golden architrave; nor did there want
Cornice or frieze, with bossy sculptures graven;
The roof was fretted gold. Not Babylon
Nor great Alcairo such magnificence
Equalled in all their glories, to enshrine
720   Belus or Serapis their gods, or seat
Their kings, when Egypt with Assyria strove
In wealth and luxury. Th' ascending pile
Stood fixed her stately height, and straight the doors,
Opening their brazen folds, discover, wide

725	Within, her ample spaces o'er the smooth
	And level pavement: from the arched roof,
	Pendent by subtle magic, many a row
	Of starry lamps and blazing cressets, fed
	With naptha and asphaltus, yielded light
730	As from a sky. The hasty multitude
	Admiring entered; and the work some praise,
	And some the architect. His hand was known
	In Heav'n by many a towered structure high,
	Where sceptred Angels held their residence,
735	And sat as Princes, whom the supreme King
	Exalted to such power, and gave to rule,
	Each in his Hierarchy, the Orders bright.
	Nor was his name unheard or unadored
	In ancient Greece; and in Ausonian land
740	Men called him Mulciber; and how he fell
	From Heav'n they fabled, thrown by angry Jove
	Sheer o'er the crystal battlements: from morn
	To noon he fell, from noon to dewy eve,
	A summer's day, and with the setting sun
745	Dropped from the zenith, like a falling star,
	On Lemnos, th' Aegaean isle. Thus they relate,
	Erring; for he with this rebellious rout
	Fell long before; nor aught availed him now
	To have built in Heav'n high towers; nor did he scape
750	By all his engines, but was headlong sent,
	With his industrious crew, to build in Hell.
	Meanwhile the winged Heralds, by command
	Of sovereign power, with awful ceremony
	And trumpet's sound, throughout the host proclaim
755	A solemn council forthwith to be held
	At Pandemonium, the high capital
	Of Satan and his peers. Their summons called

From every band and squared regiment
By place or choice the worthiest: they anon
760   With hundreds and with thousands trooping came
Attended. All access was thronged; the gates
And porches wide, but chief the spacious hall
(Though like a covered field, where champions bold
Wont ride in armed, and at the Soldan's chair
765   Defied the best of Paynim chivalry
To mortal combat, or career with lance),
Thick swarmed, both on the ground and in the air,
Brushed with the hiss of rustling wings. As bees
In spring-time, when the Sun with Taurus rides.
770   Pour forth their populous youth about the hive
In clusters; they among fresh dews and flowers
Fly to and fro, or on the smoothed plank,
The suburb of their straw-built citadel,
New rubbed with balm, expatiate, and confer
775   Their state-affairs: so thick the airy crowd
Swarmed and were straitened; till, the signal given,
Behold a wonder! They but now who seemed
In bigness to surpass Earth's giant sons,
Now less than smallest dwarfs, in narrow room
780   Throng numberless—like that Pygmean race
Beyond the Indian mount; or faery elves,
Whose midnight revels, by a forest-side
Or fountain, some belated peasant sees,
Or dreams he sees, while overhead the Moon
785   Sits arbitress, and nearer to the Earth
Wheels her pale course: they, on their mirth and dance
Intent, with jocund music charm his ear;
At once with joy and fear his heart rebounds.
Thus incorporeal Spirits to smallest forms

790   Reduced their shapes immense, and were at large,
       Though without number still, amidst the hall
       Of that infernal court. But far within,
       And in their own dimensions like themselves,
       The great Seraphic Lords and Cherubim
795   In close recess and secret conclave sat,
       A thousand demi-gods on golden seats,
       Frequent and full. After short silence then,
       And summons read, the great consult began.

BOOK II

THE ARGUMENT

The consultation begun, Satan debates whether another
battle be to be hazarded for the recovery of Heav'n: some
advise it, others dissuade: a third proposal is preferred,
mentioned before by Satan, to search the truth of that
5   prophecy or tradition in Heav'n concerning another world,
and another kind of creature equal or not much inferior to
themselves, about this time to be created: their doubt who shall
be sent on this difficult search: Satan their chief undertakes
alone the voyage, is honoured and
10   applauded. The council thus ended, the rest betake them
several ways and to several employments return. He passes on
his journey to Hell gates, finds them shut, and who sat there to
guard them, by whom at length they are opened, and discover
to him the great gulf between. Hell and
15   Heav'n; with what difficulty he passes through, directed by
Chaos, the power of that place, to the sight of this new world
which he sought.

High on a throne of royal state, which far
Outshone the wealth of Ormus and of Ind,
Or where the gorgeous East with richest hand
Showers on her kings barbaric pearl and gold,

5   Satan exalted sat, by merit raised
To that bad eminence; and, from despair
Thus high uplifted beyond hope, aspires
Beyond thus high, insatiate to pursue
Vain war with Heav'n; and, by success untaught,
10   His proud imaginations thus displayed:—
"Powers and Dominions, Deities of Heav'n!—
For, since no deep within her gulf can hold
Immortal vigour, though oppressed and fallen,
I give not Heav'n for lost: from this descent
15   Celestial Virtues rising will appear
More glorious and more dread than from no fall,
And trust themselves to fear no second fate!—
Me though just right, and the fixed laws of Heav'n,
Did first create your leader—next, free choice
20   With what besides in council or in fight
Hath been achieved of merit—yet this loss,
Thus far at least recovered, hath much more
Established in a safe, unenvied throne,
Yielded with full consent. The happier state
25   In Heav'n, which follows dignity, might draw
Envy from each inferior; but who here
Will envy whom the highest place exposes
Foremost to stand against the Thunderer's aim
Your bulwark, and condemns to greatest share
30   Of endless pain? Where there is, then, no good
For which to strive, no strife can grow up there
From faction: for none sure will claim in Hell
Precedence; none whose portion is so small
Of present pain that with ambitious mind
35   Will covet more! With this advantage, then,
To union, and firm faith, and firm accord,
More than can be in Heav'n, we now return
To claim our just inheritance of old,
Surer to prosper than prosperity

40 Could have assured us; and by what best way,
    Whether of open war or covert guile,
    We now debate. Who can advise may speak."
    He ceased; and next him Moloch, sceptred king,
    Stood up—the strongest and the fiercest Spirit
45 That fought in Heav'n, now fiercer by despair.
    His trust was with th' Eternal to be deemed
    Equal in strength, and rather than be less
    ared not to be at all; with that care lost
    Went all his fear: of God, or Hell, or worse,
50 He recked not, and these words thereafter spake:—
    "My sentence is for open war. Of wiles,
    More unexpert, I boast not: them let those
    Contrive who need, or when they need; not now.
    For, while they sit contriving, shall the rest—
55 Millions that stand in arms, and longing wait
    The signal to ascend—sit lingering here,
    Heav'n's fugitives, and for their dwelling-place
    Accept this dark opprobrious den of shame,
    The prison of his tyranny who reigns
60 By our delay? No! let us rather choose,
    Armed with Hell-flames and fury, all at once
    O'er Heav'n's high towers to force resistless way,
    Turning our tortures into horrid arms
    Against the Torturer; when, to meet the noise
65 Of his almighty engine, he shall hear
    Infernal thunder, and, for lightning, see
    Black fire and horror shot with equal rage
    Among his Angels, and his throne itself
    Mixed with Tartarean sulphur and strange fire,
70 His own invented torments. But perhaps
    The way seems difficult, and steep to scale
    With upright wing against a higher foe!
    Let such bethink them, if the sleepy drench
    Of that forgetful lake benumb not still,

75   That in our proper motion we ascend
        Up to our native seat; descent and fall
        To us is adverse. Who but felt of late,
        When the fierce foe hung on our broken rear
        Insulting, and pursued us through the Deep,
80   With what compulsion and laborious flight
        We sunk thus low? Th' ascent is easy, then;
        Th' event is feared! Should we again provoke
        Our stronger, some worse way his wrath may find
        To our destruction, if there be in Hell
85   Fear to be worse destroyed! What can be worse
        Than to dwell here, driven out from bliss, condemned
        In this abhorred deep to utter woe;
        Where pain of unextinguishable fire
        Must exercise us without hope of end
90   The vassals of his anger, when the scourge
        Inexorably, and the torturing hour,
        Calls us to penance? More destroyed than thus,
        We should be quite abolished, and expire.
        What fear we then? What doubt we to incense
95   His utmost ire? which, to the height enraged,
        Will either quite consume us, and reduce
        To nothing this essential—happier far
        Than miserable to have eternal being!—
        Or, if our substance be indeed divine,
100   And cannot cease to be, we are at worst
        On this side nothing; and by proof we feel
        Our power sufficient to disturb his Heav'n,
        And with perpetual inroads to alarm,
        Though inaccessible, his fatal throne:
105   Which, if not victory, is yet revenge."
        He ended frowning, and his look denounced
        Desperate revenge, and battle dangerous
        To less than gods. On th' other side up rose
        Belial, in act more graceful and humane.

110   A fairer person lost not Heav'n; he seemed
      For dignity composed, and high exploit.
      But all was false and hollow; though his tongue
      Dropped manna, and could make the worse appear
      The better reason, to perplex and dash
115   Maturest counsels: for his thoughts were low—
      To vice industrious, but to nobler deeds
      Timorous and slothful. Yet he pleased the ear,
      And with persuasive accent thus began:—
      "I should be much for open war, O Peers,
120   As not behind in hate, if what was urged
      Main reason to persuade immediate war
      Did not dissuade me most, and seem to cast
      Ominous conjecture on the whole success;
      When he who most excels in fact of arms,
125   In what he counsels and in what excels
      Mistrustful, grounds his courage on despair
      And utter dissolution, as the scope
      Of all his aim, after some dire revenge.
      First, what revenge? The towers of Heav'n are filled
130   With armed watch, that render all access
      Impregnable: oft on the bordering Deep
      Encamp their legions, or with obscure wing
      Scout far and wide into the realm of Night,
      Scorning surprise. Or, could we break our way
135   By force, and at our heels all Hell should rise
      With blackest insurrection to confound
      Heav'n's purest light, yet our great Enemy,
      All incorruptible, would on his throne
      Sit unpolluted, and th' ethereal mould,
140   Incapable of stain, would soon expel
      Her mischief, and purge off the baser fire,
      Victorious. Thus repulsed, our final hope
      Is flat despair: we must exasperate
      Th' Almighty Victor to spend all his rage;

145 And that must end us; that must be our cure—
  To be no more. Sad cure! for who would lose,
  Though full of pain, this intellectual being,
  Those thoughts that wander through eternity,
  To perish rather, swallowed up and lost
150 In the wide womb of uncreated Night,
  Devoid of sense and motion? And who knows,
  Let this be good, whether our angry Foe
  Can give it, or will ever? How he can
  Is doubtful; that he never will is sure.
155 Will he, so wise, let loose at once his ire,
  Belike through impotence or unaware,
  To give his enemies their wish, and end
  Them in his anger whom his anger saves
  To punish endless? "Wherefore cease we, then?"
160 Say they who counsel war; "we are decreed,
  Reserved, and destined to eternal woe;
  Whatever doing, what can we suffer more,
  What can we suffer worse?" Is this, then, worst—
  Thus sitting, thus consulting, thus in arms?
165 What when we fled amain, pursued and struck
  With Heav'n's afflicting thunder, and besought
  The Deep to shelter us? This Hell then seemed
  A refuge from those wounds. Or when we lay
  Chained on the burning lake? That sure was worse.
170 What if the breath that kindled those grim fires,
  Awaked, should blow them into sevenfold rage,
  And plunge us in the flames; or from above
  Should intermitted vengeance arm again
  His red right hand to plague us? What if all
175 Her stores were opened, and this firmament
  Of Hell should spout her cataracts of fire,
  Impendent horrors, threatening hideous fall
  One day upon our heads; while we perhaps,
  Designing or exhorting glorious war,

180   Caught in a fiery tempest, shall be hurled,
        Each on his rock transfixed, the sport and prey
        Or racking whirlwinds, or for ever sunk
        Under yon boiling ocean, wraped in chains,
        There to converse with everlasting groans,
185   Unrespited, unpitied, unreprieved,
        Ages of hopeless end? This would be worse.
        War, therefore, open or concealed, alike
        My voice dissuades; for what can force or guile
        With him, or who deceive his mind, whose eye
190   Views all things at one view? He from Heav'n's height
        All these our motions vain sees and derides,
        Not more almighty to resist our might
        Than wise to frustrate all our plots and wiles.
        Shall we, then, live thus vile—the race of Heav'n
195   Thus trampled, thus expelled, to suffer here
        Chains and these torments? Better these than worse,
        By my advice; since fate inevitable
        Subdues us, and omnipotent decree,
        The Victor's will. To suffer, as to do,
200   Our strength is equal; nor the law unjust
        That so ordains. This was at first resolved,
        If we were wise, against so great a foe
        Contending, and so doubtful what might fall.
        I laugh when those who at the spear are bold
205   And venturous, if that fail them, shrink, and fear
        What yet they know must follow—to endure
        Exile, or ignominy, or bonds, or pain,
        The sentence of their Conqueror. This is now
        Our doom; which if we can sustain and bear,
210   Our Supreme Foe in time may much remit
        His anger, and perhaps, thus far removed,
        Not mind us not offending, satisfied
        With what is punished; whence these raging fires
        Will slacken, if his breath stir not their flames.

215   Our purer essence then will overcome
       Their noxious vapour; or, inured, not feel;
       Or, changed at length, and to the place conformed
       In temper and in nature, will receive
       Familiar the fierce heat; and, void of pain,
220   This horror will grow mild, this darkness light;
       Besides what hope the never-ending flight
       Of future days may bring, what chance, what change
       Worth waiting—since our present lot appears
       For happy though but ill, for ill not worst,
225   If we procure not to ourselves more woe."
       Thus Belial, with words clothed in reason's garb,
       Counselled ignoble ease and peaceful sloth,
       Not peace; and after him thus Mammon spake:—
       "Either to disenthrone the King of Heav'n
230   We war, if war be best, or to regain
       Our own right lost. Him to unthrone we then
       May hope, when everlasting Fate shall yield
       To fickle Chance, and Chaos judge the strife.
       The former, vain to hope, argues as vain
235   The latter; for what place can be for us
       Within Heav'n's bound, unless Heav'n's Lord supreme
       We overpower? Suppose he should relent
       And publish grace to all, on promise made
       Of new subjection; with what eyes could we
240   Stand in his presence humble, and receive
       Strict laws imposed, to celebrate his throne
       With warbled hymns, and to his Godhead sing
       Forced hallelujahs, while he lordly sits
       Our envied sovereign, and his altar breathes
245   Ambrosial odours and ambrosial flowers,
       Our servile offerings? This must be our task
       In Heav'n, this our delight. How wearisome
       Eternity so spent in worship paid
       To whom we hate! Let us not then pursue,

250   By force impossible, by leave obtained
        Unacceptable, though in Heav'n, our state
        Of splendid vassalage; but rather seek
        Our own good from ourselves, and from our own
        Live to ourselves, though in this vast recess,
255   Free and to none accountable, preferring
        Hard liberty before the easy yoke
        Of servile pomp. Our greatness will appear
        Then most conspicuous when great things of small,
        Useful of hurtful, prosperous of adverse,
260   We can create, and in what place soe'er
        Thrive under evil, and work ease out of pain
        Through labour and endurance. This deep world
        Of darkness do we dread? How oft amidst
        Thick clouds and dark doth Heav'n's all-ruling Sire
265   Choose to reside, his glory unobscured,
        And with the majesty of darkness round
        Covers his throne, from whence deep thunders roar.
        Mustering their rage, and Heav'n resembles Hell!
        As he our darkness, cannot we his light
270   Imitate when we please? This desert soil
        Wants not her hidden lustre, gems and gold;
        Nor want we skill or art from whence to raise
        Magnificence; and what can Heav'n show more?
        Our torments also may, in length of time,
275   Become our elements, these piercing fires
        As soft as now severe, our temper changed
        Into their temper; which must needs remove
        The sensible of pain. All things invite
        To peaceful counsels, and the settled state
280   Of order, how in safety best we may
        Compose our present evils, with regard
        Of what we are and where, dismissing quite
        All thoughts of war. Ye have what I advise."
        He scarce had finished, when such murmur filled

285 Th' assembly as when hollow rocks retain
   The sound of blustering winds, which all night long
   Had roused the sea, now with hoarse cadence lull
   Seafaring men o'erwatched, whose bark by chance
   Or pinnace, anchors in a craggy bay
290 · After the tempest. Such applause was heard
   As Mammon ended, and his sentence pleased,
   Advising peace: for such another field
   They dreaded worse than Hell; so much the fear
   Of thunder and the sword of Michael
295 Wrought still within them; and no less desire
   To found this nether empire, which might rise,
   By policy and long process of time,
   In emulation opposite to Heav'n.
   Which when Beelzebub perceived—than whom,
300 Satan except, none higher sat—with grave
   Aspect he rose, and in his rising seemed
   A pillar of state. Deep on his front engraven
   Deliberation sat, and public care;
   And princely counsel in his face yet shone,
305 Majestic, though in ruin. Sage he stood
   With Atlantean shoulders, fit to bear
   The weight of mightiest monarchies; his look
   Drew audience and attention still as night
   Or summer's noontide air, while thus he spake:—
310 Thrones and Imperial Powers, Offspring of Heav'n,
   Ethereal Virtues! or these titles now
   Must we renounce, and, changing style, be called
   Princes of Hell? for so the popular vote
   Inclines—here to continue, and build up here
315 A growing empire; doubtless! while we dream,
   And know not that the King of Heav'n hath doomed
   This place our dungeon, not our safe retreat
   Beyond his potent arm, to live exempt
   From Heav'n's high jurisdiction, in new league

320   Banded against his throne, but to remain
In strictest bondage, though thus far removed,
Under th' inevitable curb, reserved
His captive multitude. For he, to be sure,
In height or depth, still first and last will reign
325   Sole king, and of his kingdom lose no part
By our revolt, but over Hell extend
His empire, and with iron sceptre rule
Us here, as with his golden those in Heav'n.
What sit we then projecting peace and war?
330   War hath determined us and foiled with loss
Irreparable; terms of peace yet none
Vouchsafed or sought; for what peace will be given
To us enslaved, but custody severe,
And stripes and arbitrary punishment
335   Inflicted? and what peace can we return,
But, to our power, hostility and hate,
Untamed reluctance, and revenge, though slow,
Yet ever plotting how the Conqueror least
May reap his conquest, and may least rejoice
40   In doing what we most in suffering feel?
Nor will occasion want, nor shall we need
With dangerous expedition to invade
Heav'n, whose high walls fear no assault or siege,
Or ambush from the Deep. What if we find
345   Some easier enterprise? There is a place
(If ancient and prophetic fame in Heav'n
Err not)—another World, the happy seat
Of some new race, called *Man*, about this time
To be created like to us, though less
350   In power and excellence, but favoured more
Of him who rules above; so was his will
Pronounced among the Gods, and by an oath
That shook Heav'n's whole circumference confirmed.
Thither let us bend all our thoughts, to learn

355   What creatures there inhabit, of what mould
              Or substance, how endued, and what their power
              And where their weakness: how attempted best,
              By force of subtlety. Though Heav'n be shut,
              And Heav'n's high Arbitrator sit secure
360   In his own strength, this place may lie exposed,
              The utmost border of his kingdom, left
              To their defence who hold it: here, perhaps,
              Some advantageous act may be achieved
              By sudden onset—either with Hell-fire
365   To waste his whole creation, or possess
              All as our own, and drive, as we were driven,
              The puny habitants; or, if not drive,
              Seduce them to our party, that their God
              May prove their foe, and with repenting hand
370   Abolish his own works. This would surpass
              Common revenge, and interrupt his joy
              In our confusion, and our joy upraise
              In his disturbance; when his darling sons,
              Hurled headlong to partake with us, shall curse
375   Their frail original, and faded bliss—
              Faded so soon! Advise if this be worth
              Attempting, or to sit in darkness here
              Hatching vain empires. "Thus Beelzebub
              Pleaded his devilish counsel—first devised
380   By Satan, and in part proposed: for whence,
              But from the author of all ill, could spring
              So deep a malice, to confound the race
              Of mankind in one root, and Earth with Hell
              To mingle and involve, done all to spite
385   The great Creator? But their spite still serves
              His glory to augment. The bold design
              Pleased highly those infernal States, and joy
              Sparkled in all their eyes: with full assent
              They vote: whereat his speech he thus renews:—

390   Well have ye judged, well ended long debate,
            Synod of Gods, and, like to what ye are,
            Great things resolved, which from the lowest deep
            Will once more lift us up, in spite of fate,
            Nearer our ancient seat—perhaps in view
395   Of those bright confines, whence, with neighbouring arms,
            And opportune excursion, we may chance
            Re-enter Heav'n; or else in some mild zone
            Dwell, not unvisited of Heav'n's fair light,
            Secure, and at the brightening orient beam
400   Purge off this gloom: the soft delicious air,
            To heal the scar of these corrosive fires,
            Shall breathe her balm. But, first, whom shall we send
            In search of this new World, whom shall we find
            Sufficient? who shall tempt with wandering feet
405   The dark, unbottomed, infinite Abyss,
            And through the palpable obscure find out
            His uncouth way, or spread his airy flight,
            Upborne with indefatigable wings
            Over the vast abrupt, ere he arrive
410   The happy Isle? What strength, what art, can then
            Suffice, or what evasion bear him safe,
            Through the strict senteries and stations thick
            Of Angels watching round? Here he had need
            All circumspection: and we now no less
415   Choice in our suffrage; for on whom we send
            The weight of all, and our last hope, relies."
            This said, he sat; and expectation held
            His look suspense, awaiting who appeared
            To second, or oppose, or undertake
420   The perilous attempt. But all sat mute,
            Pondering the danger with deep thoughts; and each
            In other's countenance read his own dismay,
            Astonished. None among the choice and prime
            Of those Heav'n-warring champions could be found

425   So hardy as to proffer or accept,
        Alone, the dreadful voyage; till, at last,
        Satan, whom now transcendent glory raised
        Above his fellows, with monarchal pride
        Conscious of highest worth, unmoved thus spake.
430   O Progeny of Heav'n! Empyreal Thrones!
        With reason hath deep silence and demur
        Seized us, though undismayed. Long is the way
        And hard, that out of Hell leads up to light.
        Our prison strong, this huge convex of fire,
435   Outrageous to devour, immures us round
        Ninefold; and gates of burning adamant,
        Barred over us, prohibit all egress.
        These passed, if any pass, the void profound
        Of unessential Night receives him next,
440   Wide-gaping, and with utter loss of being
        Threatens him, plunged in that abortive gulf.
        If thence he scape, into whatever world,
        Or unknown region, what remains him less
        Than unknown dangers, and as hard escape?
445   But I should ill become this throne, O Peers,
        And this imperial sovereignty, adorned
        With splendour, armed with power, if aught proposed
        And judged of public moment in the shape
        Of difficulty or danger, could deter
450   Me from attempting. Wherefore do I assume
        These royalties, and not refuse to reign,
        Refusing to accept as great a share
        Of hazard as of honour, due alike
        To him who reigns, and so much to him due
455   Of hazard more as he above the rest
        High honoured sits? Go, therefore, mighty Powers,
        Terror of Heav'n, though fallen; intend at home,
        While here shall be our home, what best may ease
        The present misery, and render Hell

460 More tolerable; if there be cure or charm
To respite, or deceive, or slack the pain
Of this ill mansion: intermit no watch
Against a wakeful foe, while I abroad
Through all the coasts of dark destruction seek
465 Deliverance for us all. This enterprise
None shall partake with me. "Thus saying, rose
The Monarch, and prevented all reply;
Prudent lest, from his resolution raised,
Others among the chief might offer now,
470 Certain to be refused, what erst they feared,
And, so refused, might in opinion stand
His rivals, winning cheap the high repute
Which he through hazard huge must earn. But they
Dreaded not more th' adventure than his voice
475 Forbidding; and at once with him they rose.
Their rising all at once was as the sound
Of thunder heard remote. Towards him they bend
With awful reverence prone, and as a God
Extol him equal to the Highest in Heav'n.
480 Nor failed they to express how much they praised
That for the general safety he despised
His own: for neither do the Spirits damned
Lose all their virtue; lest bad men should boast
Their specious deeds on earth, which glory excites,
485 Or close ambition varnished o'er with zeal.
Thus they their doubtful consultations dark
Ended, rejoicing in their matchless Chief:
As, when from mountain-tops the dusky clouds
Ascending, while the north wind sleeps, o'erspread
490 Heav'n's cheerful face, the louring element
Scowls o'er the darkened landscape snow or shower,
If chance the radiant sun, with farewell sweet,
Extend his evening beam, the fields revive,
The birds their notes renew, and bleating herds

495   Attest their joy, that hill and valley rings.
        O shame to men! Devil with devil damned
        Firm concord holds; men only disagree
        Of creatures rational, though under hope
        Of Heav'nly grace, and, God proclaiming peace,
500   Yet live in hatred, enmity, and strife
        Among themselves, and levy cruel wars
        Wasting the earth, each other to destroy:
        As if (which might induce us to accord)
        Man had not hellish foes enow besides,
505   That day and night for his destruction wait!
        The Stygian council thus dissolved; and forth
        In order came the grand infernal Peers:
        Midst came their mighty Paramount, and seemed
        Alone th' antagonist of Heav'n, nor less
510   Than Hell's dread Emperor, with pomp supreme,
        And god-like imitated state: him round
        A globe of fiery Seraphim enclosed
        With bright emblazonry, and horrent arms.
        Then of their session ended they bid cry
515   With trumpet's regal sound the great result:
        Toward the four winds four speedy Cherubim
        Put to their mouths the sounding alchemy,
        By herald's voice explained; the hollow Abyss
        Heard far and wide, and all the host of Hell
520   With deafening shout returned them loud acclaim.
        Thence more at ease their minds, and somewhat raised
        By false presumptuous hope, the ranged Powers
        Disband; and, wandering, each his several way
        Pursues, as inclination or sad choice
525   Leads him perplexed, where he may likeliest find
        Truce to his restless thoughts, and entertain
        The irksome hours, till his great Chief return.
        Part on the plain, or in the air sublime,
        Upon the wing or in swift race contend,

530   As at th' Olympian games or Pythian fields;
       Part curb their fiery steeds, or shun the goal
       With rapid wheels, or fronted brigades form:
       As when, to warn proud cities, war appears
       Waged in the troubled sky, and armies rush
535   To battle in the clouds; before each van
       Prick forth the airy knights, and couch their spears,
       Till thickest legions close; with feats of arms
       From either end of heav'n the welkin burns.
       Others, with vast Typhoean rage, more fell,
540   Rend up both rocks and hills, and ride the air
       In whirlwind; Hell scarce holds the wild uproar:—
       As when Alcides, from Oechalia crowned
       With conquest, felt th' envenomed robe, and tore
       Through pain up by the roots Thessalian pines,
545   And Lichas from the top of Oeta threw
       Into th' Euboic sea. Others, more mild,
       Retreated in a silent valley, sing
       With notes angelical to many a harp
       Their own heroic deeds, and hapless fall
550   By doom of battle, and complain that Fate
       Free Virtue should enthrall to Force or Chance.
       Their song was partial; but the harmony
       (What could it less when Spirits immortal sing?)
       Suspended Hell, and took with ravishment
555   The thronging audience. In discourse more sweet
       (For Eloquence the Soul, Song charms the Sense)
       Others apart sat on a hill retired,
       In thoughts more elevate, and reasoned high
       Of Providence, Foreknowledge, Will, and Fate—
560   Fixed fate, free will, foreknowledge absolute,
       And found no end, in wandering mazes lost.
       Of good and evil much they argued then,
       Of happiness and final misery,
       Passion and apathy, and glory and shame:

565 Vain wisdom all, and false philosophy!—
Yet, with a pleasing sorcery, could charm
Pain for a while or anguish, and excite
Fallacious hope, or arm th' obdured breast
With stubborn patience as with triple steel.
570 Another part, in squadrons and gross bands,
On bold adventure to discover wide
That dismal world, if any clime perhaps
Might yield them easier habitation, bend
Four ways their flying march, along the banks
575 Of four infernal rivers, that disgorge
Into the burning lake their baleful streams—
Abhorred Styx, the flood of deadly hate;
Sad Acheron of sorrow, black and deep;
Cocytus, named of lamentation loud
580 Heard on the rueful stream; fierce Phlegeton,
Whose waves of torrent fire inflame with rage.
Far off from these, a slow and silent stream,
Lethe, the river of oblivion, rolls
Her watery labyrinth, whereof who drinks
585 Forthwith his former state and being forgets—
Forgets both joy and grief, pleasure and pain.
Beyond this flood a frozen continent
Lies dark and wild, beat with perpetual storms
Of whirlwind and dire hail, which on firm land
590 Thaws not, but gathers heap, and ruin seems
Of ancient pile; all else deep snow and ice,
A gulf profound as that Serbonian bog
Betwixt Damiata and Mount Casius old,
Where armies whole have sunk: the parching air
595 Burns frore, and cold performs th' effect of fire.
Thither, by harpy-footed Furies haled,
At certain revolutions all the damned
Are brought; and feel by turns the bitter change
Of fierce extremes, extremes by change more fierce,

600   From beds of raging fire to starve in ice
        Their soft ethereal warmth, and there to pine
        Immovable, infixed, and frozen round
        Periods of time,—thence hurried back to fire.
        They ferry over this Lethean sound
605   Both to and fro, their sorrow to augment,
        And wish and struggle, as they pass, to reach
        The tempting stream, with one small drop to lose
        In sweet forgetfulness all pain and woe,
        All in one moment, and so near the brink;
610   But Fate withstands, and, to oppose th' attempt,
        Medusa with Gorgonian terror guards
        The ford, and of itself the water flies
        All taste of living wight, as once it fled
        The lip of Tantalus. Thus roving on
615   In confused march forlorn, th' adventurous bands,
        With shuddering horror pale, and eyes aghast,
        Viewed first their lamentable lot, and found
        No rest. Through many a dark and dreary vale
        They passed, and many a region dolorous,
620   O'er many a frozen, many a fiery alp,
        Rocks, caves, lakes, fens, bogs, dens, and shades of death—
        A universe of death, which God by curse
        Created evil, for evil only good;
        Where all life dies, death lives, and Nature breeds,
625   Perverse, all monstrous, all prodigious things,
        Abominable, unutterable, and worse
        Than fables yet have feigned or fear conceived,
        Gorgons, and Hydras, and Chimeras dire.
        Meanwhile the Adversary of God and Man,
630   Satan, with thoughts inflamed of highest design,
        Puts on swift wings, and toward the gates of Hell
        Explores his solitary flight: sometimes
        He scours the right hand coast, sometimes the left;
        Now shaves with level wing the deep, then soars

635 Up to the fiery concave towering high.
   As when far off at sea a fleet descried
   Hangs in the clouds, by equinoctial winds
   Close sailing from Bengala, or the isles
   Of Ternate and Tidore, whence merchants bring
640 Their spicy drugs; they on the trading flood,
   Through the wide Ethiopian to the Cape,
   Ply stemming nightly toward the pole: so seemed
   Far off the flying Fiend. At last appear
   Hell-bounds, high reaching to the horrid roof,
645 And thrice threefold the gates; three folds were brass,
   Three iron, three of adamantine rock,
   Impenetrable, impaled with circling fire,
   Yet unconsumed. Before the gates there sat
   On either side a formidable Shape.
650 The one seemed woman to the waist, and fair,
   But ended foul in many a scaly fold,
   Voluminous and vast—a serpent armed
   With mortal sting. About her middle round
   A cry of Hell-hounds never-ceasing barked
655 With wide Cerberean mouths full loud, and rung
   A hideous peal; yet, when they list, would creep,
   If aught disturbed their noise, into her womb,
   And kennel there; yet there still barked and howled
   Within unseen. Far less abhorred than these
660 Vexed Scylla, bathing in the sea that parts
   Calabria from the hoarse Trinacrian shore;
   Nor uglier follow the night-hag, when, called
   In secret, riding through the air she comes,
   Lured with the smell of infant blood, to dance
665 With Lapland witches, while the labouring moon
   Eclipses at their charms. The other Shape—
   If shape it might be called that shape had none
   Distinguishable in member, joint, or limb;
   Or substance might be called that shadow seemed,

670   For each seemed either—black it stood as Night,
             Fierce as ten Furies, terrible as Hell,
             And shook a dreadful dart: what seemed his head
             The likeness of a kingly crown had on.
             Satan was now at hand, and from his seat
675   The monster moving onward came as fast
             With horrid strides; Hell trembled as he strode.
             Th' undaunted Fiend what this might be admired—
             Admired, not feared (God and his Son except,
             Created thing naught valued he nor shunned),
680   And with disdainful look thus first began:—
             "Whence and what art thou, execrable Shape,
             That dar'st, though grim and terrible, advance
             Thy miscreated front athwart my way
             To yonder gates? Through them I mean to pass,
685   That be assured, without leave asked of thee.
             Retire; or taste thy folly, and learn by proof,
             Hell-born, not to contend with Spirits of Heav'n."
             To whom the Goblin, full of wrath, replied:—
             "Art thou that traitor Angel? art thou he,
690   Who first broke peace in Heav'n and faith, till then
             Unbroken, and in proud rebellious arms
             Drew after him the third part of Heav'n's sons,
             Conjured against the Highest—for which both thou
             And they, outcast from God, are here condemned
695   To waste eternal days in woe and pain?
             And reckon'st thou thyself with Spirits of Heav'n
             Hell-doomed, and breath'st defiance here and scorn,
             Where I reign king, and, to enrage thee more,
             Thy king and lord? Back to thy punishment,
700   False fugitive; and to thy speed add wings,
             Lest with a whip of scorpions I pursue
             Thy lingering, or with one stroke of this dart
             Strange horror seize thee, and pangs unfelt before."
             So spake the grisly Terror, and in shape,

705	So speaking and so threatening, grew tenfold,
	More dreadful and deform. On th' other side,
	Incensed with indignation, Satan stood
	Unterrified, and like a comet burned,
	That fires the length of Ophiuchus huge
710	In th' arctic sky, and from his horrid hair
	Shakes pestilence and war. Each at the head
	Levelled his deadly aim; their fatal hands
	No second stroke intend; and such a frown
	Each cast at th' other as when two black clouds,
715	With Heav'n's artillery fraught, came rattling on
	Over the Caspian,—then stand front to front
	Hovering a space, till winds the signal blow
	To join their dark encounter in mid-air.
	So frowned the mighty combatants that Hell
720	Grew darker at their frown; so matched they stood;
	For never but once more was wither like
	To meet so great a foe. And now great deeds
	Had been achieved, whereof all Hell had rung,
	Had not the snaky Sorceress, that sat
725	Fast by Hell-gate and kept the fatal key,
	Risen, and with hideous outcry rushed between.
	"O father, what intends thy hand," she cried,
	Against thy only son? What fury, O son,
	Possesses thee to bend that mortal dart
730	Against thy father's head? And know'st for whom?
	For him who sits above, and laughs the while
	At thee, ordained his drudge to execute
	Whate'er his wrath, which he calls justice, bids—
	His wrath, which one day will destroy ye both!"
735	She spake, and at her words the hellish Pest
	Forbore: then these to her Satan returned:—
	"So strange thy outcry, and thy words so strange
	Thou interposest, that my sudden hand,
	Prevented, spares to tell thee yet by deeds

740 What it intends, till first I know of thee
   What thing thou art, thus double-formed, and why,
   In this infernal vale first met, thou call'st
   Me father, and that phantasm call'st my son.
   I know thee not, nor ever saw till now
745 Sight more detestable than him and thee."
   T' whom thus the Portress of Hell-gate replied:—
   "Hast thou forgot me, then; and do I seem
   Now in thine eye so foul?—once deemed so fair
   In Heav'n, when at th' assembly, and in sight
750 Of all the Seraphim with thee combined
   In bold conspiracy against Heav'n's King,
   All on a sudden miserable pain
   Surprised thee, dim thine eyes and dizzy swum
   In darkness, while thy head flames thick and fast
755 Threw forth, till on the left side opening wide,
   Likest to thee in shape and countenance bright,
   Then shining heav'nly fair, a goddess armed,
   Out of thy head I sprung. Amazement seized
   All th' host of Heav'n; back they recoiled afraid
760 At first, and called me *Sin*, and for a sign
   Portentous held me; but, familiar grown,
   I pleased, and with attractive graces won
   The most averse—thee chiefly, who, full oft
   Thyself in me thy perfect image viewing,
765 Becam'st enamoured; and such joy thou took'st
   With me in secret that my womb conceived
   A growing burden. Meanwhile war arose,
   And fields were fought in Heav'n: wherein remained
   (For what could else?) to our Almighty Foe
770 Clear victory; to our part loss and rout
   Through all the Empyrean. Down they fell,
   Driven headlong from the pitch of Heav'n, down
   Into this Deep; and in the general fall
   I also: at which time this powerful key

775   Into my hands was given, with charge to keep
        These gates for ever shut, which none can pass
        Without my opening. Pensive here I sat
        Alone; but long I sat not, till my womb,
        Pregnant by thee, and now excessive grown,
780   Prodigious motion felt and rueful throes.
        At last this odious offspring whom thou seest,
        Thine own begotten, breaking violent way,
        Tore through my entrails, that, with fear and pain
        Distorted, all my nether shape thus grew
785   Transformed: but he my inbred enemy
        Forth issued, brandishing his fatal dart,
        Made to destroy. I fled, and cried out Death!
        Hell trembled at the hideous name, and sighed
        From all her caves, and back resounded Death!
790   I fled; but he pursued (though more, it seems,
        Inflamed with lust than rage), and, swifter far,
        Me overtook, his mother, all dismayed,
        And, in embraces forcible and foul
        Engendering with me, of that rape begot
795   These yelling monsters, that with ceaseless cry
        Surround me, as thou saw'st—hourly conceived
        And hourly born, with sorrow infinite
        To me; for, when they list, into the womb
        That bred them they return, and howl, and gnaw
800   My bowels, their repast; then, bursting forth
        Afresh, with conscious terrors vex me round,
        That rest or intermission none I find.
        Before mine eyes in opposition sits
        Grim Death, my son and foe, who set them on,
805   And me, his parent, would full soon devour
        For want of other prey, but that he knows
        His end with mine involved, and knows that I
        Should prove a bitter morsel, and his bane,
        Whenever that shall be: so Fate pronounced.

810   But thou, O father, I forewarn thee, shun
        His deadly arrow; neither vainly hope
        To be invulnerable in those bright arms,
        Through tempered Heav'nly; for that mortal dint,
        Save he who reigns above, none can resist."
815   She finished; and the subtle Fiend his lore
        Soon learned, now milder, and thus answered smooth:—
        "Dear daughter—since thou claim'st me for thy sire,
        And my fair son here show'st me, the dear pledge
        Of dalliance had with thee in Heav'n, and joys
820   Then sweet, now sad to mention, through dire change
        Befallen us unforeseen, unthought-of—know,
        I come no enemy, but to set free
        From out this dark and dismal house of pain
        Both him and thee, and all the Heav'nly host
825   Of Spirits that, in our just pretences armed,
        Fell with us from on high. From them I go
        This uncouth errand sole, and one for all
        Myself expose, with lonely steps to tread
        Th' unfounded Deep, and through the void immense
830   To search, with wandering quest, a place foretold
        Should be—and, by concurring signs, ere now
        Created vast and round—a place of bliss
        In the purlieus of Heav'n; and therein placed
        A race of upstart creatures, to supply
835   Perhaps our vacant room, though more removed,
        Lest Heav'n, surcharged with potent multitude,
        Might hap to move new broils. Be this, or aught
        Than this more secret, now designed, I haste
        To know; and, this once known, shall soon return,
840   And bring ye to the place where thou and Death
        Shall dwell at ease, and up and down unseen
        Wing silently the buxom air, embalmed
        With odours. There ye shall be fed and filled
        Immeasurably; all things shall be your prey."

845　He ceased; for both seemed highly pleased, and Death
　　　Grinned horrible a ghastly smile, to hear
　　　His famine should be filled, and blessed his maw
　　　Destined to that good hour. No less rejoiced
　　　His mother bad, and thus bespake her sire:—
850　"The key of this infernal Pit, by due
　　　And by command of Heav'n's all-powerful King,
　　　I keep, by him forbidden to unlock
　　　These adamantine gates; against all force
　　　Death ready stands to interpose his dart,
855　Fearless to be o'ermatched by living might.
　　　But what owe I to his commands above,
　　　Who hates me, and hath hither thrust me down
　　　Into this gloom of Tartarus profound,
　　　To sit in hateful office here confined,
860　Inhabitant of Heav'n and Heav'nly born—
　　　Here in perpetual agony and pain,
　　　With terrors and with clamours compassed round
　　　Of mine own brood, that on my bowels feed?
　　　Thou art my father, thou my author, thou
865　My being gav'st me; whom should I obey
　　　But thee? whom follow? Thou wilt bring me soon
　　　To that new world of light and bliss, among
　　　The gods who live at ease, where I shall reign
　　　At thy right hand voluptuous, as beseems
870　Thy daughter and thy darling, without end."
　　　Thus saying, from her side the fatal key,
　　　Sad instrument of all our woe, she took;
　　　And, towards the gate rolling her bestial train,
　　　Forthwith the huge portcullis high up-drew,
875　Which, but herself, not all the Stygian Powers
　　　Could once have moved; then in the key-hole turns
　　　Th' intricate wards, and every bolt and bar

Of massy iron or solid rock with ease
Unfastens. On a sudden open fly,
880 With impetuous recoil and jarring sound,
Th' infernal doors, and on their hinges grate
Harsh thunder, that the lowest bottom shook
Of Erebus. She opened; but to shut
Excelled her power: the gates wide open stood,
885 That with extended wings a bannered host,
Under spread ensigns marching, might pass through
With horse and chariots ranked in loose array;
So wide they stood, and like a furnace-mouth
Cast forth redounding smoke and ruddy flame.
890 Before their eyes in sudden view appear
The secrets of the hoary Deep—a dark
Illimitable ocean, without bound,
Without dimension; where length, breadth, and height,
And time, and place, are lost; where eldest Night
895 And Chaos, ancestors of Nature, hold
Eternal anarchy, amidst the noise
Of endless wars, and by confusion stand.
For Hot, Cold, Moist, and Dry, four champions fierce,
Strive here for mastery, and to battle bring
900 Their embryon atoms: they around the flag
Of each his faction, in their several clans,
Light-armed or heavy, sharp, smooth, swift, or slow,
Swarm populous, unnumbered as the sands
Of Barca or Cyrene's torrid soil,
905 Levied to side with warring winds, and poise
Their lighter wings. To whom these most adhere
He rules a moment: Chaos umpire sits,
And by decision more embroils the fray
By which he reigns: next him, high arbiter,
910 Chance governs all. Into this wild Abyss,
The womb of Nature, and perhaps her grave,

Of neither sea, nor shore, nor air, nor fire,
But all these in their pregnant causes mixed
Confusedly, and which thus must ever fight,
915 Unless th' Almighty Maker them ordain
His dark materials to create more worlds—
Into this wild Abyss the wary Fiend
Stood on the brink of Hell and looked a while,
Pondering his voyage; for no narrow frith
920 He had to cross. Nor was his ear less pealed
With noises loud and ruinous (to compare
Great things with small) than when Bellona storms
With all her battering engines, bent to rase
Some capital city; or less than if this frame
925 Of Heav'n were falling, and these elements
In mutiny had from her axle torn
The steadfast Earth. At last his sail-broad vans
He spread for flight, and, in the surging smoke
Uplifted, spurns the ground; thence many a league,
930 As in a cloudy chair, ascending rides
Audacious; but, that seat soon failing, meets
A vast vacuity. All unawares,
Fluttering his pennons vain, plumb-down he drops
Ten thousand fathom deep, and to this hour
935 Down had been falling, had not, by ill chance,
The strong rebuff of some tumultuous cloud,
Instinct with fire and nitre, hurried him
As many miles aloft. That fury stayed—
Quenched in a boggy Syrtis, neither sea,
940 Nor good dry land—nigh foundered, on he fares,
Treading the crude consistence, half on foot,
Half flying; behoves him now both oar and sail.
As when a gryphon through the wilderness
With winged course, o'er hill or moory dale,
945 Pursues the Arimaspian, who by stealth

Had from his wakeful custody purloined
The guarded gold; so eagerly the Fiend
O'er bog or steep, through strait, rough, dense, or rare,
With head, hands, wings, or feet, pursues his way,
950   And swims, or sinks, or wades, or creeps, or flies.
At length a universal hubbub wild
Of stunning sounds, and voices all confused,
Borne through the hollow dark, assaults his ear
With loudest vehemence. Thither he plies
955   Undaunted, to meet there whatever Power
Or Spirit of the nethermost Abyss
Might in that noise reside, of whom to ask
Which way the nearest coast of darkness lies
Bordering on light; when straight behold the throne
960   Of Chaos, and his dark pavilion spread
Wide on the wasteful Deep! With him enthroned
Sat sable-vested Night, eldest of things,
The consort of his reign; and by them stood
Orcus and Ades, and the dreaded name
965   Of Demogorgon; Rumour next, and Chance,
And Tumult, and Confusion, all embroiled,
And Discord with a thousand various mouths.
T' whom Satan, turning boldly, thus:—"Ye Powers
And Spirits of this nethermost Abyss,
970   Chaos and ancient Night, I come no spy
With purpose to explore or to disturb
The secrets of your realm; but, by constraint
Wandering this darksome desert, as my way
Lies through your spacious empire up to light,
975   Alone and without guide, half lost, I seek,
What readiest path leads where your gloomy bounds
Confine with Heav'n; or, if some other place,
From your dominion won, th' Ethereal King
Possesses lately, thither to arrive

980   I travel this profound. Direct my course:
           Directed, no mean recompense it brings
           To your behoof, if I that region lost,
           All usurpation thence expelled, reduce
           To her original darkness and your sway
985   (Which is my present journey), and once more
           Erect the standard there of ancient Night.
           Yours be th' advantage all, mine the revenge!"
           Thus Satan; and him thus the Anarch old,
           With faltering speech and visage incomposed,
990   Answered: "I know thee, stranger, who thou art—
           That mighty leading Angel, who of late
           Made head against Heav'n's King, though overthrown.
           I saw and heard; for such a numerous host
           Fled not in silence through the frighted Deep,
995   With ruin upon ruin, rout on rout,
           Confusion worse confounded; and Heav'n-gates
           Poured out by millions her victorious bands,
           Pursuing. I upon my frontiers here
           Keep residence; if all I can will serve
1000   That little which is left so to defend,
           Encroached on still through our intestine broils
           Weakening the sceptre of old Night: first, Hell,
           Your dungeon, stretching far and wide beneath;
           Now lately Heav'n and Earth, another world
1005   Hung o'er my realm, linked in a golden chain
           To that side Heav'n from whence your legions fell!
           If that way be your walk, you have not far;
           So much the nearer danger. Go, and speed;
           Havoc, and spoil, and ruin, are my gain."
1010   He ceased; and Satan stayed not to reply,
           But, glad that now his sea should find a shore,
           With fresh alacrity and force renewed

Springs upward, like a pyramid of fire,
Into the wild expanse, and through the shock
1015   Of fighting elements, on all sides round
Environed, wins his way; harder beset
And more endangered than when Argo passed
Through Bosporus betwixt the justling rocks,
Or when Ulysses on the larboard shunned
1020   Charybdis, and by th' other whirlpool steered.
So he with difficulty and labour hard
Moved on, with difficulty and labour he;
But, he once passed, soon after, when Man fell,
Strange alteration! Sin and Death amain,
1025   Following his track (such was the will of Heav'n)
Paved after him a broad and beaten way
Over the dark Abyss, whose boiling gulf
Tamely endured a bridge of wondrous length,
From Hell continued, reaching th' utmost orb
1030   Of this frail World; by which the Spirits perverse
With easy intercourse pass to and fro
To tempt or punish mortals, except whom
God and good Angels guard by special grace.
But now at last the sacred influence
1035   Of light appears, and from the walls of Heav'n
Shoots far into the bosom of dim Night
A glimmering dawn. Here Nature first begins
Her farthest verge, and Chaos to retire,
As from her outmost works, a broken foe,
1040   With tumult less and with less hostile din;
That Satan with less toil, and now with ease,
Wafts on the calmer wave by dubious light,
And, like a weather-beaten vessel, holds
Gladly the port, though shrouds and tackle torn;
1045   Or in the emptier waste, resembling air,
Weighs his spread wings, at leisure to behold

Far off th' empyreal Heav'n, extended wide
In circuit, undetermined square or round,
With opal towers and battlements adorned
1050 Of living sapphire, once his native seat;
And, fast by, hanging in a golden chain,
This pendent World, in bigness as a star
Of smallest magnitude close by the moon.
Thither, full fraught with mischievous revenge,
1055 Accursed, and in a cursed hour, he hies.

BOOK III

THE ARGUMENT

God sitting on his throne sees Satan flying towards this world, then newly created; shows him to the Son who sat at his right hand; foretells the success of Satan in perverting mankind; clears his own justice and wisdom from all

5 imputation, having created man free and able enough to have withstood his tempter; yet declares his purpose of grace towards him, in regard he fell not of his own malice, as did Satan, but by him seduced. The Son of God renders praises to his Father for the manifestation of his

10 gracious purpose towards man without the satisfaction of divine justice; man hath offended the majesty of God by aspiring to Godhead, and therefore with all his progeny devoted to death must die, unless someone can be found sufficient to answer for his offers himself a ransom for

15 man: the Father accepts him, ordains his Incarnation, pronounces his Exaltation above all names in Heav'n and earth; commands all the angels to adore him; they obey, and hymning to their harps in full choir, celebrate the Father and the Son. Meanwhile Satan alights upon the bare

20 convex of this world's outermost orb; where wandering he first finds a place since called the Limbo of Vanity; what persons and things fly up thither; thence comes to the gate of

Heav'n, described ascending by stairs, and the waters above the firmament that flow about it: his passage of that orb, but first changes himself into the shape of a meaner angel; and pretending a zealous desire to behold the new Creation and man whom God had placed here, inquires of him the place of his habitation, and is directed; alights first on Mount Niphates.

Hail, holy Light, offspring of Heav'n firstborn,
Or of the Eternal coeternal beam
May I express thee unblam'd? since God is light,
And never but in unapproached light
5   Dwelt from eternity, dwelt then in thee
Bright effluence of bright essence increate.
Or hear'st thou rather pure ethereal stream,
Whose fountain who shall tell? before the sun,
Before the Heav'ns thou wert, and at the voice
10   Of God, as with a mantle, didst invest
The rising world of waters dark and deep,
Won from the void and formless infinite.
Thee I re-visit now with bolder wing,
Escap'd the Stygian pool, though long detain'd
15   In that obscure sojourn, while in my flight
Through utter and through middle darkness borne,
With other notes than to the Orphean lyre
I sung of Chaos and eternal Night;
Taught by the Heav'nly Muse to venture down
20   The dark descent, and up to re-ascend,
Though hard and rare: Thee I revisit safe,
And feel thy sovran vital lamp; but thou
Revisit'st not these eyes, that roll in vain
To find thy piercing ray, and find no dawn;
25   So thick a drop serene hath quench'd their orbs,
Or dim suffusion veil'd. Yet not the more

Cease I to wander, where the Muses haunt,
Clear spring, or shady grove, or sunny hill,
Smit with the love of sacred song; but chief
30   Thee, Sion, and the flowery brooks beneath,
That wash thy hallow'd feet, and warbling flow,
Nightly I visit: nor sometimes forget
So were I equall'd with them in renown,
Thy sovran command, that Man should find grace;
35   Blind Thamyris, and blind Maeonides,
And Tiresias, and Phineus, prophets old:
Then feed on thoughts, that voluntary move
Harmonious numbers; as the wakeful bird
Sings darkling, and in shadiest covert hid
40   Tunes her nocturnal note. Thus with the year
Seasons return; but not to me returns
Day, or the sweet approach of even or morn,
Or sight of vernal bloom, or summer's rose,
Or flocks, or herds, or human face divine;
45   But cloud instead, and ever-during dark
Surrounds me, from the cheerful ways of men
Cut off, and for the book of knowledge fair
Presented with a universal blank
Of nature's works to me expunged and razed,
50   And wisdom at one entrance quite shut out.
So much the rather thou, celestial Light,
Shine inward, and the mind through all her powers
Irradiate; there plant eyes, all mist from thence
Purge and disperse, that I may see and tell
55   Of things invisible to mortal sight.
Now had the Almighty Father from above,
From the pure empyrean where he sits
High throned above all heighth, bent down his eye
His own works and their works at once to view:

60	About him all the Sanctities of Heav'n
	Stood thick as stars, and from his sight received
	Beatitude past utterance; on his right
	The radiant image of his glory sat,
	His only son; on earth he first beheld
65	Our two first parents, yet the only two
	Of mankind in the happy garden placed
	Reaping immortal fruits of joy and love,
	Uninterrupted joy, unrivalled love,
	In blissful solitude; he then surveyed
70	Hell and the gulf between, and Satan there
	Coasting the wall of Heav'n on this side Night
	In the dun air sublime, and ready now
	To stoop with wearied wings, and willing feet,
	On the bare outside of this world, that seemed
75	Firm land imbosomed, without firmament,
	Uncertain which, in ocean or in air.
	Him God beholding from his prospect high,
	Wherein past, present, future, he beholds,
	Thus to his only Son foreseeing spake.
80	Only begotten Son, seest thou what rage
	Transports our Adversary? whom no bounds
	Prescribed no bars of Hell, nor all the chains
	Heaped on him there, nor yet the main abyss
	Wide interrupt, can hold; so bent he seems
85	On desperate revenge, that shall redound
	Upon his own rebellious head. And now,
	Through all restraint broke loose, he wings his way
	Not far off Heav'n, in the precincts of light,
	Directly towards the new created world,
90	And man there placed, with purpose to assay
	If him by force he can destroy, or, worse,
	By some false guile pervert; and shall pervert;

For man will hearken to his glozing lies,
And easily transgress the sole command,
95   Sole pledge of his obedience: So will fall
He and his faithless progeny: Whose fault?
Whose but his own? ingrate, he had of me
All he could have; I made him just and right,
Sufficient to have stood, though free to fall.
100   Such I created all the ethereal Powers
And Spirits, both them who stood, and them who failed;
Freely they stood who stood, and fell who fell.
Not free, what proof could they have given sincere
Of true allegiance, constant faith or love,
105   Where only what they needs must do appeared,
Not what they would? What praise could they receive?
What pleasure I from such obedience paid,
When will and reason (reason also is choice)
Useless and vain, of freedom both despoiled,
110   Made passive both, had served necessity,
Not me. They therefore, as to right belonged,
So were created, nor can justly accuse
Their Maker, or their making, or their fate,
As if predestination over-rul'd
115   Their will disposed by absolute decree
Or high foreknowledge they themselves decreed
Their own revolt, not I; if I foreknew,
Foreknowledge had no influence on their fault,
Which had no less proved certain unforeknown.
120   So without least impulse or shadow of fate,
Or aught by me immutably foreseen,
They trespass, authors to themselves in all
Both what they judge, and what they choose; for so
I formed them free: and free they must remain,
125   Till they enthrall themselves; I else must change
Their nature, and revoke the high decree

Unchangeable, eternal, which ordained
Their freedom: they themselves ordained their fall.
The first sort by their own suggestion fell,
130 Self-tempted, self-depraved: Man falls, deceived
By the other first: Man therefore shall find grace,
The other none: In mercy and justice both,
Through Heav'n and Earth, so shall my glory excel;
But Mercy, first and last, shall brightest shine.
135 Thus while God spake, ambrosial fragrance filled
All Heav'n, and in the blessed Spirits elect
Sense of new joy ineffable diffused.
Beyond compare the Son of God was seen
Most glorious; in him all his Father shone
140 Substantially expressed; and in his face
Divine compassion visibly appeared,
Love without end, and without measure grace,
Which uttering, thus he to his Father spake.
O Father, gracious was that word which closed
145 Thy sov'reign command, that Man should find grace;
For which both Heav'n and earth shall high extol
Thy praises, with the innumerable sound
Of hymns and sacred songs, wherewith thy throne
Encompassed shall resound thee ever blest.
150 For should Man finally be lost, should Man,
Thy creature late so loved, thy youngest son,
Fall circumvented thus by fraud, though joined
With his own folly? that be from thee far,
That far be from thee, Father, who art judge
155 Of all things made, and judgest only right.
Or shall the Adversary thus obtain
His end, and frustrate thine? shall he fulfill
His malice, and thy goodness bring to naught,
Or proud return, though to his heavier doom,
160 Yet with revenge accomplished, and to Hell

Draw after him the whole race of mankind,
By him corrupted? or wilt thou thyself
Abolish thy creation, and unmake
For him, what for thy glory thou hast made?
165   So should thy goodness and thy greatness both
Be questioned and blasphemed without defence.
To whom the great Creator thus replied.
O son, in whom my soul hath chief delight,
Son of my bosom, Son who art alone.
170   My word, my wisdom, and effectual might,
All hast thou spoken as my thoughts are, all
As my eternal purpose hath decreed;
Man shall not quite be lost, but saved who will;
Yet not of will in him, but grace in me
175   Freely vouchsafed; once more I will renew
His lapsed powers, though forfeit; and enthralled
By sin to foul exorbitant desires;
Upheld by me, yet once more he shall stand
On even ground against his mortal foe;
180   By me upheld, that he may know how frail
His fallen condition is, and to me owe
All his deliverance, and to none but me.
Some I have chosen of peculiar grace,
Elect above the rest; so is my will:
185   The rest shall hear me call, and oft be warned
Their sinful state, and to appease betimes
The incensed Deity, while offered grace
Invites; for I will clear their senses dark,
What may suffice, and soften stony hearts
190   To pray, repent, and bring obedience due.
To prayer, repentance, and obedience due,
Though but endeavoured with sincere intent,
Mine ear shall not be slow, mine eye not shut.
And I will place within them as a guide,

195   My umpire Conscience; whom if they will hear,
Light after light, well used, they shall attain,
And to the end, persisting, safe arrive.
This my long sufferance, and my day of grace,
They who neglect and scorn, shall never taste;
200   But hard be hardened, blind be blinded more,
That they may stumble on, and deeper fall;
And none but such from mercy I exclude.
But yet all is not done; Man disobeying,
Disloyal, breaks his fealty, and sins
205   Against the high supremacy of Heav'n,
Affecting God-head, and, so losing all,
To expiate his treason hath nought left,
But to destruction sacred and devote,
He, with his whole posterity, must die,
210   Die he or justice must; unless for him
Some other able, and as willing, pay
The rigid satisfaction, death for death.
Say, Heav'nly Powers, where shall we find such love?
Which of you will be mortal, to redeem
215   Man's mortal crime, and just the unjust to save?
Dwells in all Heav'n charity so dear?
He asked, but all the Heav'nly quire stood mute,
And silence was in Heav'n: on Man's behalf
Patron or intercessor none appeared,
220   Much less that durst upon his own head draw
The deadly forfeiture, and ransom set.
And now without redemption all mankind
Must have been lost, adjudg'd to Death and Hell
By doom severe, had not the Son of God,
225   In whom the fulness dwells of love divine,
His dearest mediation thus renew'd.
Father, thy word is past, Man shall find grace;

And shall grace not find means, that finds her way,
The speediest of thy winged messengers,
230   To visit all thy creatures, and to all
Comes unprevented, unimplor'd, unsought?
Happy for Man, so coming; he her aid
Can never seek, once dead in sins, and lost;
Atonement for himself, or offering meet,
235   Indebted and undone, hath none to bring;
Behold me then: me for him, life for life
I offer: on me let thine anger fall;
Account me Man; I for his sake will leave
Thy bosom, and this glory next to thee
240   Freely put off, and for him lastly die
Well pleased; on me let Death wreak all his rage.
Under his gloomy power I shall not long
Lie vanquished. Thou hast given me to possess
Life in myself for ever; by thee I live;
245   Though now to Death I yield, and am his due,
All that of me can die, yet, that debt paid,
Thou wilt not leave me in the loathsome grave
His prey, nor suffer my unspotted soul
For ever with corruption there to dwell;
250   But I shall rise victorious, and subdue
My vanquisher, spoiled of his vaunted spoil.
Death his death's wound shall then receive, and stoop
Inglorious, of his mortal sting disarmed;
I through the ample air in triumph high
255   Shall lead Hell captive maugre Hell, and show
The powers of darkness bound. Thou, at the sight
Pleased, out of Heav'n shalt look down and smile,
While, by thee raised, I ruin all my foes;
Death last, and with his carcass glut the grave;
260   Then, with the multitude of my redeemed,
Shall enter Heav'n, long absent, and return,

Father, to see thy face, wherein no cloud
Of anger shall remain, but peace assured
And reconcilement: wrath shall be no more
265   Thenceforth, but in thy presence joy entire.
His words here ended; but his meek aspect
Silent yet spake, and breathed immortal love
To mortal men, above which only shone
Filial obedience: as a sacrifice
270   Glad to be offered, he attends the will
Of his great Father. Admiration seized
All Heav'n, what this might mean, and whither tend,
Wondering; but soon th' Almighty thus replied:
O thou in Heav'n and Earth the only peace
275   Found out for mankind under wrath, O thou
My sole complacence! Well thou know'st how dear
To me are all my works; nor Man the least,
Though last created, that for him I spare
Thee from my bosom and right hand, to save,
280   By losing thee a while, the whole race lost.
Thou, therefore, whom thou only canst redeem,
Their nature also to thy nature join;
And be thyself Man among men on Earth,
Made flesh, when time shall be, of virgin seed,
285   By wondrous birth; be thou in Adam's room
The head of all mankind, though Adam's son.
As in him perish all men, so in thee,
As from a second root, shall be restored
As many as are restored, without thee none.
290   His crime makes guilty all his sons; thy merit,
Imputed, shall absolve them who renounce
Their own both righteous and unrighteous deeds,
And live in thee transplanted, and from thee
Receive new life. So Man, as is most just,
295   Shall satisfy for Man, be judged and die,

And dying rise, and rising with him raise
His brethren, ransomed with his own dear life.
So Heav'nly love shall outdo hellish hate,
Giving to death, and dying to redeem,
300 So dearly to redeem what hellish hate
So easily destroyed, and still destroys
In those who, when they may, accept not grace.
Nor shalt thou, by descending to assume
Man's nature, lessen or degrade thine own.
305 Because thou hast, though throned in highest bliss
Equal to God, and equally enjoying
God-like fruition, quitted all, to save
A world from utter loss, and hast been found
By merit more than birthright Son of God,
310 Found worthiest to be so by being good,
Far more than great or high; because in thee
Love hath abounded more than glory abounds;
Therefore thy humiliation shall exalt
With thee thy manhood also to this throne:
315 Here shalt thou sit incarnate, here shalt reign
Both God and Man, Son both of God and Man,
Anointed universal King; all power
I give thee; reign for ever, and assume
Thy merits; under thee, as head supreme,
320 Thrones, Princedoms, Powers, Dominions, I reduce:
All knees to thee shall bow, of them that bide
In Heav'n, or Earth, or under Earth in Hell.
When thou, attended gloriously from Heav'n,
Shalt in the sky appear, and from thee send
325 The summoning Arch-Angels to proclaim
Thy dread tribunal; forthwith from all winds,
The living, and forthwith the cited dead
Of all past ages, to the general doom
Shall hasten; such a peal shall rouse their sleep.

330   Then, all thy saints assembled, thou shalt judge
       Bad Men and Angels; they, arraigned, shall sink
       Beneath thy sentence; Hell, her numbers full,
       Thenceforth shall be for ever shut. Mean while
       The world shall burn, and from her ashes spring
335   New Heav'n and Earth, wherein the just shall dwell,
       And, after all their tribulations long,
       See golden days, fruitful of golden deeds,
       With joy and peace triumphing, and fair truth.
       Then thou thy regal scepter shalt lay by,
340   For regal scepter then no more shall need,
       God shall be all in all. But, all ye Gods,
       Adore him, who to compass all this dies;
       Adore the Son, and honour him as me.
       No sooner had the Almighty ceased, but all
345   The multitude of Angels, with a shout
       Loud as from numbers without number, sweet
       As from blest voices, uttering joy, Heav'n rung
       With jubilee, and loud Hosannas filled
       The eternal regions: Lowly reverent
350   Towards either throne they bow, and to the ground
       With solemn adoration down they cast
       Their crowns inwove with amarant and gold;
       Immortal amarant, a flower which once
       In Paradise, fast by the tree of life,
355   Began to bloom; but soon for man's offence
       To Heav'n removed, where first it grew, there grows,
       And flowers aloft shading the fount of life,
       And where the river of bliss through midst of Heav'n
       Rolls o'er Elysian flowers her amber stream;
360   With these that never fade the Spirits elect
       Bind their resplendent locks inwreathed with beams;
       Now in loose garlands thick thrown off, the bright

Pavement, that like a sea of jasper shone,
Impurpled with celestial roses smiled.
365 Then, crowned again, their golden harps they took,
Harps ever tuned, that glittering by their side
Like quivers hung, and with preamble sweet
Of charming symphony they introduce
Their sacred song, and waken raptures high;
370 No voice exempt, no voice but well could join
Melodious part, such concord is in Heav'n.
Thee, Father, first they sung Omnipotent,
Immutable, Immortal, Infinite,
Eternal King; the Author of all being,
375 Fountain of light, thyself invisible
Amidst the glorious brightness where thou sit'st
Throned inaccessible, but when thou shadest
The full blaze of thy beams, and, through a cloud
Drawn round about thee like a radiant shrine,
380 Dark with excessive bright thy skirts appear,
Yet dazzle Heav'n, that brightest Seraphim
Approach not, but with both wings veil their eyes.
Thee next they sang of all creation first,
Begotten Son, Divine Similitude,
385 In whose conspicuous countenance, without cloud
Made visible, the Almighty Father shines,
Whom else no creature can behold; on thee
Impressed the effulgence of his glory abides,
Transfused on thee his ample Spirit rests.
390 He Heav'n of Heav'ns and all the Powers therein
By thee created; and by thee threw down
The aspiring Dominations: Thou that day
Thy Father's dreadful thunder didst not spare,
Nor stop thy flaming chariot-wheels, that shook
395 Heav'n's everlasting frame, while o'er the necks
Thou drovest of warring Angels disarrayed.

Back from pursuit thy Powers with loud acclaim
Thee only extolled, Son of thy Father's might,
To execute fierce vengeance on his foes,
400 Not so on Man: Him through their malice fallen,
Father of mercy and grace, thou didst not doom
So strictly, but much more to pity incline:
No sooner did thy dear and only Son
Perceive thee purposed not to doom frail Man
405 So strictly, but much more to pity inclined,
He to appease thy wrath, and end the strife
Of mercy and justice in thy face discerned,
Regardless of the bliss wherein he sat
Second to thee, offered himself to die
410 For Man's offence. O unexampled love,
Love no where to be found less than Divine!
Hail, Son of God, Saviour of Men! Thy name
Shall be the copious matter of my song
Henceforth, and never shall my heart thy praise
415 Forget, nor from thy Father's praise disjoin.
Thus they in Heav'n, above the starry sphere,
Their happy hours in joy and hymning spent.
Mean while upon the firm opacous globe
Of this round world, whose first convex divides
420 The luminous inferior orbs, enclosed
From Chaos, and the inroad of Darkness old,
Satan alighted walks: A globe far off
It seemed, now seems a boundless continent
Dark, waste, and wild, under the frown of Night
425 Starless exposed, and ever-threatening storms
Of Chaos blustering round, inclement sky;
Save on that side which from the wall of Heav'n,
Though distant far, some small reflection gains
Of glimmering air less vexed with tempest loud:
430 Here walked the Fiend at large in spacious field.

As when a vultur on Imaus bred,
Whose snowy ridge the roving Tartar bounds,
Dislodging from a region scarce of prey
To gorge the flesh of lambs or yeanling kids,
435   On hills where flocks are fed, flies toward the springs
Of Ganges or Hydaspes, Indian streams;
But in his way lights on the barren plains
Of Sericana, where Chineses drive
With sails and wind their cany waggons light:
440   So, on this windy sea of land, the Fiend
Walked up and down alone, bent on his prey;
Alone, for other creature in this place,
Living or lifeless, to be found was none;
None yet, but store hereafter from the earth
445   Up hither like aereal vapours flew
Of all things transitory and vain, when sin
With vanity had filled the works of men:
Both all things vain, and all who in vain things
Built their fond hopes of glory or lasting fame,
450   Or happiness in this or the other life;
All who have their reward on earth, the fruits
Of painful superstition and blind zeal,
Naught seeking but the praise of men, here find
Fit retribution, empty as their deeds;
455   All the unaccomplished works of Nature's hand,
Abortive, monstrous, or unkindly mixed,
Dissolved on earth, fleet hither, and in vain,
Till final dissolution, wander here;
Not in the neighbouring moon as some have dreamed;
460   Those argent fields more likely habitants,
Translated Saints, or middle Spirits hold
Betwixt the angelical and human kind.
Hither of ill-joined sons and daughters born
First from the ancient world those giants came

465   With many a vain exploit, though then renowned:
The builders next of Babel on the plain
Of Sennaar, and still with vain design,
New Babels, had they wherewithal, would build:
Others came single; he, who, to be deemed
470   A God, leaped fondly into Aetna flames,
Empedocles; and he, who, to enjoy
Plato's Elysium, leaped into the sea,
Cleombrotus; and many more too long,
Embryos, and idiots, eremites, and friars
475   White, black, and gray, with all their trumpery.
Here pilgrims roam, that strayed so far to seek
In Golgotha him dead, who lives in Heav'n;
And they, who to be sure of Paradise,
Dying, put on the weeds of Dominick,
480   Or in Franciscan think to pass disguised;
They pass the planets seven, and pass the fixed,
And that crystalline sphere whose balance weighs
The trepidation talked, and that first moved;
And now Saint Peter at Heav'n's wicket seems
485   To wait them with his keys, and now at foot
Of Heav'n's ascent they lift their feet, when lo
A violent cross wind from either coast
Blows them transverse, ten thousand leagues awry
Into the devious air: Then might ye see
490   Cowls, hoods, and habits, with their wearers, tossed
And fluttered into rags; then relics, beads,
Indulgences, dispenses, pardons, bulls,
The sport of winds: All these, upwhirled aloft,
Fly o'er the backside of the world far off
495   Into a Limbo large and broad, since called
The Paradise of Fools, to few unknown
Long after; now unpeopled, and untrod.

All this dark globe the Fiend found as he passed,
And long he wandered, till at last a gleam
500   Of dawning light turned thither-ward in haste
His travelled steps: far distant he descries
Ascending by degrees magnificent
Up to the wall of Heav'n a structure high;
At top whereof, but far more rich, appeared
505   The work as of a kingly palace-gate,
With frontispiece of diamond and gold
Embellished; thick with sparkling orient gems
The portal shone, inimitable on earth
By model, or by shading pencil, drawn.
510   These stairs were such as whereon Jacob saw
Angels ascending and descending, bands
Of guardians bright, when he from Esau fled
To Padan-Aram, in the field of Luz
Dreaming by night under the open sky
515   And waking cried, *This is the gate of Heav'n.*
Each stair mysteriously was meant, nor stood
There always, but drawn up to Heav'n sometimes
Viewless; and underneath a bright sea flowed
Of jasper, or of liquid pearl, whereon
520   Who after came from earth, failing arrived
Wafted by Angels, or flew o'er the lake
Rapt in a chariot drawn by fiery steeds.
The stairs were then let down, whether to dare
The Fiend by easy ascent, or aggravate
525   His sad exclusion from the doors of bliss:
Direct against which opened from beneath,
Just o'er the blissful seat of Paradise,
A passage down to the Earth, a passage wide,
Wider by far than that of after-times
530   Over mount Sion, and, though that were large,
Over the Promised Land to God so dear;

By which, to visit oft those happy tribes,
On high behests his angels to and fro
Passed frequent, and his eye with choice regard
535 From Paneas, the fount of Jordan's flood,
To Beersaba, where the Holy Land
Borders on Egypt and the Arabian shore;
So wide the opening seemed, where bounds were set
To darkness, such as bound the ocean wave.
540 Satan from hence, now on the lower stair,
That scaled by steps of gold to Heav'n-gate,
Looks down with wonder at the sudden view
Of all this world at once. As when a scout,
Through dark and desert ways with peril gone
545 All night; at last by break of cheerful dawn
Obtains the brow of some high-climbing hill,
Which to his eye discovers unaware
The goodly prospect of some foreign land
First seen, or some renowned metropolis
550 With glistering spires and pinnacles adorned,
Which now the rising sun gilds with his beams:
Such wonder seized, though after Heav'n seen,
The Spirit malign, but much more envy seized,
At sight of all this world beheld so fair.
555 Round he surveys (and well might, where he stood
So high above the circling canopy
Of night's extended shade,) from eastern point
Of Libra to the fleecy star that bears
Andromeda far off Atlantic seas
560 Beyond the horizon; then from pole to pole
He views in breadth, and without longer pause
Down right into the world's first region throws
His flight precipitant, and winds with ease
Through the pure marble air his oblique way
565 Amongst innumerable stars, that shone

Stars distant, but nigh hand seemed other worlds;
Or other worlds they seemed, or happy isles,
Like those Hesperian gardens famed of old,
Fortunate fields, and groves, and flowery vales,
570   Thrice happy isles; but who dwelt happy there
He staid not to inquire: Above them all
The golden sun, in splendour likest Heav'n,
Allured his eye; thither his course he bends
Through the calm firmament, (but up or down,
575   By center, or eccentric, hard to tell,
Or longitude,) where the great luminary
Aloof the vulgar constellations thick,
That from his lordly eye keep distance due,
Dispenses light from far; they, as they move
580   Their starry dance in numbers that compute
Days, months, and years, towards his all-cheering lamp
Turn swift their various motions, or are turned
By his magnetic beam, that gently warms
The universe, and to each inward part
585   With gentle penetration, though unseen,
Shoots invisible virtue even to the deep;
So wondrously was set his station bright.
There lands the Fiend, a spot like which perhaps
Astronomer in the sun's lucent orb
590   Through his glazed optic tube yet never saw.
The place he found beyond expression bright,
Compared with aught on earth, metal or stone;
Not all parts like, but all alike informed
With radiant light, as glowing iron with fire;
595   If metal, part seemed gold, part silver clear;
If stone, carbuncle most or chrysolite,
Ruby or topaz, to the twelve that shone
In Aaron's breast-plate, and a stone besides
Imagined rather oft than elsewhere seen,

600	That stone, or like to that which here below
	Philosophers in vain so long have sought,
	In vain, though by their powerful art they bind
	Volatile Hermes, and call up unbound
	In various shapes old Proteus from the sea,
605	Drained through a limbeck to his native form.
	What wonder then if fields and regions here
	Breathe forth Elixir pure, and rivers run
	Potable gold, when with one virtuous touch
	The arch-chemick sun, so far from us remote,
610	Produces, with terrestrial humour mixed,
	Here in the dark so many precious things
	Of colour glorious, and effect so rare?
	Here matter new to gaze the Devil met
	Undazzled; far and wide his eye commands;
615	For sight no obstacle found here, nor shade,
	But all sun-shine, as when his beams at noon
	Culminate from the equator, as they now
	Shot upward still direct, whence no way round
	Shadow from body opaque can fall; and the air,
620	No where so clear, sharpened his visual ray
	To objects distant far, whereby he soon
	Saw within ken a glorious Angel stand,
	The same whom John saw also in the sun:
	His back was turned, but not his brightness hid;
625	Of beaming sunny rays a golden tiar
	Circled his head, nor less his locks behind
	Illustrious on his shoulders fledge with wings
	Lay waving round; on some great charge employed
	He seemed, or fixed in cogitation deep.
630	Glad was the Spirit impure, as now in hope
	To find who might direct his wandering flight
	To Paradise, the happy seat of Man,

His journey's end and our beginning woe.
But first he casts to change his proper shape,
635   Which else might work him danger or delay:
And now a stripling Cherub he appears,
Not of the prime, yet such as in his face
Youth smiled celestial, and to every limb
Suitable grace diffused, so well he feigned:
640   Under a coronet his flowing hair
In curls on either cheek played; wings he wore
Of many a coloured plume, sprinkled with gold;
His habit fit for speed succinct, and held
Before his decent steps a silver wand.
645   He drew not nigh unheard; the Angel bright,
Ere he drew nigh, his radiant visage turned,
Admonished by his ear, and straight was known
The Arch-Angel Uriel, one of the seven
Who in God's presence, nearest to his throne,
650   Stand ready at command, and are his eyes
That run through all the Heav'ns, or down to the Earth
Bear his swift errands over moist and dry,
O'er sea and land: him Satan thus accosts.
Uriel, for thou of those seven Spirits that stand
655   In sight of God's high throne, gloriously bright,
The first art wont his great authentic will
Interpreter through highest Heav'n to bring,
Where all his sons thy embassy attend;
And here art likeliest by supreme decree
660   Like honour to obtain, and as his eye
To visit oft this new creation round;
Unspeakable desire to see, and know
All these his wondrous works, but chiefly Man,
His chief delight and favour, him for whom
665   All these his works so wonderous he ordained,
Hath brought me from the quires of Cherubim

Alone thus wandering. Brightest Seraph, tell
In which of all these shining orbs hath Man
His fixed seat, or fixed seat hath none,
670   But all these shining orbs his choice to dwell;
That I may find him, and with secret gaze
Or open admiration him behold,
On whom the great Creator hath bestowed
Worlds, and on whom hath all these graces poured;
675   That both in him and all things, as is meet,
The universal Maker we may praise;
Who justly hath driven out his rebel foes
To deepest Hell, and, to repair that loss,
Created this new happy race of Men
680   To serve him better: Wise are all his ways.
So spake the false dissembler unperceived;
For neither Man nor Angel can discern
Hypocrisy, the only evil that walks
Invisible, except to God alone,
685   By his permissive will, through Heav'n and Earth:
And oft, though wisdom wake, suspicion sleeps
At wisdom's gate, and to simplicity
Resigns her charge, while goodness thinks no ill
Where no ill seems: Which now for once beguiled
690   Uriel, though regent of the sun, and held
The sharpest-sighted Spirit of all in Heav'n;
Who to the fraudulent impostor foul,
In his uprightness, answer thus returned.
Fair Angel, thy desire, which tends to know
695   The works of God, thereby to glorify
The great Work-master, leads to no excess
That reaches blame, but rather merits praise
The more it seems excess, that led thee hither
From thy empyreal mansion thus alone,
700   To witness with thine eyes what some perhaps,

Contented with report, hear only in Heav'n:
For wonderful indeed are all his works,
Pleasant to know, and worthiest to be all
Had in remembrance always with delight;
705 But what created mind can comprehend
Their number, or the wisdom infinite
That brought them forth, but hid their causes deep?
I saw when at his word the formless mass,
This world's material mould, came to a heap:
710 Confusion heard his voice, and wild uproar
Stood ruled, stood vast infinitude confined;
Till at his second bidding Darkness fled,
Light shone, and order from disorder sprung:
Swift to their several quarters hasted then
715 The cumbrous elements, earth, flood, air, fire;
And this ethereal quintessence of Heav'n
Flew upward, spirited with various forms,
That rolled orbicular, and turned to stars
Numberless, as thou seest, and how they move;
720 Each had his place appointed, each his course;
The rest in circuit walls this universe.
Look downward on that globe, whose hither side
With light from hence, though but reflected, shines;
That place is Earth, the seat of Man; that light
725 His day, which else, as the other hemisphere,
Night would invade; but there the neighbouring moon
(So call that opposite fair star) her aid
Timely interposes, and her monthly round
Still ending, still renewing, through mid Heav'n,
730 With borrowed light her countenance triform
Hence fills and empties to enlighten the Earth,
And in her pale dominion checks the night.
That spot, to which I point, is Paradise,
Adam's abode; those lofty shades, his bower.

735   Thy way thou canst not miss, me mine requires.
        Thus said, he turned; and Satan, bowing low,
        As to superior Spirits is wont in Heav'n,
        Where honour due and reverence none neglects,
        Took leave, and toward the coast of earth beneath,
740   Down from the ecliptic, sped with hoped success,
        Throws his steep flight in many an airy wheel;
        Nor staid, till on Niphates' top he lights.

BOOK IV

THE ARGUMENT

Satan now in prospect of Eden, and nigh the place where he
must now attempt the bold enterprise which he undertook
alone against God and man, falls into many doubts with
himself, and many passions, fear, envy, and despair; but at

5   length confirms himself in evil, journeys on to Paradise,
whose outward prospect and situation is described, overleaps
the bounds, sits in the shape of a cormorant on the Tree of
Life, as highest in the garden to look about him. The garden
described; Satan's first sight of Adam and Eve;

10   his wonder at their excellent form and happy state, but with
resolution to work their Fall; overhears their discourse,
thence gathers that the Tree of Knowledge was forbidden
them to eat of, under penalty of death; and thereon intends
to found his Temptation, by seducing them to transgress:

15   then leaves them a while, to know further of their state by
some other means. Meanwhile Uriel descending on a sunbeam
warns Gabriel, who had in chare the gate of Paradise, that
some evil Spirit had escaped the deep, and passed at noon by
his sphere in the shape of a good angel

20   down to Paradise, discovered after by his furious gestures in
the mount. Gabriel promises to find him ere morning. Night
coming on, Adam and Eve, discourse of going to their rest:

their evening worship. Gabriel drawing forth his bands of night-watch to walk the round of Paradise,

25 appoints two strong angels to Adam's bower, lest the evil spirit should be there doing some harm to Adam or Eve sleeping; there they find him at the ear of Eve, tempting her in a dream, and bring him, though unwilling, to Gabriel; by whom questioned, he scornfully answers, prepares

30 resistance, but hindered by a sign from Heav'n, flies out of Paradise.

O, for that warning voice, which he, who saw
The Apocalypse, heard cry in Heav'n aloud,
Then when the Dragon, put to second rout,
Came furious down to be revenged on men,

5 *Woe to the inhabitants on earth!* that now,
While time was, our first parents had been warned
The coming of their secret foe, and 'scaped,
Haply so 'scaped his mortal snare: For now
Satan, now first inflamed with rage, came down,

10 The tempter ere the accuser of mankind,
To wreak on innocent frail Man his loss
Of that first battle, and his flight to Hell:
Yet, not rejoicing in his speed, though bold
Far off and fearless, nor with cause to boast,

15 Begins his dire attempt; which nigh the birth
Now rolling boils in his tumultuous breast,
And like a devilish engine back recoils
Upon himself; horror and doubt distract
His troubled thoughts, and from the bottom stir

20 The Hell within him; for within him Hell
He brings, and round about him, nor from Hell
One step, no more than from himself, can fly
By change of place: Now conscience wakes despair,
That slumbered; wakes the bitter memory

25   Of what he was, what is, and what must be
Worse; of worse deeds worse sufferings must ensue.
Sometimes towards Eden, which now in his view
Lay pleasant, his grieved look he fixes sad;
Sometimes towards Heav'n, and the full-blazing sun,
30   Which now sat high in his meridian tower:
Then, much revolving, thus in sighs began.
O thou, that, with surpassing glory crowned,
Lookest from thy sole dominion like the God
Of this new world; at whose sight all the stars
35   Hide their diminished heads; to thee I call,
But with no friendly voice, and add thy name,
Of Sun! to tell thee how I hate thy beams,
That bring to my remembrance from what state
I fell, how glorious once above thy sphere;
40   Till pride and worse ambition threw me down
Warring in Heav'n against Heav'n's matchless King:
Ah, wherefore! he deserved no such return
From me, whom he created what I was
In that bright eminence, and with his good
45   Upbraided none; nor was his service hard.
What could be less than to afford him praise,
The easiest recompense, and pay him thanks,
How due! yet all his good proved ill in me,
And wrought but malice; lifted up so high
50   I 'sdained subjection, and thought one step higher
Would set me highest, and in a moment quit
The debt immense of endless gratitude,
So burdensome still paying, still to owe,
Forgetful what from him I still received,
55   And understood not that a grateful mind
By owing owes not, but still pays, at once
Indebted and discharged; what burden then

O, had his powerful destiny ordained
Me some inferior Angel, I had stood
60   Then happy; no unbounded hope had raised
Ambition! Yet why not some other Power
As great might have aspired, and me, though mean,
Drawn to his part; but other Powers as great
Fell not, but stand unshaken, from within
65   Or from without, to all temptations armed.
Hadst thou the same free will and power to stand?
Thou hadst: whom hast thou then or what to accuse,
But Heav'n's free love dealt equally to all?
Be then his love accursed, since love or hate,
70   To me alike, it deals eternal woe.
Nay, cursed be thou; since against his thy will
Chose freely what it now so justly rues.
Me miserable! which way shall I fly
Infinite wrath, and infinite despair?
75   Which way I fly is Hell; myself am Hell;
And, in the lowest deep, a lower deep
Still threatening to devour me opens wide,
To which the Hell I suffer seems a Heav'n.
O, then, at last relent: Is there no place
80   Left for repentance, none for pardon left?
None left but by submission; and that word
Disdain forbids me, and my dread of shame
Among the Spirits beneath, whom I seduced
With other promises and other vaunts
85   Than to submit, boasting I could subdue
The Omnipotent. Ay me! they little know
How dearly I abide that boast so vain,
Under what torments inwardly I groan,
While they adore me on the throne of Hell.
90   With diadem and scepter high advanced,
The lower still I fall, only supreme

In misery: Such joy ambition finds.
But say I could repent, and could obtain,
By act of grace, my former state; how soon
95   Would heighth recall high thoughts, how soon unsay
What feigned submission swore? Ease would recant
Vows made in pain, as violent and void.
For never can true reconcilement grow,
Where wounds of deadly hate have pierced so deep:
100   Which would but lead me to a worse relapse
And heavier fall: so should I purchase dear
Short intermission bought with double smart.
This knows my Punisher; therefore as far
From granting he, as I from begging, peace;
105   All hope excluded thus, behold, instead
Of us out-cast, exil'd, his new delight,
Mankind created, and for him this world.
So farewell, hope; and with hope farewell, fear;
Farewell, remorse! all good to me is lost;
110   Evil, be thou my good; by thee at least
Divided empire with Heav'n's King I hold,
By thee, and more than half perhaps will reign;
As Man ere long, and this new world, shall know.
Thus while he spake, each passion dimmed his face
115   Thrice changed with pale, ire, envy, and despair;
Which marred his borrowed visage, and betrayed
Him counterfeit, if any eye beheld.
For Heav'nly minds from such distempers foul
Are ever clear. Whereof he soon aware,
120   Each perturbation smoothed with outward calm,
Artificer of fraud; and was the first
That practised falsehood under saintly show,
Deep malice to conceal, couched with revenge:
Yet not enough had practised to deceive

125	Uriel once warned; whose eye pursued him down
	The way he went, and on the Assyrian mount
	Saw him disfigured, more than could befall
	Spirit of happy sort; his gestures fierce
	He marked and mad demeanour, then alone,
130	As he supposed, all unobserved, unseen.
	So on he fares, and to the border comes
	Of Eden, where delicious Paradise,
	Now nearer, crowns with her enclosure green,
	As with a rural mound, the champaign head
135	Of a steep wilderness, whose hairy sides
	With thicket overgrown, grotesque and wild,
	Access denied; and overhead upgrew
	Insuperable height of loftiest shade,
	Cedar, and pine, and fir, and branching palm,
140	A sylvan scene, and, as the ranks ascend,
	Shade above shade, a woody theatre
	Of stateliest view. Yet higher than their tops
	The verdurous wall of Paradise up sprung;
	Which to our general sire gave prospect large
145	Into his nether empire neighbouring round.
	And higher than that wall a circling row
	Of goodliest trees, loaden with fairest fruit,
	Blossoms and fruits at once of golden hue,
	Appeared, with gay enamelled colours mixed:
150	On which the sun more glad impressed his beams
	Than in fair evening cloud, or humid bow,
	When God hath showered the earth; so lovely seemed
	That landscape: And of pure now purer air
	Meets his approach, and to the heart inspires
155	Vernal delight and joy, able to drive
	All sadness but despair: Now gentle gales,
	Fanning their odoriferous wings, dispense

Native perfumes, and whisper whence they stole
Those balmy spoils. As when to them who fail
160 Beyond the Cape of Hope, and now are past
Mozambique, off at sea north-east winds blow
Sabean odours from the spicy shore
Of Araby the blest; with such delay
Well pleased they slack their course, and many a league
165 Cheered with the grateful smell old Ocean smiles:
So entertained those odorous sweets the Fiend,
Who came their bane; though with them better pleased
Than Asmodeus with the fishy fume
That drove him, though enamoured, from the spouse
170 Of Tobit's son, and with a vengeance sent
From Media post to Egypt, there fast bound.
Now to the ascent of that steep savage hill
Satan had journeyed on, pensive and slow;
But further way found none, so thick entwined,
175 As one continued brake, the undergrowth
Of shrubs and tangling bushes had perplexed
All path of man or beast that passed that way.
One gate there only was, and that looked east
On the other side: which when the arch-felon saw,
180 Due entrance he disdained; and, in contempt,
At one flight bound high over-leaped all bound
Of hill or highest wall, and sheer within
Lights on his feet. As when a prowling wolf,
Whom hunger drives to seek new haunt for prey,
185 Watching where shepherds pen their flocks at eve
In hurdled cotes amid the field secure,
Leaps o'er the fence with ease into the fold:
Or as a thief, bent to unhoard the cash
Of some rich burgher, whose substantial doors,
190 Cross-barred and bolted fast, fear no assault,
In at the window climbs, or o'er the tiles:

So clomb this first grand thief into God's fold;
So since into his church lewd hirelings climb.
Thence up he flew, and on the tree of life,
195 The middle tree and highest there that grew,
Sat like a cormorant; yet not true life
Thereby regained, but sat devising death
To them who lived; nor on the virtue thought
Of that life-giving plant, but only used
200 For prospect, what well used had been the pledge
Of immortality. So little knows
Any, but God alone, to value right
The good before him, but perverts best things
To worst abuse, or to their meanest use.
205 Beneath him with new wonder now he views,
To all delight of human sense exposed,
In narrow room, Nature's whole wealth, yea more,
A Heav'n on Earth: For blissful Paradise
Of God the garden was, by him in the east
210 Of Eden planted; Eden stretched her line
From Auran eastward to the royal towers
Of great Seleucia, built by Grecian kings,
Or where the sons of Eden long before
Dwelt in Telassar: In this pleasant soil
215 His far more pleasant garden God ordained;
Out of the fertile ground he caused to grow
All trees of noblest kind for sight, smell, taste;
And all amid them stood the tree of life,
High eminent, blooming ambrosial fruit
220 Of vegetable gold; and next to life,
Our death, the tree of knowledge, grew fast by,
Knowledge of good bought dear by knowing ill.
Southward through Eden went a river large,
Nor changed his course, but through the shaggy hill
225 Passed underneath ingulfed; for God had thrown

That mountain as his garden-mould high raised
Upon the rapid current, which, through veins
Of porous earth with kindly thirst up-drawn,
Rose a fresh fountain, and with many a rill
230   Watered the garden; thence united fell
Down the steep glade, and met the nether flood,
Which from his darksome passage now appears,
And now, divided into four main streams,
Runs diverse, wandering many a famous realm
235   And country, whereof here needs no account;
But rather to tell how, if Art could tell,
How from that sapphire fount the crisped brooks,
Rolling on orient pearl and sands of gold,
With mazy error under pendant shades
240   Ran nectar, visiting each plant, and fed
Flowers worthy of Paradise, which not nice Art
In beds and curious knots, but Nature boon
Poured forth profuse on hill, and dale, and plain,
Both where the morning sun first warmly smote
245   The open field, and where the unpierced shade
Embrowned the noontide bowers: Thus was this place
A happy rural seat of various view;
Groves whose rich trees wept odorous gums and balm,
Others whose fruit, burnished with golden rind,
250   Hung amiable, Hesperian fables true,
If true, here only, and of delicious taste:
Betwixt them lawns, or level downs, and flocks
Grazing the tender herb, were interposed,
Or palmy hillock; or the flowery lap
255   Of some irriguous valley spread her store,
Flowers of all hue, and without thorn the rose:
Another side, umbrageous grots and caves
Of cool recess, o'er which the mantling vine
Lays forth her purple grape, and gently creeps

260	Luxuriant; mean while murmuring waters fall
	Down the slope hills, dispersed, or in a lake,
	That to the fringed bank with myrtle crowned
	Her crystal mirror holds, unite their streams.
	The birds their quire apply; airs, vernal airs,
265	Breathing the smell of field and grove, attune
	The trembling leaves, while universal Pan,
	Knit with the Graces and the Hours in dance,
	Led on the eternal Spring. Not that fair field
	Of Enna, where Proserpine gathering flowers,
270	Herself a fairer flower by gloomy Dis
	Was gathered, which cost Ceres all that pain
	To seek her through the world; nor that sweet grove
	Of Daphne by Orontes, and the inspired
	Castalian spring, might with this Paradise
275	Of Eden strive; nor that Nyseian isle
	Girt with the river Triton, where old Cham,
	Whom Gentiles Ammon call and Libyan Jove,
	Hid Amalthea, and her florid son
	Young Bacchus, from his stepdame Rhea's eye;
280	Nor where Abassin kings their issue guard,
	Mount Amara, though this by some supposed
	True Paradise under the Ethiop line
	By Nilus' head, enclosed with shining rock,
	A whole day's journey high, but wide remote
285	From this Assyrian garden, where the Fiend
	Saw, undelighted, all delight, all kind
	Of living creatures, new to sight, and strange
	Two of far nobler shape, erect and tall,
	Godlike erect, with native honour clad
290	In naked majesty seemed lords of all:
	And worthy seemed; for in their looks divine
	The image of their glorious Maker shone,

Truth, wisdom, sanctitude severe and pure,
(Severe, but in true filial freedom placed,)
295   Whence true authority in men; though both
Not equal, as their sex not equal seemed;
For contemplation he and valour formed;
For softness she and sweet attractive grace;
He for God only, she for God in him:
300   His fair large front and eye sublime declared
Absolute rule; and hyacinthine locks
Round from his parted forelock manly hung
Clustering, but not beneath his shoulders broad:
She, as a veil, down to the slender waist
305   Her unadorned golden tresses wore
Dishevelled, but in wanton ringlets waved
As the vine curls her tendrils, which implied
Subjection, but required with gentle sway,
And by her yielded, by him best received,
310   Yielded with coy submission, modest pride,
And sweet, reluctant, amorous delay.
Nor those mysterious parts were then concealed;
Then was not guilty shame, dishonest shame
Of nature's works, honour dishonourable,
315   Sin-bred, how have ye troubled all mankind
With shows instead, mere shows of seeming pure,
And banished from man's life his happiest life,
Simplicity and spotless innocence!
So passed they naked on, nor shunned the sight
320   Of God or Angel; for they thought no ill:
So hand in hand they passed, the loveliest pair,
That ever since in love's embraces met;
Adam the goodliest man of men since born
His sons, the fairest of her daughters Eve.
325   Under a tuft of shade that on a green
Stood whispering soft, by a fresh fountain side

They sat them down; and, after no more toil
Of their sweet gardening labour than sufficed
To recommend cool Zephyr, and made ease
330   More easy, wholesome thirst and appetite
More grateful, to their supper-fruits they fell,
Nectarine fruits which the compliant boughs
Yielded them, side-long as they sat recline
On the soft downy bank damasked with flowers:
335   The savoury pulp they chew, and in the rind,
Still as they thirsted, scoop the brimming stream;
Nor gentle purpose, nor endearing smiles
Wanted, nor youthful dalliance, as beseems
Fair couple, linked in happy nuptial league,
340   Alone as they. About them frisking played
All beasts of the earth, since wild, and of all chase
In wood or wilderness, forest or den;
Sporting the lion ramped, and in his paw
Dandled the kid; bears, tigers, ounces, pards,
345   Gambolled before them; the unwieldy elephant,
To make them mirth, used all his might, and wreathed
His lithe proboscis; close the serpent sly,
Insinuating, wove with Gordian twine
His braided train, and of his fatal guile
350   Gave proof unheeded; others on the grass
Couched, and now filled with pasture gazing sat,
Or bedward ruminating; for the sun,
Declined, was hasting now with prone career
To the ocean isles, and in the ascending scale
355   Of Heav'n the stars that usher evening rose:
When Satan still in gaze, as first he stood,
Scarce thus at length failed speech recovered sad.
O Hell! what do mine eyes with grief behold!
Into our room of bliss thus high advanced
360   Creatures of other mould, earth-born perhaps,

Not Spirits, yet to Heav'nly Spirits bright
Little inferior; whom my thoughts pursue
With wonder, and could love, so lively shines
In them divine resemblance, and such grace
365   The hand that formed them on their shape hath poured.
Ah! gentle pair, ye little think how nigh
Your change approaches, when all these delights
Will vanish, and deliver ye to woe;
More woe, the more your taste is now of joy;
370   Happy, but for so happy ill secured
Long to continue, and this high seat your Heav'n
Ill fenced for Heav'n to keep out such a foe
As now is entered; yet no purposed foe
To you, whom I could pity thus forlorn,
375   Though I unpitied: League with you I seek,
And mutual amity, so strait, so close,
That I with you must dwell, or you with me
Henceforth; my dwelling haply may not please,
Like this fair Paradise, your sense; yet such
380   Accept your Maker's work; he gave it me,
Which I as freely give: Hell shall unfold,
To entertain you two, her widest gates,
And send forth all her kings; there will be room,
Not like these narrow limits, to receive
385   Your numerous offspring; if no better place,
Thank him who puts me loath to this revenge
On you who wrong me not for him who wronged.
And should I at your harmless innocence
Melt, as I do, yet public reason just,
390   Honour and empire with revenge enlarged,
By conquering this new world, compels me now
To do what else, though damned, I should abhor.
So spake the Fiend, and with necessity,
The tyrant's plea, excused his devilish deeds.

395   Then from his lofty stand on that high tree
         Down he alights among the sportful herd
         Of those four-footed kinds, himself now one,
         Now other, as their shape served best his end
         Nearer to view his prey, and, unespied,
400   To mark what of their state he more might learn
         By word or action marked. About them round
         A lion now he stalks with fiery glare;
         Then as a tiger, who by chance hath spied
         In some purlieu two gentle fawns at play,
405   Straight couches close, then, rising, changes oft
         His couchant watch, as one who chose his ground,
         Whence rushing, he might surest seize them both,
         Griped in each paw: when, Adam first of men
         To first of women Eve thus moving speech,
410   Turned him, all ear to hear new utterance flow.
         Sole partner, and sole part, of all these joys,
         Dearer thyself than all; needs must the Power
         That made us, and for us this ample world,
         Be infinitely good, and of his good
415   As liberal and free as infinite;
         That raised us from the dust, and placed us here
         In all this happiness, who at his hand
         Have nothing merited, nor can perform
         Aught whereof he hath need; he who requires
420   From us no other service than to keep
         This one, this easy charge, of all the trees
         In Paradise that bear delicious fruit
         So various, not to taste that only tree
         Of knowledge, planted by the tree of life;
425   So near grows death to life, whate'er death is,
         Some dreadful thing no doubt; for well thou knowest
         God hath pronounced it death to taste that tree,

The only sign of our obedience left,
Among so many signs of power and rule
430   Conferred upon us, and dominion given
Over all other creatures that possess
Earth, air, and sea. Then let us not think hard
One easy prohibition, who enjoy
Free leave so large to all things else, and choice
435   Unlimited of manifold delights:
But let us ever praise him, and extol
His bounty, following our delightful task,
To prune these growing plants, and tend these flowers,
Which were it toilsome, yet with thee were sweet.
440   To whom thus Eve replied. O thou for whom
And from whom I was formed, flesh of thy flesh,
And without whom am to no end, my guide
And head! what thou hast said is just and right.
For we to him indeed all praises owe,
445   And daily thanks; I chiefly, who enjoy
So far the happier lot, enjoying thee
Pre-eminent by so much odds, while thou
Like consort to thyself canst no where find.
That day I oft remember, when from sleep
450   I first awaked, and found myself reposed
Under a shade on flowers, much wondering where
And what I was, whence thither brought, and how.
Not distant far from thence a murmuring sound
Of waters issued from a cave, and spread
455   Into a liquid plain, then stood unmoved
Pure as the expanse of Heav'n; I thither went
With unexperienced thought, and laid me down
On the green bank, to look into the clear
Smooth lake, that to me seemed another sky.
460   As I bent down to look, just opposite
A shape within the watery gleam appeared,

Bending to look on me: I started back,
It started back; but pleased I soon returned,
Pleased it returned as soon with answering looks
465 Of sympathy and love: There I had fixed
Mine eyes till now, and pined with vain desire,
Had not a voice thus warned me; "What thou seest,
What there thou seest, fair Creature, is thyself;
With thee it came and goes: but follow me,
470 And I will bring thee where no shadow stays
Thy coming, and thy soft embraces, he
Whose image thou art; him thou shalt enjoy
Inseparably thine, to him shalt bear
Multitudes like thyself, and thence be called
475 Mother of human race." What could I do,
But follow straight, invisibly thus led?
Till I espied thee, fair indeed and tall,
Under a platan; yet methought less fair,
Less winning soft, less amiably mild,
480 Than that smooth watery image: Back I turned;
Thou following cried'st aloud, "Return, fair Eve;
Whom fli'est thou? whom thou fli'est, of him thou art,
His flesh, his bone; to give thee being I lent
Out of my side to thee, nearest my heart,
485 Substantial life, to have thee by my side
Henceforth an individual solace dear;
Part of my soul I seek thee, and thee claim
My other half:" With that thy gentle hand
Seized mine: I yielded; and from that time see
490 How beauty is excelled by manly grace,
And wisdom, which alone is truly fair.
So spake our general mother, and with eyes
Of conjugal attraction unreproved,
And meek surrender, half-embracing leaned
495 On our first father; half her swelling breast

Naked met his, under the flowing gold
Of her loose tresses hid: he in delight
Both of her beauty, and submissive charms,
Smiled with superior love, as Jupiter
500 On Juno smiles, when he impregns the clouds
That shed Mayflowers; and pressed her matron lip
With kisses pure: Aside the Devil turned
For envy; yet with jealous leer malign
Eyed them askance, and to himself thus plained.
505 Sight hateful, sight tormenting! thus these two,
Imparadised in one another's arms,
The happier Eden, shall enjoy their fill
Of bliss on bliss; while I to Hell am thrust,
Where neither joy nor love, but fierce desire,
510 Among our other torments not the least,
Still unfulfilled with pain of longing pines.
Yet let me not forget what I have gained
From their own mouths: All is not theirs, it seems;
One fatal tree there stands, of knowledge called,
515 Forbidden them to taste: Knowledge forbidden
Suspicious, reasonless. Why should their Lord
Envy them that? Can it be sin to know?
Can it be death? And do they only stand
By ignorance? Is that their happy state,
520 The proof of their obedience and their faith?
O fair foundation laid whereon to build
Their ruin! hence I will excite their minds
With more desire to know, and to reject
Envious commands, invented with design
525 To keep them low, whom knowledge might exalt
Equal with Gods: aspiring to be such,
They taste and die: What likelier can ensue
But first with narrow search I must walk round
This garden, and no corner leave unspied;

530   A chance but chance may lead where I may meet
       Some wandering Spirit of Heav'n by fountain side,
       Or in thick shade retired, from him to draw
       What further would be learned. Live while ye may,
       Yet happy pair; enjoy, till I return,
535   Short pleasures, for long woes are to succeed!
       So saying, his proud step he scornful turned,
       But with sly circumspection, and began
       Through wood, through waste, o'er hill, o'er dale, his roam
       Mean while in utmost longitude, where Heav'n
540   With earth and ocean meets, the setting sun
       Slowly descended, and with right aspect
       Against the eastern gate of Paradise
       Levelled his evening rays: It was a rock
       Of alabaster, piled up to the clouds,
545   Conspicuous far, winding with one ascent
       Accessible from earth, one entrance high;
       The rest was craggy cliff, that overhung
       Still as it rose, impossible to climb.
       Betwixt these rocky pillars Gabriel sat,
550   Chief of the angelic guards, awaiting night;
       About him exercised heroic games
       The unarmed youth of Heav'n, but nigh at hand
       Celestial armoury, shields, helms, and spears,
       Hung high with diamond flaming, and with gold.
555   Thither came Uriel, gliding through the even
       On a sun-beam, swift as a shooting star
       In autumn thwarts the night, when vapours fired
       Impress the air, and shows the mariner
       From what point of his compass to beware
560   Impetuous winds: He thus began in haste.
       Gabriel, to thee thy course by lot hath given
       Charge and strict watch, that to this happy place

No evil thing approach or enter in.
This day at heighth of noon came to my sphere
565 A Spirit, zealous, as he seemed, to know
More of the Almighty's works, and chiefly Man,
God's latest image: I described his way
Bent all on speed, and marked his aery gait;
But in the mount that lies from Eden north,
570 Where he first lighted, soon discerned his looks
Alien from Heav'n, with passions foul obscured:
Mine eye pursued him still, but under shade
Lost sight of him: One of the banished crew,
I fear, hath ventured from the deep, to raise
575 New troubles; him thy care must be to find.
To whom the winged warrior thus returned.
Uriel, no wonder if thy perfect sight,
Amid the sun's bright circle where thou sitts,
See far and wide: In at this gate none pass
580 The vigilance here placed, but such as come
Well known from Heav'n; and since meridian hour
No creature thence: If Spirit of other sort,
So minded, have o'er-leaped these earthly bounds
On purpose, hard thou knowest it to exclude
585 Spiritual substance with corporeal bar.
But if within the circuit of these walks,
In whatsoever shape he lurk, of whom
Thou tellest, by morrow dawning I shall know.
So promised he; and Uriel to his charge
590 Returned on that bright beam, whose point now raised
Bore him slope downward to the sun now fallen
Beneath the Azores; whether the prime orb,
Incredible how swift, had thither rolled
Diurnal, or this less volubil earth,
595 By shorter flight to the east, had left him there
Arraying with reflected purple and gold

113

The clouds that on his western throne attend.
Now came still Evening on, and Twilight gray
Had in her sober livery all things clad;
600 Silence accompanied; for beast and bird,
They to their grassy couch, these to their nests
Were slunk, all but the wakeful nightingale;
She all night long her amorous descant sung;
Silence was pleased: Now glowed the firmament
605 With living sapphires: Hesperus, that led
The starry host, rode brightest, till the moon,
Rising in clouded majesty, at length
Apparent queen unveiled her peerless light,
And o'er the dark her silver mantle threw.
610 When Adam thus to Eve. Fair Consort, the hour
Of night, and all things now retired to rest,
Mind us of like repose; since God hath set
Labour and rest, as day and night, to men
Successive; and the timely dew of sleep,
615 Now falling with soft slumbrous weight, inclines
Our eye-lids: Other creatures all day long
Rove idle, unemployed, and less need rest;
Man hath his daily work of body or mind
Appointed, which declares his dignity,
620 And the regard of Heav'n on all his ways;
While other animals unactive range,
And of their doings God takes no account.
To-morrow, ere fresh morning streak the east
With first approach of light, we must be risen,
625 And at our pleasant labour, to reform
Yon flowery arbours, yonder alleys green,
Our walk at noon, with branches overgrown,
That mock our scant manuring, and require
More hands than ours to lop their wanton growth:
630 Those blossoms also, and those dropping gums,

That lie bestrown, unsightly and unsmooth,
Ask riddance, if we mean to tread with ease;
Mean while, as Nature wills, night bids us rest.
To whom thus Eve, with perfect beauty adorned
635 My Author and Disposer, what thou bidst
Unargued I obey: So God ordains;
God is thy law, thou mine: To know no more
Is woman's happiest knowledge, and her praise.
With thee conversing I forget all time;
640 All seasons, and their change, all please alike.
Sweet is the breath of Morn, her rising sweet,
With charm of earliest birds: pleasant the sun,
When first on this delightful land he spreads
His orient beams, on herb, tree, fruit, and flower,
645 Glistering with dew; fragrant the fertile earth
After soft showers; and sweet the coming on
Of grateful Evening mild; then silent Night,
With this her solemn bird, and this fair moon,
And these the gems of Heav'n, her starry train:
650 But neither breath of Morn, when she ascends
With charm of earliest birds; nor rising sun
On this delightful land; nor herb, fruit, flower,
Glistering with dew; nor fragrance after showers;
Nor grateful Evening mild; nor silent Night,
655 With this her solemn bird, nor walk by moon,
Or glittering star-light, without thee is sweet.
But wherefore all night long shine these? for whom
This glorious sight, when sleep hath shut all eyes?
To whom our general ancestor replied.
660 Daughter of God and Man, accomplished Eve,
These have their course to finish round the earth,
By morrow evening, and from land to land
In order, though to nations yet unborn,
Ministring light prepared, they set and rise;

665   Lest total Darkness should by night regain
       Her old possession, and extinguish life
       In Nature and all things; which these soft fires
       Not only enlighten, but with kindly heat
       Of various influence foment and warm,
670   Temper or nourish, or in part shed down
       Their stellar virtue on all kinds that grow
       On earth, made hereby apter to receive
       Perfection from the sun's more potent ray.
       These then, though unbeheld in deep of night,
675   Shine not in vain; nor think, though men were none,
       That Heav'n would want spectators, God want praise:
       Millions of spiritual creatures walk the earth
       Unseen, both when we wake, and when we sleep:
       All these with ceaseless praise his works behold
680   Both day and night: How often from the steep
       Of echoing hill or thicket have we heard
       Celestial voices to the midnight air,
       Sole, or responsive each to others note,
       Singing their great Creator? oft in bands
685   While they keep watch, or nightly rounding walk,
       With Heav'nly touch of instrumental sounds
       In full harmonic number joined, their songs
       Divide the night, and lift our thoughts to Heav'n.
       Thus talking, hand in hand alone they passed
690   On to their blissful bower: it was a place
       Chosen by the sov'reign Planter, when he framed
       All things to Man's delightful use; the roof
       Of thickest covert was inwoven shade
       Laurel and myrtle, and what higher grew
695   Of firm and fragrant leaf; on either side
       Acanthus, and each odorous bushy shrub,
       Fenced up the verdant wall; each beauteous flower,

Iris all hues, roses, and jessamin,
Reared high their flourished heads between, and wrought
700   Mosaic; underfoot the violet,
Crocus, and hyacinth, with rich inlay
Broidered the ground, more coloured than with stone
Of costliest emblem: Other creature here,
Bird, beast, insect, or worm, durst enter none,
705   Such was their awe of Man. In shadier bower
More sacred and sequestered, though but feigned,
Pan or Silvanus never slept, nor Nymph
Nor Faunus haunted. Here, in close recess,
With flowers, garlands, and sweet-smelling herbs,
710   Espoused Eve decked first her nuptial bed;
And Heav'nly quires the hymenean sung,
What day the genial Angel to our sire
Brought her in naked beauty more adorned,
More lovely, than Pandora, whom the Gods
715   Endowed with all their gifts, and O! too like
In sad event, when to the unwiser son
Of Japhet brought by Hermes, she ensnared
Mankind with her fair looks, to be avenged
On him who had stole Jove's authentic fire.
720   Thus, at their shady lodge arrived, both stood,
Both turned, and under open sky adored
The God that made both sky, air, earth, and Heav'n,
Which they beheld, the moon's resplendent globe,
And starry pole: Thou also madest the night,
725   Maker Omnipotent, and thou the day,
Which we, in our appointed work employed,
Have finished, happy in our mutual help
And mutual love, the crown of all our bliss
Ordained by thee; and this delicious place
730   For us too large, where thy abundance wants
Partakers, and uncropped falls to the ground.

But thou hast promised from us two a race
To fill the earth, who shall with us extol
Thy goodness infinite, both when we wake,
735   And when we seek, as now, thy gift of sleep.
This said unanimous, and other rites
Observing none, but adoration pure
Which God likes best, into their inmost bower
Handed they went; and, eased the putting off
740   These troublesome disguises which we wear,
Straight side by side were laid; nor turned, I ween,
Adam from his fair spouse, nor Eve the rites
Mysterious of connubial love refused:
Whatever hypocrites austerely talk
745   Of purity, and place, and innocence,
Defaming as impure what God declares
Pure, and commands to some, leaves free to all.
Our Maker bids increase; who bids abstain
But our Destroyer, foe to God and Man?
750   Hail, wedded Love, mysterious law, true source
Of human offspring, sole propriety
In Paradise of all things common else!
By thee adulterous Lust was driven from men
Among the bestial herds to range; by thee
755   Founded in reason, loyal, just, and pure,
Relations dear, and all the charities
Of father, son, and brother, first were known.
Far be it, that I should write thee sin or blame,
Or think thee unbefitting holiest place,
760   Perpetual fountain of domestick sweets,
Whose bed is undefiled and chaste pronounced,
Present, or past, as saints and patriarchs used.
Here Love his golden shafts employs, here lights
His constant lamp, and waves his purple wings,
765   Reigns here and revels; not in the bought smile

Of harlots, loveless, joyless, unendeared,
Casual fruition; nor in court-amours,
Mixed dance, or wanton mask, or midnight ball,
Or serenade, which the starved lover sings
770   To his proud fair, best quitted with disdain.
These, lulled by nightingales, embracing slept,
And on their naked limbs the flowery roof
Showered roses, which the morn repaired. Sleep on,
Blest pair; and O! yet happiest, if ye seek
775   No happier state, and know to know no more.
Now had night measured with her shadowy cone
Half way up hill this vast sublunar vault,
And from their ivory port the Cherubim,
Forth issuing at the accustomed hour, stood armed
780   To their night watches in warlike parade;
When Gabriel to his next in power thus spake.
Uzziel, half these draw off, and coast the south
With strictest watch; these other wheel the north;
Our circuit meets full west. As flame they part,
785   Half wheeling to the shield, half to the spear.
From these, two strong and subtle Spirits he called
That near him stood, and gave them thus in charge.
Ithuriel and Zephon, with winged speed
Search through this garden, leave unsearched no nook;
790   But chiefly where those two fair creatures lodge,
Now laid perhaps asleep, secure of harm.
This evening from the sun's decline arrived,
Who tells of some infernal Spirit seen
Hitherward bent (who could have thought?) escaped
795   The bars of Hell, on errand bad no doubt:
Such, where ye find, seise fast, and hither bring.
So saying, on he led his radiant files,
Dazzling the moon; these to the bower direct
In search of whom they sought: Him there they found

800 Squat like a toad, close at the ear of Eve,
   Assaying by his devilish art to reach
   The organs of her fancy, and with them forge
   Illusions, as he list, phantasms and dreams;
   Or if, inspiring venom, he might taint
805 The animal spirits, that from pure blood arise
   Like gentle breaths from rivers pure, thence raise
   At least distempered, discontented thoughts,
   Vain hopes, vain aims, inordinate desires,
   Blown up with high conceits ingendering pride.
810 Him thus intent Ithuriel with his spear
   Touched lightly; for no falshood can endure
   Touch of celestial temper, but returns
   Of force to its own likeness: Up he starts
   Discovered and surprised. As when a spark
815 Lights on a heap of nitrous powder, laid
   Fit for the tun some magazine to store
   Against a rumoured war, the smutty grain,
   With sudden blaze diffused, inflames the air;
   So started up in his own shape the Fiend.
820 Back stepped those two fair Angels, half amazed
   So sudden to behold the grisly king;
   Yet thus, unmoved with fear, accost him soon.
   Which of those rebel Spirits adjudged to Hell
   Comest thou, escaped thy prison? and, transformed,
825 Why sat'st thou like an enemy in wait,
   Here watching at the head of these that sleep?
   Know ye not then said Satan, filled with scorn,
   Know ye not me? ye knew me once no mate
   For you, there sitting where ye durst not soar:
830 Not to know me argues yourselves unknown,
   The lowest of your throng; or, if ye know,
   Why ask ye, and superfluous begin

Your message, like to end as much in vain?
To whom thus Zephon, answering scorn with scorn
835   Think not, revolted Spirit, thy shape the same,
Or undiminished brightness to be known,
As when thou stoodest in Heav'n upright and pure;
That glory then, when thou no more wast good,
Departed from thee; and thou resemblest now
840   Thy sin and place of doom obscure and foul.
But come, for thou, be sure, shalt give account
To him who sent us, whose charge is to keep
This place inviolable, and these from harm.
So spake the Cherub; and his grave rebuke,
845   Severe in youthful beauty, added grace
Invincible: Abashed the Devil stood,
And felt how awful goodness is, and saw
Virtue in her shape how lovely; saw, and pined
His loss; but chiefly to find here observed
850   His lustre visibly impaired; yet seemed
Undaunted. If I must contend, said he,
Best with the best, the sender, not the sent,
Or all at once; more glory will be won,
Or less be lost. Thy fear, said Zephon bold,
855   Will save us trial what the least can do
Single against thee wicked, and thence weak.
The Fiend replied not, overcome with rage;
But, like a proud steed reined, went haughty on,
Champing his iron curb: To strive or fly
860   He held it vain; awe from above had quelled
His heart, not else dismayed. Now drew they nigh
The western point, where those half-rounding guards
Just met, and closing stood in squadron joined,
A waiting next command. To whom their Chief,
865   Gabriel, from the front thus called aloud.
O friends! I hear the tread of nimble feet

Hasting this way, and now by glimpse discern
Ithuriel and Zephon through the shade;
And with them comes a third of regal port,
870   But faded splendour wan; who by his gait
And fierce demeanour seems the Prince of Hell,
Not likely to part hence without contest;
Stand firm, for in his look defiance lours.
He scarce had ended, when those two approached,
875   And brief related whom they brought, where found,
How busied, in what form and posture couched.
To whom with stern regard thus Gabriel spake.
Why hast thou, Satan, broke the bounds prescribed
To thy transgressions, and disturbed the charge
880   Of others, who approve not to transgress
By thy example, but have power and right
To question thy bold entrance on this place;
Employed, it seems, to violate sleep, and those
Whose dwelling God hath planted here in bliss!
885   To whom thus Satan with contemptuous brow.
Gabriel? thou hadst in Heav'n the esteem of wise,
And such I held thee; but this question asked
Puts me in doubt. Lives there who loves his pain!
Who would not, finding way, break loose from Hell,
890   Though thither doomed! Thou wouldst thyself, no doubt
And boldly venture to whatever place
Farthest from pain, where thou mightst hope to change
Torment with ease, and soonest recompense
Dole with delight, which in this place I sought;
895   To thee no reason, who knowest only good,
But evil hast not tried: and wilt object
His will who bounds us! Let him surer bar
His iron gates, if he intends our stay
In that dark durance: Thus much what was asked.
900   The rest is true, they found me where they say;

122

But that implies not violence or harm.
Thus he in scorn. The warlike Angel moved,
Disdainfully half smiling, thus replied.
O loss of one in Heav'n to judge of wise
905   Since Satan fell, whom folly overthrew,
And now returns him from his prison 'scaped,
Gravely in doubt whether to hold them wise
Or not, who ask what boldness brought him hither
Unlicensed from his bounds in Hell prescribed;
910   So wise he judges it to fly from pain
However, and to 'scape his punishment!
So judge thou still, presumptuous! till the wrath,
Which thou incurrest by flying, meet thy flight
Sevenfold, and scourge that wisdom back to Hell,
915   Which taught thee yet no better, that no pain
Can equal anger infinite provoked.
But wherefore thou alone? wherefore with thee
Came not all hell broke loose? or thou than they
920   Less hardy to endure? Courageous Chief!
The first in flight from pain! hadst thou alleged
To thy deserted host this cause of flight,
Thou surely hadst not come sole fugitive.
To which the Fiend thus answered, frowning stern.
925   Not that I less endure, or shrink from pain,
Insulting Angel! well thou knowest I stood
Thy fiercest, when in battle to thy aid
The blasting volleyed thunder made all speed,
And seconded thy else not dreaded spear.
930   But still thy words at random, as before,
Argue thy inexperience what behooves
From hard assays and ill successes past
A faithful leader, not to hazard all
Through ways of danger by himself untried:

935 I, therefore, I alone first undertook
 To wing the desolate abyss, and spy
 This new created world, whereof in Hell
 Fame is not silent, here in hope to find
 Better abode, and my afflicted Powers
940 To settle here on earth, or in mid air;
 Though for possession put to try once more
 What thou and thy gay legions dare against;
 Whose easier business were to serve their Lord
 High up in Heav'n, with songs to hymn his throne,
945 And practised distances to cringe, not fight,
 To whom the warriour Angel soon replied.
 To say and straight unsay, pretending first
 Wise to fly pain, professing next the spy,
 Argues no leader but a liar traced,
950 Satan, and couldst thou faithful add? O name,
 O sacred name of faithfulness profaned!
 Faithful to whom? to thy rebellious crew?
 Army of Fiends, fit body to fit head.
 Was this your discipline and faith engaged,
955 Your military obedience, to dissolve
 Allegiance to the acknowledged Power supreme?
 And thou, sly hypocrite, who now wouldst seem
 Patron of liberty, who more than thou
 Once fawned, and cringed, and servilely adored
960 Heav'n's awful Monarch? Wherefore, but in hope
 To dispossess him, and thyself to reign?
 But mark what I aread thee now, Avant;
 Fly neither whence thou fledst! If from this hour
 Within these hallowed limits thou appear,
965 Back to the infernal pit I drag thee chained,
 And seal thee so, as henceforth not to scorn
 The facile gates of Hell too slightly barred.

So threatened he; but Satan to no threats
Gave heed, but waxing more in rage replied.
970   Then when I am thy captive talk of chains,
Proud limitary Cherub! but ere then
Far heavier load thyself expect to feel
From my prevailing arm, though Heav'n's King
Ride on thy wings, and thou with thy compeers,
975   Us'd to the yoke, drawest his triumphant wheels
In progress through the road of Heav'n star-paved.
While thus he spake, the angelic squadron bright
Turned fiery red, sharpening in mooned horns
Their phalanx, and began to hem him round
980   With ported spears, as thick as when a field
Of Ceres ripe for harvest waving bends
Her bearded grove of ears, which way the wind
Sways them; the careful plowman doubting stands,
Left on the threshing floor his hopeless sheaves
985   Prove chaff. On the other side, Satan, alarmed,
Collecting all his might, dilated stood,
Like Teneriffe or Atlas, unremoved:
His stature reached the sky, and on his crest
Sat Horror plumed; nor wanted in his grasp
990   What seemed both spear and shield: Now dreadful deeds
Might have ensued, nor only Paradise
In this commotion, but the starry cope
Of Heav'n perhaps, or all the elements
At least had gone to wrack, disturbed and torn
995   With violence of this conflict, had not soon
The Eternal, to prevent such horrid fray,
Hung forth in Heav'n his golden scales, yet seen
Betwixt Astraea and the Scorpion sign,
Wherein all things created first he weighed,
1000   The pendulous round earth with balanced air
In counterpoise, now ponders all events,

Battles and realms: In these he put two weights,
The sequel each of parting and of fight:
The latter quick up flew, and kicked the beam,
1005   Which Gabriel spying, thus bespake the Fiend.
Satan, I know thy strength, and thou knowest mine;
Neither our own, but given: What folly then
To boast what arms can do? since thine no more
Than Heav'n permits, nor mine, though doubled now
1010   To trample thee as mire: For proof look up,
And read thy lot in yon celestial sign;
Where thou art weighed, and shown how light, how weak,
If thou resist. The Fiend looked up, and knew
His mounted scale aloft: Nor more; but fled
1015   Murmuring, and with him fled the shades of night.

BOOK V

THE ARGUMENT

Morning approached, Eve relates to Adam her troublesome
dream; he likes it not, yet comforts her: they come forth to
their day labours: their morning hymn at the door of their
bower. God to render man inexcusable sends Raphael to
5   admonish him of his obedience, of his free estate, of his
enemy near at hand; who he is, and why his enemy, and
whatever else may avail Adam to know. Raphael comes down
to Paradise, his appearance described, his coming discerned
by Adam afar off sitting at the door of his
10   bower; he goes out to meet him, brings him to his lodge,
entertains him with the choicest fruits of Paradise got
together by Eve; their discourse at table: Raphael performs
his message, minds Adam of his state and of his enemy;
relates at Adam's request who that enemy is, and how he
15   came to be so, beginning from his first revolt in Heav'n and
the occasion thereof; how he drew his legions after him
to the parts of the North, and there incited them to rebel
with him, persuading all but only Abdiel a Seraph, who in
argument dissuades and opposes him, then forsakes him.

Now Morn, her rosy steps in the eastern clime
Advancing, sowed the earth with orient pearl,

When Adam waked, so customed; for his sleep
Was airy-light, from pure digestion bred,
5 And temperate vapours bland, which the only sound
Of leaves and fuming rills, Aurora's fan,
Lightly dispersed, and the shrill matin song
Of birds on every bough; so much the more
His wonder was to find unwakened Eve
10 With tresses discomposed, and glowing cheek,
As through unquiet rest: He, on his side
Leaning half raised, with looks of cordial love
Hung over her enamoured, and beheld
Beauty, which, whether waking or asleep,
15 Shot forth peculiar graces; then with voice
Mild, as when Zephyrus on Flora breathes,
Her hand soft touching, whispered thus. Awake,
My fairest, my espoused, my latest found,
Heav'n's last best gift, my ever new delight!
20 Awake: The morning shines, and the fresh field
Calls us; we lose the prime, to mark how spring
Our tender plants, how blows the citron grove,
What drops the myrrh, and what the balmy reed,
How nature paints her colours, how the bee
25 Sits on the bloom extracting liquid sweet.
Such whispering waked her, but with startled eye
On Adam, whom embracing, thus she spake.
O sole in whom my thoughts find all repose,
My glory, my perfection! glad I see
30 Thy face, and morn returned; for I this night
(Such night till this I never passed) have dreamed,
If dreamed, not, as I oft am wont, of thee,
Works of day past, or morrow's next design,
But of offence and trouble, which my mind
35 Knew never till this irksome night: Methought,
Close at mine ear one called me forth to walk

With gentle voice; I thought it thine: It said,
"Why sleepest thou, Eve? now is the pleasant time,
The cool, the silent, save where silence yields
40   To the night-warbling bird, that now awake
Tunes sweetest his love-laboured song; now reigns
Full-orbed the moon, and with more pleasing light
Shadowy sets off the face of things; in vain,
If none regard; Heav'n wakes with all his eyes,
45   Whom to behold but thee, Nature's desire?
In whose sight all things joy, with ravishment
Attracted by thy beauty still to gaze."
I rose as at thy call, but found thee not;
To find thee I directed then my walk;
50   And on, methought, alone I passed through ways
That brought me on a sudden to the tree
Of interdicted knowledge: fair it seemed,
Much fairer to my fancy than by day:
And, as I wondering looked, beside it stood
55   One shaped and winged like one of those from Heav'n
By us oft seen; his dewy locks distilled
Ambrosia; on that tree he also gazed;
And "O fair plant," said he, "with fruit surcharged,
Deigns none to ease thy load, and taste thy sweet,
60   Nor God, nor Man? Is knowledge so despised?
Or envy, or what reserve forbids to taste?
Forbid who will, none shall from me withhold
Longer thy offered good; why else set here?"
This said, he paused not, but with venturous arm
65   He plucked, he tasted; me damp horrour chilled
At such bold words vouched with a deed so bold:
But he thus, overjoyed; "O fruit divine,
Sweet of thyself, but much more sweet thus cropt,
Forbidden here, it seems, as only fit

70   For Gods, yet able to make Gods of Men:
        And why not Gods of Men; since good, the more
        Communicated, more abundant grows,
        The author not impaired, but honoured more?
        Here, happy creature, fair angelic Eve!
75   Partake thou also; happy though thou art,
        Happier thou mayest be, worthier canst not be:
        Taste this, and be henceforth among the Gods
        Thyself a Goddess, not to earth confined,
        But sometimes in the air, as we, sometimes
80   Ascend to Heav'n, by merit thine, and see
        What life the Gods live there, and such live thou!"
        So saying, he drew nigh, and to me held,
        Even to my mouth of that same fruit held part
        Which he had plucked; the pleasant savoury smell
85   So quickened appetite, that I, methought,
        Could not but taste. Forthwith up to the clouds
        With him I flew, and underneath beheld
        The earth outstretched immense, a prospect wide
        And various: Wondering at my flight and change
90   To this high exaltation; suddenly
        My guide was gone, and I, methought, sunk down,
        And fell asleep; but O, how glad I waked
        To find this but a dream! Thus Eve her night
        Related, and thus Adam answered sad.
95   Best image of myself, and dearer half,
        The trouble of thy thoughts this night in sleep
        Affects me equally; nor can I like
        This uncouth dream, of evil sprung, I fear;
        Yet evil whence? in thee can harbour none,
100   Created pure. But know that in the soul
        Are many lesser faculties, that serve
        Reason as chief; among these Fancy next
        Her office holds; of all external things
        Which the five watchful senses represent,

105   She forms imaginations, airy shapes,
        Which Reason, joining or disjoining, frames
        All what we affirm or what deny, and call
        Our knowledge or opinion; then retires
        Into her private cell, when nature rests.
110   Oft in her absence mimic Fancy wakes
        To imitate her; but, misjoining shapes,
        Wild work produces oft, and most in dreams;
        Ill matching words and deeds long past or late.
        Some such resemblances, methinks, I find
115   Of our last evening's talk, in this thy dream,
        But with addition strange; yet be not sad.
        Evil into the mind of God or Man
        May come and go, so unreproved, and leave
        No spot or blame behind: Which gives me hope
120   That what in sleep thou didst abhor to dream,
        Waking thou never will consent to do.
        Be not disheartened then, nor cloud those looks,
        That wont to be more cheerful and serene,
        Than when fair morning first smiles on the world;
125   And let us to our fresh employments rise
        Among the groves, the fountains, and the flowers
        That open now their choisest bosomed smells,
        Reserved from night, and kept for thee in store.
        So cheered he his fair spouse, and she was cheered;
130   But silently a gentle tear let fall
        From either eye, and wiped them with her hair;
        Two other precious drops that ready stood,
        Each in their crystal sluice, he ere they fell
        Kissed, as the gracious signs of sweet remorse
135   And pious awe, that feared to have offended.
        So all was cleared, and to the field they haste.
        But first, from under shady arborous roof
        Soon as they forth were come to open sight
        Of day-spring, and the sun, who, scarce up-risen,

140   With wheels yet hovering o'er the ocean-brim,
      Shot parallel to the earth his dewy ray,
      Discovering in wide landscape all the east
      Of Paradise and Eden's happy plains,
      Lowly they bowed adoring, and began
145   Their orisons, each morning duly paid
      In various style; for neither various style
      Nor holy rapture wanted they to praise
      Their Maker, in fit strains pronounced, or sung
      Unmeditated; such prompt eloquence
150   Flowed from their lips, in prose or numerous verse,
      More tuneable than needed lute or harp
      To add more sweetness; and they thus began.
      These are thy glorious works, Parent of good,
      Almighty! Thine this universal frame,
155   Thus wonderous fair; Thyself how wonderous then!
      Unspeakable, who sitt'st above these Heav'ns
      To us invisible, or dimly seen
      In these thy lowest works; yet these declare
      Thy goodness beyond thought, and power divine.
160   Speak, ye who best can tell, ye sons of light,
      Angels; for ye behold him, and with songs
      And choral symphonies, day without night,
      Circle his throne rejoicing; ye in Heav'n
      On Earth join all ye Creatures to extol
165   Him first, him last, him midst, and without end.
      Fairest of stars, last in the train of night,
      If better thou belong not to the dawn,
      Sure pledge of day, that crownest the smiling morn
      With thy bright circlet, praise him in thy sphere,
170   While day arises, that sweet hour of prime.
      Thou Sun, of this great world both eye and soul,
      Acknowledge him thy greater; sound his praise
      In thy eternal course, both when thou climbest,
      And when high noon hast gained, and when thou fallest.

175   Moon, that now meetest the orient sun, now flyest,
         With the fixed Stars, fixed in their orb that flies;
         And ye five other wandering Fires, that move
         In mystic dance not without song, resound
         His praise, who out of darkness called up light.
180   Air, and ye Elements, the eldest birth
         Of Nature's womb, that in quaternion run
         Perpetual circle, multiform; and mix
         And nourish all things; let your ceaseless change
         Vary to our great Maker still new praise.
185   Ye Mists and Exhalations, that now rise
         From hill or steaming lake, dusky or gray,
         Till the sun paint your fleecy skirts with gold,
         In honour to the world's great Author rise;
         Whether to deck with clouds the uncoloured sky,
190   Or wet the thirsty earth with falling showers,
         Rising or falling still advance his praise.
         His praise, ye Winds, that from four quarters blow,
         Breathe soft or loud; and, wave your tops, ye Pines,
         With every plant, in sign of worship wave.
195   Fountains, and ye that warble, as ye flow,
         Melodious murmurs, warbling tune his praise.
         Join voices, all ye living Souls: Ye Birds,
         That singing up to Heav'n-gate ascend,
         Bear on your wings and in your notes his praise.
200   Ye that in waters glide, and ye that walk
         The earth, and stately tread, or lowly creep;
         Witness if I be silent, morn or even,
         To hill, or valley, fountain, or fresh shade,
         Made vocal by my song, and taught his praise.
205   Hail, universal Lord, be bounteous still
         To give us only good; and if the night
         Have gathered aught of evil, or concealed,
         Disperse it, as now light dispels the dark!
         So prayed they innocent, and to their thoughts

210   Firm peace recovered soon, and wonted calm.
On to their morning's rural work they haste,
Among sweet dews and flowers; where any row
Of fruit-trees over-woody reached too far
Their pampered boughs, and needed hands to check
215   Fruitless embraces: or they led the vine
To wed her elm; she, spoused, about him twines
Her marriageable arms, and with him brings
Her dower, the adopted clusters, to adorn
His barren leaves. Them thus employed beheld
220   With pity Heav'n's high King, and to him called
Raphael, the sociable Spirit, that deigned
To travel with Tobias, and secured
His marriage with the seven times-wedded maid.
Raphael, said he, thou hearest what stir on Earth
225   Satan, from Hell 'scaped through the darksome gulf,
Hath raised in Paradise; and how disturbed
This night the human pair; how he designs
In them at once to ruin all mankind.
Go therefore, half this day as friend with friend
230   Converse with Adam, in what bower or shade
Thou findest him from the heat of noon retired,
To respite his day-labour with repast,
Or with repose; and such discourse bring on,
As may advise him of his happy state,
235   Happiness in his power left free to will,
Left to his own free will, his will though free,
Yet mutable; whence warn him to beware
He swerve not, too secure: Tell him withal
His danger, and from whom; what enemy,
240   Late fallen himself from Heav'n, is plotting now
The fall of others from like state of bliss;
By violence? no, for that shall be withstood;
But by deceit and lies: This let him know,
Lest, wilfully transgressing, he pretend

245   Surprisal, unadmonished, unforewarned.
       So spake the Eternal Father, and fulfilled
       All justice: Nor delayed the winged Saint
       After his charge received; but from among
       Thousand celestial Ardours, where he stood
250   Veiled with his gorgeous wings, up springing light,
       Flew through the midst of Heav'n; the angelick quires,
       On each hand parting, to his speed gave way
       Through all the empyreal road; till, at the gate
       Of Heav'n arrived, the gate self-opened wide
255   On golden hinges turning, as by work
       Divine the sov'reign Architect had framed.
       From hence no cloud, or, to obstruct his sight,
       Star interposed, however small he sees,
       Not unconformed to other shining globes,
260   Earth, and the garden of God, with cedars crowned
       Above all hills. As when by night the glass
       Of Galileo, less assured, observes
       Imagined lands and regions in the moon:
       Or pilot, from amidst the Cyclades
265   Delos or Samos first appearing, kens
       A cloudy spot. Down thither prone in flight
       He speeds, and through the vast ethereal sky
       Sails between worlds and worlds, with steady wing
       Now on the polar winds, then with quick fan
270   Winnows the buxom air; till, within soar
       Of towering eagles, to all the fowls he seems
       A phoenix, gazed by all as that sole bird,
       When, to enshrine his reliques in the Sun's
       Bright temple, to Egyptian Thebes he flies.
275   At once on the eastern cliff of Paradise
       He lights, and to his proper shape returns
       A Seraph winged: Six wings he wore, to shade
       His lineaments divine; the pair that clad
       Each shoulder broad, came mantling o'er his breast

280	With regal ornament; the middle pair
	Girt like a starry zone his waist, and round
	Skirted his loins and thighs with downy gold
	And colours dipt in Heav'n; the third his feet
	Shadowed from either heel with feathered mail,
285	Sky-tinctured grain. Like Maia's son he stood,
	And shook his plumes, that heav'nly fragrance filled
	The circuit wide. Straight knew him all the bands
	Of Angels under watch; and to his state,
	And to his message high, in honour rise;
290	For on some message high they guessed him bound.
	Their glittering tents he passed, and now is come
	Into the blissful field, through groves of myrrh,
	And flowering odours, cassia, nard, and balm;
	A wilderness of sweets; for Nature here
295	Wantoned as in her prime, and played at will
	Her virgin fancies pouring forth more sweet,
	Wild above rule or art, enormous bliss.
	Him through the spicy forest onward come
	Adam discerned, as in the door he sat
300	Of his cool bower, while now the mounted sun
	Shot down direct his fervid rays to warm
	Earth's inmost womb, more warmth than Adam needs:
	And Eve within, due at her hour prepared
	For dinner savoury fruits, of taste to please
305	True appetite, and not disrelish thirst
	Of nectarous draughts between, from milky stream,
	Berry or grape: To whom thus Adam called.
	Haste hither, Eve, and worth thy sight behold
	Eastward among those trees, what glorious shape
310	Comes this way moving; seems another morn
	Risen on mid-noon; some great behest from Heav'n
	To us perhaps he brings, and will vouchsafe

This day to be our guest. But go with speed,
And, what thy stores contain, bring forth, and pour
315 Abundance, fit to honour and receive
Our Heav'nly stranger: Well we may afford
Our givers their own gifts, and large bestow
From large bestowed, where Nature multiplies
Her fertile growth, and by disburthening grows
320 More fruitful, which instructs us not to spare.
To whom thus Eve. Adam, earth's hallowed mould,
Of God inspired! small store will serve, where store,
All seasons, ripe for use hangs on the stalk;
Save what by frugal storing firmness gains
325 To nourish, and superfluous moist consumes:
But I will haste, and from each bough and brake,
Each plant and juciest gourd, will pluck such choice
To entertain our Angel-guest, as he
Beholding shall confess, that here on Earth
330 God hath dispensed his bounties as in Heav'n.
So saying, with dispatchful looks in haste
She turns, on hospitable thoughts intent
What choice to choose for delicacy best,
What order, so contrived as not to mix
335 Tastes, not well joined, inelegant, but bring
Taste after taste upheld with kindliest change;
Bestirs her then, and from each tender stalk
Whatever Earth, all-bearing mother, yields
In India East or West, or middle shore
340 In Pontus or the Punic coast, or where
Alcinous reigned, fruit of all kinds, in coat
Rough, or smooth rind, or bearded husk, or shell,
She gathers, tribute large, and on the board
Heaps with unsparing hand; for drink the grape
345 She crushes, inoffensive must, and meaths
From many a berry, and from sweet kernels pressed

She tempers dulcet creams; nor these to hold
Wants her fit vessels pure; then strows the ground
With rose and odours from the shrub unfumed.

350 Mean while our primitive great sire, to meet
His God-like guest, walks forth, without more train
Accompanied than with his own complete
Perfections; in himself was all his state,
More solemn than the tedious pomp that waits

355 On princes, when their rich retinue long
Of horses led, and grooms besmeared with gold,
Dazzles the croud, and sets them all agape.
Nearer his presence Adam, though not awed,
Yet with submiss approach and reverence meek,

360 As to a superior nature bowing low,
Thus said. Native of Heav'n, for other place
None can than Heav'n such glorious shape contain;
Since, by descending from the thrones above,
Those happy places thou hast deigned a while

365 To want, and honour these, vouchsafe with us
Two only, who yet by sov'reign gift possess
This spacious ground, in yonder shady bower
To rest; and what the garden choicest bears
To sit and taste, till this meridian heat

370 Be over, and the sun more cool decline.
Whom thus the angelic Virtue answered mild.
Adam, I therefore came; nor art thou such
Created, or such place hast here to dwell,
As may not oft invite, though Spirits of Heav'n,

375 To visit thee; lead on then where thy bower
O'ershades; for these mid-hours, till evening rise,
I have at will. So to the sylvan lodge
They came, that like Pomona's arbour smiled,
With flowerets decked, and fragrant smells; but Eve,

380 Undecked save with herself, more lovely fair

Than Wood-Nymph, or the fairest Goddess feigned
Of three that in mount Ida naked strove,
Stood to entertain her guest from Heav'n; no veil
She needed, virtue-proof; no thought infirm
385   Altered her cheek. On whom the Angel Hail
Bestowed, the holy salutation used
Long after to blest Mary, second Eve.
Hail, Mother of Mankind, whose fruitful womb
Shall fill the world more numerous with thy sons,
390   Than with these various fruits the trees of God
Have heaped this table!—Raised of grassy turf
Their table was, and mossy seats had round,
And on her ample square from side to side
All autumn piled, though spring and autumn here
395   Danced hand in hand. A while discourse they hold;
No fear lest dinner cool; when thus began
Our author. Heav'nly stranger, please to taste
These bounties, which our Nourisher, from whom
All perfect good, unmeasured out, descends,
400   To us for food and for delight hath caused
The earth to yield; unsavoury food perhaps
To spiritual natures; only this I know,
That one celestial Father gives to all.
To whom the Angel. Therefore what he gives
405   (Whose praise be ever sung) to Man in part
Spiritual, may of purest Spirits be found
No ingrateful food: And food alike those pure
Intelligential substances require,
As doth your rational; and both contain
410   Within them every lower faculty
Of sense, whereby they hear, see, smell, touch, taste,
Tasting concoct, digest, assimilate,
And corporeal to incorporeal turn.
For know, whatever was created, needs

415	To be sustained and fed: Of elements
	The grosser feeds the purer, earth the sea,
	Earth and the sea feed air, the air those fires
	Ethereal, and as lowest first the moon;
	Whence in her visage round those spots, unpurged
420	Vapours not yet into her substance turned.
	Nor doth the moon no nourishment exhale
	From her moist continent to higher orbs.
	The sun that light imparts to all, receives
	From all his alimental recompence
425	In humid exhalations, and at even
	Sups with the ocean. Though in Heav'n the trees
	Of life ambrosial fruitage bear, and vines
	Yield nectar; though from off the boughs each morn
	We brush mellifluous dews, and find the ground
430	Covered with pearly grain: Yet God hath here
	Varied his bounty so with new delights,
	As may compare with Heav'n; and to taste
	Think not I shall be nice. So down they sat,
	And to their viands fell; nor seemingly
435	The Angel, nor in mist, the common gloss
	Of Theologians; but with keen dispatch
	Of real hunger, and concoctive heat
	To transubstantiate: What redounds, transpires
	Through Spirits with ease; nor wonder; if by fire
440	Of sooty coal the empiric alchemist
	Can turn, or holds it possible to turn,
	Metals of drossiest ore to perfect gold,
	As from the mine. Mean while at table Eve
	Ministered naked, and their flowing cups
445	With pleasant liquors crowned: O innocence
	Deserving Paradise! if ever, then,
	Then had the sons of God excuse to have been

Enamoured at that sight; but in those hearts
Love unlibidinous reigned, nor jealousy
450   Was understood, the injured lover's hell.
Thus when with meats and drinks they had sufficed,
Not burdened nature, sudden mind arose
In Adam, not to let the occasion pass
Given him by this great conference to know
455   Of things above his world, and of their being
Who dwell in Heav'n, whose excellence he saw
Transcend his own so far; whose radiant forms,
Divine effulgence, whose high power, so far
Exceeded human; and his wary speech
460   Thus to the empyreal minister he framed.
Inhabitant with God, now know I well
Thy favour, in this honour done to Man;
Under whose lowly roof thou hast vouchsafed
To enter, and these earthly fruits to taste,
465   Food not of Angels, yet accepted so,
As that more willingly thou couldst not seem
At Heav'n's high feasts to have fed: yet what compare
To whom the winged Hierarch replied.
O Adam, One Almighty is, from whom
470   All things proceed, and up to him return,
If not depraved from good, created all
Such to perfection, one first matter all,
Endued with various forms, various degrees
Of substance, and, in things that live, of life;
475   But more refined, more spiritous, and pure,
As nearer to him placed, or nearer tending
Each in their several active spheres assigned,
Till body up to spirit work, in bounds
Proportioned to each kind. So from the root
480   Springs lighter the green stalk, from thence the leaves
More airy, last the bright consummate flower

Spirits odorous breathes: flowers and their fruit,
Man's nourishment, by gradual scale sublimed,
To vital spirits aspire, to animal,
485   To intellectual; give both life and sense,
Fancy and understanding; whence the soul
Reason receives, and reason is her being,
Discursive, or intuitive; discourse
Is oftest yours, the latter most is ours,
490   Differing but in degree, of kind the same.
Wonder not then, what God for you saw good
If I refuse not, but convert, as you
To proper substance. Time may come, when Men
With Angels may participate, and find
495   No inconvenient diet, nor too light fare;
And from these corporal nutriments perhaps
Your bodies may at last turn all to spirit,
Improved by tract of time, and, winged, ascend
Ethereal, as we; or may, at choice,
500   Here or in heav'nly Paradises dwell;
If ye be found obedient, and retain
Unalterably firm his love entire,
Whose progeny you are. Mean while enjoy
Your fill what happiness this happy state
505   Can comprehend, incapable of more.
To whom the patriarch of mankind replied.
O favourable Spirit, propitious guest,
Well hast thou taught the way that might direct
Our knowledge, and the scale of nature set
510   From center to circumference; whereon,
In contemplation of created things,
By steps we may ascend to God. But say,
What meant that caution joined, *If ye be found*
Obedient? Can we want obedience then
515   To him, or possibly his love desert,

Who formed us from the dust and placed us here
Full to the utmost measure of what bliss
Human desires can seek or apprehend?
To whom the Angel. Son of Heav'n and Earth,
520   Attend! That thou art happy, owe to God;
That thou continuest such, owe to thyself,
That is, to thy obedience; therein stand.
This was that caution given thee; be advised.
God made thee perfect, not immutable;
525   And good he made thee, but to persevere
He left it in thy power; ordained thy will
By nature free, not over-ruled by fate
Inextricable, or strict necessity:
Our voluntary service he requires,
530   Not our necessitated; such with him
Finds no acceptance, nor can find; for how
Can hearts, not free, be tried whether they serve
Willing or no, who will but what they must
By destiny, and can no other choose?
535   Myself, and all the angelic host, that stand
In sight of God, enthroned, our happy state
Hold, as you yours, while our obedience holds;
On other surety none: Freely we serve,
Because we freely love, as in our will
540   To love or not; in this we stand or fall:
And some are fallen, to disobedience fallen,
And so from Heav'n to deepest Hell; O fall
From what high state of bliss, into what woe!
To whom our great progenitor. Thy words
545   Attentive, and with more delighted ear,
Divine instructer, I have heard, than when
Cherubic songs by night from neighbouring hills
Aereal music send: Nor knew I not
To be both will and deed created free;

550   Yet that we never shall forget to love
         Our Maker, and obey him whose command
         Single is yet so just, my constant thoughts
         Assured me, and still assure: Though what thou tellest
         Hath passed in Heav'n, some doubt within me move,
555   But more desire to hear, if thou consent,
         The full relation, which must needs be strange,
         Worthy of sacred silence to be heard;
         And we have yet large day, for scarce the sun
         Hath finished half his journey, and scarce begins
560   His other half in the great zone of Heav'n.
         Thus Adam made request; and Raphael,
         After short pause assenting, thus began.
         High matter thou enjoinest me, O prime of men,
         Sad task and hard: For how shall I relate
565   To human sense the invisible exploits
         Of warring Spirits? how, without remorse,
         The ruin of so many glorious once
         And perfect while they stood? how last unfold
         The secrets of another world, perhaps
570   Not lawful to reveal? yet for thy good
         This is dispensed; and what surmounts the reach
         Of human sense, I shall delineate so,
         By likening spiritual to corporal forms,
         As may express them best; though what if Earth
575   Be but a shadow of Heav'n, and things therein
         Each to other like, more than on earth is thought?
         As yet this world was not, and Chaos wild
         Reigned where these Heav'ns now roll, where Earth now rests
         Upon her center poised; when on a day
580   (For time, though in eternity, applied
         To motion, measures all things durable
         By present, past, and future,) on such day

As Heav'n's great year brings forth, the empyreal host
Of Angels by imperial summons called,
585   Innumerable before the Almighty's throne
Forthwith, from all the ends of Heav'n, appeared
Under their Hierarchs in orders bright:
Ten thousand thousand ensigns high advanced,
Standards and gonfalons 'twixt van and rear
590   Stream in the air, and for distinction serve
Of hierarchies, of orders, and degrees;
Or in their glittering tissues bear imblazed
Holy memorials, acts of zeal and love
Recorded eminent. Thus when in orbs
595   Of circuit inexpressible they stood,
Orb within orb, the Father Infinite,
By whom in bliss embosomed sat the Son,
Amidst as from a flaming mount, whose top
Brightness had made invisible, thus spake.
600   Hear, all ye Angels, progeny of light,
Thrones, Dominations, Princedoms, Virtues, Powers;
Hear my decree, which unrevoked shall stand.
This day I have begot whom I declare
My only Son, and on this holy hill
605   Him have anointed, whom ye now behold
At my right hand; your head I him appoint;
And by myself have sworn, to him shall bow
All knees in Heav'n, and shall confess him Lord:
Under his great vice-gerent reign abide
610   United, as one individual soul,
For ever happy: Him who disobeys,
Me disobeys, breaks union, and that day,
Cast out from God and blessed vision, falls
Into utter darkness, deep engulfed, his place
615   Ordained without redemption, without end.
So spake the Omnipotent, and with his words

All seemed well pleased; all seemed, but were not all.
That day, as other solemn days, they spent
In song and dance about the sacred hill;
620   Mystical dance, which yonder starry sphere
Of planets, and of fixed, in all her wheels
Resembles nearest, mazes intricate,
Eccentric, intervolved, yet regular
Then most, when most irregular they seem;
625   And in their motions harmony divine
So smooths her charming tones, that God's own ear
Listens delighted. Evening now approached,
(For we have also our evening and our morn,
We ours for change delectable, not need;)
630   Forthwith from dance to sweet repast they turn
Desirous; all in circles as they stood,
Tables are set, and on a sudden piled
With Angels food, and rubied nectar flows
In pearl, in diamond, and massy gold,
635   Fruit of delicious vines, the growth of Heav'n.
On flowers reposed, and with fresh flowerets crowned,
They eat, they drink, and in communion sweet
Quaff immortality and joy, secure
Of surfeit, where full measure only bounds
640   Excess, before the all-bounteous King, who showered
With copious hand, rejoicing in their joy.
Now when ambrosial night with clouds exhaled
From that high mount of God, whence light and shade
Spring both, the face of brightest Heav'n had changed
645   To grateful twilight, (for night comes not there
In darker veil) and roseate dews disposed
All but the unsleeping eyes of God to rest;
Wide over all the plain, and wider far
Than all this globous earth in plain outspread,
650   (Such are the courts of God) the angelick throng,

Dispersed in bands and files, their camp extend
By living streams among the trees of life,
Pavilions numberless, and sudden reared,
Celestial tabernacles, where they slept
655   Fanned with cool winds; save those, who, in their course,
Melodious hymns about the sovran throne
Alternate all night long: but not so waked
Satan; so call him now, his former name
Is heard no more in Heav'n; he of the first,
660   If not the first Arch-Angel, great in power,
In favour and pre-eminence, yet fraught
With envy against the Son of God, that day
Honoured by his great Father, and proclaimed
Messiah King anointed, could not bear
665   Through pride that sight, and thought himself impaired.
Deep malice thence conceiving and disdain,
Soon as midnight brought on the dusky hour
Friendliest to sleep and silence, he resolved
With all his legions to dislodge, and leave
670   Unworshipped, unobeyed, the throne supreme,
Contemptuous; and his next subordinate
Awakening, thus to him in secret spake.
Sleepest thou, Companion dear? What sleep can close
Thy eye-lids? and rememberest what decree
675   Of yesterday, so late hath passed the lips
Of Heav'n's Almighty. Thou to me thy thoughts
Wast wont, I mine to thee was wont to impart;
Both waking we were one; how then can now
Thy sleep dissent? New laws thou seest imposed;
680   New laws from him who reigns, new minds may raise
In us who serve, new counsels to debate
What doubtful may ensue: More in this place
To utter is not safe. Assemble thou
Of all those myriads which we lead the chief;

685 Tell them, that by command, ere yet dim night
Her shadowy cloud withdraws, I am to haste,
And all who under me their banners wave,
Homeward, with flying march, where we possess
The quarters of the north; there to prepare
690 Fit entertainment to receive our King,
The great Messiah, and his new commands,
Who speedily through all the hierarchies
Intends to pass triumphant, and give laws.
So spake the false Arch-Angel, and infused
695 Bad influence into the unwary breast
Of his associate: He together calls,
Or several one by one, the regent Powers,
Under him Regent; tells, as he was taught,
That the Most High commanding, now ere night,
700 Now ere dim night had disencumbered Heav'n,
The great hierarchal standard was to move;
Tells the suggested cause, and casts between
Ambiguous words and jealousies, to sound
Or taint integrity: But all obeyed
705 The wonted signal, and superior voice
Of their great Potentate; for great indeed
His name, and high was his degree in Heav'n;
His countenance, as the morning-star that guides
The starry flock, allured them, and with lies
710 Drew after him the third part of Heav'n's host.
Mean while the Eternal eye, whose sight discerns
Abstrusest thoughts, from forth his holy mount,
And from within the golden lamps that burn
Nightly before him, saw without their light
715 Rebellion rising; saw in whom, how spread
Among the sons of morn, what multitudes
Were banded to oppose his high decree;

And, smiling, to his only Son thus said.
Son, thou in whom my glory I behold
720   In full resplendence, Heir of all my might,
Nearly it now concerns us to be sure
Of our Omnipotence, and with what arms
We mean to hold what anciently we claim
Of deity or empire: Such a foe
725   Is rising, who intends to erect his throne
Equal to ours, throughout the spacious north;
Nor so content, hath in his thought to try
In battle, what our power is, or our right.
Let us advise, and to this hazard draw
730   With speed what force is left, and all employ
In our defence; lest unawares we lose
This our high place, our sanctuary, our hill.
To whom the Son with calm aspect and clear,
Lightning divine, ineffable, serene,
735   Made answer. Mighty Father, thou thy foes
Justly hast in derision, and, secure,
Laughest at their vain designs and tumults vain,
Matter to me of glory, whom their hate
Illustrates, when they see all regal power
740   Given me to quell their pride, and in event
Know whether I be dextrous to subdue
Thy rebels, or be found the worst in Heav'n.
So spake the Son; but Satan, with his Powers,
Far was advanced on winged speed; an host
745   Innumerable as the stars of night,
Or stars of morning, dew-drops, which the sun
Impearls on every leaf and every flower.
Regions they passed, the mighty regencies
Of Seraphim, and Potentates, and Thrones,
750   In their triple degrees; regions to which
All thy dominion, Adam, is no more

Than what this garden is to all the earth,
And all the sea, from one entire globose
Stretched into longitude; which having passed,
755 At length into the limits of the north
They came; and Satan to his royal seat
High on a hill, far blazing, as a mount
Raised on a mount, with pyramids and towers
From diamond quarries hewn, and rocks of gold;
760 The palace of great Lucifer, (so call
That structure in the dialect of men
Interpreted,) which not long after, he
Affecting all equality with God,
In imitation of that mount whereon
765 Messiah was declared in sight of Heav'n,
The Mountain of the Congregation called;
For thither he assembled all his train,
Pretending so commanded to consult
About the great reception of their King,
770 Thither to come, and with calumnious art
Of counterfeited truth thus held their ears.
Thrones, Dominations, Princedoms, Virtues, Powers;
If these magnific titles yet remain
Not merely titular, since by decree
775 Another now hath to himself engrossed
All power, and us eclipsed under the name
Of King anointed, for whom all this haste
Of midnight-march, and hurried meeting here,
This only to consult how we may best,
780 With what may be devised of honours new,
Receive him coming to receive from us
Knee-tribute yet unpaid, prostration vile!
Too much to one! but double how endured,
To one, and to his image now proclaimed?
785 But what if better counsels might erect

Our minds, and teach us to cast off this yoke?
Will ye submit your necks, and choose to bend
The supple knee? Ye will not, if I trust
To know ye right, or if ye know yourselves
790 Natives and sons of Heav'n possessed before
By none; and if not equal all, yet free,
Equally free; for orders and degrees
Jar not with liberty, but well consist.
Who can in reason then, or right, assume
795 Monarchy over such as live by right
His equals, if in power and splendour less,
In freedom equal? or can introduce
Law and edict on us, who without law
Err not? much less for this to be our Lord,
800 And look for adoration, to the abuse
Of those imperial titles, which assert
Our being ordained to govern, not to serve.
Thus far his bold discourse without controul
Had audience; when among the Seraphim
805 Abdiel, than whom none with more zeal adored
The Deity, and divine commands obeyed,
Stood up, and in a flame of zeal severe
The current of his fury thus opposed.
O argument blasphemous, false, and proud!
810 Words which no ear ever to hear in Heav'n
Expected, least of all from thee, Ingrate,
In place thyself so high above thy peers.
Canst thou with impious obloquy condemn
The just decree of God, pronounced and sworn,
815 That to his only Son, by right endued
With regal scepter, every soul in Heav'n
Shall bend the knee, and in that honour due
Confess him rightful King? unjust, thou sayest,
Flatly unjust, to bind with laws the free,

820	And equal over equals to let reign,
	One over all with unsucceeded power.
	Shalt thou give law to God? shalt thou dispute
	With him the points of liberty, who made
	Thee what thou art, and formed the Powers of Heav'n
825	Such as he pleased, and circumscribed their being?
	Yet, by experience taught, we know how good,
	And of our good and of our dignity
	How provident he is; how far from thought
	To make us less, bent rather to exalt
830	Our happy state, under one head more near
	United. But to grant it thee unjust,
	That equal over equals monarch reign:
	Thyself, though great and glorious, dost thou count,
	Or all angelic nature joined in one,
835	Equal to him begotten Son? by whom,
	As by his Word, the Mighty Father made
	All things, even thee; and all the Spirits of Heav'n
	By him created in their bright degrees,
	Crowned them with glory, and to their glory named
840	Thrones, Dominations, Princedoms, Virtues, Powers,
	Essential Powers; nor by his reign obscured,
	But more illustrious made; since he the head
	One of our number thus reduced becomes;
	His laws our laws; all honour to him done
845	Returns our own. Cease then this impious rage,
	And tempt not these; but hasten to appease
	The incensed Father, and the incensed Son,
	While pardon may be found in time besought.
	So spake the fervent Angel; but his zeal
850	None seconded, as out of season judged,
	Or singular and rash: Whereat rejoiced
	The Apostate, and, more haughty, thus replied.

That we were formed then sayest thou? and the work
Of secondary hands, by task transferred
855 From Father to his Son? strange point and new!
Doctrine which we would know whence learned: who saw
When this creation was? rememberest thou
Thy making, while the Maker gave thee being?
We know no time when we were not as now;
860 Know none before us, self-begot, self-raised
By our own quickening power, when fatal course
Had circled his full orb, the birth mature
Of this our native Heav'n, ethereal sons.
Our puissance is our own; our own right hand
865 Shall teach us highest deeds, by proof to try
Who is our equal: Then thou shalt behold
Whether by supplication we intend
Address, and to begirt the almighty throne
Beseeching or besieging. This report,
870 These tidings carry to the anointed King;
And fly, ere evil intercept thy flight.
He said; and, as the sound of waters deep,
Hoarse murmur echoed to his words applause
Through the infinite host; nor less for that
875 The flaming Seraph fearless, though alone
Encompassed round with foes, thus answered bold.
O alienate from God, O Spirit accursed,
Forsaken of all good! I see thy fall
Determined, and thy hapless crew involved
880 In this perfidious fraud, contagion spread
Both of thy crime and punishment: Henceforth
No more be troubled how to quit the yoke
Of God's Messiah; those indulgent laws
Will not be now vouchsafed; other decrees
885 Against thee are gone forth without recall;
That golden scepter, which thou didst reject,

Is now an iron rod to bruise and break
Thy disobedience. Well thou didst advise;
Yet not for thy advice or threats I fly
890   These wicked tents devoted, lest the wrath
Impendent, raging into sudden flame,
Distinguish not: For soon expect to feel
His thunder on thy head, devouring fire.
Then who created thee lamenting learn,
895   When who can uncreate thee thou shalt know.
So spake the Seraph Abdiel, faithful found
Among the faithless, faithful only he;
Among innumerable false, unmoved,
Unshaken, unseduced, unterrified,
900   His loyalty he kept, his love, his zeal;
Nor number, nor example, with him wrought
To swerve from truth, or change his constant mind,
Though single. From amidst them forth he passed,
Long way through hostile scorn, which he sustained
905   Superior, nor of violence feared aught;
And, with retorted scorn, his back he turned
On those proud towers to swift destruction doomed.

BOOK VI

THE ARGUMENT

Raphael continues to relate how Michael and Gabriel were sent forth to battle against Satan and his angels. The first fight described: Satan and his powers retire under night: he calls a council, invents devilish engines, which in the second

5   day's fight put Michael and his angels to some disorder; but they at length pulling up mountains overwhelmed both the force and machines of Satan: yet the tumult not so ending, God on the third day sends Messiah his Son, for whom he had reserved the glory of that victory: he in

10   the power of his Father coming to the place, and causing all his legions to stand still on either side, with his chariot and thunder driving into the midst of his enemies, pursues them unable to resist towards the wall of Heav'n: which opening, they leap down with horror and confusion into

15   the place of punishment prepared for them in the deep: Messiah returns with triumph to his Father.

All night the dreadless Angel, unpursued,
Through Heav'n's wide champain held his way; till Morn,
Waked by the circling Hours, with rosy hand
Unbarred the gates of light. There is a cave

5	Within the mount of God, fast by his throne,
	Where light and darkness in perpetual round
	Lodge and dislodge by turns, which makes through Heav'n
	Grateful vicissitude, like day and night;
	Light issues forth, and at the other door
10	Obsequious darkness enters, till her hour
	To veil the Heav'n, though darkness there might well
	Seem twilight here: And now went forth the Morn
	Such as in highest Heav'n arrayed in gold
	Empyreal; from before her vanished Night,
15	Shot through with orient beams; when all the plain
	Covered with thick embattled squadrons bright,
	Chariots, and flaming arms, and fiery steeds,
	Reflecting blaze on blaze, first met his view:
	War he perceived, war in procinct; and found
20	Already known what he for news had thought
	To have reported: Gladly then he mixed
	Among those friendly Powers, who him received
	With joy and acclamations loud, that one,
	That of so many myriads fallen, yet one
25	Returned not lost. On to the sacred hill
	They led him high applauded, and present
	Before the seat supreme; from whence a voice,
	From midst a golden cloud, thus mild was heard.
	Servant of God. Well done; well hast thou fought
30	The better fight, who single hast maintained
	Against revolted multitudes the cause
	Of truth, in word mightier than they in arms;
	And for the testimony of truth hast borne
	Universal reproach, far worse to bear
35	Than violence; for this was all thy care
	To stand approved in sight of God, though worlds
	Judged thee perverse: The easier conquest now

Remains thee, aided by this host of friends,
Back on thy foes more glorious to return,
40   Than scorned thou didst depart; and to subdue
By force, who reason for their law refuse,
Right reason for their law, and for their King
Messiah, who by right of merit reigns.
Go, Michael, of celestial armies prince,
45   And thou, in military prowess next,
Gabriel, lead forth to battle these my sons
Invincible; lead forth my armed Saints,
By thousands and by millions, ranged for fight,
Equal in number to that Godless crew
50   Rebellious: Them with fire and hostile arms
Fearless assault; and, to the brow of Heav'n
Pursuing, drive them out from God and bliss,
Into their place of punishment, the gulf
Of Tartarus, which ready opens wide
55   His fiery Chaos to receive their fall.
So spake the Sovran Voice, and clouds began
To darken all the hill, and smoke to roll
In dusky wreaths, reluctant flames, the sign
Of wrath awaked; nor with less dread the loud
60   Ethereal trumpet from on high 'gan blow:
At which command the Powers militant,
That stood for Heav'n, in mighty quadrate joined
Of union irresistible, moved on
In silence their bright legions, to the sound
65   Of instrumental harmony, that breathed
Heroic ardour to adventurous deeds
Under their God-like leaders, in the cause
Of God and his Messiah. On they move
Indissolubly firm; nor obvious hill,
70   Nor straitening vale, nor wood, nor stream, divides
Their perfect ranks; for high above the ground

Their march was, and the passive air upbore
Their nimble tread; as when the total kind
Of birds, in orderly array on wing,
75 Came summoned over Eden to receive
Their names of thee; so over many a tract
Of Heav'n they marched, and many a province wide,
Tenfold the length of this terrene: At last,
Far in the horizon to the north appeared
80 From skirt to skirt a fiery region, stretched
In battailous aspect, and nearer view
Bristled with upright beams innumerable
Of rigid spears, and helmets thronged, and shields
Various, with boastful argument portrayed,
85 The banded Powers of Satan hasting on
With furious expedition; for they weened
That self-same day, by fight or by surprise,
To win the mount of God, and on his throne
To set the Envier of his state, the proud
90 Aspirer; but their thoughts proved fond and vain
In the mid way: Though strange to us it seemed
At first, that Angel should with Angel war,
And in fierce hosting meet, who wont to meet
So oft in festivals of joy and love
95 Unanimous, as sons of one great Sire,
Hymning the Eternal Father: But the shout
Of battle now began, and rushing sound
Of onset ended soon each milder thought.
High in the midst, exalted as a God,
100 The Apostate in his sun-bright chariot sat,
Idol of majesty divine, enclosed
With flaming Cherubim, and golden shields;
Then lighted from his gorgeous throne, for now
'Twixt host and host but narrow space was left,
105 A dreadful interval, and front to front

Presented stood in terrible array
Of hideous length: Before the cloudy van,
On the rough edge of battle ere it joined,
Satan, with vast and haughty strides advanced,
110   Came towering, armed in adamant and gold;
Abdiel that sight endured not, where he stood
Among the mightiest, bent on highest deeds,
And thus his own undaunted heart explores.
O Heav'n! that such resemblance of the Highest
115   Should yet remain, where faith and realty
Remain not: Wherefore should not strength and might
There fail where virtue fails, or weakest prove
Where boldest, though to fight unconquerable?
His puissance, trusting in the Almighty's aid,
120   I mean to try, whose reason I have tried
Unsound and false; nor is it aught but just,
That he, who in debate of truth hath won,
Should win in arms, in both disputes alike
Victor; though brutish that contest and foul,
125   When reason hath to deal with force, yet so
Most reason is that reason overcome.
So pondering, and from his armed peers
Forth stepping opposite, half-way he met
His daring foe, at this prevention more
130   Incensed, and thus securely him defied.
Proud, art thou met? thy hope was to have reached
The heighth of thy aspiring unopposed,
The throne of God unguarded, and his side
Abandoned, at the terror of thy power
135   Or potent tongue: Fool! not to think how vain
Against the Omnipotent to rise in arms;
Who out of smallest things could, without end,
Have raised incessant armies to defeat
Thy folly; or with solitary hand

140   Reaching beyond all limit, at one blow,
            Unaided, could have finished thee, and whelmed
            Thy legions under darkness: But thou seest
            All are not of thy train; there be, who faith
            Prefer, and piety to God, though then
145   To thee not visible, when I alone
            Seemed in thy world erroneous to dissent
            From all: My sect thou seest; now learn too late
            How few sometimes may know, when thousands err.
            Whom the grand foe, with scornful eye askance,
150   Thus answered. Ill for thee, but in wished hour
            Of my revenge, first sought for, thou returnest
            From flight, seditious Angel! to receive
            Thy merited reward, the first assay
            Of this right hand provoked, since first that tongue,
155   Inspired with contradiction, durst oppose
            A third part of the Gods, in synod met
            Their deities to assert; who, while they feel
            Vigour divine within them, can allow
            Omnipotence to none. But well thou comest
160   Before thy fellows, ambitious to win
            From me some plume, that thy success may show
            Destruction to the rest: This pause between,
            (Unanswered lest thou boast) to let thee know,
            At first I thought that Liberty and Heav'n
165   To heav'nly souls had been all one; but now
            I see that most through sloth had rather serve,
            Ministring Spirits, trained up in feast and song!
            Such hast thou armed, the minstrelsy of Heav'n,
            Servility with freedom to contend,
170   As both their deeds compared this day shall prove.
            To whom in brief thus Abdiel stern replied.
            Apostate! still thou errest, nor end wilt find

Of erring, from the path of truth remote:
Unjustly thou depravest it with the name
175   Of servitude, to serve whom God ordains,
Or Nature: God and Nature bid the same,
When he who rules is worthiest, and excels
Them whom he governs. This is servitude,
To serve the unwise, or him who hath rebelled
180   Against his worthier, as thine now serve thee,
Thyself not free, but to thyself enthralled;
Yet lewdly darest our ministring upbraid.
Reign thou in Hell, thy kingdom; let me serve
In Heav'n God ever blest, and his divine
185   Behests obey, worthiest to be obeyed;
Yet chains in Hell, not realms, expect: Mean while
From me returned, as erst thou saidst, from flight,
This greeting on thy impious crest receive.
So saying, a noble stroke he lifted high,
190   Which hung not, but so swift with tempest fell
On the proud crest of Satan, that no sight,
Nor motion of swift thought, less could his shield,
Such ruin intercept: Ten paces huge
He back recoiled; the tenth on bended knee
195   His massy spear upstaid; as if on earth
Winds under ground, or waters forcing way,
Sidelong had pushed a mountain from his seat,
Half sunk with all his pines. Amazement seised
The rebel Thrones, but greater rage, to see
200   Thus foiled their mightiest; ours joy filled, and shout,
Presage of victory, and fierce desire
Of battle: Whereat Michael bid sound
The Arch-Angel trumpet; through the vast of Heav'n
It sounded, and the faithful armies rung
205   Hosanna to the Highest: Nor stood at gaze
The adverse legions, nor less hideous joined

The horrid shock. Now storming fury rose,
And clamour such as heard in Heav'n till now
Was never; arms on armour clashing brayed
210 Horrible discord, and the madding wheels
Of brazen chariots raged; dire was the noise
Of conflict; over head the dismal hiss
Of fiery darts in flaming vollies flew,
And flying vaulted either host with fire.
215 So under fiery cope together rushed
Both battles main, with ruinous assault
And inextinguishable rage. All Heav'n
Resounded; and had Earth been then, all Earth
Had to her center shook. What wonder? when
220 Millions of fierce encountering Angels fought
On either side, the least of whom could wield
These elements, and arm him with the force
Of all their regions: How much more of power
Army against army numberless to raise
225 Dreadful combustion warring, and disturb,
Though not destroy, their happy native seat;
Had not the Eternal King Omnipotent,
From his strong hold of Heav'n, high over-ruled
And limited their might; though numbered such
230 As each divided legion might have seemed
A numerous host; in strength each armed hand
A legion; led in fight, yet leader seemed
Each warrior single as in chief, expert
When to advance, or stand, or turn the sway
235 Of battle, open when, and when to close
The ridges of grim war: No thought of flight,
None of retreat, no unbecoming deed
That argued fear; each on himself relied,
As only in his arm the moment lay
240 Of victory: Deeds of eternal fame

Were done, but infinite; for wide was spread
That war and various; sometimes on firm ground
A standing fight, then, soaring on main wing,
Tormented all the air; all air seemed then
245   Conflicting fire. Long time in even scale
The battle hung; till Satan, who that day
Prodigious power had shown, and met in arms
No equal, ranging through the dire attack
Of fighting Seraphim confused, at length
250   Saw where the sword of Michael smote, and felled
Squadrons at once; with huge two-handed sway
Brandished aloft, the horrid edge came down
Wide-wasting; such destruction to withstand
He hasted, and opposed the rocky orb
255   Of tenfold adamant, his ample shield,
A vast circumference. At his approach
The great Arch-Angel from his warlike toil
Surceased, and glad, as hoping here to end
Intestine war in Heav'n, the arch-foe subdued
260   Or captive dragged in chains, with hostile frown
And visage all inflamed first thus began.
Author of evil, unknown till thy revolt,
Unnamed in Heav'n, now plenteous as thou seest
These acts of hateful strife, hateful to all,
265   Though heaviest by just measure on thyself,
And thy adherents: How hast thou disturbed
Heav'n's blessed peace, and into nature brought
Misery, uncreated till the crime
Of thy rebellion! how hast thou instilled
270   Thy malice into thousands, once upright
And faithful, now proved false! But think not here
To trouble holy rest; Heav'n casts thee out
From all her confines. Heav'n, the seat of bliss,
Brooks not the works of violence and war.

275	Hence then, and evil go with thee along,
	Thy offspring, to the place of evil, Hell;
	Thou and thy wicked crew! there mingle broils,
	Ere this avenging sword begin thy doom,
	Or some more sudden vengeance, winged from God,
280	Precipitate thee with augmented pain.
	So spake the Prince of Angels; to whom thus
	The Adversary. Nor think thou with wind
	Of airy threats to awe whom yet with deeds
	Thou canst not. Hast thou turned the least of these
285	To flight, or if to fall, but that they rise
	Unvanquished, easier to transact with me
	That thou shouldst hope, imperious, and with threats
	To chase me hence? err not, that so shall end
	The strife which thou callest evil, but we style
290	The strife of glory; which we mean to win,
	Or turn this Heav'n itself into the Hell
	Thou fablest; here however to dwell free,
	If not to reign: Mean while thy utmost force,
	And join him named Almighty to thy aid,
295	I fly not, but have sought thee far and nigh.
	They ended parle, and both addressed for fight
	Unspeakable; for who, though with the tongue
	Of Angels, can relate, or to what things
	Liken on earth conspicuous, that may lift
300	Human imagination to such highth
	Of Godlike power? for likest Gods they seemed,
	Stood they or moved, in stature, motion, arms,
	Fit to decide the empire of great Heav'n.
	Now waved their fiery swords, and in the air
305	Made horrid circles; two broad suns their shields
	Blazed opposite, while Expectation stood
	In horror: From each hand with speed retired,

Where erst was thickest fight, the angelick throng,
And left large field, unsafe within the wind
310 Of such commotion; such as, to set forth
Great things by small, if, nature's concord broke,
Among the constellations war were sprung,
Two planets, rushing from aspect malign
Of fiercest opposition, in mid sky
315 Should combat, and their jarring spheres confound.
Together both with next to almighty arm
Up-lifted imminent, one stroke they aimed
That might determine, and not need repeat,
As not of power at once; nor odds appeared
320 In might or swift prevention: But the sword
Of Michael from the armoury of God
Was given him tempered so, that neither keen
Nor solid might resist that edge: it met
The sword of Satan, with steep force to smite
325 Descending, and in half cut sheer; nor staid,
But with swift wheel reverse, deep entering, shared
All his right side: Then Satan first knew pain,
And writhed him to and fro convolved; so sore
The griding sword with discontinuous wound
330 Passed through him: But the ethereal substance closed,
Not long divisible; and from the gash
A stream of necturous humour issuing flowed
Sanguine, such as celestial Spirits may bleed,
And all his armour stained, ere while so bright.
335 Forthwith on all sides to his aid was run
By Angels many and strong, who interposed
Defence, while others bore him on their shields
Back to his chariot, where it stood retired
From off the files of war: There they him laid
340 Gnashing for anguish, and despite, and shame,
To find himself not matchless, and his pride

Humbled by such rebuke, so far beneath
His confidence to equal God in power.
Yet soon he healed; for Spirits that live throughout
345   Vital in every part, not as frail man
In entrails, heart of head, liver or reins,
Cannot but by annihilating die;
Nor in their liquid texture mortal wound
Receive, no more than can the fluid air:
350   All heart they live, all head, all eye, all ear,
All intellect, all sense; and, as they please,
They limb themselves, and colour, shape, or size
Assume, as likes them best, condense or rare.
Mean while in other parts like deeds deserved
355   Memorial, where the might of Gabriel fought,
And with fierce ensigns pierced the deep array
Of Moloch, furious king; who him defied,
And at his chariot-wheels to drag him bound
Threatened, nor from the Holy One of Heav'n
360   Refrained his tongue blasphemous; but anon
Down cloven to the waist, with shattered arms
And uncouth pain fled bellowing. On each wing
Uriel, and Raphael, his vaunting foe,
Though huge, and in a rock of diamond armed,
365   Vanquished Adramelech, and Asmadai,
Two potent Thrones, that to be less than Gods
Disdained, but meaner thoughts learned in their flight,
Mangled with ghastly wounds through plate and mail.
Nor stood unmindful Abdiel to annoy
370   The atheist crew, but with redoubled blow
Ariel, and Arioch, and the violence
Of Ramiel scorched and blasted, overthrew.
I might relate of thousands, and their names
Eternize here on earth; but those elect
375   Angels, contented with their fame in Heav'n,

Seek not the praise of men: The other sort,
In might though wondrous and in acts of war,
Nor of renown less eager, yet by doom
Cancelled from Heav'n and sacred memory,
380   Nameless in dark oblivion let them dwell.
For strength from truth divided, and from just,
Illaudable, naught merits but dispraise
And ignominy; yet to glory aspires
Vain-glorious, and through infamy seeks fame:
385   Therefore eternal silence be their doom.
And now, their mightiest quelled, the battle swerved,
With many an inroad gored; deformed rout
Entered, and foul disorder; all the ground
With shivered armour strewn, and on a heap
390   Chariot and charioteer lay overturned,
And fiery-foaming steeds; what stood, recoiled
O'er-wearied, through the faint Satanic host
Defensive scarce, or with pale fear surprised,
Then first with fear surprised, and sense of pain,
395   Fled ignominious, to such evil brought
By sin of disobedience; till that hour
Not liable to fear, or flight, or pain.
Far otherwise the inviolable Saints,
In cubic phalanx firm, advanced entire,
400   Invulnerable, impenetrably armed;
Such high advantages their innocence
Gave them above their foes; not to have sinned,
Not to have disobeyed; in fight they stood
Unwearied, unobnoxious to be pained
405   By wound, though from their place by violence moved,
Now Night her course began, and, over Heav'n
Inducing darkness, grateful truce imposed,
And silence on the odious din of war:
Under her cloudy covert both retired,

410	Victor and vanquished: On the foughten field
	Michael and his Angels prevalent
	Encamping, placed in guard their watches round,
	Cherubic waving fires: On the other part,
	Satan with his rebellious disappeared,
415	Far in the dark dislodged; and, void of rest,
	His potentates to council called by night;
	And in the midst thus undismayed began.
	O now in danger tried, now known in arms
	Not to be overpowered, Companions dear,
420	Found worthy not of liberty alone,
	Too mean pretence! but what we more affect,
	Honour, dominion, glory, and renown;
	Who have sustained one day in doubtful fight,
	(And if one day, why not eternal days?)
425	What Heav'n's Lord had powerfullest to send
	Against us from about his throne, and judged
	Sufficient to subdue us to his will,
	But proves not so: Then fallible, it seems,
	Of future we may deem him, though till now
430	Omniscient thought. True is, less firmly armed,
	Some disadvantage we endured and pain,
	Till now not known, but, known, as soon contemned;
	Since now we find this our empyreal form
	Incapable of mortal injury,
435	Imperishable, and, though pierced with wound,
	Soon closing, and by native vigour healed.
	Of evil then so small as easy think
	The remedy; perhaps more valid arms,
	Weapons more violent, when next we meet,
440	May serve to better us, and worse our foes,
	Or equal what between us made the odds,
	In nature none: If other hidden cause

Left them superior, while we can preserve
Unhurt our minds, and understanding sound,
445   Due search and consultation will disclose.
He sat; and in the assembly next upstood
Nisroch, of Principalities the prime;
As one he stood escaped from cruel fight,
Sore toiled, his riven arms to havoc hewn,
450   And cloudy in aspect thus answering spake.
Deliverer from new Lords, leader to free
Enjoyment of our right as Gods; yet hard
For Gods, and too unequal work we find,
Against unequal arms to fight in pain,
455   Against unpained, impassive; from which evil
Ruin must needs ensue; for what avails
Valour or strength, though matchless, quelled with pain
Which all subdues, and makes remiss the hands
Of mightiest? Sense of pleasure we may well
460   Spare out of life perhaps, and not repine,
But live content, which is the calmest life:
But pain is perfect misery, the worst
Of evils, and, excessive, overturns
All patience. He, who therefore can invent
465   With what more forcible we may offend
Our yet unwounded enemies, or arm
Ourselves with like defence, to me deserves
No less than for deliverance what we owe.
Whereto with look composed Satan replied.
470   Not uninvented that, which thou aright
Believest so main to our success, I bring.
Which of us who beholds the bright surface
Of this ethereous mould whereon we stand,
This continent of spacious Heav'n, adorned
475   With plant, fruit, flower ambrosial, gems, and gold;
Whose eye so superficially surveys

These things, as not to mind from whence they grow
Deep under ground, materials dark and crude,
Of spiritous and fiery spume, till touched
480 With Heav'n's ray, and tempered, they shoot forth
So beauteous, opening to the ambient light?
These in their dark nativity the deep
Shall yield us, pregnant with infernal flame;
Which, into hollow engines, long and round,
485 Thick rammed, at the other bore with touch of fire
Dilated and infuriate, shall send forth
From far, with thundering noise, among our foes
Such implements of mischief, as shall dash
To pieces, and o'erwhelm whatever stands
490 Adverse, that they shall fear we have disarmed
The Thunderer of his only dreaded bolt.
Nor long shall be our labour; yet ere dawn,
Effect shall end our wish. Mean while revive;
Abandon fear; to strength and counsel joined
495 Think nothing hard, much less to be despaired.
He ended, and his words their drooping cheer
Enlightened, and their languished hope revived.
The invention all admired, and each, how he
To be the inventer missed; so easy it seemed
500 Once found, which yet unfound most would have thought
Impossible: Yet, haply, of thy race
In future days, if malice should abound,
Some one intent on mischief, or inspired
With devilish machination, might devise
505 Like instrument to plague the sons of men
For sin, on war and mutual slaughter bent.
Forthwith from council to the work they flew;
None arguing stood; innumerable hands
Were ready; in a moment up they turned
510 Wide the celestial soil, and saw beneath

The originals of nature in their crude
Conception; sulphurous and nitrous foam
They found, they mingled, and, with subtle art,
Concocted and adusted they reduced
515   To blackest grain, and into store conveyed:
Part hidden veins digged up (nor hath this earth
Entrails unlike) of mineral and stone,
Whereof to found their engines and their balls
Of missive ruin; part incentive reed
520   Provide, pernicious with one touch to fire.
So all ere day-spring, under conscious night,
Secret they finished, and in order set,
With silent circumspection, unespied.
Now when fair morn orient in Heav'n appeared,
525   Up rose the victor-Angels, and to arms
The matin trumpet sung: In arms they stood
Of golden panoply, refulgent host,
Soon banded; others from the dawning hills
Look round, and scouts each coast light-armed scour,
530   Each quarter to descry the distant foe,
Where lodged, or whither fled, or if for fight,
In motion or in halt: Him soon they met
Under spread ensigns moving nigh, in slow
But firm battalion; back with speediest sail
535   Zophiel, of Cherubim the swiftest wing,
Came flying, and in mid air aloud thus cried.
Arm, Warriors, arm for fight; the foe at hand,
Whom fled we thought, will save us long pursuit
This day; fear not his flight; so thick a cloud
540   He comes, and settled in his face I see
Sad resolution, and secure: Let each
His adamantine coat gird well, and each
Fit well his helm, gripe fast his orbed shield,
Borne even or high; for this day will pour down,

545   If I conjecture aught, no drizzling shower,
          But rattling storm of arrows barbed with fire.
          So warned he them, aware themselves, and soon
          In order, quit of all impediment;
          Instant without disturb they took alarm,
550   And onward moved embattled: When behold!
          Not distant far with heavy pace the foe
          Approaching gross and huge, in hollow cube
          Training his devilish enginery, impaled
          On every side with shadowing squadrons deep,
555   To hide the fraud. At interview both stood
          A while; but suddenly at head appeared
          Satan, and thus was heard commanding loud.
          Vanguard, to right and left the front unfold;
          That all may see who hate us, how we seek
560   Peace and composure, and with open breast
          Stand ready to receive them, if they like
          Our overture; and turn not back perverse:
          But that I doubt; however witness, Heav'n!
          Heav'n, witness thou anon! while we discharge
565   Freely our part: ye, who appointed stand
          Do as you have in charge, and briefly touch
          What we propound, and loud that all may hear!
          So scoffing in ambiguous words, he scarce
          Had ended; when to right and left the front
570   Divided, and to either flank retired:
          Which to our eyes discovered, new and strange,
          A triple mounted row of pillars laid
          On wheels (for like to pillars most they seemed,
          Or hollowed bodies made of oak or fir,
575   With branches lopt, in wood or mountain felled,)
          Brass, iron, stony mould, had not their mouths
          With hideous orifice gaped on us wide,

Portending hollow truce: At each behind
A Seraph stood, and in his hand a reed
580   Stood waving tipt with fire; while we, suspense,
Collected stood within our thoughts amused,
Not long; for sudden all at once their reeds
Put forth, and to a narrow vent applied
With nicest touch. Immediate in a flame,
585   But soon obscured with smoke, all Heav'n appeared,
From those deep-throated engines belched, whose roar
Embowelled with outrageous noise the air,
And all her entrails tore, disgorging foul
Their devilish glut, chained thunderbolts and hail
590   Of iron globes; which, on the victor host
Levelled, with such impetuous fury smote,
That, whom they hit, none on their feet might stand,
Though standing else as rocks, but down they fell
By thousands, Angel on Arch-Angel rolled;
595   The sooner for their arms; unarmed, they might
Have easily, as Spirits, evaded swift
By quick contraction or remove; but now
Foul dissipation followed, and forced rout;
Nor served it to relax their serried files.
600   What should they do? if on they rushed, repulse
Repeated, and indecent overthrow
Doubled, would render them yet more despised,
And to their foes a laughter; for in view
Stood ranked of Seraphim another row,
605   In posture to displode their second tire
Of thunder: Back defeated to return
They worse abhorred. Satan beheld their plight,
And to his mates thus in derision called.
O Friends! why come not on these victors proud
610   Ere while they fierce were coming; and when we,
To entertain them fair with open front

And breast, (what could we more?) propounded terms
Of composition, straight they changed their minds,
Flew off, and into strange vagaries fell,
615 As they would dance; yet for a dance they seemed
Somewhat extravagant and wild; perhaps
For joy of offered peace: But I suppose,
If our proposals once again were heard,
We should compel them to a quick result.
620 To whom thus Belial, in like gamesome mood.
Leader! the terms we sent were terms of weight,
Of hard contents, and full of force urged home;
Such as we might perceive amused them all,
And stumbled many: Who receives them right,
625 Had need from head to foot well understand;
Not understood, this gift they have besides,
They show us when our foes walk not upright.
So they among themselves in pleasant vein
Stood scoffing, hightened in their thoughts beyond
630 All doubt of victory: Eternal Might
To match with their inventions they presumed
So easy, and of his thunder made a scorn,
And all his host derided, while they stood
A while in trouble: But they stood not long;
635 Rage prompted them at length, and found them arms
Against such hellish mischief fit to oppose.
Forthwith (behold the excellence, the power,
Which God hath in his mighty Angels placed!)
Their arms away they threw, and to the hills
640 (For Earth hath this variety from Heav'n
Of pleasure situate in hill and dale,)
Light as the lightning glimpse they ran, they flew;
From their foundations loosening to and fro,
They plucked the seated hills, with all their load,
645 Rocks, waters, woods, and by the shaggy tops

Up-lifting bore them in their hands: Amaze,
Be sure, and terror, seized the rebel host,
When coming towards them so dread they saw
The bottom of the mountains upward turned;
650   Till on those cursed engines' triple-row
They saw them whelmed, and all their confidence
Under the weight of mountains buried deep;
Themselves invaded next, and on their heads
Main promontories flung, which in the air
655   Came shadowing, and oppressed whole legions armed;
Their armour helped their harm, crushed in and bruised
Into their substance pent, which wrought them pain
Implacable, and many a dolorous groan;
Long struggling underneath, ere they could wind
660   Out of such prison, though Spirits of purest light,
Purest at first, now gross by sinning grown.
The rest, in imitation, to like arms
Betook them, and the neighbouring hills uptore:
So hills amid the air encountered hills,
665   Hurled to and fro with jaculation dire;
That under ground they fought in dismal shade;
Infernal noise! war seemed a civil game
To this uproar; horrid confusion heaped
Upon confusion rose: And now all Heav'n
670   Had gone to wrack, with ruin overspread;
Had not the Almighty Father, where he sits
Shrined in his sanctuary of Heav'n secure,
Consulting on the sum of things, foreseen
This tumult, and permitted all, advised:
675   That his great purpose he might so fulfil,
To honour his anointed Son avenged
Upon his enemies, and to declare
All power on him transferred: Whence to his Son,
The Assessour of his throne, he thus began.

680   Effulgence of my glory, Son beloved,
        Son, in whose face invisible is beheld
        Visibly, what by Deity I am;
        And in whose hand what by decree I do,
        Second Omnipotence! two days are past,
685   Two days, as we compute the days of Heav'n,
        Since Michael and his Powers went forth to tame
        These disobedient: Sore hath been their fight,
        As likeliest was, when two such foes met armed;
        For to themselves I left them; and thou knowest,
690   Equal in their creation they were formed,
        Save what sin hath impaired; which yet hath wrought
        Insensibly, for I suspend their doom;
        Whence in perpetual fight they needs must last
        Endless, and no solution will be found:
695   War wearied hath performed what war can do,
        And to disordered rage let loose the reins
        With mountains, as with weapons, armed; which makes
        Wild work in Heav'n, and dangerous to the main.
        Two days are therefore past, the third is thine;
700   For thee I have ordained it; and thus far
        Have suffered, that the glory may be thine
        Of ending this great war, since none but Thou
        Can end it. Into thee such virtue and grace
        Immense I have transfused, that all may know
705   In Heav'n and Hell thy power above compare;
        And, this perverse commotion governed thus,
        To manifest thee worthiest to be Heir
        Of all things; to be Heir, and to be King
        By sacred unction, thy deserved right.
710   Go then, Thou Mightiest, in thy Father's might;
        Ascend my chariot, guide the rapid wheels
        That shake Heav'n's basis, bring forth all my war,

My bow and thunder, my almighty arms
Gird on, and sword upon thy puissant thigh;
715   Pursue these sons of darkness, drive them out
From all Heav'n's bounds into the utter deep:
There let them learn, as likes them, to despise
God, and Messiah his anointed King.
He said, and on his Son with rays direct
720   Shone full; he all his Father full expressed
Ineffably into his face received;
And thus the Filial Godhead answering spake.
O Father, O Supreme of heav'nly Thrones,
First, Highest, Holiest, Best; thou always seek'st
725   To glorify thy Son, I always thee,
As is most just: This I my glory account,
My exaltation, and my whole delight,
That thou, in me well pleased, declarest thy will
Fulfilled, which to fulfil is all my bliss.
730   Scepter and power, thy giving, I assume,
And gladlier shall resign, when in the end
Thou shalt be all in all, and I in thee
For ever; and in me all whom thou lovest:
But whom thou hatest, I hate, and can put on
735   Thy terrors, as I put thy mildness on,
Image of thee in all things; and shall soon,
Armed with thy might, rid Heav'n of these rebelled;
To their prepared ill mansion driven down,
To chains of darkness, and the undying worm;
740   That from thy just obedience could revolt,
Whom to obey is happiness entire.
Then shall thy Saints unmixed, and from the impure
Far separate, circling thy holy mount,
Unfeigned Halleluiahs to thee sing,
745   Hymns of high praise, and I among them Chief.
So said, he, o'er his scepter bowing, rose

From the right hand of Glory where he sat;
And the third sacred morn began to shine,
Dawning through Heav'n. Forth rushed with whirlwind sound
750 The chariot of Paternal Deity,
Flashing thick flames, wheel within wheel undrawn,
Itself instinct with Spirit, but convoyed
By four Cherubic shapes; four faces each
Had wonderous; as with stars, their bodies all
755 And wings were set with eyes; with eyes the wheels
Of beryl, and careering fires between;
Over their heads a crystal firmament,
Whereon a sapphire throne, inlaid with pure
Amber, and colours of the showery arch.
760 He, in celestial panoply all armed
Of radiant Urim, work divinely wrought,
Ascended; at his right hand Victory
Sat eagle-winged; beside him hung his bow
And quiver with three-bolted thunder stored;
765 And from about him fierce effusion rolled
Of smoke, and bickering flame, and sparkles dire:
Attended with ten thousand thousand Saints,
He onward came; far off his coming shone;
And twenty thousand (I their number heard)
770 Chariots of God, half on each hand, were seen;
He on the wings of Cherub rode sublime
On the crystalline sky, in sapphire throned,
Illustrious far and wide; but by his own
First seen: Them unexpected joy surprised,
775 When the great ensign of Messiah blazed
Aloft by Angels borne, his sign in Heav'n;
Under whose conduct Michael soon reduced
His army, circumfused on either wing,
Under their Head embodied all in one.
780 Before him Power Divine his way prepared;

At his command the uprooted hills retired
Each to his place; they heard his voice, and went
Obsequious; Heav'n his wonted face renewed,
And with fresh flowerets hill and valley smiled.
785 This saw his hapless foes, but stood obdured,
And to rebellious fight rallied their Powers,
Insensate, hope conceiving from despair.
In heav'nly Spirits could such perverseness dwell?
But to convince the proud what signs avail,
790 Or wonders move the obdurate to relent?
They, hardened more by what might most reclaim,
Grieving to see his glory, at the sight
Took envy; and, aspiring to his highth,
Stood re-embattled fierce, by force or fraud
795 Weening to prosper, and at length prevail
Against God and Messiah, or to fall
In universal ruin last; and now
To final battle drew, disdaining flight,
Or faint retreat; when the great Son of God
800 To all his host on either hand thus spake.
Stand still in bright array, ye Saints; here stand,
Ye Angels armed; this day from battle rest:
Faithful hath been your warfare, and of God
Accepted, fearless in his righteous cause;
805 And as ye have received, so have ye done,
Invincibly: But of this cursed crew
The punishment to other hand belongs;
Vengeance is his, or whose he sole appoints:
Number to this day's work is not ordained,
810 Nor multitude; stand only, and behold
God's indignation on these godless poured
By me; not you, but me, they have despised,
Yet envied; against me is all their rage,
Because the Father, to whom in Heav'n s'preme

815   Kingdom, and power, and glory appertains,
        Hath honoured me, according to his will.
        Therefore to me their doom he hath assigned;
        That they may have their wish, to try with me
        In battle which the stronger proves; they all,
820   Or I alone against them; since by strength
        They measure all, of other excellence
        Not emulous, nor care who them excels;
        Nor other strife with them do I vouchsafe.
        So spake the Son, and into terror changed
825   His countenance too severe to be beheld,
        And full of wrath bent on his enemies.
        At once the Four spread out their starry wings
        With dreadful shade contiguous, and the orbs
        Of his fierce chariot rolled, as with the sound
830   Of torrent floods, or of a numerous host.
        He on his impious foes right onward drove,
        Gloomy as night; under his burning wheels
        The steadfast empyrean shook throughout,
        All but the throne itself of God. Full soon
835   Among them he arrived; in his right hand
        Grasping ten thousand thunders, which he sent
        Before him, such as in their souls infixed
        Plagues: They, astonished, all resistance lost,
        All courage; down their idle weapons dropt:
840   O'er shields, and helms, and helmed heads he rode
        Of Thrones and mighty Seraphim prostrate,
        That wished the mountains now might be again
        Thrown on them, as a shelter from his ire.
        Nor less on either side tempestuous fell
845   His arrows, from the fourfold-visaged Four
        Distinct with eyes, and from the living wheels
        Distinct alike with multitude of eyes;

One Spirit in them ruled; and every eye
Glared lightning, and shot forth pernicious fire
850   Among the accursed, that withered all their strength,
And of their wonted vigour left them drained,
Exhausted, spiritless, afflicted, fallen.
Yet half his strength he put not forth, but checked
His thunder in mid volley; for he meant
855   Not to destroy, but root them out of Heav'n:
The overthrown he raised, and as a herd
Of goats or timorous flock together thronged
Drove them before him thunder-struck, pursued
With terrors, and with furies, to the bounds
860   And crystal wall of Heav'n; which, opening wide,
Rolled inward, and a spacious gap disclosed
Into the wasteful deep: The monstrous sight
Struck them with horror backward, but far worse
Urged them behind: Headlong themselves they threw
865   Down from the verge of Heav'n; eternal wrath
Burnt after them to the bottomless pit.
Hell heard the unsufferable noise, Hell saw
Heav'n ruining from Heav'n, and would have fled
Affrighted; but strict Fate had cast too deep
870   Her dark foundations, and too fast had bound.
Nine days they fell: Confounded Chaos roared,
And felt tenfold confusion in their fall
Through his wild anarchy, so huge a rout
encumbered him with ruin: Hell at last
875   Yawning received them whole, and on them closed;
Hell, their fit habitation, fraught with fire
Unquenchable, the house of woe and pain.
Disburdened Heav'n rejoiced, and soon repaired
Her mural breach, returning whence it rolled.
880   Sole victor, from the expulsion of his foes,
Messiah his triumphal chariot turned:

To meet him all his Saints, who silent stood
Eye-witnesses of his almighty acts,
With jubilee advanced; and, as they went,
885   Shaded with branching palm, each Order bright,
Sung triumph, and him sung victorious King,
Son, Heir, and Lord, to him dominion given,
Worthiest to reign: He, celebrated, rode
Triumphant through mid Heav'n, into the courts
890   And temple of his Mighty Father throned
On high; who into glory him received,
Where now he sits at the right hand of bliss.
Thus, measuring things in Heav'n by things on Earth,
At thy request, and that thou mayest beware
895   By what is past, to thee I have revealed
What might have else to human race been hid;
The discord which befell, and war in Heav'n
Among the angelic Powers, and the deep fall
Of those too high aspiring, who rebelled
900   With Satan; he who envies now thy state,
Who now is plotting how he may seduce
Thee also from obedience, that, with him
Bereaved of happiness, thou mayest partake
His punishment, eternal misery;
905   Which would be all his solace and revenge,
As a despite done against the Most High,
Thee once to gain companion of his woe.
But listen not to his temptations, warn
Thy weaker; let it profit thee to have heard,
910   By terrible example, the reward
Of disobedience; firm they might have stood,
Yet fell; remember, and fear to transgress.

BOOK VII

THE ARGUMENT

Raphael at the request of Adam relates how and wherefore
this world was first created; that God, after the expelling of
Satan and his angels out of Heav'n, declared his pleasure to
create another world and other creatures to dwell

5   therein; sends his Son with glory and attendance of angels to
perform the work of Creation in six days: the angels celebrate
with hymns the performance thereof, and his reascension
into Heav'n.

     Descend from Heav'n, Urania, by that name
     If rightly thou art called, whose voice divine
     Following, above the Olympian hill I soar,
     Above the flight of Pegasean wing!
5   The meaning, not the name, I call: for thou
     Nor of the Muses nine, nor on the top
     Of old Olympus dwellest; but, Heav'nly-born,
     Before the hills appeared, or fountain flowed,
     Thou with eternal Wisdom didst converse,
10   Wisdom thy sister, and with her didst play
     In presence of the Almighty Father, pleased
     With thy celestial song. Up led by thee

Into the Heav'n of Heav'ns I have presumed,
An earthly guest, and drawn empyreal air,
15 Thy tempering: with like safety guided down
Return me to my native element:
Lest from this flying steed unreined, (as once
Bellerophon, though from a lower clime,)
Dismounted, on the Aleian field I fall,
20 Erroneous there to wander, and forlorn.
Half yet remains unsung, but narrower bound
Within the visible diurnal sphere;
Standing on earth, not rapt above the pole,
More safe I sing with mortal voice, unchanged
25 To hoarse or mute, though fallen on evil days,
On evil days though fallen, and evil tongues;
In darkness, and with dangers compassed round,
And solitude; yet not alone, while thou
Visitest my slumbers nightly, or when morn
30 Purples the east: still govern thou my song,
Urania, and fit audience find, though few.
But drive far off the barbarous dissonance
Of Bacchus and his revellers, the race
Of that wild rout that tore the Thracian bard
35 In Rhodope, where woods and rocks had ears
To rapture, till the savage clamour drowned
Both harp and voice; nor could the Muse defend
Her son. So fail not thou, who thee implores:
For thou art heav'nly, she an empty dream.
40 Say, Goddess, what ensued when Raphael,
The affable Arch-Angel, had forewarned
Adam, by dire example, to beware
Apostasy, by what befell in Heav'n
To those apostates; lest the like befall
45 In Paradise to Adam or his race,
Charged not to touch the interdicted tree,

If they transgress, and slight that sole command,
So easily obeyed amid the choice
Of all tastes else to please their appetite,
50   Though wandering. He, with his consorted Eve,
The story heard attentive, and was filled
With admiration and deep muse, to hear
Of things so high and strange; things, to their thought
So unimaginable, as hate in Heav'n,
55   And war so near the peace of God in bliss,
With such confusion: but the evil, soon
Driven back, redounded as a flood on those
From whom it sprung; impossible to mix
With blessedness. Whence Adam soon repealed
60   The doubts that in his heart arose: and now
Led on, yet sinless, with desire to know
What nearer might concern him, how this world
Of Heav'n and Earth conspicuous first began;
When, and whereof created; for what cause;
65   What within Eden, or without, was done
Before his memory; as one whose drouth
Yet scarce allayed still eyes the current stream,
Whose liquid murmur heard new thirst excites,
Proceeded thus to ask his heav'nly guest.
70   Great things, and full of wonder in our ears,
Far differing from this world, thou hast revealed,
Divine interpreter! by favour sent
Down from the empyrean, to forewarn
Us timely of what might else have been our loss,
75   Unknown, which human knowledge could not reach;
For which to the infinitely Good we owe
Immortal thanks, and his admonishment
Receive, with solemn purpose to observe
Immutably his sovreign will, the end

80   Of what we are. But since thou hast vouchsafed
            Gently, for our instruction, to impart
            Things above earthly thought, which yet concerned
            Our knowing, as to highest wisdom seemed,
            Deign to descend now lower, and relate
85   What may no less perhaps avail us known,
            How first began this Heav'n which we behold
            Distant so high, with moving fires adorned
            Innumerable; and this which yields or fills
            All space, the ambient air wide interfused
90   Embracing round this florid Earth; what cause
            Moved the Creator, in his holy rest
            Through all eternity, so late to build
            In Chaos; and the work begun, how soon
            Absolved; if unforbid thou mayest unfold
95   What we, not to explore the secrets ask
            Of his eternal empire, but the more
            To magnify his works, the more we know.
            And the great light of day yet wants to run
            Much of his race though steep; suspense in Heav'n,
100   Held by thy voice, thy potent voice, he hears,
            And longer will delay to hear thee tell
            His generation, and the rising birth
            Of Nature from the unapparent Deep:
            Or if the star of evening and the moon
105   Haste to thy audience, Night with her will bring,
            Silence; and Sleep, listening to thee, will watch;
            Or we can bid his absence, till thy song
            End, and dismiss thee ere the morning shine.
            Thus Adam his illustrious guest besought:
110   And thus the Godlike Angel answered mild.
            This also thy request, with caution asked,
            Obtain; though to recount almighty works

What words or tongue of Seraph can suffice,
Or heart of man suffice to comprehend?
115   Yet what thou canst attain, which best may serve
To glorify the Maker, and infer
Thee also happier, shall not be withheld
Thy hearing; such commission from above
I have received, to answer thy desire
120   Of knowledge within bounds; beyond, abstain
To ask; nor let thine own inventions hope
Things not revealed, which the invisible King,
Only Omniscient, hath suppressed in night;
To none communicable in Earth or Heav'n:
125   Enough is left besides to search and know.
But knowledge is as food, and needs no less
Her temperance over appetite, to know
In measure what the mind may well contain;
Oppresses else with surfeit, and soon turns
130   Wisdom to folly, as nourishment to wind.
Know then, that, after Lucifer from Heav'n
(So call him, brighter once amidst the host
Of Angels, than that star the stars among,)
Fell with his flaming legions through the deep
135   Into his place, and the great Son returned
Victorious with his Saints, the Omnipotent
Eternal Father from his throne beheld
Their multitude, and to his Son thus spake.
At least our envious Foe hath failed, who thought
140   All like himself rebellious, by whose aid
This inaccessible high strength, the seat
Of Deity supreme, us dispossessed,
He trusted to have seized, and into fraud
Drew many, whom their place knows here no more:
145   Yet far the greater part have kept, I see,
Their station; Heav'n, yet populous, retains

Number sufficient to possess her realms
Though wide, and this high temple to frequent
With ministeries due, and solemn rites:
150 But, lest his heart exalt him in the harm
Already done, to have dispeopled Heav'n,
My damage fondly deemed, I can repair
That detriment, if such it be to lose
Self-lost; and in a moment will create
155 Another world, out of one man a race
Of men innumerable, there to dwell,
Not here; till, by degrees of merit raised,
They open to themselves at length the way
Up hither, under long obedience tried;
160 And Earth be changed to Heav'n, and Heav'n to Earth,
One kingdom, joy and union without end.
Mean while inhabit lax, ye Powers of Heav'n;
And thou my Word, begotten Son, by thee
This I perform; speak thou, and be it done!
165 My overshadowing Spirit and Might with thee
I send along; ride forth, and bid the Deep
Within appointed bounds be Heav'n and Earth;
Boundless the Deep, because I Am who fill
Infinitude, nor vacuous the space.
170 Though I, uncircumscribed myself, retire,
And put not forth my goodness, which is free
To act or not, Necessity and Chance
Approach not me, and what I will is Fate.
So spake the Almighty, and to what he spake
175 His Word, the Filial Godhead, gave effect.
Immediate are the acts of God, more swift
Than time or motion, but to human ears
Cannot without process of speech be told,
So told as earthly notion can receive.
180 Great triumph and rejoicing was in Heav'n,

When such was heard declared the Almighty's will;
Glory they sung to the Most High, good will
To future men, and in their dwellings peace;
Glory to Him, whose just avenging ire
185   Had driven out the ungodly from his sight
And the habitations of the just; to Him
Glory and praise, whose wisdom had ordained
Good out of evil to create; instead
Of Spirits malign, a better race to bring
190   Into their vacant room, and thence diffuse
His good to worlds and ages infinite.
So sang the Hierarchies: Mean while the Son
On his great expedition now appeared,
Girt with Omnipotence, with radiance crowned
195   Of Majesty Divine; sapience and love
Immense, and all his Father in him shone.
About his chariot numberless were poured
Cherub, and Seraph, Potentates, and Thrones,
And Virtues, winged Spirits, and chariots winged
200   From the armory of God; where stand of old
Myriads, between two brazen mountains lodged
Against a solemn day, harnessed at hand,
Celestial equipage; and now came forth
Spontaneous, for within them Spirit lived,
205   Attendant on their Lord: Heav'n opened wide
Her ever-during gates, harmonious sound
On golden hinges moving, to let forth
The King of Glory, in his powerful Word
And Spirit, coming to create new worlds.
210   On heav'nly ground they stood; and from the shore
They viewed the vast immeasurable abyss
Outrageous as a sea, dark, wasteful, wild,
Up from the bottom turned by furious winds
And surging waves, as mountains, to assault

215   Heav'n's heighth, and with the center mix the pole.
           Silence, ye troubled Waves, and thou Deep, peace,
           Said then the Omnific Word; your discord end!
           Nor staid; but, on the wings of Cherubim
           Uplifted, in paternal glory rode
           Far into Chaos, and the world unborn;
220   For Chaos heard his voice: Him all his train
           Followed in bright procession, to behold
           Creation, and the wonders of his might.
           Then staid the fervid wheels, and in his hand
225   He took the golden compasses, prepared
           In God's eternal store, to circumscribe
           This universe, and all created things:
           One foot he centered, and the other turned
           Round through the vast profundity obscure;
230   And said, Thus far extend, thus far thy bounds,
           This be thy just circumference, O World!
           Thus God the Heav'n created, thus the Earth,
           Matter unformed and void: Darkness profound
           Covered the abyss: but on the watery calm
235   His brooding wings the Spirit of God outspread,
           And vital virtue infused, and vital warmth
           Throughout the fluid mass; but downward purged
           The black tartareous cold infernal dregs,
           Adverse to life: then founded, then conglobed
240   Like things to like; the rest to several place
           Disparted, and between spun out the air;
           And Earth self-balanced on her center hung.
           Let there be light, said God; and forthwith Light
           Ethereal, first of things, quintessence pure,
245   Sprung from the deep; and from her native east
           To journey through the airy gloom began,
           Sphered in a radiant cloud, for yet the sun

Was not; she in a cloudy tabernacle
Sojourned the while. God saw the light was good;
250   And light from darkness by the hemisphere
Divided: light the Day, and darkness Night,
He named. Thus was the first day even and morn:
Nor past uncelebrated, nor unsung
By the celestial quires, when orient light
255   Exhaling first from darkness they beheld;
Birth-day of Heav'n and Earth; with joy and shout
The hollow universal orb they filled,
And touched their golden harps, and hymning praised
God and his works; Creator him they sung,
260   Both when first evening was, and when first morn.
Again, God said, Let there be firmament
Amid the waters, and let it divide
The waters from the waters; and God made
The firmament, expanse of liquid, pure,
265   Transparent, elemental air, diffused
In circuit to the uttermost convex
Of this great round; partition firm and sure,
The waters underneath from those above
Dividing: for as earth, so he the world
270   Built on circumfluous waters calm, in wide
Crystalline ocean, and the loud misrule
Of Chaos far removed; lest fierce extremes
Contiguous might distemper the whole frame:
And Heav'n he named the Firmament: So even
275   And morning chorus sung the second day.
The Earth was formed, but in the womb as yet
Of waters, embryon immature involved,
Appeared not: over all the face of Earth
Main ocean flowed, not idle; but, with warm
280   Prolific humour softening all her globe,
Fermented the great mother to conceive,

Satiate with genial moisture; when God said,
Be gathered now ye waters under Heav'n
Into one place, and let dry land appear.
285   Immediately the mountains huge appear
Emergent, and their broad bare backs upheave
Into the clouds; their tops ascend the sky:
So high as heaved the tumid hills, so low
Down sunk a hollow bottom broad and deep,
290   Capacious bed of waters: Thither they
Hasted with glad precipitance, uprolled,
As drops on dust conglobing from the dry:
Part rise in crystal wall, or ridge direct,
For haste; such flight the great command impressed
295   On the swift floods: As armies at the call
Of trumpet (for of armies thou hast heard)
Troop to their standard; so the watery throng,
Wave rolling after wave, where way they found,
If steep, with torrent rapture, if through plain,
300   Soft-ebbing; nor withstood them rock or hill;
But they, or under ground, or circuit wide
With serpent error wandering, found their way,
And on the washy ooze deep channels wore;
Easy, ere God had bid the ground be dry,
305   All but within those banks, where rivers now
Stream, and perpetual draw their humid train.
The dry land, Earth; and the great receptacle
Of congregated waters, he called Seas:
And saw that it was good; and said, Let the Earth
310   Put forth the verdant grass, herb yielding seed,
And fruit-tree yielding fruit after her kind,
Whose seed is in herself upon the Earth.
He scarce had said, when the bare Earth, till then
Desert and bare, unsightly, unadorned,
315   Brought forth the tender grass, whose verdure clad

Her universal face with pleasant green;
Then herbs of every leaf, that sudden flowered
Opening their various colours, and made gay
Her bosom, smelling sweet: and, these scarce blown,
320   Forth flourished thick the clustering vine, forth crept
The swelling gourd, up stood the corny reed
Embattled in her field, and the humble shrub,
And bush with frizzled hair implicit: Last
Rose, as in dance, the stately trees, and spread
325   Their branches hung with copious fruit, or gemmed
Their blossoms: With high woods the hills were crowned;
With tufts the valleys, and each fountain side;
With borders long the rivers: that Earth now
Seemed like to Heav'n, a seat where Gods might dwell,
330   Or wander with delight, and love to haunt
Her sacred shades: though God had yet not rained
Upon the Earth, and man to till the ground
None was; but from the Earth a dewy mist
Went up, and watered all the ground, and each
335   Plant of the field; which, ere it was in the Earth,
God made, and every herb, before it grew
On the green stem: God saw that it was good:
So even and morn recorded the third day.
Again the Almighty spake, Let there be lights
340   High in the expanse of Heav'n, to divide
The day from night; and let them be for signs,
For seasons, and for days, and circling years;
And let them be for lights, as I ordain
Their office in the firmament of Heav'n,
345   To give light on the Earth; and it was so.
And God made two great lights, great for their use
To Man, the greater to have rule by day,
The less by night, altern; and made the stars,
And set them in the firmament of Heav'n

350	To illuminate the Earth, and rule the day
	In their vicissitude, and rule the night,
	And light from darkness to divide. God saw,
	Surveying his great work, that it was good:
	For of celestial bodies first the sun
355	A mighty sphere he framed, unlightsome first,
	Though of ethereal mould: then formed the moon
	Globose, and every magnitude of stars,
	And sowed with stars the Heav'n, thick as a field:
	Of light by far the greater part he took,
360	Transplanted from her cloudy shrine, and placed
	In the sun's orb, made porous to receive
	And drink the liquid light; firm to retain
	Her gathered beams, great palace now of light.
	Hither, as to their fountain, other stars
365	Repairing, in their golden urns draw light,
	And hence the morning-planet gilds her horns;
	By tincture or reflection they augment
	Their small peculiar, though from human sight
	So far remote, with diminution seen,
370	First in his east the glorious lamp was seen,
	Regent of day, and all the horizon round
	Invested with bright rays, jocund to run
	His longitude through Heav'n's high road; the gray
375	Dawn, and the Pleiades, before him danced,
	Shedding sweet influence: Less bright the moon,
	But opposite in levelled west was set,
	His mirror, with full face borrowing her light
	From him; for other light she needed none
	In that aspect, and still that distance keeps
380	Till night; then in the east her turn she shines,
	Revolved on Heav'n's great axle, and her reign
	With thousand lesser lights dividual holds,

With thousand thousand stars, that then appeared
Spangling the hemisphere: Then first adorned
385   With their bright luminaries that set and rose,
Glad evening and glad morn crowned the fourth day.
And God said, Let the waters generate
Reptile with spawn abundant, living soul:
And let fowl fly above the Earth, with wings
390   Displayed on the open firmament of Heav'n.
And God created the great whales, and each
Soul living, each that crept, which plenteously
The waters generated by their kinds;
And every bird of wing after his kind;
395   And saw that it was good, and blessed them, saying.
Be fruitful, multiply, and in the seas,
And lakes, and running streams, the waters fill;
And let the fowl be multiplied, on the Earth.
Forthwith the sounds and seas, each creek and bay,
400   With fry innumerable swarm, and shoals
Of fish that with their fins, and shining scales,
Glide under the green wave, in sculls that oft
Bank the mid sea: part single, or with mate,
Graze the sea-weed their pasture, and through groves
405   Of coral stray; or, sporting with quick glance,
Show to the sun their waved coats dropt with gold;
Or, in their pearly shells at ease, attend
Moist nutriment; or under rocks their food
In jointed armour watch: on smooth the seal
410   And bended dolphins play: part huge of bulk
Wallowing unwieldy, enormous in their gait,
Tempest the ocean: there leviathan,
Hugest of living creatures, on the deep
Stretched like a promontory sleeps or swims,
415   And seems a moving land; and at his gills
Draws in, and at his trunk spouts out, a sea.

Mean while the tepid caves, and fens, and shores,
Their brood as numerous hatch, from the egg that soon
Bursting with kindly rupture forth disclosed
420   Their callow young; but feathered soon and fledge
They summed their pens; and, soaring the air sublime,
With clang despised the ground, under a cloud
In prospect; there the eagle and the stork
On cliffs and cedar tops their eyries build:
425   Part loosely wing the region, part more wise
In common, ranged in figure, wedge their way,
Intelligent of seasons, and set forth
Their airy caravan, high over seas
Flying, and over lands, with mutual wing
430   Easing their flight; so steers the prudent crane
Her annual voyage, borne on winds; the air
Floats as they pass, fanned with unnumbered plumes:
From branch to branch the smaller birds with song
Solaced the woods, and spread their painted wings
435   Till even; nor then the solemn nightingale
Ceased warbling, but all night tun'd her soft lays:
Others, on silver lakes and rivers, bathed
Their downy breast; the swan with arched neck,
Between her white wings mantling proudly, rows
440   Her state with oary feet; yet oft they quit
The dank, and, rising on stiff pennons, tower
The mid aerial sky: Others on ground
Walked firm; the crested cock whose clarion sounds
The silent hours, and the other whose gay train
445   Adorns him, coloured with the florid hue
Of rainbows and starry eyes. The waters thus
With fish replenished, and the air with fowl,
Evening and morn solemnized the fifth day.
The sixth, and of creation last, arose
450   With evening harps and matin; when God said,

Let the Earth bring forth soul living in her kind,
Cattle, and creeping things, and beast of the Earth,
Each in their kind. The Earth obeyed, and straight
Opening her fertile womb teemed at a birth
455   Innumerous living creatures, perfect forms,
Limbed and full grown: Out of the ground up rose,
As from his lair, the wild beast where he wons
In forest wild, in thicket, brake, or den;
Among the trees in pairs they rose, they walked:
460   The cattle in the fields and meadows green:
Those rare and solitary, these in flocks
Pasturing at once, and in broad herds upsprung.
The grassy clods now calved; now half appeared
The tawny lion, pawing to get free
465   His hinder parts, then springs as broke from bonds,
And rampant shakes his brinded mane; the ounce,
The libbard, and the tiger, as the mole
Rising, the crumbled earth above them threw
In hillocks: The swift stag from under ground
470   Bore up his branching head: Scarce from his mould
Behemoth biggest born of earth upheaved
His vastness: Fleeced the flocks and bleating rose,
As plants: Ambiguous between sea and land
The river-horse, and scaly crocodile.
475   At once came forth whatever creeps the ground,
Insect or worm: those waved their limber fans
For wings, and smallest lineaments exact
In all the liveries decked of summer's pride
With spots of gold and purple, azure and green:
480   These, as a line, their long dimension drew,
Streaking the ground with sinuous trace; not all
Minims of nature; some of serpent-kind,
Wonderous in length and corpulence, involved
Their snaky folds, and added wings. First crept

485   The parsimonious emmet, provident
        Of future; in small room large heart enclosed;
        Pattern of just equality perhaps
        Hereafter, joined in her popular tribes
        Of commonalty: Swarming next appeared
490   The female bee, that feeds her husband drone
        Deliciously, and builds her waxen cells
        With honey stored: The rest are numberless,
        And thou their natures knowest, and gavest them names,
        Needless to thee repeated; nor unknown
495   The serpent, subtlest beast of all the field,
        Of huge extent sometimes, with brazen eyes
        And hairy mane terrific, though to thee
        Not noxious, but obedient at thy call.
        Now Heav'n in all her glory shone, and rolled
500   Her motions, as the great first Mover's hand
        First wheeled their course: Earth in her rich attire
        Consummate lovely smiled; air, water, earth,
        By fowl, fish, beast, was flown, was swum, was walked,
        Frequent; and of the sixth day yet remained:
505   There wanted yet the master-work, the end
        Of all yet done; a creature, who, not prone
        And brute as other creatures, but endued
        With sanctity of reason, might erect
        His stature, and upright with front serene
510   Govern the rest, self-knowing; and from thence
        Magnanimous to correspond with Heav'n,
        But grateful to acknowledge whence his good
        Descends, thither with heart, and voice, and eyes
        Directed in devotion, to adore
515   And worship God Supreme, who made him chief
        Of all his works: therefore the Omnipotent
        Eternal Father (for where is not he

Present?) thus to his Son audibly spake.

Let us make now Man in our image, Man

520 In our similitude, and let them rule

Over the fish and fowl of sea and air,

Beast of the field, and over all the Earth,

And every creeping thing that creeps the ground.

This said, he formed thee, Adam, thee, O Man,

525 Dust of the ground, and in thy nostrils breathed

The breath of life; in his own image he

Created thee, in the image of God

Express; and thou becamest a living soul.

Male he created thee; but thy consort

530 Female, for race; then blessed mankind, and said,

Be fruitful, multiply, and fill the Earth;

Subdue it, and throughout dominion hold

Over fish of the sea, and fowl of the air,

And every living thing that moves on the Earth.

535 Wherever thus created, for no place

Is yet distinct by name, thence, as thou knowest,

He brought thee into this delicious grove,

This garden, planted with the trees of God,

Delectable both to behold and taste;

540 And freely all their pleasant fruit for food

Gave thee; all sorts are here that all the Earth yields,

Variety without end; but of the tree,

Which, tasted, works knowledge of good and evil,

Thou mayest not; in the day thou eatest, thou diest;

545 Death is the penalty imposed; beware,

And govern well thy appetite; lest Sin

Surprise thee, and her black attendant Death.

Here finished he, and all that he had made

Viewed, and behold all was entirely good;

550 So even and morn accomplished the sixth day:

Yet not till the Creator from his work

Desisting, though unwearied, up returned,
Up to the Heav'n of Heav'ns, his high abode;
Thence to behold this new created world,
555 The addition of his empire, how it showed
In prospect from his throne, how good, how fair,
Answering his great idea. Up he rode
Followed with acclamation, and the sound
Symphonious of ten thousand harps, that tuned
560 Angelic harmonies: The earth, the air
Resounded, (thou rememberest, for thou heardst,)
The Heav'ns and all the constellations rung,
The planets in their station listening stood,
While the bright pomp ascended jubilant.
565 Open, ye everlasting gates! they sung,
Open, ye Heav'ns! your living doors; let in
The great Creator from his work returned
Magnificent, his six days work, a World;
Open, and henceforth oft; for God will deign
570 To visit oft the dwellings of just men,
Delighted; and with frequent intercourse
Thither will send his winged messengers
On errands of supernal grace. So sung
The glorious train ascending: He through Heav'n,
575 That opened wide her blazing portals, led
To God's eternal house direct the way;
A broad and ample road, whose dust is gold
And pavement stars, as stars to thee appear,
Seen in the galaxy, that milky way,
580 Which nightly, as a circling zone, thou seest
Powdered with stars. And now on Earth the seventh
Evening arose in Eden, for the sun
Was set, and twilight from the east came on,
Forerunning night; when at the holy mount
585 Of Heav'n's high-seated top, the imperial throne

Of Godhead, fixed for ever firm and sure,
The Filial Power arrived, and sat him down
With his great Father; for he also went
Invisible, yet staid, (such privilege
590 Hath Omnipresence) and the work ordained,
Author and End of all things; and, from work
Now resting, blessed and hallowed the seventh day,
As resting on that day from all his work,
But not in silence holy kept: the harp
595 Had work and rested not; the solemn pipe,
And dulcimer, all organs of sweet stop,
All sounds on fret by string or golden wire,
Tempered soft tunings, intermixed with voice
Choral or unison: of incense clouds,
600 Fuming from golden censers, hid the mount.
Creation and the six days acts they sung:
Great are thy works, Jehovah! infinite
Thy power! what thought can measure thee, or tongue
Relate thee! Greater now in thy return
605 Than from the giant Angels: Thee that day
Thy thunders magnified; but to create
Is greater than created to destroy.
Who can impair thee, Mighty King, or bound
Thy empire! Easily the proud attempt
610 Of Spirits apostate, and their counsels vain,
Thou hast repelled; while impiously they thought
Thee to diminish, and from thee withdraw
The number of thy worshippers. Who seeks
To lessen thee, against his purpose serves
615 To manifest the more thy might: his evil
Thou usest, and from thence createst more good.
Witness this new-made world, another Heav'n
From Heav'n-gate not far, founded in view
On the clear hyaline, the glassy sea;

620   Of amplitude almost immense, with stars
       Numerous, and every star perhaps a world
       Of destined habitation; but thou knowest
       Their seasons: among these the seat of Men,
       Earth, with her nether ocean circumfused,
625   Their pleasant dwelling-place. Thrice happy Men,
       And sons of Men, whom God hath thus advanced!
       Created in his image, there to dwell
       And worship him; and in reward to rule
       Over his works, on earth, in sea, or air,
630   And multiply a race of worshippers
       Holy and just: Thrice happy, if they know
       Their happiness, and persevere upright!
       So sung they, and the empyrean rung
       With halleluiahs: Thus was sabbath kept.
635   And thy request think now fulfilled, that asked
       How first this world and face of things began,
       And what before thy memory was done
       From the beginning; that posterity,
       Informed by thee, might know: If else thou seekest
640   Aught, not surpassing human measure, say.

BOOK VIII

THE ARGUMENT

Adam inquires concerning celestial motions, is doubtfully
answered, and exhorted to search rather things more
worthy of knowledge: Adam assents, and still desirous to
detain Raphael, relates to him what he remembered wince
5   his own creation, his placing in Paradise, his talk with God
concerning solitude and fit society, his first meeting and
nuptials with Eve, his discourse with the angel thereupon; who
after admonitions repeated departs.

     The Angel ended, and in Adam's ear
     So charming left his voice, that he a while
     Thought him still speaking, still stood fixed to hear;
     Then, as new waked, thus gratefully replied.
5   What thanks sufficient, or what recompence
     Equal, have I to render thee, divine
     Historian, who thus largely hast allayed
     The thirst I had of knowledge, and vouchsafed
     This friendly condescension to relate
10   Things, else by me unsearchable; now heard
     With wonder, but delight, and, as is due,
     With glory attributed to the high

Creator! Something yet of doubt remains,
Which only thy solution can resolve.
15 When I behold this goodly frame, this world,
Of Heav'n and Earth consisting; and compute
Their magnitudes; this Earth, a spot, a grain,
An atom, with the firmament compared
And all her numbered stars, that seem to roll
20 Spaces incomprehensible, (for such
Their distance argues, and their swift return
Diurnal,) merely to officiate light
Round this opacous Earth, this punctual spot,
One day and night; in all her vast survey
25 Useless besides; reasoning I oft admire,
How Nature wise and frugal could commit
Such disproportions, with superfluous hand
So many nobler bodies to create,
Greater so manifold, to this one use,
30 For aught appears, and on their orbs impose
Such restless revolution day by day
Repeated; while the sedentary Earth,
That better might with far less compass move,
Served by more noble than herself, attains
35 Her end without least motion, and receives,
As tribute, such a sumless journey brought
Of incorporeal speed, her warmth and light;
Speed, to describe whose swiftness number fails.
So spake our sire, and by his countenance seemed
40 Entering on studious thoughts abstruse; which Eve
Perceiving, where she sat retired in sight,
With lowliness majestic from her seat,
And grace that won who saw to wish her stay,
Rose, and went forth among her fruits and flowers,
45 To visit how they prospered, bud and bloom,
Her nursery; they at her coming sprung,
And, touched by her fair tendance, gladlier grew.

Yet went she not, as not with such discourse
Delighted, or not capable her ear
50   Of what was high: such pleasure she reserved,
Adam relating, she sole auditress;
Her husband the relater she preferred
Before the Angel, and of him to ask
Chose rather; he, she knew, would intermix
55   Grateful digressions, and solve high dispute
With conjugal caresses: from his lip
Not words alone pleased her. O! when meet now
Such pairs, in love and mutual honour joined?
With Goddess-like demeanour forth she went,
60   Not unattended; for on her, as Queen,
A pomp of winning Graces waited still,
And from about her shot darts of desire
Into all eyes, to wish her still in sight.
And Raphael now, to Adam's doubt proposed,
65   Benevolent and facile thus replied.
To ask or search, I blame thee not; for Heav'n
Is as the book of God before thee set,
Wherein to read his wondrous works, and learn
His seasons, hours, or days, or months, or years:
70   This to attain, whether Heav'n move or Earth,
Imports not, if thou reckon right; the rest
From Man or Angel the great Architect
Did wisely to conceal, and not divulge
His secrets to be scanned by them who ought
75   Rather admire; or, if they list to try
Conjecture, he his fabric of the Heav'ns
Hath left to their disputes, perhaps to move
His laughter at their quaint opinions wide
Hereafter; when they come to model Heav'n
80   And calculate the stars, how they will wield
The mighty frame; how build, unbuild, contrive
To save appearances; how gird the sphere

With centric and eccentric scribbled o'er,
Cycle and epicycle, orb in orb:
85   Already by thy reasoning this I guess,
Who art to lead thy offspring, and supposest
That bodies bright and greater should not serve
The less not bright, nor Heav'n such journeys run,
Earth sitting still, when she alone receives
90   The benefit: Consider first, that great
Or bright infers not excellence: the Earth
Though, in comparison of Heav'n, so small,
Nor glistering, may of solid good contain
More plenty than the sun that barren shines;
95   Whose virtue on itself works no effect,
But in the fruitful Earth; there first received,
His beams, unactive else, their vigour find.
Yet not to Earth are those bright luminaries
Officious; but to thee, Earth's habitant.
100   And for the Heav'n's wide circuit, let it speak
The Maker's high magnificence, who built
So spacious, and his line stretched out so far;
That Man may know he dwells not in his own;
An edifice too large for him to fill,
105   Lodged in a small partition; and the rest
Ordained for uses to his Lord best known.
The swiftness of those circles attribute,
Though numberless, to his Omnipotence,
That to corporeal substances could add
110   Speed almost spiritual: Me thou thinkest not slow,
Who since the morning-hour set out from Heav'n
Where God resides, and ere mid-day arrived
In Eden; distance inexpressible
By numbers that have name. But this I urge,
115   Admitting motion in the Heav'ns, to show
Invalid that which thee to doubt it moved;
Not that I so affirm, though so it seem

To thee who hast thy dwelling here on Earth.
God, to remove his ways from human sense,
120 Placed Heav'n from Earth so far, that earthly sight,
If it presume, might err in things too high,
And no advantage gain. What if the sun
Be center to the world; and other stars,
By his attractive virtue and their own
125 Incited, dance about him various rounds?
Their wandering course now high, now low, then hid,
Progressive, retrograde, or standing still,
In six thou seest; and what if seventh to these
The planet earth, so steadfast though she seem,
130 Insensibly three different motions move?
Which else to several spheres thou must ascribe,
Moved contrary with thwart obliquities;
Or save the sun his labour, and that swift
Nocturnal and diurnal rhomb supposed,
135 Invisible else above all stars, the wheel
Of day and night; which needs not thy belief,
If earth, industrious of herself, fetch day
Travelling east, and with her part averse
From the sun's beam meet night, her other part
140 Still luminous by his ray. What if that light,
Sent from her through the wide transpicuous air,
To the terrestrial moon be as a star,
Enlightening her by day, as she by night
This earth? reciprocal, if land be there,
145 Fields and inhabitants: Her spots thou seest
As clouds, and clouds may rain, and rain produce
Fruits in her softened soil for some to eat
Allotted there; and other suns perhaps,
With their attendant moons, thou wilt descry,
150 Communicating male and female light;
Which two great sexes animate the world,
Stored in each orb perhaps with some that live.

For such vast room in Nature unpossessed
By living soul, desart and desolate,
155 Only to shine, yet scarce to contribute
Each orb a glimpse of light, conveyed so far
Down to this habitable, which returns
Light back to them, is obvious to dispute.
But whether thus these things, or whether not;
160 whether the sun, predominant in Heav'n,
Rise on the earth; or earth rise on the sun;
He from the east his flaming road begin;
Or she from west her silent course advance,
With inoffensive pace that spinning sleeps
165 On her soft axle, while she paces even,
And bears thee soft with the smooth hair along;
Sollicit not thy thoughts with matters hid;
Leave them to God above; him serve, and fear!
Of other creatures, as him pleases best,
170 Wherever placed, let him dispose; joy thou
In what he gives to thee, this Paradise
And thy fair Eve; Heav'n is for thee too high
To know what passes there; be lowly wise:
Think only what concerns thee, and thy being;
175 Dream not of other worlds, what creatures there
Live, in what state, condition, or degree;
Contented that thus far hath been revealed
Not of Earth only, but of highest Heav'n.
To whom thus Adam, cleared of doubt, replied.
180 How fully hast thou satisfied me, pure
Intelligence of Heav'n, Angel serene!
And, freed from intricacies, taught to live
The easiest way; nor with perplexing thoughts
To interrupt the sweet of life, from which
185 God hath bid dwell far off all anxious cares,
And not molest us; unless we ourselves

Seek them with wandering thoughts, and notions vain.
But apt the mind or fancy is to rove
Unchecked, and of her roving is no end;
190 Till warned, or by experience taught, she learn,
That, not to know at large of things remote
From use, obscure and subtle; but, to know
That which before us lies in daily life,
Is the prime wisdom: What is more, is fume,
195 Or emptiness, or fond impertinence:
And renders us, in things that most concern,
Unpractised, unprepared, and still to seek.
Therefore from this high pitch let us descend
A lower flight, and speak of things at hand
200 Useful; whence, haply, mention may arise
Of something not unseasonable to ask,
By sufferance, and thy wonted favour, deigned.
Thee I have heard relating what was done
Ere my remembrance: now, hear me relate
205 My story, which perhaps thou hast not heard;
And day is not yet spent; till then thou seest
How subtly to detain thee I devise;
Inviting thee to hear while I relate;
Fond! were it not in hope of thy reply:
210 For, while I sit with thee, I seem in Heav'n;
And sweeter thy discourse is to my ear
Than fruits of palm-tree pleasantest to thirst
And hunger both, from labour, at the hour
Of sweet repast; they satiate, and soon fill,
215 Though pleasant; but thy words, with grace divine
Imbued, bring to their sweetness no satiety.
To whom thus Raphael answered heav'nly meek.
Nor are thy lips ungraceful, Sire of men,
Nor tongue ineloquent; for God on thee
220 Abundantly his gifts hath also poured

Inward and outward both, his image fair:
Speaking, or mute, all comeliness and grace
Attends thee; and each word, each motion, forms;
Nor less think we in Heav'n of thee on Earth
225 Than of our fellow-servant, and inquire
Gladly into the ways of God with Man:
For God, we see, hath honoured thee, and set
On Man his equal love: Say therefore on;
For I that day was absent, as befell,
230 Bound on a voyage uncouth and obscure,
Far on excursion toward the gates of Hell;
Squared in full legion (such command we had)
To see that none thence issued forth a spy,
Or enemy, while God was in his work;
235 Lest he, incensed at such eruption bold,
Destruction with creation might have mixed.
Not that they durst without his leave attempt;
But us he sends upon his high behests
For state, as Sovran King; and to inure
240 Our prompt obedience. Fast we found, fast shut,
The dismal gates, and barricadoed strong;
But long ere our approaching heard within
Noise, other than the sound of dance or song,
Torment, and loud lament, and furious rage.
245 Glad we returned up to the coasts of light
Ere sabbath-evening: so we had in charge.
But thy relation now; for I attend,
Pleased with thy words no less than thou with mine.
So spake the Godlike Power, and thus our Sire.
250 For Man to tell how human life began
Is hard; for who himself beginning knew
Desire with thee still longer to converse
Induced me. As new waked from soundest sleep,
Soft on the flowery herb I found me laid,

255 In balmy sweat; which with his beams the sun
 Soon dried, and on the reeking moisture fed.
 Straight toward Heav'n my wondering eyes I turned,
 And gazed a while the ample sky; till, raised
 By quick instinctive motion, up I sprung,
260 As thitherward endeavouring, and upright
 Stood on my feet: about me round I saw
 Hill, dale, and shady woods, and sunny plains,
 And liquid lapse of murmuring streams; by these,
 Creatures that lived and moved, and walked, or flew;
265 Birds on the branches warbling; all things smiled;
 With fragrance and with joy my heart o'erflowed.
 Myself I then perused, and limb by limb
 Surveyed, and sometimes went, and sometimes ran
 With supple joints, as lively vigour led:
270 But who I was, or where, or from what cause,
 Knew not; to speak I tried, and forthwith spake;
 My tongue obeyed, and readily could name
 Whate'er I saw. Thou Sun, said I, fair light,
 And thou enlightened Earth, so fresh and gay,
275 Ye Hills, and Dales, ye Rivers, Woods, and Plains,
 And ye that live and move, fair Creatures, tell,
 Tell, if ye saw, how I came thus, how here?—
 Not of myself;—by some great Maker then,
 In goodness and in power pre-eminent:
280 Tell me, how may I know him, how adore,
 From whom I have that thus I move and live,
 And feel that I am happier than I know.—
 While thus I called, and strayed I knew not whither,
 From where I first drew air, and first beheld
285 This happy light; when, answer none returned,
 On a green shady bank, profuse of flowers,
 Pensive I sat me down: There gentle sleep

First found me, and with soft oppression seized
My drowsed sense, untroubled, though I thought
290 I then was passing to my former state
Insensible, and forthwith to dissolve:
When suddenly stood at my head a dream,
Whose inward apparition gently moved
My fancy to believe I yet had being,
295 And lived: One came, methought, of shape divine,
And said, "Thy mansion wants thee, Adam; rise,
First Man, of men innumerable ordained
First Father! called by thee, I come thy guide
To the garden of bliss, thy seat prepared."
300 So saying, by the hand he took me raised,
And over fields and waters, as in air
Smooth-sliding without step, last led me up
A woody mountain; whose high top was plain,
A circuit wide, enclosed, with goodliest trees
305 Planted, with walks, and bowers; that what I saw
Of Earth before scarce pleasant seemed. Each tree,
Loaden with fairest fruit that hung to the eye
Tempting, stirred in me sudden appetite
To pluck and eat; whereat I waked, and found
310 Before mine eyes all real, as the dream
Had lively shadowed: Here had new begun
My wandering, had not he, who was my guide
Up hither, from among the trees appeared,
Presence Divine. Rejoicing, but with awe,
315 In adoration at his feet I fell
Submiss: He reared me, and "Whom thou soughtest I am,"
Said mildly, "Author of all this thou seest
Above, or round about thee, or beneath.
This Paradise I give thee, count it thine
320 To till and keep, and of the fruit to eat:
Of every tree that in the garden grows

Eat freely with glad heart; fear here no dearth:
But of the tree whose operation brings
Knowledge of good and ill, which I have set
325   The pledge of thy obedience and thy faith,
Amid the garden by the tree of life,
Remember what I warn thee, shun to taste,
And shun the bitter consequence: for know,
The day thou eatest thereof, my sole command
330   Transgressed, inevitably thou shalt die,
From that day mortal; and this happy state
Shalt lose, expelled from hence into a world
Of woe and sorrow." Sternly he pronounced
The rigid interdiction, which resounds
335   Yet dreadful in mine ear, though in my choice
Not to incur; but soon his clear aspect
Returned, and gracious purpose thus renewed.
"Not only these fair bounds, but all the Earth
To thee and to thy race I give; as lords
340   Possess it, and all things that therein live,
Or live in sea, or air; beast, fish, and fowl.
In sign whereof, each bird and beast behold
After their kinds; I bring them to receive
From thee their names, and pay thee fealty
345   With low subjection; understand the same
Of fish within their watery residence,
Not hither summoned, since they cannot change
Their element, to draw the thinner air."
As thus he spake, each bird and beast behold
350   Approaching two and two; these cowering low
With blandishment; each bird stooped on his wing.
I named them, as they passed, and understood
Their nature, with such knowledge God endued
My sudden apprehension: But in these

355   I found not what methought I wanted still;
         And to the heav'nly Vision thus presumed.
         O, by what name, for thou above all these,
         Above mankind, or aught than mankind higher,
         Surpassest far my naming; how may I
360   Adore thee, Author of this universe,
         And all this good to man? for whose well being
         So amply, and with hands so liberal,
         Thou hast provided all things: But with me
         I see not who partakes. In solitude
365   What happiness, who can enjoy alone,
         Or, all enjoying, what contentment find?
         Thus I presumptuous; and the Vision bright,
         As with a smile more brightened, thus replied.
         What callest thou solitude? Is not the Earth
370   With various living creatures, and the air
         Replenished, and all these at thy command
         To come and play before thee? Knowest thou not
         Their language and their ways? They also know,
         And reason not contemptibly: With these
375   Find pastime, and bear rule; thy realm is large.
         So spake the Universal Lord, and seemed
         So ordering: I, with leave of speech implored,
         And humble deprecation, thus replied.
         Let not my words offend thee, Heav'nly Power;
380   My Maker, be propitious while I speak.
         Hast thou not made me here thy substitute,
         And these inferiour far beneath me set?
         Among unequals what society
         Can sort, what harmony, or true delight?
385   Which must be mutual, in proportion due
         Given and received; but, in disparity
         The one intense, the other still remiss,

Cannot well suit with either, but soon prove
Tedious alike: Of fellowship I speak
390   Such as I seek, fit to participate
All rational delight: wherein the brute
Cannot be human consort: They rejoice
Each with their kind, lion with lioness;
So fitly them in pairs thou hast combined:
395   Much less can bird with beast, or fish with fowl
So well converse, nor with the ox the ape;
Worse then can man with beast, and least of all.
Whereto the Almighty answered, not displeased.
A nice and subtle happiness, I see,
400   Thou to thyself proposest, in the choice
Of thy associates, Adam! and wilt taste
No pleasure, though in pleasure, solitary.
What thinkest thou then of me, and this my state?
Seem I to thee sufficiently possessed
405   Of happiness, or not? who am alone
From all eternity; for none I know
Second to me or like, equal much less.
How have I then with whom to hold converse,
Save with the creatures which I made, and those
410   To me inferior, infinite descents
Beneath what other creatures are to thee?
He ceased; I lowly answered. To attain
The highth and depth of thy eternal ways
All human thoughts come short, Supreme of things!
415   Thou in thyself art perfect, and in thee
Is no deficience found: Not so is Man,
But in degree; the cause of his desire
By conversation with his like to help
Or solace his defects. No need that thou
420   Shouldst propagate, already Infinite;
And through all numbers absolute, though One:

But Man by number is to manifest
His single imperfection, and beget
Like of his like, his image multiplied,
425 In unity defective; which requires
Collateral love, and dearest amity.
Thou in thy secrecy although alone,
Best with thyself accompanied, seekest not
Social communication; yet, so pleased,
430 Canst raise thy creature to what heighth thou wilt
Of union or communion, deified:
I, by conversing, cannot these erect
From prone; nor in their ways complacence find.
Thus I emboldened spake, and freedom used
435 Permissive, and acceptance found; which gained
This answer from the gracious Voice Divine.
Thus far to try thee, Adam, I was pleased;
And find thee knowing, not of beasts alone,
Which thou hast rightly named, but of thyself;
440 Expressing well the spirit within thee free,
My image, not imparted to the brute;
Whose fellowship therefore unmeet for thee
Good reason was thou freely shouldst dislike;
And be so minded still: I, ere thou spakest,
445 Knew it not good for Man to be alone;
And no such company as then thou sawest
Intended thee; for trial only brought,
To see how thou couldest judge of fit and meet:
What next I bring shall please thee, be assured,
450 Thy likeness, thy fit help, thy other self,
Thy wish exactly to thy heart's desire.
He ended, or I heard no more; for now
My earthly by his heav'nly overpowered,
Which it had long stood under, strained to the highth
455 In that celestial colloquy sublime,

As with an object that excels the sense
Dazzled and spent, sunk down; and sought repair
Of sleep, which instantly fell on me, called
By Nature as in aid, and closed mine eyes.
460   Mine eyes he closed, but open left the cell
Of fancy, my internal sight; by which,
Abstract as in a trance, methought I saw,
Though sleeping, where I lay, and saw the shape
Still glorious before whom awake I stood:
465   Who stooping opened my left side, and took
From thence a rib, with cordial spirits warm,
And life-blood streaming fresh; wide was the wound,
But suddenly with flesh filled up and healed:
The rib he formed and fashioned with his hands;
470   Under his forming hands a creature grew,
Man-like, but different sex; so lovely fair,
That what seemed fair in all the world, seemed now
Mean, or in her summed up, in her contained
And in her looks; which from that time infused
475   Sweetness into my heart, unfelt before,
And into all things from her air inspired
The spirit of love and amorous delight.
She disappeared, and left me dark; I waked
To find her, or for ever to deplore
480   Her loss, and other pleasures all abjure:
When out of hope, behold her, not far off,
Such as I saw her in my dream, adorned
With what all Earth or Heav'n could bestow
To make her amiable: On she came,
485   Led by her heav'nly Maker, though unseen,
And guided by his voice; nor uninformed
Of nuptial sanctity, and marriage rites:
Grace was in all her steps, Heav'n in her eye,
In every gesture dignity and love.

490   I, overjoyed, could not forbear aloud.
This turn hath made amends; thou hast fulfilled
Thy words, Creator bounteous and benign,
Giver of all things fair! but fairest this
Of all thy gifts! nor enviest. I now see
495   Bone of my bone, flesh of my flesh, myself
Before me: Woman is her name; of Man
Extracted: for this cause he shall forego
Father and mother, and to his wife adhere;
And they shall be one flesh, one heart, one soul.
500   She heard me thus; and though divinely brought,
Yet innocence, and virgin modesty,
Her virtue, and the conscience of her worth,
That would be wooed, and not unsought be won,
Not obvious, not obtrusive, but, retired,
505   The more desirable; or, to say all,
Nature herself, though pure of sinful thought,
Wrought in her so, that, seeing me, she turned:
I followed her; she what was honour knew,
And with obsequious majesty approved
510   My pleaded reason. To the nuptial bower
I led her blushing like the morn: All Heav'n,
And happy constellations, on that hour
Shed their selectest influence; the Earth
Gave sign of gratulation, and each hill;
515   Joyous the birds; fresh gales and gentle airs
Whispered it to the woods, and from their wings
Flung rose, flung odours from the spicy shrub,
Disporting, till the amorous bird of night
Sung spousal, and bid haste the evening-star
520   On his hill top, to light the bridal lamp.
Thus have I told thee all my state, and brought
My story to the sum of earthly bliss,

Which I enjoy; and must confess to find
In all things else delight indeed, but such
525   As, used or not, works in the mind no change,
Nor vehement desire; these delicacies
I mean of taste, sight, smell, herbs, fruits, and flowers,
Walks, and the melody of birds: but here
Far otherwise, transported I behold,
530   Transported touch; here passion first I felt,
Commotion strange! in all enjoyments else
Superior and unmoved; here only weak
Against the charm of Beauty's powerful glance.
Or Nature failed in me, and left some part
535   Not proof enough such object to sustain;
Or, from my side subducting, took perhaps
More than enough; at least on her bestowed
Too much of ornament, in outward show
Elaborate, of inward less exact.
540   For well I understand in the prime end
Of Nature her the inferior, in the mind
And inward faculties, which most excel;
In outward also her resembling less
His image who made both, and less expressing
545   The character of that dominion given
O'er other creatures: Yet when I approach
Her loveliness, so absolute she seems
And in herself complete, so well to know
Her own, that what she wills to do or say,
550   Seems wisest, virtuousest, discreetest, best:
All higher knowledge in her presence falls
Degraded; Wisdom in discourse with her
Loses discountenanced, and like Folly shows;
Authority and Reason on her wait,
555   As one intended first, not after made
Occasionally; and, to consummate all,

Greatness of mind and Nobleness their seat
Build in her loveliest, and create an awe
About her, as a guard angelic placed.
560 To whom the Angel with contracted brow.
Accuse not Nature, she hath done her part;
Do thou but thine; and be not diffident
Of Wisdom; she deserts thee not, if thou
Dismiss not her, when most thou needest her nigh,
565 By attributing overmuch to things
Less excellent, as thou thyself perceivest.
For, what admirest thou, what transports thee so,
An outside? fair, no doubt, and worthy well
Thy cherishing, thy honouring, and thy love;
570 Not thy subjection: Weigh with her thyself;
Then value: Oft-times nothing profits more
Than self-esteem, grounded on just and right
Well managed; of that skill the more thou knowest,
The more she will acknowledge thee her head,
575 And to realities yield all her shows:
Made so adorn for thy delight the more,
So awful, that with honour thou mayest love
Thy mate, who sees when thou art seen least wise.
But if the sense of touch, whereby mankind
580 Is propagated, seem such dear delight
Beyond all other; think the same vouchsafed
To cattle and each beast; which would not be
To them made common and divulged, if aught
Therein enjoyed were worthy to subdue
585 The soul of man, or passion in him move.
What higher in her society thou findest
Attractive, human, rational, love still;
In loving thou dost well, in passion not,
Wherein true love consists not: Love refines
590 The thoughts, and heart enlarges; hath his seat

In reason, and is judicious; is the scale
By which to heav'nly love thou mayest ascend,
Not sunk in carnal pleasure; for which cause,
Among the beasts no mate for thee was found.
595   To whom thus, half abashed, Adam replied.
Neither her outside formed so fair, nor aught
In procreation common to all kinds,
(Though higher of the genial bed by far,
And with mysterious reverence I deem,)
600   So much delights me, as those graceful acts,
Those thousand decencies, that daily flow
From all her words and actions mixed with love
And sweet compliance, which declare unfeigned
Union of mind, or in us both one soul;
605   Harmony to behold in wedded pair
More grateful than harmonious sound to the ear.
Yet these subject not; I to thee disclose
What inward thence I feel, not therefore foiled,
Who meet with various objects, from the sense
610   Variously representing; yet, still free,
Approve the best, and follow what I approve.
To love, thou blamest me not; for Love, thou sayest,
Leads up to Heav'n, is both the way and guide;
Bear with me then, if lawful what I ask:
615   Love not the heav'nly Spirits, and how their love
Express they? by looks only? or do they mix
Irradiance, virtual or immediate touch?
To whom the Angel, with a smile that glowed
Celestial rosy red, Love's proper hue,
620   Answered. Let it suffice thee that thou knowest
Us happy, and without love no happiness.
Whatever pure thou in the body enjoyest,
(And pure thou wert created) we enjoy
In eminence; and obstacle find none

625 Of membrane, joint, or limb, exclusive bars;
Easier than air with air, if Spirits embrace,
Total they mix, union of pure with pure
Desiring, nor restrained conveyance need,
As flesh to mix with flesh, or soul with soul.
630 But I can now no more; the parting sun
Beyond the Earth's green Cape and verdant Isles
Hesperian sets, my signal to depart.
Be strong, live happy, and love! But, first of all,
Him, whom to love is to obey, and keep
635 His great command; take heed lest passion sway
Thy judgement to do aught, which else free will
Would not admit: thine, and of all thy sons,
The weal or woe in thee is placed; beware!
I in thy persevering shall rejoice,
640 And all the Blest: Stand fast; to stand or fall
Free in thine own arbitrament it lies.
Perfect within, no outward aid require;
And all temptation to transgress repel.
So saying, he arose; whom Adam thus
645 Followed with benediction. Since to part,
Go, heav'nly guest, ethereal Messenger,
Sent from whose sovereign goodness I adore!
Gentle to me and affable hath been
Thy condescension, and shall be honoured ever
650 With grateful memory: Thou to mankind
Be good and friendly still, and oft return!
So parted they; the Angel up to Heav'n
From the thick shade, and Adam to his bower.

BOOK IX

THE ARGUMENT

Satan having compassed the earth, with meditated guile
returns as a mist by night into Paradise, enters into the serpent
sleeping. Adam and Eve in the morning go forth to their
labours, which Eve proposes to divide in several
5   places, each laboring apart: Adam consents not, alleging the
danger, lest that Enemy, of whom they were forewarned,
should attempt her found alone: Eve loath to be thought not
circumspect or firm enough, urges her going apart, the rather
desirous to make trial of her strength; Adam at
10   last yields: the serpent finds her alone; his subtle approach, first
gazing, then speaking, with much flattery extolling Eve above
all other creatures. Eve wondering to hear the serpent speak,
asks how he attained to human speech and such understanding
not till now; the serpent
15   answers, that by tasting of a certain tree in the garden he
attained both to speech and reason, till then void of both:
Eve requires him to bring her to that tree, and finds it to be
the Tree of Knowledge forbidden: the serpent now grown
bolder, with many wiles and arguments induces her
20   at length to ear; she pleased with the taste deliberates a while
whether to impart thereof to Adam or not, at last brings him

of the fruit, relates what persuaded her to eat thereof: Adam at first amazed, but perceiving her lost, resolves through vehemence of love to perish with her; and
25   extenuating the trespass eats also of the fruit: the effects thereof in them both; they seek to cover their nakedness; then fall to variance and accusation of one another.

No more of talk where God or Angel guest
With Man, as with his friend, familiar us'd,
To sit indulgent, and with him partake
Rural repast; permitting him the while
5   Venial discourse unblam'd. I now must change
Those notes to tragic; foul distrust, and breach
Disloyal on the part of Man, revolt,
And disobedience: on the part of Heav'n
Now alienated, distance and distaste,
10   Anger and just rebuke, and judgement given,
That brought into this world a world of woe,
Sin and her shadow Death, and Misery
Death's harbinger: Sad task! yet argument
Not less but more heroic than the wrath
15   Of stern Achilles on his foe pursued
Thrice fugitive about Troy wall; or rage
Of Turnus for Lavinia disespous'd;
Or Neptune's ire, or Juno's, that so long
Perplexed the Greek, and Cytherea's son:
20   If answerable style I can obtain
Of my celestial patroness, who deigns
Her nightly visitation unimplor'd,
And dictates to me slumbering; or inspires
Easy my unpremeditated verse:
25   Since first this subject for heroic song
Pleas'd me long choosing, and beginning late;
Not sedulous by nature to indite

Wars, hitherto the only argument
Heroic deem'd chief mastery to dissect
30   With long and tedious havoc fabled knights
In battles feign'd; the better fortitude
Of patience and heroick martyrdom
Unsung; or to describe races and games,
Or tilting furniture, imblazon'd shields,
35   Impresses quaint, caparisons and steeds,
Bases and tinsel trappings, gorgeous knights
At joust and tournament; then marshall'd feast
Serv'd up in hall with sewers and seneshals;
The skill of artifice or office mean,
40   Not that which justly gives heroic name
To person, or to poem. Me, of these
Nor skill'd nor studious, higher argument
Remains; sufficient of itself to raise
That name, unless an age too late, or cold
45   Climate, or years, damp my intended wing
Depress'd; and much they may, if all be mine,
Not hers, who brings it nightly to my ear.
The sun was sunk, and after him the star
Of Hesperus, whose office is to bring
50   Twilight upon the earth, short arbiter
'Twixt day and night, and now from end to end
Night's hemisphere had veil'd the horizon round:
When satan, who late fled before the threats
Of Gabriel out of Eden, now improv'd
55   In meditated fraud and malice, bent
On Man's destruction, maugre what might hap
Of heavier on himself, fearless returned
By night he fled, and at midnight returned
From compassing the earth; cautious of day,
60   Since Uriel, regent of the sun, descried
His entrance, and foreworned the Cherubim

That kept their watch; thence full of anguish driven,
The space of seven continued nights he rode
With darkness; thrice the equinoctial line
65 He circled; four times crossed the car of night
From pole to pole, traversing each colure;
On the eighth returned; and, on the coast averse
From entrance or Cherubic watch, by stealth
Found unsuspected way. There was a place,
70 Now not, though sin, not time, first wrought the change,
Where Tigris, at the foot of Paradise,
Into a gulf shot under ground, till part
Rose up a fountain by the tree of life:
In with the river sunk, and with it rose
75 Satan, involved in rising mist; then sought
Where to lie hid; sea he had searched, and land,
From Eden over Pontus and the pool
Maeotis, up beyond the river Ob;
Downward as far antarctic; and in length,
80 West from Orontes to the ocean barred
At Darien; thence to the land where flows
Ganges and Indus: Thus the orb he roamed
With narrow search; and with inspection deep
Considered every creature, which of all
85 Most opportune might serve his wiles; and found
The Serpent subtlest beast of all the field.
Him after long debate, irresolute
Of thoughts revolved, his final sentence chose
Fit vessel, fittest imp of fraud, in whom
90 To enter, and his dark suggestions hide
From sharpest sight: for, in the wily snake
Whatever sleights, none would suspicious mark,
As from his wit and native subtlety
Proceeding; which, in other beasts observed,

95   Doubt might beget of diabolic power
       Active within, beyond the sense of brute.
       Thus he resolved, but first from inward grief
       His bursting passion into plaints thus poured.
100   More justly, seat worthier of Gods, as built
       With second thoughts, reforming what was old!
       O Earth, how like to Heav'n, if not preferred
       For what God, after better, worse would build?
       Terrestrial Heav'n, danced round by other Heav'ns
       That shine, yet bear their bright officious lamps,
105   Light above light, for thee alone, as seems,
       In thee concentring all their precious beams
       Of sacred influence! As God in Heav'n
       Is center, yet extends to all; so thou,
       Centring, receivest from all those orbs: in thee,
110   Not in themselves, all their known virtue appears
       Productive in herb, plant, and nobler birth
       Of creatures animate with gradual life
       Of growth, sense, reason, all summed up in Man.
       With what delight could I have walked thee round,
115   If I could joy in aught, sweet interchange
       Of hill, and valley, rivers, woods, and plains,
       Now land, now sea and shores with forest crowned,
       Rocks, dens, and caves! But I in none of these
       Find place or refuge; and the more I see
120   Pleasures about me, so much more I feel
       Torment within me, as from the hateful siege
       Of contraries: all good to me becomes
       Bane, and in Heav'n much worse would be my state.
       But neither here seek I, no nor in Heav'n
125   To dwell, unless by mastering Heav'n's Supreme;
       Nor hope to be myself less miserable
       By what I seek, but others to make such

As I, though thereby worse to me redound:
For only in destroying I find ease
130 To my relentless thoughts; and, him destroyed,
Or won to what may work his utter loss,
For whom all this was made, all this will soon
Follow, as to him linked in weal or woe;
In woe then; that destruction wide may range:
135 To me shall be the glory sole among
The infernal Powers, in one day to have marred
What he, Almighty styled, six nights and days
Continued making; and who knows how long
Before had been contriving? though perhaps
140 Not longer than since I, in one night, freed
From servitude inglorious well nigh half
The angelic name, and thinner left the throng
Of his adorers: He, to be avenged,
And to repair his numbers thus impaired,
145 Whether such virtue spent of old now failed
More Angels to create, if they at least
Are his created, or, to spite us more,
Determined to advance into our room
A creature formed of earth, and him endow,
150 Exalted from so base original,
With heav'nly spoils, our spoils: What he decreed,
He effected; Man he made, and for him built
Magnificent this world, and earth his seat,
Him lord pronounced; and, O indignity!
155 Subjected to his service angel-wings,
And flaming ministers to watch and tend
Their earthly charge: Of these the vigilance
I dread; and, to elude, thus wrapped in mist
Of midnight vapour glide obscure, and pry
160 In every bush and brake, where hap may find
The serpent sleeping; in whose mazy folds

To hide me, and the dark intent I bring.
O foul descent! that I, who erst contended
With Gods to sit the highest, am now constrained
165   Into a beast; and, mixed with bestial slime,
This essence to incarnate and imbrute,
That to the heighth of Deity aspired!
But what will not ambition and revenge
Descend to? Who aspires, must down as low
170   As high he soared; obnoxious, first or last,
To basest things. Revenge, at first though sweet,
Bitter ere long, back on itself recoils:
Let it; I reck not, so it light well aimed,
Since higher I fall short, on him who next
175   Provokes my envy, this new favourite
Of Heav'n, this man of clay, son of despite,
Whom, us the more to spite, his Maker raised
From dust: Spite then with spite is best repaid.
So saying, through each thicket dank or dry,
180   Like a black mist low-creeping, he held on
His midnight-search, where soonest he might find
The serpent; him fast-sleeping soon he found
In labyrinth of many a round self-rolled,
His head the midst, well stored with subtle wiles:
185   Not yet in horrid shade or dismal den,
Nor nocent yet; but, on the grassy herb,
Fearless unfeared he slept: in at his mouth
The Devil entered; and his brutal sense,
In heart or head, possessing, soon inspired
190   With act intelligential; but his sleep
Disturbed not, waiting close the approach of morn.
Now, when as sacred light began to dawn
In Eden on the humid flowers, that breathed
Their morning incense, when all things, that breathe,

195　From the Earth's great altar send up silent praise
To the Creator, and his nostrils fill
With grateful smell, forth came the human pair,
And joined their vocal worship to the quire
Of creatures wanting voice; that done, partake
200　The season prime for sweetest scents and airs:
Then commune, how that day they best may ply
Their growing work: for much their work out-grew
The hands' dispatch of two gardening so wide,
And Eve first to her husband thus began.
205　Adam, well may we labour still to dress
This garden, still to tend plant, herb, and flower,
Our pleasant task enjoined; but, till more hands
Aid us, the work under our labour grows,
Luxurious by restraint; what we by day
210　Lop overgrown, or prune, or prop, or bind,
One night or two with wanton growth derides
Tending to wild. Thou therefore now advise,
Or bear what to my mind first thoughts present:
Let us divide our labours; thou, where choice
215　Leads thee, or where most needs, whether to wind
The woodbine round this arbour, or direct
The clasping ivy where to climb; while I,
In yonder spring of roses intermixed
With myrtle, find what to redress till noon:
220　For, while so near each other thus all day
Our task we choose, what wonder if so near
Looks intervene and smiles, or object new
Casual discourse draw on; which intermits
Our day's work, brought to little, though begun
225　Early, and the hour of supper comes unearned?
To whom mild answer Adam thus returned.
Sole Eve, associate sole, to me beyond
Compare above all living creatures dear!
Well hast thou motioned, well thy thoughts employed,

230 How we might best fulfil the work which here
God hath assigned us; nor of me shalt pass
Unpraised: for nothing lovelier can be found
In woman, than to study houshold good,
And good works in her husband to promote.
235 Yet not so strictly hath our Lord imposed
Labour, as to debar us when we need
Refreshment, whether food, or talk between,
Food of the mind, or this sweet intercourse
Of looks and smiles; for smiles from reason flow,
240 To brute denied, and are of love the food;
Love, not the lowest end of human life.
For not to irksome toil, but to delight,
He made us, and delight to reason joined.
These paths and bowers doubt not but our joint hands
245 Will keep from wilderness with ease, as wide
As we need walk, till younger hands ere long
Assist us; But, if much converse perhaps
Thee satiate, to short absence I could yield:
For solitude sometimes is best society,
250 And short retirement urges sweet return.
But other doubt possesses me, lest harm
Befall thee severed from me; for thou knowest
What hath been warned us, what malicious foe
Envying our happiness, and of his own
255 Despairing, seeks to work us woe and shame
By sly assault; and somewhere nigh at hand
Watches, no doubt, with greedy hope to find
His wish and best advantage, us asunder;
Hopeless to circumvent us joined, where each
260 To other speedy aid might lend at need:
Whether his first design be to withdraw
Our fealty from God, or to disturb
Conjugal love, than which perhaps no bliss
Enjoyed by us excites his envy more;

265   Or this, or worse, leave not the faithful side
        That gave thee being, still shades thee, and protects.
        The wife, where danger or dishonour lurks,
        Safest and seemliest by her husband stays,
        Who guards her, or with her the worst endures.
270   To whom the virgin majesty of Eve,
        As one who loves, and some unkindness meets,
        With sweet austere composure thus replied.
        Offspring of Heav'n and Earth, and all Earth's Lord!
        That such an enemy we have, who seeks
275   Our ruin, both by thee informed I learn,
        And from the parting Angel over-heard,
        As in a shady nook I stood behind,
        Just then returned at shut of evening flowers.
        But, that thou shouldst my firmness therefore doubt
280   To God or thee, because we have a foe
        May tempt it, I expected not to hear.
        His violence thou fearest not, being such
        As we, not capable of death or pain,
        Can either not receive, or can repel.
285   His fraud is then thy fear; which plain infers
        Thy equal fear, that my firm faith and love
        Can by his fraud be shaken or seduced;
        Thoughts, which how found they harbour in thy breast,
        Adam, mis-thought of her to thee so dear?
290   To whom with healing words Adam replied.
        Daughter of God and Man, immortal Eve!
        For such thou art; from sin and blame entire:
        Not diffident of thee do I dissuade
        Thy absence from my sight, but to avoid
295   The attempt itself, intended by our foe.
        For he who tempts, though in vain, at least asperses
        The tempted with dishonour foul; supposed

Not incorruptible of faith, not proof
Against temptation: Thou thyself with scorn
300   And anger wouldst resent the offered wrong,
Though ineffectual found: misdeem not then,
If such affront I labour to avert
From thee alone, which on us both at once
The enemy, though bold, will hardly dare;
305   Or daring, first on me the assault shall light.
Nor thou his malice and false guile contemn;
Subtle he needs must be, who could seduce
Angels; nor think superfluous other's aid.
I, from the influence of thy looks, receive
310   Access in every virtue; in thy sight
More wise, more watchful, stronger, if need were
Of outward strength; while shame, thou looking on,
Shame to be overcome or over-reached,
Would utmost vigour raise, and raised unite.
315   Why shouldst not thou like sense within thee feel
When I am present, and thy trial choose
With me, best witness of thy virtue tried?
So spake domestic Adam in his care
And matrimonial love; but Eve, who thought
320   Less attributed to her faith sincere,
Thus her reply with accent sweet renewed.
If this be our condition, thus to dwell
In narrow circuit straitened by a foe,
Subtle or violent, we not endued
325   Single with like defence, wherever met;
How are we happy, still in fear of harm?
But harm precedes not sin: only our foe,
Tempting, affronts us with his foul esteem
Of our integrity: his foul esteem

330   Sticks no dishonour on our front, but turns
Foul on himself; then wherefore shunned or feared
By us? who rather double honour gain
From his surmise proved false; find peace within,
Favour from Heav'n, our witness, from the event.
335   And what is faith, love, virtue, unassayed
Alone, without exterior help sustained?
Let us not then suspect our happy state
Left so imperfect by the Maker wise,
As not secure to single or combined.
340   Frail is our happiness, if this be so,
And Eden were no Eden, thus exposed.
To whom thus Adam fervently replied.
O Woman, best are all things as the will
Of God ordained them: His creating hand
345   Nothing imperfect or deficient left
Of all that he created, much less Man,
Or aught that might his happy state secure,
Secure from outward force; within himself
The danger lies, yet lies within his power:
350   Against his will he can receive no harm.
But God left free the will; for what obeys
Reason, is free; and Reason he made right,
But bid her well be ware, and still erect;
Lest, by some fair-appearing good surprised,
355   She dictate false; and mis-inform the will
To do what God expressly hath forbid.
Not then mistrust, but tender love, enjoins,
That I should mind thee oft; and mind thou me.
Firm we subsist, yet possible to swerve;
360   Since Reason not impossibly may meet
Some specious object by the foe suborned,
And fall into deception unaware,

Not keeping strictest watch, as she was warned.
365 Seek not temptation then, which to avoid
Were better, and most likely if from me
Thou sever not: Trial will come unsought.
Wouldst thou approve thy constancy, approve
First thy obedience; the other who can know,
Not seeing thee attempted, who attest?
370 But, if thou think, trial unsought may find
Us both securer than thus warned thou seemest,
Go; for thy stay, not free, absents thee more;
Go in thy native innocence, rely
On what thou hast of virtue; summon all!
375 For God towards thee hath done his part, do thine.
So spake the patriarch of mankind; but Eve
Persisted; yet submiss, though last, replied.
With thy permission then, and thus forewarned
Chiefly by what thy own last reasoning words
380 Touched only; that our trial, when least sought,
May find us both perhaps far less prepared,
The willinger I go, nor much expect
A foe so proud will first the weaker seek;
So bent, the more shall shame him his repulse.
385 Thus saying, from her husband's hand her hand
Soft she withdrew; and, like a Wood-Nymph light,
Oread or Dryad, or of Delia's train,
Betook her to the groves; but Delia's self
In gait surpassed, and Goddess-like deport,
390 Though not as she with bow and quiver armed,
But with such gardening tools as Art yet rude,
Guiltless of fire, had formed, or Angels brought.
To Pales, or Pomona, thus adorned,
Likest she seemed, Pomona when she fled

395   Vertumnus, or to Ceres in her prime,
          Yet virgin of Proserpina from Jove.
          Her long with ardent look his eye pursued
          Delighted, but desiring more her stay.
          Oft he to her his charge of quick return
400   Repeated; she to him as oft engaged
          To be returned by noon amid the bower,
          And all things in best order to invite
          Noontide repast, or afternoon's repose.
          O much deceived, much failing, hapless Eve,
405   hou never from that hour in Paradise
          Foundst either sweet repast, or sound repose;
          Such ambush, hid among sweet flowers and shades,
          Waited with hellish rancour imminent
410   To intercept thy way, or send thee back
          Despoiled of innocence, of faith, of bliss!
          For now, and since first break of dawn, the Fiend,
          Mere serpent in appearance, forth was come;
          And on his quest, where likeliest he might find
415   The only two of mankind, but in them
          The whole included race, his purposed prey.
          In bower and field he sought, where any tuft
          Of grove or garden-plot more pleasant lay,
          Their tendance, or plantation for delight;
420   By fountain or by shady rivulet
          He sought them both, but wished his hap might find
          Eve separate; he wished, but not with hope
          Of what so seldom chanced; when to his wish,
          Beyond his hope, Eve separate he spies,
425   Veiled in a cloud of fragrance, where she stood,
          Half spied, so thick the roses blushing round
          About her glowed, oft stooping to support
          Each flower of slender stalk, whose head, though gay
          Carnation, purple, azure, or specked with gold,

430   Hung drooping unsustained; them she upstays
             Gently with myrtle band, mindless the while
             Herself, though fairest unsupported flower,
             From her best prop so far, and storm so nigh.
             Nearer he drew, and many a walk traversed
435   Of stateliest covert, cedar, pine, or palm;
             Then voluble and bold, now hid, now seen,
             Among thick-woven arborets, and flowers
             Imbordered on each bank, the hand of Eve:
             Spot more delicious than those gardens feigned
440   Or of revived Adonis, or renowned
             Alcinous, host of old Laertes' son;
             Or that, not mystick, where the sapient king
             Held dalliance with his fair Egyptian spouse.
             Much he the place admired, the person more.
445   As one who long in populous city pent,
             Where houses thick and sewers annoy the air,
             Forth issuing on a summer's morn, to breathe
             Among the pleasant villages and farms
             Adjoined, from each thing met conceives delight;
450   The smell of grain, or tedded grass, or kine,
             Or dairy, each rural sight, each rural sound;
             If chance, with nymph-like step, fair virgin pass,
             What pleasing seemed, for her now pleases more;
             She most, and in her look sums all delight:
455   Such pleasure took the Serpent to behold
             This flowery plat, the sweet recess of Eve
             Thus early, thus alone: Her heav'nly form
             Angelic, but more soft, and feminine,
             Her graceful innocence, her every air
460   Of gesture, or least action, overawed
             His malice, and with rapine sweet bereaved
             His fierceness of the fierce intent it brought:

That space the Evil-one abstracted stood
From his own evil, and for the time remained
465   Stupidly good; of enmity disarmed,
Of guile, of hate, of envy, of revenge:
But the hot Hell that always in him burns,
Though in mid Heav'n, soon ended his delight,
And tortures him now more, the more he sees
470   Of pleasure, not for him ordained: then soon
Fierce hate he recollects, and all his thoughts
Of mischief, gratulating, thus excites.
Thoughts, whither have ye led me! with what sweet
Compulsion thus transported, to forget
475   What hither brought us! hate, not love; nor hope
Of Paradise for Hell, hope here to taste
Of pleasure; but all pleasure to destroy,
Save what is in destroying; other joy
To me is lost. Then, let me not let pass
480   Occasion which now smiles; behold alone
The woman, opportune to all attempts,
Her husband, for I view far round, not nigh,
Whose higher intellectual more I shun,
And strength, of courage haughty, and of limb
485   Heroic built, though of terrestrial mould;
Foe not informidable! exempt from wound,
I not; so much hath Hell debased, and pain
Enfeebled me, to what I was in Heav'n.
She fair, divinely fair, fit love for Gods!
490   Not terrible, though terror be in love
And beauty, not approached by stronger hate,
Hate stronger, under show of love well feigned;
The way which to her ruin now I tend.
So spake the enemy of mankind, enclosed
495   In serpent, inmate bad! and toward Eve
Addressed his way: not with indented wave,

Prone on the ground, as since; but on his rear,
Circular base of rising folds, that towered
Fold above fold, a surging maze! his head
500 Crested aloft, and carbuncle his eyes;
With burnished neck of verdant gold, erect
Amidst his circling spires, that on the grass
Floated redundant: pleasing was his shape
And lovely; never since of serpent-kind
505 Lovelier, not those that in Illyria changed,
Hermione and Cadmus, or the god
In Epidaurus; nor to which transformed
Ammonian Jove, or Capitoline, was seen;
He with Olympias; this with her who bore
510 Scipio, the heighth of Rome. With tract oblique
At first, as one who sought access, but feared
To interrupt, side-long he works his way.
As when a ship, by skilful steersmen wrought
Nigh river's mouth or foreland, where the wind
515 Veers oft, as oft so steers, and shifts her sail:
So varied he, and of his tortuous train
Curled many a wanton wreath in sight of Eve,
To lure her eye; she, busied, heard the sound
Of rustling leaves, but minded not, as used
520 To such disport before her through the field,
From every beast; more duteous at her call,
Than at Circean call the herd disguised.
He, bolder now, uncalled before her stood,
But as in gaze admiring: oft he bowed
525 His turret crest, and sleek enamelled neck,
Fawning; and licked the ground whereon she trod.
His gentle dumb expression turned at length
The eye of Eve to mark his play; he, glad
Of her attention gained, with serpent-tongue

530   Organic, or impulse of vocal air,
            His fraudulent temptation thus began.
            Wonder not, sovreign Mistress, if perhaps
            Thou canst, who art sole wonder! much less arm
            Thy looks, the Heav'n of mildness, with disdain,
535   Displeased that I approach thee thus, and gaze
            Insatiate; I thus single; nor have feared
            Thy awful brow, more awful thus retired.
            Fairest resemblance of thy Maker fair,
            Thee all things living gaze on, all things thine
540   By gift, and thy celestial beauty adore
            With ravishment beheld! there best beheld,
            Where universally admired; but here
            In this enclosure wild, these beasts among,
            Beholders rude, and shallow to discern
545   Half what in thee is fair, one man except,
            Who sees thee? and what is one? who should be seen
            A Goddess among Gods, adored and served
            By Angels numberless, thy daily train.
            So glozed the Tempter, and his proem tuned:
550   Into the heart of Eve his words made way,
            Though at the voice much marvelling; at length,
            Not unamazed, she thus in answer spake.
            What may this mean? language of man pronounced
            By tongue of brute, and human sense expressed?
555   The first, at least, of these I thought denied
            To beasts; whom God, on their creation-day,
            Created mute to all articulate sound:
            The latter I demur; for in their looks
            Much reason, and in their actions, oft appears.
560   Thee, Serpent, subtlest beast of all the field
            I knew, but not with human voice endued;
            Redouble then this miracle, and say,

How camest thou speakable of mute, and how
To me so friendly grown above the rest
565   Of brutal kind, that daily are in sight?
Say, for such wonder claims attention due.
To whom the guileful Tempter thus replied.
Empress of this fair world, resplendent Eve!
Easy to me it is to tell thee all
570   What thou commandest; and right thou shouldst be obeyed:
I was at first as other beasts that graze
The trodden herb, of abject thoughts and low,
As was my food; nor aught but food discerned
Or sex, and apprehended nothing high:
575   Till, on a day roving the field, I chanced
A goodly tree far distant to behold
Loaden with fruit of fairest colours mixed,
Ruddy and gold: I nearer drew to gaze;
When from the boughs a savoury odour blown,
580   Grateful to appetite, more pleased my sense
Than smell of sweetest fennel, or the teats
Of ewe or goat dropping with milk at even,
Unsucked of lamb or kid, that tend their play.
To satisfy the sharp desire I had
585   Of tasting those fair apples, I resolved
Not to defer; hunger and thirst at once,
Powerful persuaders, quickened at the scent
Of that alluring fruit, urged me so keen.
About the mossy trunk I wound me soon;
590   For, high from ground, the branches would require
Thy utmost reach or Adam's: Round the tree
All other beasts that saw, with like desire
Longing and envying stood, but could not reach.
Amid the tree now got, where plenty hung

595 Tempting so nigh, to pluck and eat my fill
I spared not; for, such pleasure till that hour,
At feed or fountain, never had I found.
Sated at length, ere long I might perceive
Strange alteration in me, to degree
600 Of reason in my inward powers; and speech
Wanted not long; though to this shape retained.
Thenceforth to speculations high or deep
I turned my thoughts, and with capacious mind
Considered all things visible in Heav'n,
605 Or Earth, or Middle; all things fair and good:
But all that fair and good in thy divine
Semblance, and in thy beauty's heav'nly ray,
United I beheld; no fair to thine
Equivalent or second! which compelled
610 Me thus, though importune perhaps, to come
And gaze, and worship thee of right declared
Sovran of creatures, universal Dame!
So talked the spirited sly Snake; and Eve,
Yet more amazed, unwary thus replied.
615 Serpent, thy overpraising leaves in doubt
The virtue of that fruit, in thee first proved:
But say, where grows the tree? from hence how far?
For many are the trees of God that grow
In Paradise, and various, yet unknown
620 To us; in such abundance lies our choice,
As leaves a greater store of fruit untouched,
Still hanging incorruptible, till men
Grow up to their provision, and more hands
Help to disburden Nature of her birth.
625 To whom the wily Adder, blithe and glad.
Empress, the way is ready, and not long;
Beyond a row of myrtles, on a flat,

Fast by a fountain, one small thicket past
Of blowing myrrh and balm: if thou accept
630   My conduct, I can bring thee thither soon
Lead then, said Eve. He, leading, swiftly rolled
In tangles, and made intricate seem straight,
To mischief swift. Hope elevates, and joy
Brightens his crest; as when a wandering fire,
635   Compact of unctuous vapour, which the night
Condenses, and the cold environs round,
Kindled through agitation to a flame,
Which oft, they say, some evil Spirit attends,
Hovering and blazing with delusive light,
640   Misleads the amazed night-wanderer from his way
To bogs and mires, and oft through pond or pool;
There swallowed up and lost, from succour far.
So glistered the dire Snake, and into fraud
Led Eve, our credulous mother, to the tree
645   Of prohibition, root of all our woe;
Which when she saw, thus to her guide she spake.
Serpent, we might have spared our coming hither,
Fruitless to me, though fruit be here to excess,
The credit of whose virtue rest with thee;
650   Wondrous indeed, if cause of such effects.
But of this tree we may not taste nor touch;
God so commanded, and left that command
Sole daughter of his voice; the rest, we live
Law to ourselves; our reason is our law.
655   To whom the Tempter guilefully replied.
Indeed! hath God then said that of the fruit
Of all these garden-trees ye shall not eat,
Yet Lords declared of all in earth or air?
To whom thus Eve, yet sinless. Of the fruit

660   Of each tree in the garden we may eat;
But of the fruit of this fair tree amidst
The garden, God hath said, Ye shall not eat
Thereof, nor shall ye touch it, lest ye die.
She scarce had said, though brief, when now more bold

665   The Tempter, but with show of zeal and love
To Man, and indignation at his wrong,
New part puts on; and, as to passion moved,
Fluctuates disturbed, yet comely and in act
Raised, as of some great matter to begin.

670   As when of old some orator renowned,
In Athens or free Rome, where eloquence
Flourished, since mute! to some great cause addressed,
Stood in himself collected; while each part,
Motion, each act, won audience ere the tongue;

675   Sometimes in heighth began, as no delay
Of preface brooking, through his zeal of right:
So standing, moving, or to heighth up grown,
The Tempter, all impassioned, thus began.
O sacred, wise, and wisdom-giving Plant,

680   Mother of science! now I feel thy power
Within me clear; not only to discern
Things in their causes, but to trace the ways
Of highest agents, deemed however wise.
Queen of this universe! do not believe

685   Those rigid threats of death: ye shall not die:
How should you? by the fruit? it gives you life
To knowledge; by the threatener? look on me,
Me, who have touched and tasted; yet both live,
And life more perfect have attained than Fate

690   Meant me, by venturing higher than my lot.
Shall that be shut to Man, which to the Beast
Is open? or will God incense his ire

For such a petty trespass? and not praise
Rather your dauntless virtue, whom the pain
695   Of death denounced, whatever thing death be,
Deterred not from achieving what might lead
To happier life, knowledge of good and evil;
Of good, how just? of evil, if what is evil
Be real, why not known, since easier shunned?
700   God therefore cannot hurt ye, and be just;
Not just, not God; not feared then, nor obeyed:
Your fear itself of death removes the fear.
Why then was this forbid? Why, but to awe;
Why, but to keep ye low and ignorant,
705   His worshippers? He knows that in the day
Ye eat thereof, your eyes that seem so clear,
Yet are but dim, shall perfectly be then
Opened and cleared, and ye shall be as Gods,
Knowing both good and evil, as they know.
710   That ye shall be as Gods, since I as Man,
Internal Man, is but proportion meet;
I, of brute, human; ye, of human, Gods.
So ye shall die perhaps, by putting off
Human, to put on Gods; death to be wished,
715   Though threatened, which no worse than this can bring.
And what are Gods, that Man may not become
As they, participating God-like food?
The Gods are first, and that advantage use
On our belief, that all from them proceeds:
720   I question it; for this fair earth I see,
Warmed by the sun, producing every kind;
Them, nothing: if they all things, who enclosed
Knowledge of good and evil in this tree,
That whoso eats thereof, forthwith attains

725   Wisdom without their leave? and wherein lies
          The offence, that Man should thus attain to know?
          What can your knowledge hurt him, or this tree
          Impart against his will, if all be his?
          Or is it envy? and can envy dwell
730   In heav'nly breasts? These, these, and many more
          Causes import your need of this fair fruit.
          Goddess humane, reach then, and freely taste!
          He ended; and his words, replete with guile,
          Into her heart too easy entrance won:
735   Fixed on the fruit she gazed, which to behold
          Might tempt alone; and in her ears the sound
          Yet rung of his persuasive words, impregned
          With reason, to her seeming, and with truth:
          Mean while the hour of noon drew on, and waked
740   An eager appetite, raised by the smell
          So savoury of that fruit, which with desire,
          Inclinable now grown to touch or taste,
          Solicited her longing eye; yet first
          Pausing a while, thus to herself she mused.
745   Great are thy virtues, doubtless, best of fruits,
          Though kept from man, and worthy to be admired;
          Whose taste, too long forborne, at first assay
          Gave elocution to the mute, and taught
          The tongue not made for speech to speak thy praise:
750   Thy praise he also, who forbids thy use,
          Conceals not from us, naming thee the tree
          Of knowledge, knowledge both of good and evil;
          Forbids us then to taste! but his forbidding
          Commends thee more, while it infers the good
755   By thee communicated, and our want:
          For good unknown sure is not had; or, had
          And yet unknown, is as not had at all.

In plain then, what forbids he but to know,
Forbids us good, forbids us to be wise?
760   Such prohibitions bind not. But, if death
Bind us with after-bands, what profits then
Our inward freedom? In the day we eat
Of this fair fruit, our doom is, we shall die!
How dies the Serpent? he hath eaten and lives,
765   And knows, and speaks, and reasons, and discerns,
Irrational till then. For us alone
Was death invented? or to us denied
This intellectual food, for beasts reserved?
For beasts it seems: yet that one beast which first
770   Hath tasted envies not, but brings with joy
The good befallen him, author unsuspect,
Friendly to man, far from deceit or guile.
What fear I then? rather, what know to fear
Under this ignorance of good and evil,
775   Of God or death, of law or penalty?
Here grows the cure of all, this fruit divine,
Fair to the eye, inviting to the taste,
Of virtue to make wise: What hinders then
To reach, and feed at once both body and mind?
780   So saying, her rash hand in evil hour
Forth reaching to the fruit, she plucked, she eat!
Earth felt the wound; and Nature from her seat,
Sighing through all her works, gave signs of woe,
That all was lost. Back to the thicket slunk
785   The guilty Serpent; and well might; for Eve,
Intent now wholly on her taste, naught else
Regarded; such delight till then, as seemed,
In fruit she never tasted, whether true
Or fancied so, through expectation high

790   Of knowledge; not was Godhead from her thought.
      Greedily she engorged without restraint,
      And knew not eating death: Satiate at length,
      And heightened as with wine, jocund and boon,
      Thus to herself she pleasingly began.
795   O soveign, virtuous, precious of all trees
      In Paradise! of operation blest
      To sapience, hitherto obscured, infamed.
      And thy fair fruit let hang, as to no end
      Created; but henceforth my early care,
800   Not without song, each morning, and due praise,
      Shall tend thee, and the fertile burden ease
      Of thy full branches offered free to all;
      Till, dieted by thee, I grow mature
      In knowledge, as the Gods, who all things know;
805   Though others envy what they cannot give:
      For, had the gift been theirs, it had not here
      Thus grown. Experience, next, to thee I owe,
      Best guide; not following thee, I had remained
      In ignorance; thou openest wisdom's way,
810   And givest access, though secret she retire.
      And I perhaps am secret: Heav'n is high,
      High, and remote to see from thence distinct
      Each thing on Earth; and other care perhaps
      May have diverted from continual watch
815   Our great Forbidder, safe with all his spies
      About him. But to Adam in what sort
      Shall I appear? shall I to him make known
      As yet my change, and give him to partake
      Full happiness with me, or rather not,
820   But keeps the odds of knowledge in my power
      Without copartner? so to add what wants
      In female sex, the more to draw his love,

And render me more equal; and perhaps,
A thing not undesirable, sometime
825 Superior; for, inferior, who is free
This may be well: But what if God have seen,
And death ensue? then I shall be no more!
And Adam, wedded to another Eve,
Shall live with her enjoying, I extinct;
830 A death to think! Confirmed then I resolve,
Adam shall share with me in bliss or woe:
So dear I love him, that with him all deaths
I could endure, without him live no life.
So saying, from the tree her step she turned;
835 But first low reverence done, as to the Power
That dwelt within, whose presence had infused
Into the plant sciential sap, derived
From nectar, drink of Gods. Adam the while,
Waiting desirous her return, had wove
840 Of choicest flowers a garland, to adorn
Her tresses, and her rural labours crown;
As reapers oft are wont their harvest-queen.
Great joy he promised to his thoughts, and new
Solace in her return, so long delayed:
845 Yet oft his heart, divine of something ill,
Misgave him; he the faltering measure felt;
And forth to meet her went, the way she took
That morn when first they parted: by the tree
Of knowledge he must pass; there he her met,
850 Scarce from the tree returning; in her hand
A bough of fairest fruit, that downy smiled,
New gathered, and ambrosial smell diffused.
To him she hasted; in her face excuse
Came prologue, and apology too prompt;

855 Which, with bland words at will, she thus addressed.
Hast thou not wondered, Adam, at my stay?
Thee I have missed, and thought it long, deprived
Thy presence; agony of love till now
Not felt, nor shall be twice; for never more
860 Mean I to try, what rash untried I sought,
The pain of absence from thy sight. But strange
Hath been the cause, and wonderful to hear:
This tree is not, as we are told, a tree
Of danger tasted, nor to evil unknown
865 Opening the way, but of divine effect
To open eyes, and make them Gods who taste;
And hath been tasted such: The serpent wise,
Or not restrained as we, or not obeying,
Hath eaten of the fruit; and is become,
870 Not dead, as we are threatened, but thenceforth
Endued with human voice and human sense,
Reasoning to admiration; and with me
Persuasively hath so prevailed, that I
Have also tasted, and have also found
875 The effects to correspond; opener mine eyes,
Dim erst, dilated spirits, ampler heart,
And growing up to Godhead; which for thee
Chiefly I sought, without thee can despise.
For bliss, as thou hast part, to me is bliss;
880 Tedious, unshared with thee, and odious soon.
Thou therefore also taste, that equal lot
May join us, equal joy, as equal love;
Lest, thou not tasting, different degree
Disjoin us, and I then too late renounce
885 Deity for thee, when Fate will not permit.
Thus Eve with countenance blithe her story told;
But in her cheek distemper flushing glowed.

On the other side Adam, soon as he heard
The fatal trespass done by Eve, amazed,
890   Astonied stood and blank, while horror chill
Ran through his veins, and all his joints relaxed;
From his slack hand the garland wreathed for Eve
Down dropt, and all the faded roses shed:
Speechless he stood and pale, till thus at length
895   First to himself he inward silence broke.
O fairest of Creation, last and best
Of all God's works, Creature in whom excelled
Whatever can to sight or thought be formed,
Holy, divine, good, amiable, or sweet!
900   How art thou lost! how on a sudden lost,
Defaced, deflowered, and now to death devote!
Rather, how hast thou yielded to transgress
The strict forbiddance, how to violate
The sacred fruit forbidden! Some cursed fraud
905   Of enemy hath beguiled thee, yet unknown,
And me with thee hath ruined; for with thee
Certain my resolution is to die:
How can I live without thee! how forego
Thy sweet converse, and love so dearly joined,
910   To live again in these wild woods forlorn!
Should God create another Eve, and I
Another rib afford, yet loss of thee
Would never from my heart: no, no! I feel
The link of Nature draw me: flesh of flesh,
915   Bone of my bone thou art, and from thy state
Mine never shall be parted, bliss or woe.
So having said, as one from sad dismay
Recomforted, and after thoughts disturbed
Submitting to what seemed remediless,

920	Thus in calm mood his words to Eve he turned.
	Bold deed thou hast presumed, adventurous Eve,
	And peril great provoked, who thus hast dared,
	Had it been only coveting to eye
	That sacred fruit, sacred to abstinence,
925	Much more to taste it under ban to touch.
	But past who can recall, or done undo?
	Not God Omnipotent, nor Fate; yet so
	Perhaps thou shalt not die, perhaps the fact
	Is not so heinous now, foretasted fruit,
930	Profaned first by the serpent, by him first
	Made common, and unhallowed, ere our taste;
	Nor yet on him found deadly; yet he lives;
	Lives, as thou saidst, and gains to live, as Man,
	Higher degree of life; inducement strong
935	To us, as likely tasting to attain
	Proportional ascent; which cannot be
	But to be Gods, or Angels, demi-Gods.
	Nor can I think that God, Creator wise,
	Though threatening, will in earnest so destroy
940	Us his prime creatures, dignified so high,
	Set over all his works; which in our fall,
	For us created, needs with us must fail,
	Dependant made; so God shall uncreate,
	Be frustrate, do, undo, and labour lose;
945	Not well conceived of God, who, though his power
	Creation could repeat, yet would be loath
	Us to abolish, lest the Adversary
	Triumph, and say; "Fickle their state whom God
	Most favours; who can please him long? Me first
950	He ruined, now Mankind; whom will he next?"
	Matter of scorn, not to be given the Foe.
	However I with thee have fixed my lot,

Certain to undergo like doom: If death
Consort with thee, death is to me as life;
955   So forcible within my heart I feel
The bond of Nature draw me to my own;
My own in thee, for what thou art is mine;
Our state cannot be severed; we are one,
One flesh; to lose thee were to lose myself.
960   So Adam; and thus Eve to him replied.
O glorious trial of exceeding love,
Illustrious evidence, example high!
Engaging me to emulate; but, short
Of thy perfection, how shall I attain,
965   Adam, from whose dear side I boast me sprung,
And gladly of our union hear thee speak,
One heart, one soul in both; whereof good proof
This day affords, declaring thee resolved,
Rather than death, or aught than death more dread,
970   Shall separate us, linked in love so dear,
To undergo with me one guilt, one crime,
If any be, of tasting this fair fruit;
Whose virtue for of good still good proceeds,
Direct, or by occasion, hath presented
975   This happy trial of thy love, which else
So eminently never had been known?
Were it I thought death menaced would ensue
This my attempt, I would sustain alone
The worst, and not persuade thee, rather die
980   Deserted, than oblige thee with a fact
Pernicious to thy peace; chiefly assured
Remarkably so late of thy so true,
So faithful, love unequalled: but I feel
Far otherwise the event; not death, but life

985   Augmented, opened eyes, new hopes, new joys,
           Taste so divine, that what of sweet before
           Hath touched my sense, flat seems to this, and harsh.
           On my experience, Adam, freely taste,
           And fear of death deliver to the winds.
990   So saying, she embraced him, and for joy
           Tenderly wept; much won, that he his love
           Had so ennobled, as of choice to incur
           Divine displeasure for her sake, or death.
           In recompense (for such compliance bad
995   Such recompense best merits) from the bough
           She gave him of that fair enticing fruit
           With liberal hand: he scrupled not to eat,
           Against his better knowledge; not deceived,
           But fondly overcome with female charm.
1000   Earth trembled from her entrails, as again
           In pangs; and Nature gave a second groan;
           Sky loured; and, muttering thunder, some sad drops
           Wept at completing of the mortal sin
           Original: while Adam took no thought,
1005   Eating his fill; nor Eve to iterate
           Her former trespass feared, the more to sooth
           Him with her loved society; that now,
           As with new wine intoxicated both,
           They swim in mirth, and fancy that they feel
1010   Divinity within them breeding wings,
           Wherewith to scorn the earth: But that false fruit
           Far other operation first displayed,
           Carnal desire inflaming; he on Eve
           Began to cast lascivious eyes; she him
1015   As wantonly repaid; in lust they burn:
           Till Adam thus 'gan Eve to dalliance move.
           Eve, now I see thou art exact of taste,

And elegant, of sapience no small part;
Since to each meaning savour we apply,
1020 And palate call judicious; I the praise
Yield thee, so well this day thou hast purveyed.
Much pleasure we have lost, while we abstained
From this delightful fruit, nor known till now
True relish, tasting; if such pleasure be
1025 In things to us forbidden, it might be wished,
For this one tree had been forbidden ten.
But come, so well refreshed, now let us play,
As meet is, after such delicious fare;
For never did thy beauty, since the day
1030 I saw thee first and wedded thee, adorned
With all perfections, so inflame my sense
With ardour to enjoy thee, fairer now
Than ever; bounty of this virtuous tree!
So said he, and forbore not glance or toy
1035 Of amorous intent; well understood
Of Eve, whose eye darted contagious fire.
Her hand he seized; and to a shady bank,
Thick over-head with verdant roof embowered,
He led her nothing loth; flowers were the couch,
1040 Pansies, and violets, and asphodel,
And hyacinth; Earth's freshest softest lap.
There they their fill of love and love's disport
Took largely, of their mutual guilt the seal,
The solace of their sin; till dewy sleep
1045 Oppressed them, wearied with their amorous play,
Soon as the force of that fallacious fruit,
That with exhilarating vapour bland
About their spirits had played, and inmost powers
Made err, was now exhaled; and grosser sleep,

1050   Bred of unkindly fumes, with conscious dreams
        Encumbered, now had left them; up they rose
        As from unrest; and, each the other viewing,
        Soon found their eyes how opened, and their minds
        How darkened; innocence, that as a veil
1055   Had shadowed them from knowing ill, was gone;
        Just confidence, and native righteousness,
        And honour, from about them, naked left
        To guilty Shame; he covered, but his robe
        Uncovered more. So rose the Danite strong,
1060   Herculean Samson, from the harlot-lap
        Of Philistean Dalilah, and waked
        Shorn of his strength. They destitute and bare
        Of all their virtue: Silent, and in face
        Confounded, long they sat, as strucken mute:
1065   Till Adam, though not less than Eve abashed,
        At length gave utterance to these words constrained.
        O Eve, in evil hour thou didst give ear
        To that false worm, of whomsoever taught
        To counterfeit Man's voice; true in our fall,
1070   False in our promised rising; since our eyes
        Opened we find indeed, and find we know
        Both good and evil; good lost, and evil got;
        Bad fruit of knowledge, if this be to know;
        Which leaves us naked thus, of honour void,
1075   Of innocence, of faith, of purity,
        Our wonted ornaments now soiled and stained,
        And in our faces evident the signs
        Of foul concupiscence; whence evil store;
        Even shame, the last of evils; of the first
1080   Be sure then.——How shall I behold the face
        Henceforth of God or Angel, erst with joy
        And rapture so oft beheld? Those heav'nly shapes

Will dazzle now this earthly with their blaze
Insufferably bright. O! might I here
1085 In solitude live savage; in some glade
Obscured, where highest woods, impenetrable
To star or sun-light, spread their umbrage broad
And brown as evening: Cover me, ye Pines!
Ye Cedars, with innumerable boughs
1090 Hide me, where I may never see them more!—
But let us now, as in bad plight, devise
What best may for the present serve to hide
The parts of each from other, that seem most
To shame obnoxious, and unseemliest seen;
1095 Some tree, whose broad smooth leaves together sewed,
And girded on our loins, may cover round
Those middle parts; that this new comer, Shame,
There sit not, and reproach us as unclean.
So counselled he, and both together went
1100 Into the thickest wood; there soon they chose
The fig-tree; not that kind for fruit renowned,
But such as at this day, to Indians known,
In Malabar or Deccan spreads her arms
Branching so broad and long, that in the ground
1105 The bended twigs take root, and daughters grow
About the mother tree, a pillared shade
High over-arched, and echoing walks between:
There oft the Indian herdsman, shunning heat,
Shelters in cool, and tends his pasturing herds
1110 At loop-holes cut through thickest shade: Those leaves
They gathered, broad as Amazonian targe;
And, with what skill they had, together sewed,
To gird their waist; vain covering, if to hide
Their guilt and dreaded shame! O, how unlike

1115 To that first naked glory! Such of late
 Columbus found the American, so girt
 With feathered cincture; naked else, and wild
 Among the trees on isles and woody shores.
 Thus fenced, and, as they thought, their shame in part
1120 Covered, but not at rest or ease of mind,
 They sat them down to weep; nor only tears
 Rained at their eyes, but high winds worse within
 Began to rise, high passions, anger, hate,
 Mistrust, suspicion, discord; and shook sore
1125 Their inward state of mind, calm region once
 And full of peace, now tossed and turbulent:
 For Understanding ruled not, and the Will
 Heard not her lore; both in subjection now
 To sensual Appetite, who from beneath
1130 Usurping over sovreign Reason claimed
 Superior sway: From thus distempered breast,
 Adam, estranged in look and altered style,
 Speech intermitted thus to Eve renewed.
 Would thou hadst hearkened to my words, and staid
1135 With me, as I besought thee, when that strange
 Desire of wandering, this unhappy morn,
 I know not whence possessed thee; we had then
 Remained still happy; not, as now, despoiled
 Of all our good; shamed, naked, miserable!
1140 Let none henceforth seek needless cause to approve
 The faith they owe; when earnestly they seek
 Such proof, conclude, they then begin to fail.
 To whom, soon moved with touch of blame, thus Eve.
 What words have passed thy lips, Adam severe!
1145 Imputest thou that to my default, or will
 Of wandering, as thou callest it, which who knows
 But might as ill have happened thou being by,

Or to thyself perhaps? Hadst thou been there,
Or here the attempt, thou couldst not have discerned
1150   Fraud in the Serpent, speaking as he spake;
No ground of enmity between us known,
Why he should mean me ill, or seek to harm.
Was I to have never parted from thy side?
As good have grown there still a lifeless rib.
1155   Being as I am, why didst not thou, the head,
Command me absolutely not to go,
Going into such danger, as thou saidst?
Too facile then, thou didst not much gainsay;
Nay, didst permit, approve, and fair dismiss.
1160   Hadst thou been firm and fixed in thy dissent,
Neither had I transgressed, nor thou with me.
To whom, then first incensed, Adam replied.
Is this the love, is this the recompence
Of mine to thee, ingrateful Eve! expressed
1165   Immutable, when thou wert lost, not I;
Who might have lived, and joyed immortal bliss,
Yet willingly chose rather death with thee?
And am I now upbraided as the cause
Of thy transgressing? Not enough severe,
1170   It seems, in thy restraint: What could I more
I warned thee, I admonished thee, foretold
The danger, and the lurking enemy
That lay in wait; beyond this, had been force;
And force upon free will hath here no place.
1175   But confidence then bore thee on; secure
Either to meet no danger, or to find
Matter of glorious trial; and perhaps
I also erred, in overmuch admiring
What seemed in thee so perfect, that I thought

1180   No evil durst attempt thee; but I rue
        The error now, which is become my crime,
        And thou the accuser. Thus it shall befall
        Him, who, to worth in women overtrusting,
        Lets her will rule: restraint she will not brook;
1185   And, left to herself, if evil thence ensue,
        She first his weak indulgence will accuse.
        Thus they in mutual accusation spent
        The fruitless hours, but neither self-condemning;
        And of their vain contest appeared no end.

BOOK X

THE ARGUMENT

Man's transgression known, the guardian angels forsake
Paradise, and return up to Heav'n to approve their vigilance,
and are approved, God declaring that the entrance of Satan
could not be by them prevented. He sends his Son to
5   judge the transgressors, who descends and gives sentence
accordingly; then in pity clothes them both, and reascends. Sin
and Death sitting till then at the gates of Hell, by wondrous
sympathy feeling the success of Satan in this new world, and
the sin by man there committed, resolve to sit no
10   longer confined in Hell, but to follow Satan their sire up to
the place of man: to make the way easier from Hell to this
world to and fro, they pave a broad highway or bridge over
Chaos, according to the track that Satan first made; then
preparing for earth, they meet him proud of his success
15   returning to Hell; their mutual gratulation. Satan arrives at
Pandaemonium, in full assembly relates with himself also
suddenly into serpents, according to his doom given in
Paradise; then deluded with a show of the Forbidden Tree
springing up before them, they greedily reaching to take
20   of the fruit, chew dust and bitter ashes. The proceedings
of Sin and Death; God foretells the final victory of his Son
over them, and the renewing of all things; but for the present

commands his angels to make several alterations in the heav'ns and elements. Adam more and more
25   perceiving his fallen condition heavily bewails, rejects the condolement of Eve; she persists and at length appeases him: then to evade the curse likely to fall on their offspring, proposes to Adam violent ways which he approves not, but conceiving better hope, puts her in mind of the late
30   promise made them, that her seed should be revenged on the serpent, and exhorts her with him to seek peace of the offended Deity, by repentance and supplication.

Mean while the heinous and despiteful act
Of Satan, done in Paradise; and how
He, in the serpent, had perverted Eve,
Her husband she, to taste the fatal fruit,
5   Was known in Heav'n; for what can 'scape the eye
Of God all-seeing, or deceive his heart
Omniscient? who, in all things wise and just,
Hindered not Satan to attempt the mind
Of Man, with strength entire and free will armed,
10   Complete to have discovered and repulsed
Whatever wiles of foe or seeming friend.
For still they knew, and ought to have still remembered,
The high injunction, not to taste that fruit,
Whoever tempted; which they not obeying,
15   (Incurred what could they less?) the penalty;
And, manifold in sin, deserved to fall.
Up into Heav'n from Paradise in haste
The angelic guards ascended, mute, and sad,
For Man; for of his state by this they knew,
20   Much wondering how the subtle Fiend had stolen
Entrance unseen. Soon as the unwelcome news
From Earth arrived at Heav'n-gate, displeased
All were who heard; dim sadness did not spare
That time celestial visages, yet, mixed

25 With pity, violated not their bliss.
    About the new-arrived, in multitudes
    The ethereal people ran, to hear and know
    How all befel: They towards the throne supreme,
    Accountable, made haste, to make appear,
30 With righteous plea, their utmost vigilance
    And easily approved; when the Most High
    Eternal Father, from his secret cloud,
    Amidst in thunder uttered thus his voice.
    Assembled Angels, and ye Powers returned
35 From unsuccessful charge; be not dismayed,
    Nor troubled at these tidings from the earth,
    Which your sincerest care could not prevent;
    Foretold so lately what would come to pass,
    When first this tempter crossed the gulf from Hell.
40 I told ye then he should prevail, and speed
    On his bad errand; Man should be seduced,
    And flattered out of all, believing lies
    Against his Maker; no decree of mine
    Concurring to necessitate his fall,
45 Or touch with lightest moment of impulse
    His free will, to her own inclining left
    In even scale. But fallen he is; and now
    What rests, but that the mortal sentence pass
    On his transgression,—death denounced that day?
50 Which he presumes already vain and void,
    Because not yet inflicted, as he feared,
    By some immediate stroke; but soon shall find
    Forbearance no acquittance, ere day end.
    Justice shall not return as bounty scorned.
55 But whom send I to judge them? whom but thee,
    Vicegerent Son? To thee I have transferred
    All judgement, whether in Heav'n, or Earth, or Hell.

Easy it may be seen that I intend
Mercy colleague with justice, sending thee
60   Man's friend, his Mediator, his designed
Both ransom and Redeemer voluntary,
And destined Man himself to judge Man fallen.
So spake the Father; and, unfolding bright
Toward the right hand his glory, on the Son
65   Blazed forth unclouded Deity: He full
Resplendent all his Father manifest
Expressed, and thus divinely answered mild.
Father Eternal, thine is to decree;
Mine, both in Heav'n and Earth, to do thy will
70   Supreme; that thou in me, thy Son beloved,
Mayest ever rest well pleased. I go to judge
On earth these thy transgressours; but thou knowest,
Whoever judged, the worst on me must light,
When time shall be; for so I undertook
75   Before thee; and, not repenting, this obtain
Of right, that I may mitigate their doom
On me derived; yet I shall temper so
Justice with mercy, as may illustrate most
Them fully satisfied, and thee appease.
80   Attendance none shall need, nor train, where none
Are to behold the judgement, but the judged,
Those two; the third best absent is condemned,
Convict by flight, and rebel to all law:
Conviction to the serpent none belongs.
85   Thus saying, from his radiant seat he rose
Of high collateral glory: Him Thrones, and Powers,
Princedoms, and Dominations ministrant,
Accompanied to Heav'n-gate; from whence
Eden, and all the coast, in prospect lay.
90   Down he descended straight; the speed of Gods
Time counts not, though with swiftest minutes winged.

Now was the sun in western cadence low
From noon, and gentle airs, due at their hour,
To fan the earth now waked, and usher in
95   The evening cool; when he, from wrath more cool,
Came the mild Judge, and Intercessor both,
To sentence Man: The voice of God they heard
Now walking in the garden, by soft winds
Brought to their ears, while day declined; they heard,
100   And from his presence hid themselves among
The thickest trees, both man and wife; till God,
Approaching, thus to Adam called aloud.
Where art thou, Adam, wont with joy to meet
My coming seen far off? I miss thee here,
105   Not pleased, thus entertained with solitude,
Where obvious duty ere while appeared unsought:
Or come I less conspicuous, or what change
Absents thee, or what chance detains?—Come forth!
He came; and with him Eve, more loth, though first
110   To offend; discountenanced both, and discomposed;
Love was not in their looks, either to God,
Or to each other; but apparent guilt,
And shame, and perturbation, and despair,
Anger, and obstinacy, and hate, and guile.
115   Whence Adam, faltering long, thus answered brief.
I heard thee in the garden, and of thy voice
Afraid, being naked, hid myself. To whom
The gracious Judge without revile replied.
My voice thou oft hast heard, and hast not feared,
120   But still rejoiced; how is it now become
So dreadful to thee? That thou art naked, who
Hath told thee? Hast thou eaten of the tree,
Whereof I gave thee charge thou shouldst not eat?
To whom thus Adam sore beset replied.

125	O Heav'n! in evil strait this day I stand
	Before my Judge; either to undergo
	Myself the total crime, or to accuse
	My other self, the partner of my life;
	Whose failing, while her faith to me remains,
130	I should conceal, and not expose to blame
	By my complaint: but strict necessity
	Subdues me, and calamitous constraint;
	Lest on my head both sin and punishment,
	However insupportable, be all
135	Devolved; though should I hold my peace, yet thou
	Wouldst easily detect what I conceal.—
	This Woman, whom thou madest to be my help,
	And gavest me as thy perfect gift, so good,
	So fit, so acceptable, so divine,
140	That from her hand I could suspect no ill,
	And what she did, whatever in itself,
	Her doing seemed to justify the deed;
	She gave me of the tree, and I did eat.
	To whom the Sovran Presence thus replied.
145	Was she thy God, that her thou didst obey
	Before his voice? or was she made thy guide,
	Superiour, or but equal, that to her
	Thou didst resign thy manhood, and the place
	Wherein God set thee above her made of thee,
150	And for thee, whose perfection far excelled
	Hers in all real dignity? Adorned
	She was indeed, and lovely, to attract
	Thy love, not thy subjection; and her gifts
	Were such, as under government well seemed;
155	Unseemly to bear rule; which was thy part
	And person, hadst thou known thyself aright.
	So having said, he thus to Eve in few.
	Say, Woman, what is this which thou hast done?
	To whom sad Eve, with shame nigh overwhelmed,

160   Confessing soon, yet not before her Judge
         Bold or loquacious, thus abashed replied.
         The Serpent me beguiled, and I did eat.
         Which when the Lord God heard, without delay
         To judgement he proceeded on the accused
165   Serpent, though brute; unable to transfer
         The guilt on him, who made him instrument
         Of mischief, and polluted from the end
         Of his creation; justly then accursed,
         As vitiated in nature: More to know
170   Concerned not Man, (since he no further knew)
         Nor altered his offence; yet God at last
         To Satan first in sin his doom applied,
         Though in mysterious terms, judged as then best:
         And on the Serpent thus his curse let fall.
175   Because thou hast done this, thou art accursed
         Above all cattle, each beast of the field;
         Upon thy belly groveling thou shalt go,
         And dust shalt eat all the days of thy life.
         Between thee and the woman I will put
180   Enmity, and between thine and her seed;
         Her seed shall bruise thy head, thou bruise his heel.
         So spake this oracle, then verified
         When Jesus, Son of Mary, second Eve,
         Saw Satan fall, like lightning, down from Heav'n,
185   Prince of the air; then, rising from his grave
         Spoiled Principalities and Powers, triumphed
         In open show; and, with ascension bright,
         Captivity led captive through the air,
         The realm itself of Satan, long usurped;
190   Whom he shall tread at last under our feet;
         Even he, who now foretold his fatal bruise;
         And to the Woman thus his sentence turned.

Thy sorrow I will greatly multiply
By thy conception; children thou shalt bring
195   In sorrow forth; and to thy husband's will
Thine shall submit; he over thee shall rule.
On Adam last thus judgement he pronounced.
Because thou hast hearkened to the voice of thy wife,
And eaten of the tree, concerning which
200   I charged thee, saying, Thou shalt not eat thereof:
Cursed is the ground for thy sake; thou in sorrow
Shalt eat thereof, all the days of thy life;
Thorns also and thistles it shall bring thee forth
Unbid; and thou shalt eat the herb of the field;
205   In the sweat of thy face shalt thou eat bread,
Till thou return unto the ground; for thou
Out of the ground wast taken, know thy birth,
For dust thou art, and shalt to dust return.
So judged he Man, both Judge and Saviour sent;
210   And the instant stroke of death, denounced that day,
Removed far off; then, pitying how they stood
Before him naked to the air, that now
Must suffer change, disdained not to begin
Thenceforth the form of servant to assume;
215   As when he washed his servants feet; so now,
As father of his family, he clad
Their nakedness with skins of beasts, or slain,
Or as the snake with youthful coat repaid;
And thought not much to clothe his enemies;
220   Nor he their outward only with the skins
Of beasts, but inward nakedness, much more.
Opprobrious, with his robe of righteousness,
Arraying, covered from his Father's sight.
To him with swift ascent he up returned,
225   Into his blissful bosom reassumed
In glory, as of old; to him appeased

All, though all-knowing, what had passed with Man
Recounted, mixing intercession sweet.
Mean while, ere thus was sinned and judged on Earth,
230   Within the gates of Hell sat Sin and Death,
In counterview within the gates, that now
Stood open wide, belching outrageous flame
Far into Chaos, since the Fiend passed through,
Sin opening; who thus now to Death began.
235   O Son, why sit we here each other viewing
Idly, while Satan, our great author, thrives
In other worlds, and happier seat provides
.For us, his offspring dear? It cannot be
But that success attends him; if mishap,
240   Ere this he had returned, with fury driven
By his avengers; since no place like this
Can fit his punishment, or their revenge.
Methinks I feel new strength within me rise,
Wings growing, and dominion given me large
245   Beyond this deep; whatever draws me on,
Or sympathy, or some connatural force,
Powerful at greatest distance to unite,
With secret amity, things of like kind,
By secretest conveyance. Thou, my shade
250   Inseparable, must with me along;
For Death from Sin no power can separate.
But, lest the difficulty of passing back
Stay his return perhaps over this gulf
Impassable, impervious; let us try
255   Adventurous work, yet to thy power and mine
Not unagreeable, to found a path
Over this main from Hell to that new world,
Where Satan now prevails; a monument
Of merit high to all the infernal host,

260	Easing their passage hence, for intercourse,
	Or transmigration, as their lot shall lead.
	Nor can I miss the way, so strongly drawn
	By this new-felt attraction and instinct.
	Whom thus the meager Shadow answered soon.
265	Go, whither Fate, and inclination strong,
	Leads thee; I shall not lag behind, nor err
	The way, thou leading; such a scent I draw
	Of carnage, prey innumerable, and taste
	The savour of death from all things there that live:
270	Nor shall I to the work thou enterprisest
	Be wanting, but afford thee equal aid.
	So saying, with delight he snuffed the smell
	Of mortal change on earth. As when a flock
	Of ravenous fowl, though many a league remote,
275	Against the day of battle, to a field,
	Where armies lie encamped, come flying, lured
	With scent of living carcasses designed
	For death, the following day, in bloody fight:
	So scented the grim Feature, and upturned
280	His nostril wide into the murky air;
	Sagacious of his quarry from so far.
	Then both from out Hell-gates, into the waste
	Wide anarchy of Chaos, damp and dark,
	Flew diverse; and with power (their power was great)
285	Hovering upon the waters, what they met
	Solid or slimy, as in raging sea
	Tossed up and down, together crowded drove,
	From each side shoaling towards the mouth of Hell;
	As when two polar winds, blowing adverse
290	Upon the Cronian sea, together drive
	Mountains of ice, that stop the imagined way
	Beyond Petsora eastward, to the rich

Cathaian coast. The aggregated soil
Death with his mace petrific, cold and dry,
295   As with a trident, smote; and fixed as firm
As Delos, floating once; the rest his look
Bound with Gorgonian rigour not to move;
And with Asphaltic slime, broad as the gate,
Deep to the roots of Hell the gathered beach
300   They fastened, and the mole immense wrought on
Over the foaming deep high-arched, a bridge
Of length prodigious, joining to the wall
Immoveable of this now fenceless world,
Forfeit to Death; from hence a passage broad,
305   Smooth, easy, inoffensive, down to Hell.
So, if great things to small may be compared,
Xerxes, the liberty of Greece to yoke,
From Susa, his Memnonian palace high,
Came to the sea: and, over Hellespont
310   Bridging his way, Europe with Asia joined,
And scourged with many a stroke the indignant waves.
Now had they brought the work by wonderous art
Pontifical, a ridge of pendant rock,
Over the vexed abyss, following the track
315   Of Satan to the self-same place where he
First lighted from his wing, and landed safe
From out of Chaos, to the outside bare
Of this round world: With pins of adamant
And chains they made all fast, too fast they made
320   And durable! And now in little space
The confines met of empyrean Heav'n,
And of this World; and, on the left hand, Hell
With long reach interposed; three several ways
In sight, to each of these three places led.
325   And now their way to Earth they had descried,
To Paradise first tending; when, behold!

Satan, in likeness of an Angel bright,
Betwixt the Centaur and the Scorpion steering
His zenith, while the sun in Aries rose:
330 Disguised he came; but those his children dear
Their parent soon discerned, though in disguise.
He, after Eve seduced, unminded slunk
Into the wood fast by; and, changing shape,
To observe the sequel, saw his guileful act
335 By Eve, though all unweeting, seconded
Upon her husband; saw their shame that sought
Vain covertures; but when he saw descend
The Son of God to judge them, terrified
He fled; not hoping to escape, but shun
340 The present; fearing, guilty, what his wrath
Might suddenly inflict; that past, returned
By night, and listening where the hapless pair
Sat in their sad discourse, and various plaint,
Thence gathered his own doom; which understood
345 Not instant, but of future time, with joy
And tidings fraught, to Hell he now returned;
And at the brink of Chaos, near the foot
Of this new wonderous pontifice, unhoped
Met, who to meet him came, his offspring dear.
350 Great joy was at their meeting, and at sight
Of that stupendous bridge his joy increased.
Long he admiring stood, till Sin, his fair
Enchanting daughter, thus the silence broke.
O Parent, these are thy magnific deeds,
355 Thy trophies! which thou viewest as not thine own;
Thou art their author, and prime architect:
For I no sooner in my heart divined,
My heart, which by a secret harmony
Still moves with thine, joined in connexion sweet,
360 That thou on earth hadst prospered, which thy looks

Now also evidence, but straight I felt,
Though distant from thee worlds between, yet felt,
That I must after thee, with this thy son;
Such fatal consequence unites us three!
365 Hell could no longer hold us in our bounds,
Nor this unvoyageable gulf obscure
Detain from following thy illustrious track.
Thou hast achieved our liberty, confined
Within Hell-gates till now; thou us impowered
370 To fortify thus far, and overlay,
With this portentous bridge, the dark abyss.
Thine now is all this world; thy virtue hath won
What thy hands builded not; thy wisdom gained
With odds what war hath lost, and fully avenged
375 Our foil in Heav'n; here thou shalt monarch reign,
There didst not; there let him still victor sway,
As battle hath adjudged; from this new world
Retiring, by his own doom alienated;
And henceforth monarchy with thee divide
380 Of all things, parted by the empyreal bounds,
His quadrature, from thy orbicular world;
Or try thee now more dangerous to his throne.
Whom thus the Prince of darkness answered glad.
Fair Daughter, and thou Son and Grandchild both;
385 High proof ye now have given to be the race
Of Satan (for I glory in the name,
Antagonist of Heav'n's Almighty King,)
Amply have merited of me, of all
The infernal empire, that so near Heav'n's door
390 Triumphal with triumphal act have met,
Mine, with this glorious work; and made one realm,
Hell and this world, one realm, one continent
Of easy thorough-fare. Therefore, while I
Descend through darkness, on your road with ease,

395   To my associate Powers, them to acquaint
              With these successes, and with them rejoice;
              You two this way, among these numerous orbs,
              All yours, right down to Paradise descend;
              There dwell, and reign in bliss; thence on the earth
400   Dominion exercise and in the air,
              Chiefly on Man, sole lord of all declared;
              Him first make sure your thrall, and lastly kill.
              My substitutes I send ye, and create
              Plenipotent on earth, of matchless might
405   Issuing from me: on your joint vigour now
              My hold of this new kingdom all depends,
              Through Sin to Death exposed by my exploit.
              If your joint power prevail, the affairs of Hell
              No detriment need fear; go, and be strong!
410   So saying he dismissed them; they with speed
              Their course through thickest constellations held,
              Spreading their bane; the blasted stars looked wan,
              And planets, planet-struck, real eclipse
              Then suffered. The other way Satan went down
415   The causey to Hell-gate: On either side
              Disparted Chaos overbuilt exclaimed,
              And with rebounding surge the bars assailed,
              That scorned his indignation: Through the gate,
              Wide open and unguarded, Satan passed,
420   And all about found desolate; for those,
              Appointed to sit there, had left their charge,
              Flown to the upper world; the rest were all
              Far to the inland retired, about the walls
              Of Pandemonium; city and proud seat
425   Of Lucifer, so by allusion called
              Of that bright star to Satan paragoned;
              There kept their watch the legions, while the Grand

In council sat, solicitous what chance
Might intercept their emperor sent; so he
430 Departing gave command, and they observed.
As when the Tartar from his Russian foe,
By Astracan, over the snowy plains,
Retires; or Bactrin Sophi, from the horns
Of Turkish crescent, leaves all waste beyond
435 The realm of Aladule, in his retreat
To Tauris or Casbeen: So these, the late
Heav'n-banished host, left desart utmost Hell
Many a dark league, reduced in careful watch
Round their metropolis; and now expecting
440 Each hour their great adventurer, from the search
Of foreign worlds: He through the midst unmarked,
In show plebeian Angel militant
Of lowest order, passed; and from the door
Of that Plutonian hall, invisible
445 Ascended his high throne; which, under state
Of richest texture spread, at the upper end
Was placed in regal lustre. Down a while
He sat, and round about him saw unseen:
At last, as from a cloud, his fulgent head
450 And shape star-bright appeared, or brighter; clad
With what permissive glory since his fall
Was left him, or false glitter: All amazed
At that so sudden blaze the Stygian throng
Bent their aspect, and whom they wished beheld,
455 Their mighty Chief returned: loud was the acclaim:
Forth rushed in haste the great consulting peers,
Raised from their dark Divan, and with like joy
Congratulant approached him; who with hand
Silence, and with these words attention, won.
460 Thrones, Dominations, Princedoms, Virtues, Powers;
For in possession such, not only of right,

I call ye, and declare ye now; returned
Successful beyond hope, to lead ye forth
Triumphant out of this infernal pit
465 Abominable, accursed, the house of woe,
And dungeon of our tyrant: Now possess,
As Lords, a spacious world, to our native Heav'n
Little inferior, by my adventure hard
With peril great achieved. Long were to tell
470 What I have done; what suffered; with what pain
Voyaged th' unreal, vast, unbounded deep
Of horrible confusion; over which
By Sin and Death a broad way now is paved,
To expedite your glorious march; but I
475 Toiled out my uncouth passage, forced to ride
The untractable abyss, plunged in the womb
Of unoriginal Night and Chaos wild;
That, jealous of their secrets, fiercely opposed
My journey strange, with clamorous uproar
480 Protesting Fate supreme; thence how I found
The new created world, which fame in Heav'n
Long had foretold, a fabric wonderful
Of absolute perfection! therein Man
Placed in a Paradise, by our exile
485 Made happy: Him by fraud I have seduced
From his Creator; and, the more to encrease
Your wonder, with an apple; he, thereat
Offended, worth your laughter! hath given up
Both his beloved Man, and all his world,
490 To Sin and Death a prey, and so to us,
Without our hazard, labour, or alarm;
To range in, and to dwell, and over Man
To rule, as over all he should have ruled.
True is, me also he hath judged, or rather
495 Me not, but the brute serpent in whose shape

Man I deceived: that which to me belongs,
Is enmity which he will put between
Me and mankind; I am to bruise his heel;
His seed, when is not set, shall bruise my head:
A world who would not purchase with a bruise,
Or much more grievous pain?—Ye have the account
Of my performance: What remains, ye Gods,
But up, and enter now into full bliss?
So having said, a while he stood, expecting
Their universal shout, and high applause,
To fill his ear; when, contrary, he hears
On all sides, from innumerable tongues,
A dismal universal hiss, the sound
Of public scorn; he wondered, but not long
Had leisure, wondering at himself now more,
His visage drawn he felt to sharp and spare;
His arms clung to his ribs; his legs entwining
Each other, till supplanted down he fell
A monstrous serpent on his belly prone,
Reluctant, but in vain; a greater power
Now ruled him, punished in the shape he sinned,
According to his doom: he would have spoke,
But hiss for hiss returned with forked tongue
To forked tongue; for now were all transformed
Alike, to serpents all, as accessories
To his bold riot: Dreadful was the din
Of hissing through the hall, thick swarming now
With complicated monsters head and tail,
Scorpion, and Asp, and Amphisbaena dire,
Cerastes horned, Hydrus, and Elops drear,
And Dipsas; (not so thick swarmed once the soil
Bedropt with blood of Gorgon, or the isle
Ophiusa,) but still greatest he the midst,
Now Dragon grown, larger than whom the sun

500

505

510

515

520

525

530 Engendered in the Pythian vale or slime,
  Huge Python, and his power no less he seemed
  Above the rest still to retain; they all
  Him followed, issuing forth to the open field,
  Where all yet left of that revolted rout,
535 Heav'n-fallen, in station stood or just array;
  Sublime with expectation when to see
  In triumph issuing forth their glorious Chief;
  They saw, but other sight instead! a croud
  Of ugly serpents; horrour on them fell,
540 And horrid sympathy; for, what they saw,
  They felt themselves, now changing; down their arms,
  Down fell both spear and shield; down they as fast;
  And the dire hiss renewed, and the dire form
  Catched, by contagion; like in punishment,
545 As in their crime. Thus was the applause they meant,
  Turned to exploding hiss, triumph to shame
  Cast on themselves from their own mouths. There stood
  A grove hard by, sprung up with this their change,
  His will who reigns above, to aggravate
550 Their penance, laden with fair fruit, like that
  Which grew in Paradise, the bait of Eve
  Used by the Tempter: on that prospect strange
  Their earnest eyes they fixed, imagining
  For one forbidden tree a multitude
555 Now risen, to work them further woe or shame;
  Yet, parched with scalding thirst and hunger fierce,
  Though to delude them sent, could not abstain;
  But on they rolled in heaps, and, up the trees
  Climbing, sat thicker than the snaky locks
560 That curled Megaera: greedily they plucked
  The fruitage fair to sight, like that which grew
  Near that bituminous lake where Sodom flamed;

This more delusive, not the touch, but taste
Deceived; they, fondly thinking to allay
565   Their appetite with gust, instead of fruit
Chewed bitter ashes, which the offended taste
With spattering noise rejected: oft they assayed,
Hunger and thirst constraining; drugged as oft,
With hatefullest disrelish writhed their jaws,
570   With soot and cinders filled; so oft they fell
Into the same illusion, not as Man
Whom they triumphed once lapsed. Thus were they plagued
And worn with famine, long and ceaseless hiss,
Till their lost shape, permitted, they resumed;
575   Yearly enjoined, some say, to undergo,
This annual humbling certain numbered days,
To dash their pride, and joy, for Man seduced.
However, some tradition they dispersed
Among the Heathen, of their purchase got,
580   And fabled how the Serpent, whom they called
Ophion, with Eurynome, the wide—
Encroaching Eve perhaps, had first the rule
Of high Olympus; thence by Saturn driven
And Ops, ere yet Dictaean Jove was born.
585   Mean while in Paradise the hellish pair
Too soon arrived; Sin, there in power before,
Once actual; now in body, and to dwell
Habitual habitant; behind her Death,
Close following pace for pace, not mounted yet
590   On his pale horse: to whom Sin thus began.
Second of Satan sprung, all-conquering Death!
What thinkest thou of our empire now, though earned
With travel difficult, not better far
Than still at Hell's dark threshold to have sat watch,
595   Unnamed, undreaded, and thyself half starved?
Whom thus the Sin-born monster answered soon.

To me, who with eternal famine pine,
Alike is Hell, or Paradise, or Heav'n;
There best, where most with ravine I may meet;
600 Which here, though plenteous, all too little seems
To stuff this maw, this vast unhide-bound corps.
To whom the incestuous mother thus replied.
Thou therefore on these herbs, and fruits, and flowers,
Feed first; on each beast next, and fish, and fowl;
605 No homely morsels! and, whatever thing
The scythe of Time mows down, devour unspared;
Till I, in Man residing, through the race,
His thoughts, his looks, words, actions, all infect;
And season him thy last and sweetest prey.
610 This said, they both betook them several ways,
Both to destroy, or unimmortal make
All kinds, and for destruction to mature
Sooner or later; which the Almighty seeing,
From his transcendent seat the Saints among,
615 To those bright Orders uttered thus his voice.
See, with what heat these dogs of Hell advance
To waste and havoc yonder world, which I
So fair and good created; and had still
Kept in that state, had not the folly of Man
620 Let in these wasteful furies, who impute
Folly to me; so doth the Prince of Hell
And his adherents, that with so much ease
I suffer them to enter and possess
A place so heav'nly; and, conniving, seem
625 To gratify my scornful enemies,
That laugh, as if, transported with some fit
Of passion, I to them had quitted all,
At random yielded up to their misrule;
And know not that I called, and drew them thither,
630 My Hell-hounds, to lick up the draff and filth

Which Man's polluting sin with taint hath shed
On what was pure; til, crammed and gorged, nigh burst
With sucked and glutted offal, at one sling
Of thy victorious arm, well-pleasing Son,
635   Both Sin, and Death, and yawning Grave, at last,
Through Chaos hurled, obstruct the mouth of Hell
For ever, and seal up his ravenous jaws.
Then Heav'n and Earth renewed shall be made pure
To sanctity, that shall receive no stain:
640   Till then, the curse pronounced on both precedes.
He ended, and the heav'nly audience loud
Sung Halleluiah, as the sound of seas,
Through multitude that sung: Just are thy ways,
Righteous are thy decrees on all thy works;
645   Who can extenuate thee? Next, to the Son,
Destined Restorer of mankind, by whom
New Heav'n and Earth shall to the ages rise,
Or down from Heav'n descend.—Such was their song;
While the Creator, calling forth by name
650   His mighty Angels, gave them several charge,
As sorted best with present things. The sun
Had first his precept so to move, so shine,
As might affect the earth with cold and heat
Scarce tolerable; and from the north to call
655   Decrepit winter; from the south to bring
Solstitial summer's heat. To the blank moon
Her office they prescribed; to the other five
Their planetary motions, and aspects,
In sextile, square, and trine, and opposite,
660   Of noxious efficacy, and when to join
In synod unbenign; and taught the fixed
Their influence malignant when to shower,
Which of them rising with the sun, or falling,
Should prove tempestuous: To the winds they set

665   Their corners, when with bluster to confound
Sea, air, and shore; the thunder when to roll
With terror through the dark aerial hall.
Some say, he bid his Angels turn askanse
The poles of earth, twice ten degrees and more,
670   From the sun's axle; they with labour pushed
Oblique the centric globe: Some say, the sun
Was bid turn reins from the equinoctial road
Like distant breadth to Taurus with the seven
Atlantic Sisters, and the Spartan Twins,
675   Up to the Tropic Crab: thence down amain
By Leo, and the Virgin, and the Scales,
As deep as Capricorn; to bring in change
Of seasons to each clime; else had the spring
Perpetual smiled on earth with vernant flowers,
680   Equal in days and nights, except to those
Beyond the polar circles; to them day
Had unbenighted shone, while the low sun,
To recompense his distance, in their sight
Had rounded still the horizon, and not known
685   Or east or west; which had forbid the snow
From cold Estotiland, and south as far
Beneath Magellan. At that tasted fruit
The sun, as from Thyestean banquet, turned
His course intended; else, how had the world
690   Inhabited, though sinless, more than now,
Avoided pinching cold and scorching heat?
These changes in the Heav'ns, though slow, produced
Like change on sea and land; sideral blast,
Vapour, and mist, and exhalation hot,
695   Corrupt and pestilent: Now from the north
Of Norumbega, and the Samoed shore,
Bursting their brazen dungeon, armed with ice,
And snow, and hail, and stormy gust and flaw,
Boreas, and Caecias, and Argestes loud,

700 And Thrascias, rend the woods, and seas upturn;
 With adverse blast upturns them from the south
 Notus, and Afer black with thunderous clouds
 From Serraliona; thwart of these, as fierce,
 Forth rush the Levant and the Ponent winds,
705 Eurus and Zephyr, with their lateral noise,
 Sirocco and Libecchio. Thus began
 Outrage from lifeless things; but Discord first,
 Daughter of Sin, among the irrational
 Death introduced, through fierce antipathy:
710 Beast now with beast 'gan war, and fowl with fowl,
 And fish with fish; to graze the herb all leaving,
 Devoured each other; nor stood much in awe
 Of Man, but fled him; or, with countenance grim,
 Glared on him passing. These were from without
715 The growing miseries, which Adam saw
 Already in part, though hid in gloomiest shade,
 To sorrow abandoned, but worse felt within;
 And, in a troubled sea of passion tost,
 Thus to disburden sought with sad complaint.
720 O miserable of happy! Is this the end
 Of this new glorious world, and me so late
 The glory of that glory, who now become
 Accursed, of blessed? hide me from the face
 Of God, whom to behold was then my highth
725 Of happiness!—Yet well, if here would end
 The misery; I deserved it, and would bear
 My own deservings; but this will not serve:
 All that I eat or drink, or shall beget,
 Is propagated curse. O voice, once heard
730 Delightfully, Increase and multiply;
 Now death to hear! for what can I encrease,
 Or multiply, but curses on my head?
 Who of all ages to succeed, but, feeling

The evil on him brought by me, will curse
735   My head? Ill fare our ancestor impure,
For this we may thank Adam! but his thanks
Shall be the execration: so, besides
Mine own that bide upon me, all from me
Shall with a fierce reflux on me rebound;
740   On me, as on their natural center, light
Heavy, though in their place. O fleeting joys
Of Paradise, dear bought with lasting woes!
Did I request thee, Maker, from my clay
To mould me Man? did I solicit thee
745   From darkness to promote me, or here place
In this delicious garden? As my will
Concurred not to my being, it were but right
And equal to reduce me to my dust;
Desirous to resign and render back
750   All I received; unable to perform
Thy terms too hard, by which I was to hold
The good I sought not. To the loss of that,
Sufficient penalty, why hast thou added
The sense of endless woes? Inexplicable
755   Thy justice seems; yet to say truth, too late
I thus contest; then should have been refused
Those terms whatever, when they were proposed:
Thou didst accept them; wilt thou enjoy the good,
Then cavil the conditions? And, though God
760   Made thee without thy leave, what if thy son
Prove disobedient, and reproved, retort,
"Wherefore didst thou beget me? I sought it not!"
Wouldst thou admit for his contempt of thee
That proud excuse? yet him not thy election,
765   But natural necessity begot.
God made thee of choice his own, and of his own
To serve him; thy reward was of his grace;

Thy punishment then, justly is at his will.
Be it so, for I submit; his doom is fair,
770   That dust I am, and shall to dust return.
O welcome hour whenever! Why delays
His hand to execute what his decree
Fixed on this day? Why do I overlive,
Why am I mocked with death, and lengthened out
775   To deathless pain? How gladly would I meet
Mortality my sentence, and be earth
Insensible! How glad would lay me down
As in my mother's lap! There I should rest,
And sleep secure; his dreadful voice no more
780   Would thunder in my ears; no fear of worse
To me, and to my offspring, would torment me
With cruel expectation. Yet one doubt
Pursues me still, lest all I cannot die;
Lest that pure breath of life, the spirit of Man
785   Which God inspired, cannot together perish
With this corporeal clod; then, in the grave,
Or in some other dismal place, who knows
But I shall die a living death? O thought
Horrid, if true! Yet why? It was but breath
790   Of life that sinned; what dies but what had life
And sin? The body properly had neither,
All of me then shall die: let this appease
The doubt, since human reach no further knows.
For though the Lord of all be infinite,
795   Is his wrath also? Be it, Man is not so,
But mortal doomed. How can he exercise
Wrath without end on Man, whom death must end?
Can he make deathless death? That were to make
Strange contradiction, which to God himself
800   Impossible is held; as argument
Of weakness, not of power. Will he draw out,

For anger's sake, finite to infinite,
In punished Man, to satisfy his rigour,
Satisfied never? That were to extend
805 His sentence beyond dust and Nature's law;
By which all causes else, according still
To the reception of their matter, act;
Not to the extent of their own sphere. But say
That death be not one stroke, as I supposed,
810 Bereaving sense, but endless misery
From this day onward; which I feel begun
Both in me, and without me; and so last
To perpetuity;—Ay me! that fear
Comes thundering back with dreadful revolution
815 On my defenceless head; both Death and I
Am found eternal, and incorporate both;
Nor I on my part single; in me all
Posterity stands cursed: Fair patrimony
That I must leave ye, Sons! O, were I able
820 To waste it all myself, and leave ye none!
So disinherited, how would you bless
Me, now your curse! Ah, why should all mankind,
For one man's fault, thus guiltless be condemned,
It guiltless? But from me what can proceed,
825 But all corrupt; both mind and will depraved
Not to do only, but to will the same
With me? How can they then acquitted stand
In sight of God? Him, after all disputes,
Forced I absolve: all my evasions vain,
830 And reasonings, though through mazes, lead me still
But to my own conviction: first and last
On me, me only, as the source and spring
Of all corruption, all the blame lights due;
So might the wrath! Fond wish! couldst thou support
835 That burden, heavier than the earth to bear;

Than all the world much heavier, though divided
With that bad Woman? Thus, what thou desirest,
And what thou fearest, alike destroys all hope
Of refuge, and concludes thee miserable
840   Beyond all past example and future;
To Satan only like both crime and doom.
O Conscience! into what abyss of fears
And horrors hast thou driven me; out of which
I find no way, from deep to deeper plunged!
845   Thus Adam to himself lamented loud,
Through the still night; not now, as ere Man fell,
Wholesome, and cool, and mild, but with black air
Accompanied; with damps, and dreadful gloom;
Which to his evil conscience represented
850   All things with double terror: On the ground
Outstretched he lay, on the cold ground; and oft
Cursed his creation; Death as oft accused
Of tardy execution, since denounced
The day of his offence. Why comes not Death,
855   Said he, with one thrice-acceptable stroke
To end me? Shall Truth fail to keep her word,
Justice Divine not hasten to be just?
But Death comes not at call; Justice Divine
Mends not her slowest pace for prayers or cries,
860   O woods, O fountains, hillocks, dales, and bowers!
With other echo late I taught your shades
To answer, and resound far other song.—
Whom thus afflicted when sad Eve beheld,
Desolate where she sat, approaching nigh,
865   Soft words to his fierce passion she assayed:
But her with stern regard he thus repelled.
Out of my sight, thou Serpent! That name best
Befits thee with him leagued, thyself as false
And hateful; nothing wants, but that thy shape,

870	Like his, and colour serpentine, may show
	Thy inward fraud; to warn all creatures from thee
	Henceforth; lest that too heav'nly form, pretended
	To hellish falsehood, snare them! But for thee
	I had persisted happy; had not thy pride
875	And wandering vanity, when least was safe,
	Rejected my forewarning, and disdained
	Not to be trusted; longing to be seen,
	Though by the Devil himself; him overweening
	To over-reach; but, with the serpent meeting,
880	Fooled and beguiled; by him thou, I by thee
	To trust thee from my side; imagined wise,
	Constant, mature, proof against all assaults;
	And understood not all was but a show,
	Rather than solid virtue; all but a rib
885	Crooked by nature, bent, as now appears,
	More to the part sinister, from me drawn;
	Well if thrown out, as supernumerary
	To my just number found. O! why did God,
	Creator wise, that peopled highest Heav'n
890	With Spirits masculine, create at last
	This novelty on earth, this fair defect
	Of nature, and not fill the world at once
	With Men, as Angels, without feminine;
	Or find some other way to generate
895	Mankind? This mischief had not been befallen,
	And more that shall befall; innumerable
	Disturbances on earth through female snares,
	And strait conjunction with this sex: for either
	He never shall find out fit mate, but such
900	As some misfortune brings him, or mistake;
	Or whom he wishes most shall seldom gain
	Through her perverseness, but shall see her gained

By a far worse; or, if she love, withheld
By parents; or his happiest choice too late
905 Shall meet, already linked and wedlock-bound
To a fell adversary, his hate or shame:
Which infinite calamity shall cause
To human life, and household peace confound.
He added not, and from her turned; but Eve,
910 Not so repulsed, with tears that ceased not flowing
And tresses all disordered, at his feet
Fell humble; and, embracing them, besought
His peace, and thus proceeded in her plaint.
Forsake me not thus, Adam! witness Heav'n
915 What love sincere, and reverence in my heart
I bear thee, and unweeting have offended,
Unhappily deceived! Thy suppliant
I beg, and clasp thy knees; bereave me not,
Whereon I live, thy gentle looks, thy aid,
920 Thy counsel, in this uttermost distress,
My only strength and stay: Forlorn of thee,
Whither shall I betake me, where subsist?
While yet we live, scarce one short hour perhaps,
Between us two let there be peace; both joining,
925 As joined in injuries, one enmity
Against a foe by doom express assigned us,
That cruel Serpent: On me exercise not
Thy hatred for this misery befallen;
On me already lost, me than thyself
930 More miserable! Both have sinned; but thou
Against God only; I against God and thee;
And to the place of judgement will return,
There with my cries importune Heav'n; that all
The sentence, from thy head removed, may light
935 On me, sole cause to thee of all this woe;
Me, me only, just object of his ire!

289

She ended weeping; and her lowly plight,
Immoveable, till peace obtained from fault
Acknowledged and deplored, in Adam wrought
940 Commiseration: Soon his heart relented
Towards her, his life so late, and sole delight,
Now at his feet submissive in distress;
Creature so fair his reconcilement seeking,
His counsel, whom she had displeased, his aid:
945 As one disarmed, his anger all he lost,
And thus with peaceful words upraised her soon.
Unwary, and too desirous, as before,
So now of what thou knowest not, who desirest
The punishment all on thyself; alas!
950 Bear thine own first, ill able to sustain
His full wrath, whose thou feelest as yet least part,
And my displeasure bearest so ill. If prayers
Could alter high decrees, I to that place
Would speed before thee, and be louder heard,
955 That on my head all might be visited;
Thy frailty and infirmer sex forgiven,
To me committed, and by me exposed.
But rise;—let us no more contend, nor blame
Each other, blamed enough elsewhere; but strive
960 In offices of love, how we may lighten
Each other's burden, in our share of woe;
Since this day's death denounced, if aught I see,
Will prove no sudden, but a slow-paced evil;
A long day's dying, to augment our pain;
965 And to our seed (O hapless seed!) derived.
To whom thus Eve, recovering heart, replied.
Adam, by sad experiment I know
How little weight my words with thee can find,
Found so erroneous; thence by just event
970 Found so unfortunate: Nevertheless,

Restored by thee, vile as I am, to place
Of new acceptance, hopeful to regain
Thy love, the sole contentment of my heart
Living or dying, from thee I will not hide
975   What thoughts in my unquiet breast are risen,
Tending to some relief of our extremes,
Or end; though sharp and sad, yet tolerable,
As in our evils, and of easier choice.
If care of our descent perplex us most,
980   Which must be born to certain woe, devoured
By Death at last; and miserable it is
To be to others cause of misery,
Our own begotten, and of our loins to bring
Into this cursed world a woeful race,
985   That after wretched life must be at last
Food for so foul a monster; in thy power
It lies, yet ere conception to prevent
The race unblest, to being yet unbegot.
Childless thou art, childless remain:
990   So DeathShall be deceived his glut, and with us two
Be forced to satisfy his ravenous maw.
But if thou judge it hard and difficult,
Conversing, looking, loving, to abstain
From love's due rights, nuptial embraces sweet;
995   And with desire to languish without hope,
Before the present object languishing
With like desire; which would be misery
And torment less than none of what we dread;
Then, both ourselves and seed at once to free
1000   From what we fear for both, let us make short,—
Let us seek Death;—or, he not found, supply
With our own hands his office on ourselves:
Why stand we longer shivering under fears,
That show no end but death, and have the power,

1005 Of many ways to die the shortest choosing,
   Destruction with destruction to destroy?—
   She ended here, or vehement despair
   Broke off the rest: so much of death her thoughts
   Had entertained, as dyed her cheeks with pale.
1010 But Adam, with such counsel nothing swayed,
   To better hopes his more attentive mind
   Labouring had raised; and thus to Eve replied.
   Eve, thy contempt of life and pleasure seems
   To argue in thee something more sublime
1015 And excellent, than what thy mind contemns;
   But self-destruction therefore sought, refutes
   That excellence thought in thee; and implies,
   Not thy contempt, but anguish and regret
   For loss of life and pleasure overloved.
1020 Or if thou covet death, as utmost end
   Of misery, so thinking to evade
   The penalty pronounced; doubt not but God
   Hath wiselier armed his vengeful ire, than so
   To be forestalled; much more I fear lest death,
1025 So snatched, will not exempt us from the pain
   We are by doom to pay; rather, such acts
   Of contumacy will provoke the Highest
   To make death in us live: Then let us seek
   Some safer resolution, which methinks
1030 I have in view, calling to mind with heed
   Part of our sentence, that thy seed shall bruise
   The Serpent's head; piteous amends! unless
   Be meant, whom I conjecture, our grand foe,
   Satan; who, in the serpent, hath contrived
1035 Against us this deceit: To crush his head
   Would be revenge indeed! which will be lost
   By death brought on ourselves, or childless days
   Resolved, as thou proposest; so our foe
   Shal 'scape his punishment ordained, and we

1040   Instead shall double ours upon our heads.
       No more be mentioned then of violence
       Against ourselves; and wilful barrenness,
       That cuts us off from hope; and savours only
       Rancour and pride, impatience and despite,
1045   Reluctance against God and his just yoke
       Laid on our necks. Remember with what mild
       And gracious temper he both heard, and judged,
       Without wrath or reviling; we expected
       Immediate dissolution, which we thought
1050   Was meant by death that day; when lo! to thee
       Pains only in child-bearing were foretold,
       And bringing forth; soon recompensed with joy,
       Fruit of thy womb: On me the curse aslope
       Glanced on the ground; with labour I must earn
1055   My bread; what harm? Idleness had been worse;
       My labour will sustain me; and, lest cold
       Or heat should injure us, his timely care
       Hath, unbesought, provided; and his hands
       Clothed us unworthy, pitying while he judged;
1060   How much more, if we pray him, will his ear
       Be open, and his heart to pity incline,
       And teach us further by what means to shun
       The inclement seasons, rain, ice, hail, and snow!
       Which now the sky, with various face, begins
1065   To show us in this mountain; while the winds
       Blow moist and keen, shattering the graceful locks
       Of these fair spreading trees; which bids us seek
       Some better shroud, some better warmth to cherish
       Our limbs benummed, ere this diurnal star
1070   Leave cold the night, how we his gathered beams
       Reflected may with matter sere foment;
       Or, by collision of two bodies, grind

The air attrite to fire; as late the clouds
Justling, or pushed with winds, rude in their shock,
1075   Tine the slant lightning; whose thwart flame, driven down
Kindles the gummy bark of fir or pine;
And sends a comfortable heat from far,
Which might supply the sun: Such fire to use,
And what may else be remedy or cure
1080   To evils which our own misdeeds have wrought,
He will instruct us praying, and of grace
Beseeching him; so as we need not fear
To pass commodiously this life, sustained
By him with many comforts, till we end
1085   In dust, our final rest and native home.
What better can we do, than, to the place
Repairing where he judged us, prostrate fall
Before him reverent; and there confess
Humbly our faults, and pardon beg; with tears
1090   Watering the ground, and with our sighs the air
Frequenting, sent from hearts contrite, in sign
Of sorrow unfeigned, and humiliation meek.
Undoubtedly he will relent, and turn
From his displeasure; in whose look serene,
1095   When angry most he seemed and most severe,
What else but favour, grace, and mercy, shone?
So spake our father penitent; nor Eve
Felt less remorse: they, forthwith to the place
Repairing where he judged them, prostrate fell
1100   Before him reverent; and both confessed
Humbly their faults, and pardon begged; with tears
Watering the ground, and with their sighs the air
Frequenting, sent from hearts contrite, in sign
Of sorrow unfeigned, and humiliation meek.

BOOK XI

THE ARGUMENT

The Son of God presents to his Father the prayers of our first parents now repenting, and intercedes for them: God accepts them, but declares that they must no longer abide I Paradise; sends Michael with a band of Cherubim

5   to dispossess them; but first to reveal to Adam future things: Michael's coming down. Adam shows to Eve certain ominous signs; he denounces their departure. Eve's lamentation. Adam pleads, but submits; the angel leads him up to a high hill, sets before him in vision what shall

10   happen till the Flood.

Thus they, in lowliest plight, repentant stood
Praying; for from the mercy-seat above
Prevenient grace descending had removed
The stony from their hearts, and made new flesh
5   Regenerate grow instead; that sighs now breathed
Unutterable; which the Spirit of prayer
Inspired, and winged for Heav'n with speedier flight
Than loudest oratory: Yet their port
Not of mean suitors; nor important less
10   Seemed their petition, than when the ancient pair
In fables old, less ancient yet than these,

Deucalion and chaste Pyrrha, to restore
The race of mankind drowned, before the shrine
Of Themis stood devout. To Heav'n their prayers
15   Flew up, nor missed the way, by envious winds
Blown vagabond or frustrate: in they passed
Dimensionless through heav'nly doors; then clad
With incense, where the golden altar fumed,
By their great intercessor, came in sight
20   Before the Father's throne: them the glad Son
Presenting, thus to intercede began.
See Father, what first-fruits on earth are sprung
From thy implanted grace in Man; these sighs
And prayers, which in this golden censer mixed
25   With incense, I thy priest before thee bring;
Fruits of more pleasing savour, from thy seed
Sown with contrition in his heart, than those
Which, his own hand manuring, all the trees
Of Paradise could have produced, ere fallen
30   From innocence. Now therefore, bend thine ear
To supplication; hear his sighs, though mute;
Unskilful with what words to pray, let me
Interpret for him; me, his advocate
And propitiation; all his works on me,
35   Good, or not good, ingraft; my merit those
Shall perfect, and for these my death shall pay.
Accept me; and, in me, from these receive
The smell of peace toward mankind: let him live
Before thee reconciled, at least his days
40   Numbered, though sad; till death, his doom, (which I
To mitigate thus plead, not to reverse,)
To better life shall yield him: where with me
All my redeemed may dwell in joy and bliss;
Made one with me, as I with thee am one.
45   To whom the Father, without cloud, serene.

All thy request for Man, accepted Son,
Obtain; all thy request was my decree:
But, longer in that Paradise to dwell,
The law I gave to Nature him forbids:
50   Those pure immortal elements, that know,
No gross, no unharmonious mixture foul,
Eject him, tainted now; and purge him off,
As a distemper, gross, to air as gross,
And mortal food; as may dispose him best
55   For dissolution wrought by sin, that first
Distempered all things, and of incorrupt
Corrupted. I, at first, with two fair gifts
Created him endowed; with happiness,
And immortality: that fondly lost,
60   This other served but to eternize woe;
Till I provided death: so death becomes
His final remedy; and, after life,
Tried in sharp tribulation, and refined
By faith and faithful works, to second life,
65   Waked in the renovation of the just,
Resigns him up with Heav'n and Earth renewed.
But let us call to synod all the Blest,
Through Heav'n's wide bounds: from them I will not hide
My judgements; how with mankind I proceed,
70   As how with peccant Angels late they saw,
And in their state, though firm, stood more confirmed.
He ended, and the Son gave signal high
To the bright minister that watched; he blew
His trumpet, heard in Oreb since perhaps
75   When God descended, and perhaps once more
To sound at general doom. The angelic blast
Filled all the regions: from their blissful bowers
Of amarantine shade, fountain or spring,
By the waters of life, where'er they sat

80   In fellowships of joy, the sons of light
          Hasted, resorting to the summons high;
          And took their seats; till from his throne supreme
          The Almighty thus pronounced his sovran will.
          O Sons, like one of us Man is become

85   To know both good and evil, since his taste
          Of that defended fruit; but let him boast
          His knowledge of good lost, and evil got;
          Happier! had it sufficed him to have known
          Good by itself, and evil not at all.

90   He sorrows now, repents, and prays contrite,
          My motions in him; longer than they move,
          His heart I know, how variable and vain,
          Self-left. Lest therefore his now bolder hand
          Reach also of the tree of life, and eat,

95   And live for ever, dream at least to live
          For ever, to remove him I decree,
          And send him from the garden forth to till
          The ground whence he was taken, fitter soil.
          Michael, this my behest have thou in charge;

100   Take to thee from among the Cherubim
          Thy choice of flaming warriours, lest the Fiend,
          Or in behalf of Man, or to invade
          Vacant possession, some new trouble raise:
          Haste thee, and from the Paradise of God

105   Without remorse drive out the sinful pair;
          From hallowed ground the unholy; and denounce
          To them, and to their progeny, from thence
          Perpetual banishment. Yet, lest they faint
          At the sad sentence rigorously urged,

110   (For I behold them softened, and with tears
          Bewailing their excess,) all terrour hide.
          If patiently thy bidding they obey,

Dismiss them not disconsolate; reveal
To Adam what shall come in future days,
115   As I shall thee enlighten; intermix
My covenant in the Woman's seed renewed;
So send them forth, though sorrowing, yet in peace:
And on the east side of the garden place,
Where entrance up from Eden easiest climbs,
120   Cherubic watch; and of a sword the flame
Wide-waving; all approach far off to fright,
And guard all passage to the tree of life:
Lest Paradise a receptacle prove
To Spirits foul, and all my trees their prey;
125   With whose stolen fruit Man once more to delude.
He ceased; and the arch-angelic Power prepared
For swift descent; with him the cohort bright
Of watchful Cherubim: four faces each
Had, like a double Janus; all their shape
130   Spangled with eyes more numerous than those
Of Argus, and more wakeful than to drowse,
Charmed with Arcadian pipe, the pastoral reed
Of Hermes, or his opiate rod. Mean while,
To re-salute the world with sacred light,
135   Leucothea waked; and with fresh dews embalmed
The earth; when Adam and first matron Eve
Had ended now their orisons, and found
Strength added from above; new hope to spring
Out of despair; joy, but with fear yet linked;
140   Which thus to Eve his welcome words renewed.
Eve, easily my faith admit, that all
The good which we enjoy from Heav'n descends;
But, that from us aught should ascend to Heav'n
So prevalent as to concern the mind
145   Of God high-blest, or to incline his will,
Hard to belief may seem; yet this will prayer

Or one short sigh of human breath, upborne
Even to the seat of God. For since I sought
By prayer the offended Deity to appease;
150 Kneeled, and before him humbled all my heart;
Methought I saw him placable and mild,
Bending his ear; persuasion in me grew
That I was heard with favour; peace returned
Home to my breast, and to my memory
155 His promise, that thy seed shall bruise our foe;
Which, then not minded in dismay, yet now
Assures me that the bitterness of death
Is past, and we shall live. Whence hail to thee,
Eve rightly called, mother of all mankind,
160 Mother of all things living, since by thee
Man is to live; and all things live for Man.
To whom thus Eve with sad demeanour meek.
Ill-worthy I such title should belong
To me transgressor; who, for thee ordained
165 A help, became thy snare; to me reproach
Rather belongs, distrust, and all dispraise:
But infinite in pardon was my Judge,
That I, who first brought death on all, am graced
The source of life; next favourable thou,
170 Who highly thus to entitle me vouchsaf'st,
Far other name deserving. But the field
To labour calls us, now with sweat imposed,
Though after sleepless night; for see! the morn,
All unconcerned with our unrest, begins
175 Her rosy progress smiling: let us forth;
I never from thy side henceforth to stray,
Where'er our day's work lies, though now enjoined
Laborious, till day droop; while here we dwell,
What can be toilsome in these pleasant walks?
180 Here let us live, though in fallen state, content.

So spake, so wished much humbled Eve; but Fate
Subscribed not: Nature first gave signs, impressed
On bird, beast, air; air suddenly eclipsed,
After short blush of morn; nigh in her sight
185 The bird of Jove, stooped from his aery tour,
Two birds of gayest plume before him drove;
Down from a hill the beast that reigns in woods,
First hunter then, pursued a gentle brace,
Goodliest of all the forest, hart and hind;
190 Direct to the eastern gate was bent their flight.
Adam observed, and with his eye the chase
Pursuing, not unmoved, to Eve thus spake.
O Eve, some further change awaits us nigh,
Which Heav'n, by these mute signs in Nature, shows
195 Forerunners of his purpose; or to warn
Us, haply too secure, of our discharge
From penalty, because from death released
Some days: how long, and what till then our life,
Who knows? or more than this, that we are dust,
200 And thither must return, and be no more?
Why else this double object in our sight
Of flight pursued in the air, and o'er the ground,
One way the self-same hour? why in the east
Darkness ere day's mid-course, and morning-light
205 More orient in yon western cloud, that draws
O'er the blue firmament a radiant white,
And slow descends with something heav'nly fraught?
He erred not; for by this the heav'nly bands
Down from a sky of jasper lighted now
210 In Paradise, and on a hill made halt;
A glorious apparition, had not doubt
And carnal fear that day dimmed Adam's eye.
Not that more glorious, when the Angels met
Jacob in Mahanaim, where he saw

215   The field pavilioned with his guardians bright;
        Nor that, which on the flaming mount appeared
        In Dothan, covered with a camp of fire,
        Against the Syrian king, who to surprise
        One man, assassin-like, had levied war,
220   War unproclaimed. The princely Hierarch
        In their bright stand there left his Powers, to seize
        Possession of the garden; he alone,
        To find where Adam sheltered, took his way,
        Not unperceived of Adam; who to Eve,
225   While the great visitant approached, thus spake.
        Eve, now expect great tidings, which perhaps
        Of us will soon determine, or impose
        New laws to be observed; for I descry,
        From yonder blazing cloud that veils the hill,
230   One of the heav'nly host; and, by his gait,
        None of the meanest; some great Potentate
        Or of the Thrones above; such majesty
        Invests him coming! yet not terrible,
        That I should fear; nor sociably mild,
235   As Raphael, that I should much confide;
        But solemn and sublime; whom not to offend,
        With reverence I must meet, and thou retire.
        He ended: and the Arch-Angel soon drew nigh,
        Not in his shape celestial, but as man
240   Clad to meet man; over his lucid arms
        A military vest of purple flowed,
        Livelier than Meliboean, or the grain
        Of Sarra, worn by kings and heroes old
        In time of truce; Iris had dipt the woof;
245   His starry helm unbuckled showed him prime
        In manhood where youth ended; by his side,
        As in a glistering zodiac, hung the sword,

Satan's dire dread; and in his hand the spear.
Adam bowed low; he, kingly, from his state
250   Inclined not, but his coming thus declared.
Adam, Heav'n's high behest no preface needs:
Sufficient that thy prayers are heard; and Death,
Then due by sentence when thou didst transgress,
Defeated of his seizure many days
255   Given thee of grace; wherein thou mayest repent,
And one bad act with many deeds well done
Mayest cover: Well may then thy Lord, appeased,
Redeem thee quite from Death's rapacious claim;
But longer in this Paradise to dwell
260   Permits not: to remove thee I am come,
And send thee from the garden forth to till
The ground whence thou wast taken, fitter soil.
He added not; for Adam at the news
Heart-struck with chilling gripe of sorrow stood,
265   That all his senses bound; Eve, who unseen
Yet all had heard, with audible lament
Discovered soon the place of her retire.
O unexpected stroke, worse than of Death!
Must I thus leave thee Paradise? thus leave
270   Thee, native soil! these happy walks and shades,
Fit haunt of Gods? where I had hope to spend,
Quiet though sad, the respite of that day
That must be mortal to us both. O flowers,
That never will in other climate grow,
275   My early visitation, and my last
At even, which I bred up with tender hand
From the first opening bud, and gave ye names,
Who now shall rear ye to the sun, or rank
Your tribes, and water from the ambrosial fount?
280   Thee lastly, nuptial bower! by me adorned
With what to sight or smell was sweet! from thee

How shall I part, and whither wander down
Into a lower world; to this obscure
And wild, how shall we breathe in other air
285   Less pure, accustomed to immortal fruits?
Whom thus the Angel interrupted mild.
Lament not, Eve, but patiently resign
What justly thou hast lost, nor set thy heart,
Thus over-fond, on that which is not thine:
290   Thy going is not lonely; with thee goes
Thy husband; whom to follow thou art bound;
Where he abides, think there thy native soil.
Adam, by this from the cold sudden damp
Recovering, and his scattered spirits returned,
295   To Michael thus his humble words addressed.
Celestial, whether among the Thrones, or named
Of them the highest; for such of shape may seem
Prince above princes! gently hast thou told
Thy message, which might else in telling wound,
300   And in performing end us; what besides
Of sorrow, and dejection, and despair,
Our frailty can sustain, thy tidings bring,
Departure from this happy place, our sweet
Recess, and only consolation left
305   Familiar to our eyes! all places else
Inhospitable appear, and desolate;
Nor knowing us, nor known: And, if by prayer
Incessant I could hope to change the will
Of Him who all things can, I would not cease
310   To weary him with my assiduous cries:
But prayer against his absolute decree
No more avails than breath against the wind,
Blown stifling back on him that breathes it forth:
Therefore to his great bidding I submit.
315   This most afflicts me, that, departing hence,

As from his face I shall be hid, deprived
His blessed countenance: Here I could frequent
With worship place by place where he vouchsafed
Presence Divine; and to my sons relate,
320   On this mount he appeared; under this tree
Stood visible; among these pines his voice
I heard; here with him at this fountain talked:
So many grateful altars I would rear
Of grassy turf, and pile up every stone
325   Of lustre from the brook, in memory,
Or monument to ages; and theron
Offer sweet-smelling gums, and fruits, and flowers:
In yonder nether world where shall I seek
His bright appearances, or foot-step trace?
330   For though I fled him angry, yet recalled
To life prolonged and promised race, I now
Gladly behold though but his utmost skirts
Of glory; and far off his steps adore.
To whom thus Michael with regard benign.
335   Adam, thou knowest Heav'n his, and all the Earth;
Not this rock only; his Omnipresence fills
Land, sea, and air, and every kind that lives,
Fomented by his virtual power and warmed:
All the earth he gave thee to possess and rule,
340   No despicable gift; surmise not then
His presence to these narrow bounds confined
Of Paradise, or Eden: this had been
Perhaps thy capital seat, from whence had spread
All generations; and had hither come
345   From all the ends of the earth, to celebrate
And reverence thee, their great progenitor.
But this pre-eminence thou hast lost, brought down
To dwell on even ground now with thy sons:
Yet doubt not but in valley, and in plain,

350	God is, as here; and will be found alike
	Present; and of his presence many a sign
	Still following thee, still compassing thee round
	With goodness and paternal love, his face
	Express, and of his steps the track divine.
355	Which that thou mayest believe, and be confirmed
	Ere thou from hence depart; know, I am sent
	To show thee what shall come in future days
	To thee, and to thy offspring: good with bad
	Expect to hear; supernal grace contending
360	With sinfulness of men; thereby to learn
	True patience, and to temper joy with fear
	And pious sorrow; equally inured
	By moderation either state to bear,
	Prosperous or adverse: so shalt thou lead
365	Safest thy life, and best prepared endure
	Thy mortal passage when it comes.—Ascend
	This hill; let Eve (for I have drenched her eyes)
	Here sleep below; while thou to foresight wakest;
	As once thou slepest, while she to life was formed.
370	To whom thus Adam gratefully replied.
	Ascend, I follow thee, safe Guide, the path
	Thou leadest me; and to the hand of Heav'n submit,
	However chastening; to the evil turn
	My obvious breast; arming to overcome
375	By suffering, and earn rest from labour won,
	If so I may attain.—So both ascend
	In the visions of God. It was a hill,
	Of Paradise the highest; from whose top
	The hemisphere of earth, in clearest ken,
380	Stretched out to the amplest reach of prospect lay.
	Not higher that hill, nor wider looking round,
	Whereon, for different cause, the Tempter set

Our second Adam, in the wilderness;
To show him all Earth's kingdoms, and their glory.
385   His eye might there command wherever stood
City of old or modern fame, the seat
Of mightiest empire, from the destined walls
Of Cambalu, seat of Cathaian Can,
And Samarchand by Oxus, Temir's throne,
390   To Paquin of Sinaean kings; and thence
To Agra and Lahor of great Mogul,
Down to the golden Chersonese; or where
The Persian in Ecbatan sat, or since
In Hispahan; or where the Russian Ksar
395   In Mosco; or the Sultan in Bizance,
Turchestan-born; nor could his eye not ken
The empire of Negus to his utmost port
Ercoco, and the less maritim kings
Mombaza, and Quiloa, and Melind,
400   And Sofala, thought Ophir, to the realm
Of Congo, and Angola farthest south;
Or thence from Niger flood to Atlas mount
The kingdoms of Almansor, Fez and Sus,
Morocco, and Algiers, and Tremisen;
405   On Europe thence, and where Rome was to sway
The world: in spirit perhaps he also saw
Rich Mexico, the seat of Montezume,
And Cusco in Peru, the richer seat
Of Atabalipa; and yet unspoiled
410   Guiana, whose great city Geryon's sons
Call El Dorado. But to nobler sights
Michael from Adam's eyes the film removed,
Which that false fruit that promised clearer sight
Had bred; then purged with euphrasy and rue
415   The visual nerve, for he had much to see;
And from the well of life three drops instilled.

So deep the power of these ingredients pierced,
Even to the inmost seat of mental sight,
That Adam, now enforced to close his eyes,
420   Sunk down, and all his spirits became entranced;
But him the gentle Angel by the hand
Soon raised, and his attention thus recalled.
Adam, now ope thine eyes; and first behold
The effects, which thy original crime hath wrought
425   In some to spring from thee; who never touched
The excepted tree; nor with the snake conspired;
Nor sinned thy sin; yet from that sin derive
Corruption, to bring forth more violent deeds.
His eyes he opened, and beheld a field,
430   Part arable and tilth, whereon were sheaves
New reaped; the other part sheep-walks and folds;
I' the midst an altar as the land-mark stood,
Rustick, of grassy sord; thither anon
A sweaty reaper from his tillage brought
435   First fruits, the green ear, and the yellow sheaf,
Unculled, as came to hand; a shepherd next,
More meek, came with the firstlings of his flock,
Choicest and best; then, sacrificing, laid
The inwards and their fat, with incense strowed,
440   On the cleft wood, and all due rights performed:
His offering soon propitious fire from Heav'n
Consumed with nimble glance, and grateful steam;
The other's not, for his was not sincere;
Whereat he inly raged, and, as they talked,
445   Smote him into the midriff with a stone
That beat out life; he fell; and, deadly pale,
Groaned out his soul with gushing blood effused.
Much at that sight was Adam in his heart
Dismayed, and thus in haste to the Angel cried.
450   O Teacher, some great mischief hath befallen

To that meek man, who well had sacrificed;
Is piety thus and pure devotion paid?
To whom Michael thus, he also moved, replied.
These two are brethren, Adam, and to come
455   Out of thy loins; the unjust the just hath slain,
For envy that his brother's offering found
From Heav'n acceptance; but the bloody fact
Will be avenged; and the other's faith, approved,
Lose no reward; though here thou see him die,
460   Rolling in dust and gore. To which our sire.
Alas! both for the deed, and for the cause!
But have I now seen Death? Is this the way
I must return to native dust? O sight
Of terror, foul and ugly to behold,
465   Horrid to think, how horrible to feel!
To whom thus Michael. Death thou hast seen
In his first shape on Man; but many shapes
Of Death, and many are the ways that lead
To his grim cave, all dismal; yet to sense
470   More terrible at the entrance, than within.
Some, as thou sawest, by violent stroke shall die;
By fire, flood, famine, by intemperance more
In meats and drinks, which on the earth shall bring
Diseases dire, of which a monstrous crew
475   Before thee shall appear; that thou mayest know
What misery the inabstinence of Eve
Shall bring on Men. Immediately a place
Before his eyes appeared, sad, noisome, dark;
A lazar-house it seemed; wherein were laid
480   Numbers of all diseased; all maladies
Of ghastly spasm, or racking torture, qualms
Of heart-sick agony, all feverous kinds,
Convulsions, epilepsies, fierce catarrhs,
Intestine stone and ulcer, colic-pangs,

485   Demoniac frenzy, moping melancholy,
        And moon-struck madness, pining atrophy,
        Marasmus, and wide-wasting pestilence,
        Dropsies, and asthmas, and joint-racking rheums.
        Dire was the tossing, deep the groans; Despair
490   Tended the sick busiest from couch to couch;
        And over them triumphant Death his dart
        Shook, but delayed to strike, though oft invoked
        With vows, as their chief good, and final hope.
        Sight so deform what heart of rock could long
495   Dry-eyed behold? Adam could not, but wept,
        Though not of woman born; compassion quelled
        His best of man, and gave him up to tears
        A space, till firmer thoughts restrained excess;
        And, scarce recovering words, his plaint renewed.
500   O miserable mankind, to what fall
        Degraded, to what wretched state reserved!
        Better end here unborn. Why is life given
        To be thus wrested from us? rather, why
        Obtruded on us thus? who, if we knew
505   What we receive, would either no accept
        Life offered, or soon beg to lay it down;
        Glad to be so dismissed in peace. Can thus
        The image of God in Man, created once
        So goodly and erect, though faulty since,
510   To such unsightly sufferings be debased
        Under inhuman pains? Why should not Man,
        Retaining still divine similitude
        In part, from such deformities be free,
        And, for his Maker's image sake, exempt?
515   Their Maker's image, answered Michael, then
        Forsook them, when themselves they vilified
        To serve ungoverned Appetite; and took

His image whom they served, a brutish vice,
Inductive mainly to the sin of Eve.
520 Therefore so abject is their punishment,
Disfiguring not God's likeness, but their own;
Or if his likeness, by themselves defaced;
While they pervert pure Nature's healthful rules
To loathsome sickness; worthily, since they
525 God's image did not reverence in themselves.
I yield it just, said Adam, and submit.
But is there yet no other way, besides
These painful passages, how we may come
To death, and mix with our connatural dust?
530 There is, said Michael, if thou well observe
The rule of *Not too much*; by temperance taught,
In what thou eatest and drinkest; seeking from thence
Due nourishment, not gluttonous delight,
Till many years over thy head return:
535 So mayest thou live; till, like ripe fruit, thou drop
Into thy mother's lap; or be with ease
Gathered, nor harshly plucked; for death mature:
This is Old Age; but then, thou must outlive
Thy youth, thy strength, thy beauty; which will change
540 To withered, weak, and gray; thy senses then,
Obtuse, all taste of pleasure must forego,
To what thou hast; and, for the air of youth,
Hopeful and cheerful, in thy blood will reign
A melancholy damp of cold and dry
545 To weigh thy spirits down, and last consume
The balm of life. To whom our ancestor.
Henceforth I fly not death, nor would prolong
Life much; bent rather, how I may be quit,
Fairest and easiest, of this cumbrous charge;
550 Which I must keep till my appointed day
Of rendering up, and patiently attend

My dissolution. Michael replied.
Nor love thy life, nor hate; but what thou livest
Live well; how long, or short, permit to Heav'n:
555　And now prepare thee for another sight.
He looked, and saw a spacious plain, whereon
Were tents of various hue; by some, were herds
Of cattle grazing; others, whence the sound
Of instruments, that made melodious chime,
560　Was heard, of harp and organ; and, who moved
Their stops and chords, was seen; his volant touch,
Instinct through all proportions, low and high,
Fled and pursued transverse the resonant fugue.
In other part stood one who, at the forge
565　Labouring, two massy clods of iron and brass
Had melted, (whether found where casual fire
Had wasted woods on mountain or in vale,
Down to the veins of earth; thence gliding hot
To some cave's mouth; or whether washed by stream
570　From underground;) the liquid ore he drained
Into fit moulds prepared; from which he formed
First his own tools; then, what might else be wrought
Fusil or graven in metal. After these,
But on the hither side, a different sort
575　From the high neighbouring hills, which was their seat,
Down to the plain descended; by their guise
Just men they seemed, and all their study bent
To worship God aright, and know his works
Not hid; nor those things last, which might preserve
580　Freedom and peace to Men; they on the plain
Long had not walked, when from the tents, behold!
A bevy of fair women, richly gay
In gems and wanton dress; to the harp they sung
Soft amorous ditties, and in dance came on:
585　The men, though grave, eyed them; and let their eyes

Rove without rein; till, in the amorous net
Fast caught, they liked; and each his liking chose;
And now of love they treat, till the evening-star,
Love's harbinger, appeared; then, all in heat
590 They light the nuptial torch, and bid invoke
Hymen, then first to marriage rites invoked:
With feast and music all the tents resound.
Such happy interview, and fair event
Of love and youth not lost, songs, garlands, flowers,
595 And charming symphonies, attached the heart
Of Adam, soon inclined to admit delight,
The bent of nature; which he thus expressed.
True opener of mine eyes, prime Angel blest;
Much better seems this vision, and more hope
600 Of peaceful days portends, than those two past;
Those were of hate and death, or pain much worse;
Here Nature seems fulfilled in all her ends.
To whom thus Michael. Judge not what is best
By pleasure, though to nature seeming meet;
605 Created, as thou art, to nobler end
Holy and pure, conformity divine.
Those tents thou sawest so pleasant, were the tents
Of wickedness, wherein shall dwell his race
Who slew his brother; studious they appear
610 Of arts that polish life, inventers rare;
Unmindful of their Maker, though his Spirit
Taught them; but they his gifts acknowledged none.
Yet they a beauteous offspring shall beget;
For that fair female troop thou sawest, that seemed
615 Of Goddesses, so blithe, so smooth, so gay,
Yet empty of all good wherein consists
Woman's domestic honour and chief praise;
Bred only and completed to the taste
Of lustful appetence, to sing, to dance,

620 To dress, and troll the tongue, and roll the eye:
To these that sober race of men, whose lives
Religious titled them the sons of God,
Shall yield up all their virtue, all their fame
Ignobly, to the trains and to the smiles
625 Of these fair atheists; and now swim in joy,
Erelong to swim at large; and laugh, for which
The world erelong a world of tears must weep.
To whom thus Adam, of short joy bereft.
O pity and shame, that they, who to live well
630 Entered so fair, should turn aside to tread
Paths indirect, or in the mid way faint!
But still I see the tenor of Man's woe
Holds on the same, from Woman to begin.
From Man's effeminate slackness it begins,
635 Said the Angel, who should better hold his place
By wisdom, and superior gifts received.
But now prepare thee for another scene.
He looked, and saw wide territory spread
Before him, towns, and rural works between;
640 Cities of men with lofty gates and towers,
Concourse in arms, fierce faces threatening war,
Giants of mighty bone and bold emprise;
Part wield their arms, part curb the foaming steed,
Single or in array of battle ranged
645 Both horse and foot, nor idly mustering stood;
One way a band select from forage drives
A herd of beeves, fair oxen and fair kine,
From a fat meadow ground; or fleecy flock,
Ewes and their bleating lambs over the plain,
650 Their booty; scarce with life the shepherds fly,
But call in aid, which makes a bloody fray;
With cruel tournament the squadrons join;

Where cattle pastured late, now scattered lies
With carcasses and arms the ensanguined field,
655 Deserted: Others to a city strong
Lay siege, encamped; by battery, scale, and mine,
Assaulting; others from the wall defend
With dart and javelin, stones, and sulphurous fire;
On each hand slaughter, and gigantic deeds.
660 In other part the sceptred heralds call
To council, in the city-gates; anon
Gray-headed men and grave, with warriors mixed,
Assemble, and harangues are heard; but soon,
In factious opposition; till at last,
665 Of middle age one rising, eminent
In wise deport, spake much of right and wrong,
Of justice, or religion, truth, and peace,
And judgement from above: him old and young
Exploded, and had seized with violent hands,
670 Had not a cloud descending snatched him thence
Unseen amid the throng: so violence
Proceeded, and oppression, and sword-law,
Through all the plain, and refuge none was found.
Adam was all in tears, and to his guide
675 Lamenting turned full sad; O! what are these,
Death's ministers, not men? who thus deal death
Inhumanly to men, and multiply
Ten thousandfold the sin of him who slew
His brother: for of whom such massacre
680 Make they, but of their brethren; men of men
But who was that just man, whom had not Heav'n
Rescued, had in his righteousness been lost?
To whom thus Michael. These are the product
Of those ill-mated marriages thou sawest;
685 Where good with bad were matched, who of themselves
Abhor to join; and, by imprudence mixed,

Produce prodigious births of body or mind.
Such were these giants, men of high renown;
For in those days might only shall be admired,
690 And valour and heroic virtue called;
To overcome in battle, and subdue
Nations, and bring home spoils with infinite
Man-slaughter, shall be held the highest pitch
Of human glory; and for glory done
695 Of triumph, to be styled great conquerors
Patrons of mankind, Gods, and sons of Gods;
Destroyers rightlier called, and plagues of men.
Thus fame shall be achieved, renown on earth;
And what most merits fame, in silence hid.
700 But he, the seventh from thee, whom thou beheldst
The only righteous in a world preverse,
And therefore hated, therefore so beset
With foes, for daring single to be just,
And utter odious truth, that God would come
705 To judge them with his Saints; him the Most High
Rapt in a balmy cloud with winged steeds
Did, as thou sawest, receive, to walk with God
High in salvation and the climes of bliss,
Exempt from death; to show thee what reward
710 Awaits the good; the rest what punishment;
Which now direct thine eyes and soon behold.
He looked, and saw the face of things quite changed;
The brazen throat of war had ceased to roar;
All now was turned to jollity and game,
715 To luxury and riot, feast and dance;
Marrying or prostituting, as befel,
Rape or adultery, where passing fair
Allured them; thence from cups to civil broils.
At length a reverend sire among them came,
720 And of their doings great dislike declared,

And testified against their ways; he oft
Frequented their assemblies, whereso met,
Triumphs or festivals; and to them preached
Conversion and repentance, as to souls
725 In prison, under judgements imminent:
But all in vain: which when he saw, he ceased
Contending, and removed his tents far off;
Then, from the mountain hewing timber tall,
Began to build a vessel of huge bulk;
730 Measured by cubit, length, and breadth, and heighth;
Smeared round with pitch; and in the side a door
Contrived; and of provisions laid in large,
For man and beast: when lo, a wonder strange!
Of every beast, and bird, and insect small,
735 Came sevens, and pairs; and entered in as taught
Their order: last the sire and his three sons,
With their four wives; and God made fast the door.
Mean while the south-wind rose, and, with black wings
Wide-hovering, all the clouds together drove
740 From under Heav'n; the hills to their supply
Vapour, and exhalation dusk and moist,
Sent up amain; and now the thickened sky
Like a dark ceiling stood; down rushed the rain
Impetuous; and continued, till the earth
745 No more was seen: the floating vessel swum
Uplifted, and secure with beaked prow
Rode tilting o'er the waves; all dwellings else
Flood overwhelmed, and them with all their pomp
Deep under water rolled; sea covered sea,
750 Sea without shore; and in their palaces,
Where luxury late reigned, sea-monsters whelped
And stabled; of mankind, so numerous late,
All left, in one small bottom swum imbarked.
How didst thou grieve then, Adam, to behold

755   The end of all thy offspring, end so sad,
            Depopulation! Thee another flood,
            Of tears and sorrow a flood, thee also drowned,
            And sunk thee as thy sons; till, gently reared
            By the Angel, on thy feet thou stoodest at last,
760   Though comfortless; as when a father mourns
            His children, all in view destroyed at once;
            And scarce to the Angel utter'dst thus thy plaint.
            O visions ill foreseen! Better had I
            Lived ignorant of future! so had borne
765   My part of evil only, each day's lot
            Enough to bear; those now, that were dispensed
            The burden of many ages, on me light
            At once, by my foreknowledge gaining birth
            Abortive, to torment me ere their being,
770   With thought that they must be. Let no man seek
            Henceforth to be foretold, what shall befall
            Him or his children; evil he may be sure,
            Which neither his foreknowing can prevent;
            And he the future evil shall no less
775   In apprehension than in substance feel,
            Grievous to bear: but that care now is past,
            Man is not whom to warn: those few escaped
            Famine and anguish will at last consume,
            Wandering that watery desert: I had hope,
780   When violence was ceased, and war on earth,
            All would have then gone well; peace would have crowned
            With length of happy days the race of Man;
            But I was far deceived; for now I see
            Peace to corrupt no less than war to waste.
785   How comes it thus? unfold, celestial Guide,
            And whether here the race of Man will end.
            To whom thus Michael. Those, whom last thou sawest

In triumph and luxurious wealth, are they
First seen in acts of prowess eminent
790 And great exploits, but of true virtue void;
Who, having spilt much blood, and done much wast
Subduing nations, and achieved thereby
Fame in the world, high titles, and rich prey;
Shall change their course to pleasure, ease, and sloth,
795 Surfeit, and lust; till wantonness and pride
Raise out of friendship hostile deeds in peace.
The conquered also, and enslaved by war,
Shall, with their freedom lost, all virtue lose
And fear of God; from whom their piety feigned
800 In sharp contest of battle found no aid
Against invaders; therefore, cooled in zeal,
Thenceforth shall practice how to live secure,
Worldly or dissolute, on what their lords
Shall leave them to enjoy; for the earth shall bear
805 More than enough, that temperance may be tried:
So all shall turn degenerate, all depraved;
Justice and temperance, truth and faith, forgot;
One man except, the only son of light
In a dark age, against example good,
810 Against allurement, custom, and a world
Offended: fearless of reproach and scorn,
Or violence, he of their wicked ways
Shall them admonish; and before them set
The paths of righteousness, how much more safe
815 And full of peace; denouncing wrath to come
On their impenitence; and shall return
Of them derided, but of God observed
The one just man alive; by his command
Shall build a wondrous ark, as thou beheldst,
820 To save himself, and household, from amidst
A world devote to universal wrack.

No sooner he, with them of man and beast
Select for life, shall in the ark be lodged,
And sheltered round; but all the cataracts
825   Of Heav'n set open on the Earth shall pour
Rain, day and night; all fountains of the deep,
Broke up, shall heave the ocean to usurp
Beyond all bounds; till inundation rise
Above the highest hills: Then shall this mount
830   Of Paradise by might of waves be moved
Out of his place, pushed by the horned flood,
With all his verdure spoiled, and trees adrift,
Down the great river to the opening gulf,
And there take root an island salt and bare,
835   The haunt of seals, and orcs, and sea-mews' clang:
To teach thee that God attributes to place
No sanctity, if none be thither brought
By men who there frequent, or therein dwell.
And now, what further shall ensue, behold.
840   He looked, and saw the ark hull on the flood,
Which now abated; for the clouds were fled,
Driven by a keen north-wind, that, blowing dry,
Wrinkled the face of deluge, as decayed;
And the clear sun on his wide watery glass
845   Gazed hot, and of the fresh wave largely drew,
As after thirst; which made their flowing shrink
From standing lake to tripping ebb, that stole
With soft foot towards the deep; who now had stopt
His sluices, as the Heav'n his windows shut.
850   The ark no more now floats, but seems on ground,
Fast on the top of some high mountain fixed.
And now the tops of hills, as rocks, appear;
With clamour thence the rapid currents drive,
Towards the retreating sea, their furious tide.
855   Forthwith from out the ark a raven flies,

And after him, the surer messenger,
A dove sent forth once and again to spy
Green tree or ground, whereon his foot may light:
The second time returning, in his bill
860   An olive-leaf he brings, pacific sign:
Anon dry ground appears, and from his ark
The ancient sire descends, with all his train;
Then with uplifted hands, and eyes devout,
Grateful to Heav'n, over his head beholds
865   A dewy cloud, and in the cloud a bow
Conspicuous with three lifted colours gay,
Betokening peace from God, and covenant new.
Whereat the heart of Adam, erst so sad,
Greatly rejoiced; and thus his joy broke forth.
870   O thou, who future things canst represent
As present, heav'nly Instructor! I revive
At this last sight; assured that Man shall live,
With all the creatures, and their seed preserve.
Far less I now lament for one whole world
875   Of wicked sons destroyed, than I rejoice
For one man found so perfect, and so just,
That God vouchsafes to raise another world
From him, and all his anger to forget.
But say, what mean those coloured streaks in Heav'n
880   Distended, as the brow of God appeased?
Or serve they, as a flowery verge, to bind
The fluid skirts of that same watery cloud,
Lest it again dissolve, and shower the earth?
To whom the Arch-Angel. Dextrously thou aimest;
885   So willingly doth God remit his ire,
Though late repenting him of Man depraved;
Grieved at his heart, when looking down he saw
The whole earth filled with violence, and all flesh
Corrupting each their way; yet, those removed,

890 Such grace shall one just man find in his sight,
   That he relents, not to blot out mankind;
   And makes a covenant never to destroy
   The earth again by flood; nor let the sea
   Surpass his bounds; nor rain to drown the world,
895 With man therein or beast; but, when he brings
   Over the earth a cloud, will therein set
   His triple-coloured bow, whereon to look,
   And call to mind his covenant: Day and night,
   Seed-time and harvest, heat and hoary frost,
900 Shall hold their course; till fire purge all things new,
   Both Heav'n and Earth, wherein the just shall dwell.

BOOK XII

THE ARGUMENT

The angel Michael continues from the Flood to relate what
shall succeed; then, in the mention of Abraham, comes by
degrees to explain, who that Seed of the Woman shall be,
which was promised Adam and Eve in the Fall; his
5   Incarnation, Death, Resurrection, and Ascension; the state of
the Church till his second coming. Adam, greatly satisfied and
recomforted by these relations, and promises descends the hill
with Michael; wakens Eve, who all this while had slept, but
with gentle dreams composed to
10   quietness of mind and submission. Michael in either hand leads
them out of Paradise, the fiery sword waving behind them,
and the Cherubim taking their stations to guard the place.

As one who in his journey bates at noon,
Though bent on speed; so here the Arch-Angel paused
Betwixt the world destroyed and world restored,
If Adam aught perhaps might interpose;
5   Then, with transition sweet, new speech resumes.
Thus thou hast seen one world begin, and end;
And Man, as from a second stock, proceed.
Much thou hast yet to see; but I perceive
Thy mortal sight to fail; objects divine

10   Must needs impair and weary human sense:
Henceforth what is to come I will relate;
Thou therefore give due audience, and attend.
This second source of Men, while yet but few,
And while the dread of judgement past remains
15   Fresh in their minds, fearing the Deity,
With some regard to what is just and right
Shall lead their lives, and multiply apace;
Labouring the soil, and reaping plenteous crop,
Corn, wine, and oil; and, from the herd or flock,
20   Oft sacrificing bullock, lamb, or kid,
With large wine-offerings poured, and sacred feast,
Shall spend their days in joy unblamed; and dwell
Long time in peace, by families and tribes,
Under paternal rule: till one shall rise
25   Of proud ambitious heart; who, not content
With fair equality, fraternal state,
Will arrogate dominion undeserved
Over his brethren, and quite dispossess
Concord and law of nature from the earth;
30   Hunting (and men not beasts shall be his game)
With war, and hostile snare, such as refuse
Subjection to his empire tyrannous:
A mighty hunter thence he shall be styled
Before the Lord; as in despite of Heav'n,
35   Or from Heav'n, claiming second sovranty;
And from rebellion shall derive his name,
Though of rebellion others he accuse.
He with a crew, whom like ambition joins
With him or under him to tyrannize,
40   Marching from Eden towards the west, shall find
The plain, wherein a black bituminous gurge
Boils out from under ground, the mouth of Hell:

Of brick, and of that stuff, they cast to build
A city and tower, whose top may reach to Heav'n;
45   And get themselves a name; lest, far dispersed
In foreign lands, their memory be lost;
Regardless whether good or evil fame.
But God, who oft descends to visit men
Unseen, and through their habitations walks
50   To mark their doings, them beholding soon,
Comes down to see their city, ere the tower
Obstruct Heav'n-towers, and in derision sets
Upon their tongues a various spirit, to rase
Quite out their native language; and, instead,
55   To sow a jangling noise of words unknown:
Forthwith a hideous gabble rises loud,
Among the builders; each to other calls
Not understood; till hoarse, and all in rage,
As mocked they storm: great laughter was in Heav'n,
60   And looking down, to see the hubbub strange,
And hear the din: Thus was the building left
Ridiculous, and the work Confusion named.
Whereto thus Adam, fatherly displeased.
O execrable son! so to aspire
65   Above his brethren; to himself assuming
Authority usurped, from God not given:
He gave us only over beast, fish, fowl,
Dominion absolute; that right we hold
By his donation; but man over men
70   He made not lord; such title to himself
Reserving, human left from human free.
But this usurper his encroachment proud
Stays not on Man; to God his tower intends
Siege and defiance: Wretched man! what food
75   Will he convey up thither, to sustain
Himself and his rash army; where thin air

Above the clouds will pine his entrails gross,
And famish him of breath, if not of bread?
To whom thus Michael. Justly thou abhorrest
80   That son, who on the quiet state of men
Such trouble brought, affecting to subdue
Rational liberty; yet know withal,
Since thy original lapse, true liberty
Is lost, which always with right reason dwells
85   Twinned, and from her hath no dividual being:
Reason in man obscured, or not obeyed,
Immediately inordinate desires,
And upstart passions, catch the government
From reason; and to servitude reduce
90   Man, till then free. Therefore, since he permits
Within himself unworthy powers to reign
Over free reason, God, in judgement just,
Subjects him from without to violent lords;
Who oft as undeservedly enthrall
95   His outward freedom: Tyranny must be;
Though to the tyrant thereby no excuse.
Yet sometimes nations will decline so low
From virtue, which is reason, that no wrong,
But justice, and some fatal curse annexed,
100   Deprives them of their outward liberty;
Their inward lost: Witness the irreverent son
Of him who built the ark; who, for the shame
Done to his father, heard this heavy curse,
Servant of servants, on his vicious race.
105   Thus will this latter, as the former world,
Still tend from bad to worse; till God at last,
Wearied with their iniquities, withdraw
His presence from among them, and avert
His holy eyes; resolving from thenceforth
110   To leave them to their own polluted ways;

And one peculiar nation to select
From all the rest, of whom to be invoked,
A nation from one faithful man to spring:
Him on this side Euphrates yet residing,
115   Bred up in idol-worship: O, that men
(Canst thou believe?) should be so stupid grown,
While yet the patriarch lived, who 'scaped the flood,
As to forsake the living God, and fall
To worship their own work in wood and stone
120   For Gods! Yet him God the Most High vouchsafes
To call by vision, from his father's house,
His kindred, and false Gods, into a land
Which he will show him; and from him will raise
A mighty nation; and upon him shower
125   His benediction so, that in his seed
All nations shall be blest: he straight obeys;
Not knowing to what land, yet firm believes:
I see him, but thou canst not, with what faith
He leaves his Gods, his friends, and native soil,
130   Ur of Chaldea, passing now the ford
To Haran; after him a cumbrous train
Of herds and flocks, and numerous servitude;
Not wandering poor, but trusting all his wealth
With God, who called him, in a land unknown.
135   Canaan he now attains; I see his tents
Pitched about Sechem, and the neighbouring plain
Of Moreh; there by promise he receives
Gift to his progeny of all that land,
From Hameth northward to the Desart south;
140   (Things by their names I call, though yet unnamed;)
From Hermon east to the great western Sea;
Mount Hermon, yonder sea; each place behold
In prospect, as I point them; on the shore
Mount Carmel; here, the double-founted stream,

145 Jordan, true limit eastward; but his sons
   Shall dwell to Senir, that long ridge of hills.
   This ponder, that all nations of the earth
   Shall in his seed be blessed: By that seed
   Is meant thy great Deliverer, who shall bruise
150 The Serpent's head; whereof to thee anon
   Plainlier shall be revealed. This patriarch blest,
   Whom *faithful Abraham* due time shall call,
   A son, and of his son a grand-child, leaves;
   Like him in faith, in wisdom, and renown:
155 The grandchild, with twelve sons increased, departs
   From Canaan to a land hereafter called
   Egypt, divided by the river Nile
   See where it flows, disgorging at seven mouths
   Into the sea. To sojourn in that land
160 He comes, invited by a younger son
   In time of dearth, a son whose worthy deeds
   Raise him to be the second in that realm
   Of Pharaoh. There he dies, and leaves his race
   Growing into a nation, and now grown
165 Suspected to a sequent king, who seeks
   To stop their overgrowth, as inmate guests
   Too numerous; whence of guests he makes them slaves
   Inhospitably, and kills their infant males:
   Till by two brethren (these two brethren call
170 Moses and Aaron) sent from God to claim
   His people from enthralment, they return,
   With glory and spoil, back to their promised land.
   But first, the lawless tyrant, who denies
   To know their God, or message to regard,
175 Must be compelled by signs and judgements dire;
   To blood unshed the rivers must be turned;
   Frogs, lice, and flies, must all his palace fill

With loathed intrusion, and fill all the land;
His cattle must of rot and murren die;
180   Botches and blains must all his flesh emboss,
And all his people; thunder mixed with hail,
Hail mixed with fire, must rend the Egyptians sky,
And wheel on the earth, devouring where it rolls;
What it devours not, herb, or fruit, or grain,
185   A darksome cloud of locusts swarming down
Must eat, and on the ground leave nothing green;
Darkness must overshadow all his bounds,
Palpable darkness, and blot out three days;
Last, with one midnight stroke, all the first-born
190   Of Egypt must lie dead. Thus with ten wounds
The river-dragon tamed at length submits
To let his sojourners depart, and oft
Humbles his stubborn heart; but still, as ice
More hardened after thaw; till, in his rage
195   Pursuing whom he late dismissed, the sea
Swallows him with his host; but them lets pass,
As on dry land, between two crystal walls;
Awed by the rod of Moses so to stand
Divided, till his rescued gain their shore:
200   Such wondrous power God to his saint will lend,
Though present in his Angel; who shall go
Before them in a cloud, and pillar of fire;
By day a cloud, by night a pillar of fire;
To guide them in their journey, and remove
205   Behind them, while the obdurate king pursues:
All night he will pursue; but his approach
Darkness defends between till morning watch;
Then through the fiery pillar, and the cloud,
God looking forth will trouble all his host,
210   And craze their chariot-wheels: when by command
Moses once more his potent rod extends

Over the sea; the sea his rod obeys;
On their embattled ranks the waves return,
And overwhelm their war: The race elect
215 Safe toward Canaan from the shore advance
Through the wild Desert, not the readiest way;
Lest, entering on the Canaanite alarmed,
War terrify them inexpert, and fear
Return them back to Egypt, choosing rather
220 Inglorious life with servitude; for life
To noble and ignoble is more sweet
Untrained in arms, where rashness leads not on.
This also shall they gain by their delay
In the wide wilderness; there they shall found
225 Their government, and their great senate choose
Through the twelve tribes, to rule by laws ordained:
God from the mount of Sinai, whose gray top
Shall tremble, he descending, will himself
In thunder, lightning, and loud trumpets' sound,
230 Ordain them laws; part, such as appertain
To civil justice; part, religious rites
Of sacrifice; informing them, by types
And shadows, of that destined Seed to bruise
The Serpent, by what means he shall achieve
235 Mankind's deliverance. But the voice of God
To mortal ear is dreadful: They beseech
That Moses might report to them his will,
And terrour cease; he grants what they besought,
Instructed that to God is no access
240 Without Mediator, whose high office now
Moses in figure bears; to introduce
One greater, of whose day he shall foretel,
And all the Prophets in their age the times
Of great Messiah shall sing. Thus, laws and rites
245 Established, such delight hath God in Men

Obedient to his will, that he vouchsafes
Among them to set up his tabernacle;
The Holy One with mortal Men to dwell:
By his prescript a sanctuary is framed
250   Of cedar, overlaid with gold; therein
An ark, and in the ark his testimony,
The records of his covenant; over these
A mercy-seat of gold, between the wings
Of two bright Cherubim; before him burn
255   Seven lamps as in a zodiac representing
The heav'nly fires; over the tent a cloud
Shall rest by day, a fiery gleam by night;
Save when they journey, and at length they come,
Conducted by his Angel, to the land
260   Promised to Abraham and his seed:—The rest
Were long to tell; how many battles fought
How many kings destroyed; and kingdoms won;
Or how the sun shall in mid Heav'n stand still
A day entire, and night's due course adjourn,
265   Man's voice commanding, "Sun, in Gibeon stand,
And thou moon in the vale of Aialon,
Till Israel overcome!" so call the third
From Abraham, son of Isaac; and from him
His whole descent, who thus shall Canaan win.
270   Here Adam interposed. O sent from Heav'n,
Enlightener of my darkness, gracious things
Thou hast revealed; those chiefly, which concern
Just Abraham and his seed: now first I find
Mine eyes true-opening, and my heart much eased;
275   Erewhile perplexed with thoughts, what would become
Of me and all mankind: But now I see
His day, in whom all nations shall be blest;
Favour unmerited by me, who sought
Forbidden knowledge by forbidden means.

280   This yet I apprehend not, why to those
        Among whom God will deign to dwell on earth
        So many and so various laws are given;
        So many laws argue so many sins
        Among them; how can God with such reside?
285   To whom thus Michael. Doubt not but that sin
        Will reign among them, as of thee begot;
        And therefore was law given them, to evince
        Their natural pravity, by stirring up
        Sin against law to fight: that when they see
290   Law can discover sin, but not remove,
        Save by those shadowy expiations weak,
        The blood of bulls and goats, they may conclude
        Some blood more precious must be paid for Man;
        Just for unjust; that, in such righteousness
295   To them by faith imputed, they may find
        Justification towards God, and peace
        Of conscience; which the law by ceremonies
        Cannot appease; nor Man the mortal part
        Perform; and, not performing, cannot live.
300   So law appears imperfect; and but given
        With purpose to resign them, in full time,
        Up to a better covenant; disciplined
        From shadowy types to truth; from flesh to spirit;
        From imposition of strict laws to free
305   Acceptance of large grace; from servile fear
        To filial; works of law to works of faith.
        And therefore shall not Moses, though of God
        Highly beloved, being but the minister
        Of law, his people into Canaan lead;
310   But Joshua, whom the Gentiles Jesus call,
        His name and office bearing, who shall quell
        The adversary-Serpent, and bring back

Through the world's wilderness long-wandered Man
Safe to eternal Paradise of rest.
315   Mean while they, in their earthly Canaan placed,
Long time shall dwell and prosper, but when sins
National interrupt their publick peace,
Provoking God to raise them enemies;
From whom as oft he saves them penitent
320   By Judges first, then under Kings; of whom
The second, both for piety renowned
And puissant deeds, a promise shall receive
Irrevocable, that his regal throne
For ever shall endure; the like shall sing
325   All Prophecy, that of the royal stock
Of David (so I name this king) shall rise
A Son, the Woman's seed to thee foretold,
Foretold to Abraham, as in whom shall trust
All nations; and to kings foretold, of kings
330   The last; for of his reign shall be no end.
But first, a long succession must ensue;
And his next son, for wealth and wisdom famed,
The clouded ark of God, till then in tents
Wandering, shall in a glorious temple enshrine.
335   Such follow him, as shall be registered
Part good, part bad; of bad the longer scroll;
Whose foul idolatries, and other faults
Heaped to the popular sum, will so incense
God, as to leave them, and expose their land,
340   Their city, his temple, and his holy ark,
With all his sacred things, a scorn and prey
To that proud city, whose high walls thou sawest
Left in confusion; Babylon thence called.
There in captivity he lets them dwell
345   The space of seventy years; then brings them back,
Remembering mercy, and his covenant sworn

To David, stablished as the days of Heav'n.
Returned from Babylon by leave of kings
Their lords, whom God disposed, the house of God
350   They first re-edify; and for a while
In mean estate live moderate; till, grown
In wealth and multitude, factious they grow;
But first among the priests dissention springs,
Men who attend the altar, and should most
355   Endeavour peace: their strife pollution brings
Upon the temple itself: at last they seize
The scepter, and regard not David's sons;
Then lose it to a stranger, that the true
Anointed King Messiah might be born
360   Barred of his right; yet at his birth a star,
Unseen before in Heav'n, proclaims him come;
And guides the eastern sages, who inquire
His place, to offer incense, myrrh, and gold:
His place of birth a solemn Angel tells
365   To simple shepherds, keeping watch by night;
They gladly thither haste, and by a quire
Of squadroned Angels hear his carol sung.
A virgin is his mother, but his sire
The power of the Most High: He shall ascend
370   The throne hereditary, and bound his reign
With Earth's wide bounds, his glory with the Heav'ns.
He ceased, discerning Adam with such joy
Surcharged, as had like grief been dewed in tears,
Without the vent of words; which these he breathed.
375   O prophet of glad tidings, finisher
Of utmost hope! now clear I understand
What oft my steadiest thoughts have searched in vain;
Why our great Expectation should be called
The seed of Woman: Virgin Mother, hail,
380   High in the love of Heav'n; yet from my loins

Thou shalt proceed, and from thy womb the Son
Of God Most High: so God with Man unites!
Needs must the Serpent now his capital bruise
Expect with mortal pain: Say where and when
385   Their fight, what stroke shall bruise the victor's heel.
To whom thus Michael. Dream not of their fight,
As of a duel, or the local wounds
Of head or heel: Not therefore joins the Son
Manhood to Godhead, with more strength to foil
390   Thy enemy; nor so is overcome
Satan, whose fall from Heav'n, a deadlier bruise,
Disabled, not to give thee thy death's wound:
Which he, who comes thy Saviour, shall recure,
Not by destroying Satan, but his works
395   In thee, and in thy seed: Nor can this be,
But by fulfilling that which thou didst want,
Obedience to the law of God, imposed
On penalty of death, and suffering death;
The penalty to thy transgression due,
400   And due to theirs which out of thine will grow:
So only can high Justice rest appaid.
The law of God exact he shall fulfil
Both by obedience and by love, though love
Alone fulfil the law; thy punishment
405   He shall endure, by coming in the flesh
To a reproachful life, and cursed death;
Proclaiming life to all who shall believe
In his redemption; and that his obedience,
Imputed, becomes theirs by faith; his merits
410   To save them, not their own, though legal, works.
For this he shall live hated, be blasphemed,
Seized on by force, judged, and to death condemned
A shameful and accursed, nailed to the cross
By his own nation; slain for bringing life:

415   But to the cross he nails thy enemies,
The law that is against thee, and the sins
Of all mankind, with him there crucified,
Never to hurt them more who rightly trust
In this his satisfaction; so he dies,
420   But soon revives; Death over him no power
Shall long usurp; ere the third dawning light
Return, the stars of morn shall see him rise
Out of his grave, fresh as the dawning light,
Thy ransom paid, which Man from death redeems,
425   His death for Man, as many as offered life
Neglect not, and the benefit embrace
By faith not void of works: This God-like act
Annuls thy doom, the death thou shouldst have died,
In sin for ever lost from life; this act
430   Shall bruise the head of Satan, crush his strength,
Defeating Sin and Death, his two main arms;
And fix far deeper in his head their stings
Than temporal death shall bruise the victor's heel,
Or theirs whom he redeems; a death, like sleep,
435   A gentle wafting to immortal life.
Nor after resurrection shall he stay
Longer on earth, than certain times to appear
To his disciples, men who in his life
Still followed him; to them shall leave in charge
440   To teach all nations what of him they learned
And his salvation; them who shall believe
Baptizing in the profluent stream, the sign
Of washing them from guilt of sin to life
Pure, and in mind prepared, if so befall,
445   For death, like that which the Redeemer died.
All nations they shall teach; for, from that day,
Not only to the sons of Abraham's loins

Salvation shall be preached, but to the sons
Of Abraham's faith wherever through the world;
450   So in his seed all nations shall be blest.
Then to the Heav'n of Heav'ns he shall ascend
With victory, triumphing through the air
Over his foes and thine; there shall surprise
The Serpent, prince of air, and drag in chains
455   Through all his realm, and there confounded leave;
Then enter into glory, and resume
His seat at God's right hand, exalted high
Above all names in Heav'n; and thence shall come,
When this world's dissolution shall be ripe,
460   With glory and power to judge both quick and dead;
To judge the unfaithful dead, but to reward
His faithful, and receive them into bliss,
Whether in Heav'n or Earth; for then the Earth
Shall all be Paradise, far happier place
465   Than this of Eden, and far happier days.
So spake the Arch-Angel Michael; then paused,
As at the world's great period; and our sire,
Replete with joy and wonder, thus replied.
O Goodness infinite, Goodness immense!
470   That all this good of evil shall produce,
And evil turn to good; more wonderful
Than that which by creation first brought forth
Light out of darkness! Full of doubt I stand,
Whether I should repent me now of sin
475   By me done, and occasioned; or rejoice
Much more, that much more good thereof shall spring;
To God more glory, more good-will to Men
From God, and over wrath grace shall abound.
But say, if our Deliverer up to Heav'n
480   Must re-ascend, what will betide the few
His faithful, left among the unfaithful herd,

The enemies of truth? Who then shall guide
His people, who defend? Will they not deal
Worse with his followers than with him they dealt?

485 Be sure they will, said the Angel; but from Heav'n
He to his own a Comforter will send,
The promise of the Father, who shall dwell
His Spirit within them; and the law of faith,
Working through love, upon their hearts shall write,

490 To guide them in all truth; and also arm
With spiritual armour, able to resist
Satan's assaults, and quench his fiery darts;
What man can do against them, not afraid,
Though to the death; against such cruelties

495 With inward consolations recompensed,
And oft supported so as shall amaze
Their proudest persecutors: For the Spirit,
Poured first on his Apostles, whom he sends
To evangelize the nations, then on all

500 Baptized, shall them with wondrous gifts endue
To speak all tongues, and do all miracles,
As did their Lord before them. Thus they win
Great numbers of each nation to receive
With joy the tidings brought from Heav'n: At length

505 Their ministry performed, and race well run,
Their doctrine and their story written left,
They die; but in their room, as they forewarn,
Wolves shall succeed for teachers, grievous wolves,
Who all the sacred mysteries of Heav'n

510 To their own vile advantages shall turn
Of lucre and ambition; and the truth
With superstitions and traditions taint,
Left only in those written records pure,
Though not but by the Spirit understood.

515 Then shall they seek to avail themselves of names,

Places, and titles, and with these to join
Secular power; though feigning still to act
By spiritual, to themselves appropriating
The Spirit of God, promised alike and given
520   To all believers; and, from that pretence,
Spiritual laws by carnal power shall force
On every conscience; laws which none shall find
Left them enrolled, or what the Spirit within
Shall on the heart engrave. What will they then
525   But force the Spirit of Grace itself, and bind
His consort Liberty? what, but unbuild
His living temples, built by faith to stand,
Their own faith, not another's? for, on earth,
Who against faith and conscience can be heard
530   Infallible? yet many will presume:
Whence heavy persecution shall arise
On all, who in the worship persevere
Of spirit and truth; the rest, far greater part,
Will deem in outward rites and specious forms
535   Religion satisfied; Truth shall retire
Bestuck with slanderous darts, and works of faith
Rarely be found: So shall the world go on,
To good malignant, to bad men benign;
Under her own weight groaning; till the day
540   Appear of respiration to the just,
And vengeance to the wicked, at return
Of him so lately promised to thy aid,
The Woman's Seed; obscurely then foretold,
Now ampler known thy Saviour and thy Lord;
545   Last, in the clouds, from Heav'n to be revealed
In glory of the Father, to dissolve
Satan with his perverted world; then raise
From the conflagrant mass, purged and refined,
New Heav'ns, new Earth, ages of endless date,

550   Founded in righteousness, and peace, and love;
             To bring forth fruits, joy and eternal bliss.
             He ended; and thus Adam last replied.
             How soon hath thy prediction, Seer blest,
             Measured this transient world, the race of time,
555   Till time stand fixed! Beyond is all abyss,
             Eternity, whose end no eye can reach.
             Greatly-instructed I shall hence depart;
             Greatly in peace of thought; and have my fill
             Of knowledge, what this vessel can contain;
560   Beyond which was my folly to aspire.
             Henceforth I learn, that to obey is best,
             And love with fear the only God; to walk
             As in his presence; ever to observe
             His providence; and on him sole depend,
565   Merciful over all his works, with good
             Still overcoming evil, and by small
             Accomplishing great things, by things deemed weak
             Subverting worldly strong, and worldly wise
             By simply meek: that suffering for truth's sake
570   Is fortitude to highest victory,
             And, to the faithful, death the gate of life;
             Taught this by his example, whom I now
             Acknowledge my Redeemer ever blest.
             To whom thus also the Angel last replied.
575   This having learned, thou hast attained the sum
             Of wisdom; hope no higher, though all the stars
             Thou knewest by name, and all the ethereal powers,
             All secrets of the deep, all Nature's works,
             Or works of God in Heav'n, air, earth, or sea,
580   And all the riches of this world enjoyedst,
             And all the rule, one empire; only add
             Deeds to thy knowledge answerable; add faith,

Add virtue, patience, temperance; add love,
By name to come called charity, the soul
585   Of all the rest: then wilt thou not be loth
To leave this Paradise, but shalt possess
A Paradise within thee, happier far.—
Let us descend now therefore from this top
Of speculation; for the hour precise
590   Exacts our parting hence; and see the guards,
By me encamped on yonder hill, expect
Their motion; at whose front a flaming sword,
In signal of remove, waves fiercely round:
We may no longer stay: go, waken Eve;
595   Her also I with gentle dreams have calmed
Portending good, and all her spirits composed
To meek submission: thou, at season fit,
Let her with thee partake what thou hast heard;
Chiefly what may concern her faith to know,
600   The great deliverance by her seed to come
(For by the Woman's seed) on all mankind:
That ye may live, which will be many days,
Both in one faith unanimous, though sad,
With cause, for evils past; yet much more cheered
605   With meditation on the happy end.
He ended, and they both descend the hill;
Descended, Adam to the bower, where Eve
Lay sleeping, ran before; but found her waked;
And thus with words not sad she him received.
610   Whence thou returnest, and whither wentest, I know;
For God is also in sleep; and dreams advise,
Which he hath sent propitious, some great good
Presaging, since with sorrow and heart's distress
Wearied I fell asleep: But now lead on;
615   In me is no delay; with thee to go,
Is to stay here; without thee here to stay,

Is to go hence unwilling; thou to me
Art all things under Heav'n, all places thou,
Who for my wilful crime art banished hence.
620   This further consolation yet secure
I carry hence; though all by me is lost,
Such favour I unworthy am vouchsafed,
By me the Promised Seed shall all restore.
So spake our mother Eve; and Adam heard
625   Well pleased, but answered not: For now, too nigh
The Arch-Angel stood; and, from the other hill
To their fixed station, all in bright array
The Cherubim descended; on the ground
Gliding meteorous, as evening-mist
630   Risen from a river o'er the marish glides,
And gathers ground fast at the labourer's heel
Homeward returning. High in front advanced,
The brandished sword of God before them blazed,
Fierce as a comet; which with torrid heat,
635   And vapour as the Libyan air adust,
Began to parch that temperate clime; whereat
In either hand the hastening Angel caught
Our lingering parents, and to the eastern gate
Led them direct, and down the cliff as fast
640   To the subjected plain; then disappeared.
They, looking back, all the eastern side beheld
Of Paradise, so late their happy seat,
Waved over by that flaming brand; the gate
With dreadful faces thronged, and fiery arms:
645   Some natural tears they dropped, but wiped them soon;
The world was all before them, where to choose
Their place of rest, and Providence their guide:
They, hand in hand, with wandering steps and slow,
Through Eden took their solitary way.

PARADISE REGAINED

BOOK I

I, who erewhile the happy Garden sung
By one man's disobedience lost, now sing
Recovered Paradise to all mankind,
By one man's firm obedience fully tried
Through all temptation, and the Tempter foiled
In all his wiles, defeated and repulsed,
And Eden raised in the waste Wilderness.
Thou Spirit, who led'st this glorious Eremite
Into the desert, his victorious field
Against the spiritual foe, and brought'st him thence
By proof the undoubted Son of God, inspire,
As thou art wont, my prompted song, else mute,
And bear through highth or depth of Nature's bounds,
With prosperous wing full summed, to tell of deeds
Above heroic, though in secret done,
And unrecorded left through many an age:
Worthy to have not remained so long unsung.
Now had the great Proclaimer, with a voice
More awful than the sound of trumpet, cried
Repentance, and Heaven's kingdom nigh at hand
To all baptized. To his great baptism flocked
With awe the regions round, and with them came
From Nazareth the son of Joseph deemed
To the flood Jordan—came as then obscure,

10

20

345

Unmarked, unknown. But him the Baptist soon
Descried, divinely warned, and witness bore
As to his worthier, and would have resigned
To him his heavenly office. Nor was long
His witness unconfirmed: on him baptized
30   Heaven opened, and in likeness of a Dove
The Spirit descended, while the Father's voice
From Heaven pronounced him his beloved Son.
That heard the Adversary, who, roving still
About the world, at that assembly famed
Would not be last, and, with the voice divine
Nigh thunder-struck, the exalted man to whom
Such high attest was given a while surveyed
With wonder; then, with envy fraught and rage,
Flies to his place, nor rests, but in mid air
40   To council summons all his mighty Peers,
Within thick clouds and dark tenfold involved,
A gloomy consistory; and them amidst,
With looks aghast and sad, he thus bespake:—
"O ancient Powers of Air and this wide World
(For much more willingly I mention Air,
This our old conquest, than remember Hell,
Our hated habitation), well ye know
How many ages, as the years of men,
This Universe we have possessed, and ruled
50   In manner at our will the affairs of Earth,
Since Adam and his facile consort Eve
Lost Paradise, deceived by me, though since
With dread attending when that fatal wound
Shall be inflicted by the seed of Eve
Upon my head. Long the decrees of Heaven
Delay, for longest time to Him is short;
And now, too soon for us, the circling hours

This dreaded time have compassed, wherein we
Must bide the stroke of that long-threatened wound
60   (At least, if so we can, and by the head
Broken be not intended all our power
To be infringed, our freedom and our being
In this fair empire won of Earth and Air)—
For this ill news I bring: The Woman's Seed,
Destined to this, is late of woman born.
His birth to our just fear gave no small cause;
But his growth now to youth's full flower, displaying
All virtue, grace and wisdom to achieve
Things highest, greatest, multiplies my fear.
70   Before him a great Prophet, to proclaim
His coming, is sent harbinger, who all
Invites, and in the consecrated stream
Pretends to wash off sin, and fit them so
Purified to receive him pure, or rather
To do him honour as their King. All come,
And he himself among them was baptized—
Not thence to be more pure, but to receive
The testimony of Heaven, that who he is
Thenceforth the nations may not doubt. I saw
80   The Prophet do him reverence; on him, rising
Out of the water, Heaven above the clouds
Unfold her crystal doors; thence on his head
A perfet Dove descend (whate'er it meant);
And out of Heaven the sovraign voice I heard,
'This is my Son beloved,—in him am pleased.'
His mother, than, is mortal, but his Sire
He who obtains the monarchy of Heaven;
And what will He not do to advance his Son?
His first-begot we know, and sore have felt,
90   When his fierce thunder drove us to the Deep;
Who this is we must learn, for Man he seems

In all his lineaments, though in his face
The glimpses of his Father's glory shine.
Ye see our danger on the utmost edge
Of hazard, which admits no long debate,
But must with something sudden be opposed
(Not force, but well-couched fraud, well-woven snares),
Ere in the head of nations he appear,
Their king, their leader, and supreme on Earth.
100   I, when no other durst, sole undertook
The dismal expedition to find out
And ruin Adam, and the exploit performed
Successfully: a calmer voyage now
Will waft me; and the way found prosperous once
Induces best to hope of like success."
He ended, and his words impression left
Of much amazement to the infernal crew,
Distracted and surprised with deep dismay
At these sad tidings. But no time was then
110   For long indulgence to their fears or grief:
Unanimous they all commit the care
And management of this man enterprise
To him, their great Dictator, whose attempt
At first against mankind so well had thrived
In Adam's overthrow, and led their march
From Hell's deep-vaulted den to dwell in light,
Regents, and potentates, and kings, yea gods,
Of many a pleasant realm and province wide.
So to the coast of Jordan he directs
120   His easy steps, girded with snaky wiles,
Where he might likeliest find this new-declared,
This man of men, attested Son of God,
Temptation and all guile on him to try—
So to subvert whom he suspected raised

To end his reign on Earth so long enjoyed:
But, contrary, unweeting he fulfilled
The purposed counsel, pre-ordained and fixed,
Of the Most High, who, in full frequence bright
Of Angels, thus to Gabriel smiling spake:—

130   "Gabriel, this day, by proof, thou shalt behold,
Thou and all Angels conversant on Earth
With Man or men's affairs, how I begin
To verify that solemn message late,
On which I sent thee to the Virgin pure
In Galilee, that she should bear a son,
Great in renown, and called the Son of God.
Then told'st her, doubting how these things could be
To her a virgin, that on her should come
The Holy Ghost, and the power of the Highest

140   O'ershadow her. This Man, born and now upgrown,
To shew him worthy of his birth divine
And high prediction, henceforth I expose
To Satan; let him tempt, and now assay
His utmost subtlety, because he boasts
And vaunts of his great cunning to the throng
Of his Apostasy. He might have learnt
Less overweening, since he failed in Job,
Whose constant perseverance overcame
Whate'er his cruel malice could invent.

150   He now shall know I can produce a man,
Of female seed, far abler to resist
All his solicitations, and at length
All his vast force, and drive him back to Hell—
Winning by conquest what the first man lost
By fallacy surprised. But first I mean
To exercise him in the Wilderness;
There he shall first lay down the rudiments

Of his great warfare, ere I send him forth
To conquer Sin and Death, the two grand foes.
160   By humiliation and strong sufferance
His weakness shall o'ercome Satanic strength,
And all the world, and mass of sinful flesh;
That all the Angels and aethereal Powers—
They now, and men hereafter—may discern
From what consummate virtue I have chose
This perfet man, by merit called my Son,
To earn salvation for the sons of men."
So spake the Eternal Father, and all Heaven
Admiring stood a space; then into hymns
170   Burst forth, and in celestial measures moved,
Circling the throne and singing, while the hand
Sung with the voice, and this the argument:—
"Victory and triumph to the Son of God,
Now entering his great duel, not of arms,
But to vanquish by wisdom hellish wiles!
The Father knows the Son; therefore secure
Ventures his filial virtue, though untried,
Against whate'er may tempt, whate'er seduce,
Allure, or terrify, or undermine.
180   Be frustrate, all ye stratagems of Hell,
And, devilish machinations, come to nought!"
So they in Heaven their odes and vigils tuned.
Meanwhile the Son of God, who yet some days
Lodged in Bethabara, where John baptized,
Musing and much revolving in his breast
How best the mighty work he might begin
Of Saviour to mankind, and which way first
Publish his godlike office now mature,
One day forth walked alone, the Spirit leading
190   And his deep thoughts, the better to converse
With solitude, till, far from track of men,

Thought following thought, and step by step led on,
He entered now the bordering Desert wild,
And, with dark shades and rocks environed round,
His holy meditations thus pursued:—
"O what a multitude of thoughts at once
Awakened in me swarm, while I consider
What from within I feel myself, and hear
What from without comes often to my ears,
200   Ill sorting with my present state compared!
When I was yet a child, no childish play
To me was pleasing; all my mind was set
Serious to learn and know, and thence to do,
What might be public good; myself I thought
Born to that end, born to promote all truth,
All righteous things. Therefore, above my years,
The Law of God I read, and found it sweet;
Made it my whole delight, and in it grew
To such perfection that, ere yet my age
210   Had measured twice six years, at our great Feast
I went into the Temple, there to hear
The teachers of our Law, and to propose
What might improve my knowledge or their own,
And was admired by all. Yet this not all
To which my spirit aspired. Victorious deeds
Flamed in my heart, heroic acts—one while
To rescue Israel from the Roman yoke;
Then to subdue and quell, o'er all the earth,
Brute violence and proud tyrannic power,
220   Till truth were freed, and equity restored:
Yet held it more humane, more heavenly, first
By winning words to conquer willing hearts,
And make persuasion do the work of fear;
At least to try, and teach the erring soul,
Not wilfully misdoing, but unware

Misled; the stubborn only to subdue.
These growing thoughts my mother soon perceiving,
By words at times cast forth, inly rejoiced,
And said to me apart, 'High are thy thoughts,
230   O Son! but nourish them, and let them soar
To what highth sacred virtue and true worth
Can raise them, though above example high;
By matchless deeds express thy matchless Sire.
For know, thou art no son of mortal man;
Though men esteem thee low of parentage,
Thy Father is the Eternal King who rules
All Heaven and Earth, Angels and sons of men.
A messenger from God foretold thy birth
Conceived in me a virgin; he foretold
240   Thou shouldst be great, and sit on David's throne,
And of thy kingdom there should be no end.
At thy nativity a glorious quire
Of Angels, in the fields of Bethlehem, sung
To shepherds, watching at their folds by night,
And told them the Messiah now was born,
Where they might see him; and to thee they came,
Directed to the manger where thou lay'st;
For in the inn was left no better room.
A Star, not seen before, in heaven appearing,
250   Guided the Wise Men thither from the East,
To honour thee with incense, myrrh, and gold;
By whose bright course led on they found the place,
Affirming it thy star, new-graven in heaven,
By which they knew thee King of Israel born.
Just Simeon and prophetic Anna, warned
By vision, found thee in the Temple, and spake,
Before the altar and the vested priest,
Like things of thee to all that present stood.'
This having heart, straight I again revolved

260   The Law and Prophets, searching what was writ
Concerning the Messiah, to our scribes
Known partly, and soon found of whom they spake
I am—this chiefly, that my way must lie
Through many a hard assay, even to the death,
Ere I the promised kingdom can attain,
Or work redemption for mankind, whose sins'
Full weight must be transferred upon my head.
Yet, neither thus disheartened or dismayed,
The time prefixed I waited; when behold

270   The Baptist (of whose birth I oft had heard,
Not knew by sight) now come, who was to come
Before Messiah, and his way prepare!
I, as all others, to his baptism came,
Which I believed was from above; but he
Straight knew me, and with loudest voice proclaimed
Me him (for it was shewn him so from Heaven)—
Me him whose harbinger he was; and first
Refused on me his baptism to confer,
As much his greater, and was hardly won.

280   But, as I rose out of the laving stream,
Heaven opened her eternal doors, from whence
The Spirit descended on me like a Dove;
And last, the sum of all, my Father's voice,
Audibly heard from Heaven, pronounced me his,
Me his beloved Son, in whom alone
He was well pleased: by which I knew the time
Now full, that I no more should live obscure,
But openly begin, as best becomes
The authority which I derived from Heaven.

290   And now by some strong motion I am led
Into this wilderness; to what intent
I learn not yet. Perhaps I need not know;
For what concerns my knowledge God reveals."

So spake our Morning Star, then in his rise,
And, looking round, on every side beheld
A pathless desert, dusk with horrid shades.
The way he came, not having marked return,
Was difficult, by human steps untrod;
And he still on was led, but with such thoughts
300   Accompanied of things past and to come
Lodged in his breast as well might recommend
Such solitude before choicest society.
Full forty days he passed—whether on hill
Sometimes, anon in shady vale, each night
Under the covert of some ancient oak
Or cedar to defend him from the dew,
Or harboured in one cave, is not revealed;
Nor tasted human food, nor hunger felt,
Till those days ended; hungered then at last
310   Among wild beasts. They at his sight grew mild,
Nor sleeping him nor waking harmed; his walk
The fiery serpent fled and noxious worm;
The lion and fierce tiger glared aloof.
But now an aged man in rural weeds,
Following, as seemed, the quest of some stray eye,
Or withered sticks to gather, which might serve
Against a winter's day, when winds blow keen,
To warm him wet returned from field at eve,
He saw approach; who first with curious eye
320   Perused him, then with words thus uttered spake:—
"Sir, what ill chance hath brought thee to this place,
So far from path or road of men, who pass
In troop or caravan? for single none
Durst ever, who returned, and dropt not here
His carcass, pined with hunger and with droughth.
I ask the rather, and the more admire,
For that to me thou seem'st the man whom late

Our new baptizing Prophet at the ford
Of Jordan honoured so, and called thee Son
330   Of God. I saw and heard, for we sometimes
Who dwell this wild, constrained by want, come forth
To town or village nigh (nighest is far),
Where aught we hear, and curious are to hear,
What happens new; fame also finds us out."
To whom the Son of God:—"Who brought me hither
Will bring me hence; no other guide I seek."
"By miracle he may," replied the swain;
"What other way I see not; for we here
Live on tough roots and stubs, to thirst inured
340   More than the camel, and to drink go far—
Men to much misery and hardship born.
But, if thou be the Son of God, command
That out of these hard stones be made thee bread;
So shalt thou save thyself, and us relieve
With food, whereof we wretched seldom taste."
He ended, and the Son of God replied:—
"Think'st thou such force in bread? Is it not written
(For I discern thee other than thou seem'st),
Man lives not by bread only, but each word
350   Proceeding from the mouth of God, who fed
Our fathers here with manna? In the Mount
Moses was forty days, nor eat nor drank;
And forty days Eliah without food
Wandered this barren waste; the same I now.
Why dost thou, then, suggest to me distrust
Knowing who I am, as I know who thou art?"
Whom thus answered the Arch-Fiend, now undisguised:—
"'Tis true, I am that Spirit unfortunate
Who, leagued with millions more in rash revolt,
360   Kept not my happy station, but was driven
With them from bliss to the bottomless Deep—

Yet to that hideous place not so confined
By rigour unconniving but that oft,
Leaving my dolorous prison, I enjoy
Large liberty to round this globe of Earth,
Or range in the Air; nor from the Heaven of Heavens
Hath he excluded my resort sometimes.
I came, among the Sons of God, when he
Gave up into my hands Uzzean Job,
370   To prove him, and illustrate his high worth;
And, when to all his Angels he proposed
To draw the proud king Ahab into fraud,
That he might fall in Ramoth, they demurring,
I undertook that office, and the tongues
Of all his flattering prophets glibbed with lies
To his destruction, as I had in charge:
For what he bids I do. Though I have lost
Much lustre of my native brightness, lost
To be beloved of God, I have not lost
380   To love, at least contemplate and admire,
What I see excellent in good, or fair,
Or virtuous; I should so have lost all sense.
What can be then less in me than desire
To see thee and approach thee, whom I know
Declared the Son of God, to hear attent
Thy wisdom, and behold thy godlike deeds?
Men generally think me much a foe
To all mankind. Why should I? they to me
Never did wrong or violence. By them
390   I lost not what I lost; rather by them
I gained what I have gained, and with them dwell
Copartner in these regions of the World,
If not disposer—lend them oft my aid,
Oft my advice by presages and signs,
And answers, oracles, portents, and dreams,

Whereby they may direct their future life.
Envy, they say, excites me, thus to gain
Companions of my misery and woe!
At first it may be; but, long since with woe
400   Nearer acquainted, now I feel by proof
That fellowship in pain divides not smart,
Nor lightens aught each man's peculiar load;
Small consolation, then, were Man adjoined.
This wounds me most (what can it less?) that Man,
Man fallen, shall be restored, I never more."
To whom our Saviour sternly thus replied:—
"Deservedly thou griev'st, composed of lies
From the beginning, and in lies wilt end,
Who boast'st release from Hell, and leave to come
410   Into the Heaven of Heavens. Thou com'st, indeed,
As a poor miserable captive thrall
Comes to the place where he before had sat
Among the prime in splendour, now deposed,
Ejected, emptied, gazed, unpitied, shunned,
A spectacle of ruin, or of scorn,
To all the host of Heaven. The happy place
Imparts to thee no happiness, no joy—
Rather inflames thy torment, representing
Lost bliss, to thee no more communicable;
420   So never more in Hell than when in Heaven.
But thou art serviceable to Heaven's King!
Wilt thou impute to obedience what thy fear
Extorts, or pleasure to do ill excites?
What but thy malice moved thee to misdeem
Of righteous Job, then cruelly to afflict him
With all inflictions? but his patience won.
The other service was thy chosen task,
To be a liar in four hundred mouths;
For lying is thy sustenance, thy food.

430	Yet thou pretend'st to truth! all oracles
	By thee are given, and what confessed more true
	Among the nations? That hath been thy craft,
	By mixing somewhat true to vent more lies.
	But what have been thy answers? what but dark,
	Ambiguous, and with double sense deluding,
	Which they who asked have seldom understood,
	And, not well understood, as good not known?
	Who ever, by consulting at thy shrine,
	Returned the wiser, or the more instruct
440	To fly or follow what concerned him most,
	And run not sooner to his fatal snare?
	For God hath justly given the nations up
	To thy delusions; justly, since they fell
	Idolatrous. But, when his purpose is
	Among them to declare his providence,
	To thee not known, whence hast thou then thy truth,
	But from him, or his Angels president
	In every province, who, themselves disdaining
	To approach thy temples, give thee in command
450	What, to the smallest tittle, thou shalt say
	To thy adorers? Thou, with trembling fear,
	Or like a fawning parasite, obey'st;
	Then to thyself ascrib'st the truth foretold.
	But this thy glory shall be soon retrenched;
	No more shalt thou by oracling abuse
	The Gentiles; henceforth oracles are ceased,
	And thou no more with pomp and sacrifice
	Shalt be enquired at Delphos or elsewhere—
	At least in vain, for they shall find thee mute.
460	God hath now sent his living Oracle
	Into the world to teach his final will,
	And sends his Spirit of Truth henceforth to dwell

In pious hearts, an inward oracle
To all truth requisite for men to know."
So spake our Saviour; but the subtle Fiend,
Though inly stung with anger and disdain,
Dissembled, and this answer smooth returned:—
"Sharply thou hast insisted on rebuke,
And urged me hard with doings which not will,
470   But misery, hath wrested from me. Where
Easily canst thou find one miserable,
And not inforced oft-times to part from truth,
If it may stand him more in stead to lie,
Say and unsay, feign, flatter, or abjure?
But thou art placed above me; thou art Lord;
From thee I can, and must, submiss, endure
Cheek or reproof, and glad to scape so quit.
Hard are the ways of truth, and rough to walk,
Smooth on the tongue discoursed, pleasing to the ear,
480   And tunable as sylvan pipe or song;
What wonder, then, if I delight to hear
Her dictates from thy mouth? most men admire
Virtue who follow not her lore. Permit me
To hear thee when I come (since no man comes),
And talk at least, though I despair to attain.
Thy Father, who is holy, wise, and pure,
Suffers the hypocrite or atheous priest
To tread his sacred courts, and minister
About his altar, handling holy things,
490   Praying or vowing, and voutsafed his voice
To Balaam reprobate, a prophet yet
Inspired: disdain not such access to me."
To whom our Saviour, with unaltered brow:—
"Thy coming hither, though I know thy scope,
I bid not, or forbid. Do as thou find'st

Permission from above; thou canst not more."
He added not; and Satan, bowling low
His gray dissimulation, disappeared,
Into thin air diffused: for now began
500   Night with her sullen wing to double-shade
The desert; fowls in their clay nests were couched;
And now wild beasts came forth the woods to roam.

BOOK II

Meanwhile the new-baptized, who yet remained
At Jordan with the Baptist, and had seen
Him whom they heard so late expressly called
Jesus Messiah, Son of God, declared,
And on that high authority had believed,
And with him talked, and with him lodged—I mean
Andrew and Simon, famous after known,
With others, though in Holy Writ not named—
Now missing him, their joy so lately found,
10   So lately found and so abruptly gone,
Began to doubt, and doubted many days,
And, as the days increased, increased their doubt.
Sometimes they thought he might be only shewn,
And for a time caught up to God, as once
Moses was in the Mount and missing long,
And the great Thisbite, who on fiery wheels
Rode up to Heaven, yet once again to come.
Therefore, as those young prophets then with care
Sought lost Eliah, so in each place these
20   Nigh to Bethabara—in Jericho
The city of palms, AEnon, and Salem old,
Machaerus, and each town or city walled
On this side the broad lake Genezaret,
Or in Peraea—but returned in vain.

Then on the bank of Jordan, by a creek,
Where winds with reeds and osiers whispering play,
Plain fishermen (no greater men them call),
Close in a cottage low together got,
Their unexpected loss and plaints outbreathed:—
30   "Alas, from what high hope to what relapse
Unlooked for are we fallen! Our eyes beheld
Messiah certainly now come, so long
Expected of our fathers; we have heard
His words, his wisdom full of grace and truth.
'Now, now, for sure, deliverance is at hand;
The kingdom shall to Israel be restored:'
Thus we rejoiced, but soon our joy is turned
Into perplexity and new amaze.
For whither is he gone? what accident
40   Hath rapt him from us? will he now retire
After appearance, and again prolong
Our expectation? God of Israel,
Send thy Messiah forth; the time is come.
Behold the kings of the earth, how they oppress
Thy Chosen, to what highth their power unjust
They have exalted, and behind them cast
All fear of Thee; arise, and vindicate
Thy glory; free thy people from their yoke!
But let us wait; thus far He hath performed—
50   Sent his Anointed, and to us revealed him
By his great Prophet pointed at and shown
In public, and with him we have conversed.
Let us be glad of this, and all our fears
Lay on his providence; He will not fail,
Nor will withdraw him now, nor will recall—
Mock us with his blest sight, then snatch him hence:
Soon we shall see our hope, our joy, return."

Thus they out of their plaints new hope resume
To find whom at the first they found unsought.
60   But to his mother Mary, when she saw
Others returned from baptism, not her Son,
Nor left at Jordan tidings of him none,
Within her breast though calm, her breast though pure,
Motherly cares and fears got head, and raised
Some troubled thoughts, which she in sighs thus clad:—
"Oh, what avails me now that honour high,
To have conceived of God, or that salute,
'Hail, highly favoured, among women blest!'
While I to sorrows am no less advanced,
70   And fears as eminent above the lot
Of other women, by the birth I bore:
In such a season born, when scarce a shed
Could be obtained to shelter him or me
From the bleak air? A stable was our warmth,
A manger his; yet soon enforced to fly
Thence into Egypt, till the murderous king
Were dead, who sought his life, and, missing, filled
With infant blood the streets of Bethlehem.
From Egypt home returned, in Nazareth
80   Hath been our dwelling many years; his life
Private, unactive, calm, contemplative,
Little suspicious to any king. But now,
Full grown to man, acknowledged, as I hear,
By John the Baptist, and in public shewn,
Son owned from Heaven by his Father's voice,
I looked for some great change. To honour? no;
But trouble, as old Simeon plain foretold,
That to the fall and rising he should be
Of many in Israel, and to a sign
90   Spoken against—that through my very soul
A sword shall pierce. This is my favoured lot,

My exaltation to afflictions high!
Afflicted I may be, it seems, and blest!
I will not argue that, nor will repine.
But where delays he now? Some great intent
Conceals him. When twelve years he scarce had seen,
I lost him, but so found as well I saw
He could not lose himself, but went about
His Father's business. What he meant I mused—
100   Since understand; much more his absence now
Thus long to some great purpose he obscures.
But I to wait with patience am inured;
My heart hath been a storehouse long of things
And sayings laid up, pretending strange events."
Thus Mary, pondering oft, and oft to mind
Recalling what remarkably had passed
Since first her Salutation heard, with thoughts
Meekly composed awaited the fulfilling:
The while her Son, tracing the desert wild,
110   Sole, but with holiest meditations fed,
Into himself descended, and at once
All his great work to come before him set—
How to begin, how to accomplish best
His end of being on Earth, and mission high.
For Satan, with sly preface to return,
Had left him vacant, and with speed was gone
Up to the middle region of thick air,
Where all his Potentates in council sate.
There, without sign of boast, or sign of joy,
120   Solicitous and blank, he thus began:—
"Princes, Heaven's ancient Sons, AEthereal Thrones—
Daemonian Spirits now, from the element
Each of his reign allotted, rightlier called
Powers of Fire, Air, Water, and Earth beneath
(So may we hold our place and these mild seats

Without new trouble!)—such an enemy
Is risen to invade us, who no less
Threatens than our expulsion down to Hell.
I, as I undertook, and with the vote
130   Consenting in full frequence was impowered,
Have found him, viewed him, tasted him; but find
Far other labour to be undergone
Than when I dealt with Adam, first of men,
Though Adam by his wife's allurement fell,
However to this Man inferior far—
If he be Man by mother's side, at least
With more than human gifts from Heaven adorned,
Perfections absolute, graces divine,
And amplitude of mind to greatest deeds.
140   Therefore I am returned, lest confidence
Of my success with Eve in Paradise
Deceive ye to persuasion over-sure
Of like succeeding here. I summon all
Rather to be in readiness with hand
Or counsel to assist, lest I, who erst
Thought none my equal, now be overmatched."
So spake the old Serpent, doubting, and from all
With clamour was assured their utmost aid
At his command; when from amidst them rose
150   Belial, the dissolutest Spirit that fell,
The sensualest, and, after Asmodai,
The fleshliest Incubus, and thus advised:—
"Set women in his eye and in his walk,
Among daughters of men the fairest found.
Many are in each region passing fair
As the noon sky, more like to goddesses
Than mortal creatures, graceful and discreet,
Expert in amorous arts, enchanting tongues
Persuasive, virgin majesty with mild

160   And sweet allayed, yet terrible to approach,
Skilled to retire, and in retiring draw
Hearts after them tangled in amorous nets.
Such object hath the power to soften and tame
Severest temper, smooth the rugged'st brow,
Enerve, and with voluptuous hope dissolve,
Draw out with credulous desire, and lead
At will the manliest, resolutest breast,
As the magnetic hardest iron draws.
Women, when nothing else, beguiled the heart

170   Of wisest Solomon, and made him build,
And made him bow, to the gods of his wives."
To whom quick answer Satan thus returned:—
"Belial, in much uneven scale thou weigh'st
All others by thyself. Because of old
Thou thyself doat'st on womankind, admiring
Their shape, their colour, and attractive grace,
None are, thou think'st, but taken with such toys.
Before the Flood, thou, with thy lusty crew,
False titled Sons of God, roaming the Earth,

180   Cast wanton eyes on the daughters of men,
And coupled with them, and begot a race.
Have we not seen, or by relation heard,
In courts and regal chambers how thou lurk'st,
In wood or grove, by mossy fountain-side,
In valley or green meadow, to waylay
Some beauty rare, Calisto, Clymene,
Daphne, or Semele, Antiopa,
Or Amymone, Syrinx, many more
Too long—then lay'st thy scapes on names adored,

190   Apollo, Neptune, Jupiter, or Pan,
Satyr, or Faun, or Silvan? But these haunts
Delight not all. Among the sons of men
How many have with a smile made small account

Of beauty and her lures, easily scorned
All her assaults, on worthier things intent!
Remember that Pellean conqueror,
A youth, how all the beauties of the East
He slightly viewed, and slightly overpassed;
How he surnamed of Africa dismissed,
200   In his prime youth, the fair Iberian maid.
For Solomon, he lived at ease, and, full
Of honour, wealth, high fare, aimed not beyond
Higher design than to enjoy his state;
Thence to the bait of women lay exposed.
But he whom we attempt is wiser far
Than Solomon, of more exalted mind,
Made and set wholly on the accomplishment
Of greatest things. What woman will you find,
Though of this age the wonder and the fame,
210   On whom his leisure will voutsafe an eye
Of fond desire? Or should she, confident,
As sitting queen adored on Beauty's throne,
Descend with all her winning charms begirt
To enamour, as the zone of Venus once
Wrought that effect on Jove (so fables tell),
How would one look from his majestic brow,
Seated as on the top of Virtue's hill,
Discountenance her despised, and put to rout
All her array, her female pride deject,
220   Or turn to reverent awe! For Beauty stands
In the admiration only of weak minds
Led captive; cease to admire, and all her plumes
Fall flat, and shrink into a trivial toy,
At every sudden slighting quite abashed.
Therefore with manlier objects we must try
His constancy—with such as have more shew
Of worth, of honour, glory, and popular praise

(Rocks whereon greatest men have oftest wrecked);
Or that which only seems to satisfy
230   Lawful desires of nature, not beyond.
And now I know he hungers, where no food
Is to be found, in the wide Wilderness:
The rest commit to me; I shall let pass
No advantage, and his strength as oft assay."
He ceased, and heard their grant in loud acclaim;
Then forthwith to him takes a chosen band
Of Spirits likest to himself in guile,
To be at hand and at his beck appear,
If cause were to unfold some active scene
240   Of various persons, each to know his part;
Then to the desert takes with these his flight,
Where still, from shade to shade, the Son of God,
After forty days' fasting, had remained,
Now hungering first, and to himself thus said:—
"Where will this end? Four times ten days I have passed
Wandering this woody maze, and human food
Nor tasted, nor had appetite. That fast
To virtue I impute not, or count part
Of what I suffer here. If nature need not,
250   Or God support nature without repast,
Though needing, what praise is it to endure?
But now I feel I hunger; which declares
Nature hath need of what she asks. Yet God
Can satisfy that need some other way,
Though hunger still remain. So it remain
Without this body's wasting, I content me,
And from the sting of famine fear no harm;
Nor mind it, fed with better thoughts, that feed
Me hungering more to do my Father's will."
260   It was the hour of night, when thus the Son
Communed in silent walk, then laid him down

Under the hospitable covert nigh
Of trees thick interwoven. There he slept,
And dreamed, as appetite is wont to dream,
Of meats and drinks, nature's refreshment sweet.
Him thought he by the brook of Cherith stood,
And saw the ravens with their horny beaks
Food to Elijah bringing even and morn—
Though ravenous, taught to abstain from what they brought;
270   He saw the Prophet also, how he fled
Into the desert, and how there he slept
Under a juniper—then how, awaked,
He found his supper on the coals prepared,
And by the Angel was bid rise and eat,
And eat the second time after repose,
The strength whereof sufficed him forty days:
Sometimes that with Elijah he partook,
Or as a guest with Daniel at his pulse.
Thus wore out night; and now the harald Lark
280   Left his ground-nest, high towering to descry
The Morn's approach, and greet her with his song.
As lightly from his grassy couch up rose
Our Saviour, and found all was but a dream;
Fasting he went to sleep, and fasting waked.
Up to a hill anon his steps he reared,
From whose high top to ken the prospect round,
If cottage were in view, sheep-cote, or herd;
But cottage, herd, or sheep-cote, none he saw—
Only in a bottom saw a pleasant grove,
290   With chaunt of tuneful birds resounding loud.
Thither he bent his way, determined there
To rest at noon, and entered soon the shade
High-roofed, and walks beneath, and alleys brown,
That opened in the midst a woody scene;
Nature's own work it seemed (Nature taught Art),

369

And, to a superstitious eye, the haunt
Of wood-gods and wood-nymphs. He viewed it round;
When suddenly a man before him stood,
Not rustic as before, but seemlier clad,
300   As one in city or court or palace bred,
And with fair speech these words to him addressed:—
"With granted leave officious I return,
But much more wonder that the Son of God
In this wild solitude so long should bide,
Of all things destitute, and, well I know,
Not without hunger. Others of some note,
As story tells, have trod this wilderness:
The fugitive Bond-woman, with her son,
Outcast Nebaioth, yet found here relief
310   By a providing Angel; all the race
Of Israel here had famished, had not God
Rained from heaven manna; and that Prophet bold,
Native of Thebez, wandering here, was fed
Twice by a voice inviting him to eat.
Of thee those forty days none hath regard,
Forty and more deserted here indeed."
To whom thus Jesus:—"What conclud'st thou hence?
They all had need; I, as thou seest, have none."
"How hast thou hunger then?" Satan replied.
320   "Tell me, if food were now before thee set,
Wouldst thou not eat?" "Thereafter as I like
the giver," answered Jesus. "Why should that
Cause thy refusal?" said the subtle Fiend.
"Hast thou not right to all created things?
Owe not all creatures, by just right, to thee
Duty and service, nor to stay till bid,
But tender all their power? Nor mention I
Meats by the law unclean, or offered first
To idols—those young Daniel could refuse;

330   Nor proffered by an enemy—though who
        Would scruple that, with want oppressed? Behold,
        Nature ashamed, or, better to express,
        Troubled, that thou shouldst hunger, hath purveyed
        From all the elements her choicest store,
        To treat thee as beseems, and as her Lord
        With honour. Only deign to sit and eat."
        He spake no dream; for, as his words had end,
        Our Saviour, lifting up his eyes, beheld,
        In ample space under the broadest shade,
340   A table richly spread in regal mode,
        With dishes piled and meats of noblest sort
        And savour—beasts of chase, or fowl of game,
        In pastry built, or from the spit, or boiled,
        Grisamber-steamed; all fish, from sea or shore,
        Freshet or purling brook, of shell or fin,
        And exquisitest name, for which was drained
        Pontus, and Lucrine bay, and Afric coast.
        Alas! how simple, to these cates compared,
        Was that crude Apple that diverted Eve!
350   And at a stately sideboard, by the wine,
        That fragrant smell diffused, in order stood
        Tall stripling youths rich-clad, of fairer hue
        Than Ganymed or Hylas; distant more,
        Under the trees now tripped, now solemn stood,
        Nymphs of Diana's train, and Naiades
        With fruits and flowers from Amalthea's horn,
        And ladies of the Hesperides, that seemed
        Fairer than feigned of old, or fabled since
        Of faery damsels met in forest wide
360   By knights of Logres, or of Lyones,
        Lancelot, or Pelleas, or Pellenore.
        And all the while harmonious airs were heard
        Of chiming strings or charming pipes; and winds

Of gentlest gale Arabian odours fanned
From their soft wings, and Flora's earliest smells.
Such was the splendour; and the Tempter now
His invitation earnestly renewed:—
"What doubts the Son of God to sit and eat?
These are not fruits forbidden; no interdict

370   Defends the touching of these viands pure;
Their taste no knowledge works, at least of evil,
But life preserves, destroys life's enemy,
Hunger, with sweet restorative delight.
All these are Spirits of air, and woods, and springs,
Thy gentle ministers, who come to pay
Thee homage, and acknowledge thee their Lord.
What doubt'st thou, Son of God? Sit down and eat."
To whom thus Jesus temperately replied:—
"Said'st thou not that to all things I had right?

380   And who withholds my power that right to use?
Shall I receive by gift what of my own,
When and where likes me best, I can command?
I can at will, doubt not, as soon as thou,
Command a table in this wilderness,
And call swift flights of Angels ministrant,
Arrayed in glory, on my cup to attend:
Why shouldst thou, then, obtrude this diligence
In vain, where no acceptance it can find?
And with my hunger what hast thou to do?

390   Thy pompous delicacies I contemn,
And count thy specious gifts no gifts, but guiles."
To whom thus answered Satan, male-content:—
"That I have also power to give thou seest;
If of that power I bring thee voluntary
What I might have bestowed on whom I pleased,
And rather opportunely in this place
Chose to impart to thy apparent need,

Why shouldst thou not accept it? But I see
What I can do or offer is suspect.
400   Of these things others quickly will dispose,
Whose pains have earned the far-fet spoil." With that
Both table and provision vanished quite,
With sound of harpies' wings and talons heard;
Only the importune Tempter still remained,
And with these words his temptation pursued:—
"By hunger, that each other creature tames,
Thou art not to be harmed, therefore not moved;
Thy temperance, invincible besides,
For no allurement yields to appetite;
410   And all thy heart is set on high designs,
High actions. But wherewith to be achieved?
Great acts require great means of enterprise;
Thou art unknown, unfriended, low of birth,
A carpenter thy father known, thyself
Bred up in poverty and straits at home,
Lost in a desert here and hunger-bit.
Which way, or from what hope, dost thou aspire
To greatness? whence authority deriv'st?
What followers, what retinue canst thou gain,
420   Or at thy heels the dizzy multitude,
Longer than thou canst feed them on thy cost?
Money brings honour, friends, conquest, and realms.
What raised Antipater the Edomite,
And his son Herod placed on Juda's throne,
Thy throne, but gold, that got him puissant friends?
Therefore, if at great things thou wouldst arrive,
Get riches first, get wealth, and treasure heap—
Not difficult, if thou hearken to me.
Riches are mine, fortune is in my hand;
430   They whom I favour thrive in wealth amain,
While virtue, valour, wisdom, sit in want."

To whom thus Jesus patiently replied:—
"Yet wealth without these three is impotent
To gain dominion, or to keep it gained—
Witness those ancient empires of the earth,
In highth of all their flowing wealth dissolved;
But men endued with these have oft attained,
In lowest poverty, to highest deeds—
Gideon, and Jephtha, and the shepherd lad
440   Whose offspring on the throne of Juda sate
So many ages, and shall yet regain
That seat, and reign in Israel without end.
Among the Heathen (for throughout the world
To me is not unknown what hath been done
Worthy of memorial) canst thou not remember
Quintius, Fabricius, Curius, Regulus?
For I esteem those names of men so poor,
Who could do mighty things, and could contemn
Riches, though offered from the hand of kings.
450   And what in me seems wanting but that I
May also in this poverty as soon
Accomplish what they did, perhaps and more?
Extol not riches, then, the toil of fools,
The wise man's cumbrance, if not snare; more apt
To slacken virtue and abate her edge
Than prompt her to do aught may merit praise.
What if with like aversion I reject
Riches and realms! Yet not for that a crown,
Golden in shew, is but a wreath of thorns,
460   Brings dangers, troubles, cares, and sleepless nights,
To him who wears the regal diadem,
When on his shoulders each man's burden lies;
For therein stands the office of a king,
His honour, virtue, merit, and chief praise,
That for the public all this weight he bears.

Yet he who reigns within himself, and rules
Passions, desires, and fears, is more a king—
Which every wise and virtuous man attains;
And who attains not, ill aspires to rule
470   Cities of men, or headstrong multitudes,
Subject himself to anarchy within,
Or lawless passions in him, which he serves.
But to guide nations in the way of truth
By saving doctrine, and from error lead
To know, and, knowing, worship God aright,
Is yet more kingly. This attracts the soul,
Governs the inner man, the nobler part;
That other o'er the body only reigns,
And oft by force—which to a generous mind
480   So reigning can be no sincere delight.
Besides, to give a kingdom hath been thought
Greater and nobler done, and to lay down
Far more magnanimous, than to assume.
Riches are needless, then, both for themselves,
And for thy reason why they should be sought—
To gain a sceptre, oftest better missed."

BOOK III

So spake the Son of God; and Satan stood
A while as mute, confounded what to say,
What to reply, confuted and convinced
Of his weak arguing and fallacious drift;
At length, collecting all his serpent wiles,
With soothing words renewed, him thus accosts:—
"I see thou know'st what is of use to know,
What best to say canst say, to do canst do;
Thy actions to thy words accord; thy words
10   To thy large heart give utterance due; thy heart
Contains of good, wise, just, the perfet shape.
Should kings and nations from thy mouth consult,
Thy counsel would be as the oracle
Urim and Thummim, those oraculous gems
On Aaron's breast, or tongue of Seers old
Infallible; or, wert thou sought to deeds
That might require the array of war, thy skill
Of conduct would be such that all the world
Could not sustain thy prowess, or subsist
20   In battle, though against thy few in arms.
These godlike virtues wherefore dost thou hide?
Affecting private life, or more obscure
In savage wilderness, wherefore deprive
All Earth her wonder at thy acts, thyself

The fame and glory—glory, the reward
That sole excites to high attempts the flame
Of most erected spirits, most tempered pure
AEthereal, who all pleasures else despise,
All treasures and all gain esteem as dross,
30   And dignities and powers, all but the highest?
Thy years are ripe, and over-ripe. The son
Of Macedonian Philip had ere these
Won Asia, and the throne of Cyrus held
At his dispose; young Scipio had brought down
The Carthaginian pride; young Pompey quelled
The Pontic king, and in triumph had rode.
Yet years, and to ripe years judgment mature,
Quench not the thirst of glory, but augment.
Great Julius, whom now all the world admires,
40   The more he grew in years, the more inflamed
With glory, wept that he had lived so long
Ingloroious. But thou yet art not too late."
To whom our Saviour calmly thus replied:—
"Thou neither dost persuade me to seek wealth
For empire's sake, nor empire to affect
For glory's sake, by all thy argument.
For what is glory but the blaze of fame,
The people's praise, if always praise unmixed?
And what the people but a herd confused,
50   A miscellaneous rabble, who extol
Things vulgar, and, well weighed, scarce worth the praise?
They praise and they admire they know not what,
And know not whom, but as one leads the other;
And what delight to be by such extolled,
To live upon their tongues, and be their talk?
Of whom to be dispraised were no small praise—
His lot who dares be singularly good.

The intelligent among them and the wise
Are few, and glory scarce of few is raised.
60   This is true glory and renown—when God,
Looking on the Earth, with approbation marks
The just man, and divulges him through Heaven
To all his Angels, who with true applause
Recount his praises. Thus he did to Job,
When, to extend his fame through Heaven and Earth,
As thou to thy reproach may'st well remember,
He asked thee, 'Hast thou seen my servant Job?'
Famous he was in Heaven; on Earth less known,
Where glory is false glory, attributed
70   To things not glorious, men not worthy of fame.
They err who count it glorious to subdue
By conquest far and wide, to overrun
Large countries, and in field great battles win,
Great cities by assault. What do these worthies
But rob and spoil, burn, slaughter, and enslave
Peaceable nations, neighbouring or remote,
Made captive, yet deserving freedom more
Than those their conquerors, who leave behind
Nothing but ruin wheresoe'er they rove,
80   And all the flourishing works of peace destroy;
Then swell with pride, and must be titled Gods,
Great benefactors of mankind, Deliverers,
Worshipped with temple, priest, and sacrifice?
One is the son of Jove, of Mars the other;
Till conqueror Death discover them scarce men,
Rowling in brutish vices, and deformed,
Violent or shameful death their due reward.
But, if there be in glory aught of good;
It may be means far different be attained,
90   Without ambition, war, or violence—
By deeds of peace, by wisdom eminent,

By patience, temperance. I mention still
Him whom thy wrongs, with saintly patience borne,
Made famous in a land and times obscure;
Who names not now with honour patient Job?
Poor Socrates, (who next more memorable?)
By what he taught and suffered for so doing,
For truth's sake suffering death unjust, lives now
Equal in fame to proudest conquerors.
100   Yet, if for fame and glory aught be done,
Aught suffered—if young African for fame
His wasted country freed from Punic rage—
The deed becomes unpraised, the man at least,
And loses, though but verbal, his reward.
Shall I seek glory, then, as vain men seek,
Oft not deserved? I seek not mine, but His
Who sent me, and thereby witness whence I am."
To whom the Tempter, murmuring, thus replied:—
"Think not so slight of glory, therein least
110   Resembling thy great Father. He seeks glory,
And for his glory all things made, all things
Orders and governs; nor content in Heaven,
By all his Angels glorified, requires
Glory from men, from all men, good or bad,
Wise or unwise, no difference, no exemption.
Above all sacrifice, or hallowed gift,
Glory he requires, and glory he receives,
Promiscuous from all nations, Jew, or Greek,
Or Barbarous, nor exception hath declared;
120   From us, his foes pronounced, glory he exacts."
To whom our Saviour fervently replied:
"And reason; since his Word all things produced,
Though chiefly not for glory as prime end,
But to shew forth his goodness, and impart
His good communicable to every soul

Freely; of whom what could He less expect
Than glory and benediction—that is, thanks—
The slightest, easiest, readiest recompense
From them who could return him nothing else,
130 And, not returning that, would likeliest render
Contempt instead, dishonour, obloquy?
Hard recompense, unsuitable return
For so much good, so much beneficence!
But why should man seek glory, who of his own
Hath nothing, and to whom nothing belongs
But condemnation, ignominy, and shame—
Who, for so many benefits received,
Turned recreant to God, ingrate and false,
And so of all true good himself despoiled;
140 Yet, sacrilegious, to himself would take
That which to God alone of right belongs?
Yet so much bounty is in God, such grace,
That who advances his glory, not their own,
Them he himself to glory will advance."
So spake the Son of God; and here again
Satan had not to answer, but stood struck
With guilt of his own sin—for he himself,
Insatiable of glory, had lost all;
Yet of another plea bethought him soon:—
150 "Of glory, as thou wilt," said he, "so deem;
Worth or not worth the seeking, let it pass.
But to a Kingdom thou art born—ordained
To sit upon thy father David's throne,
By mother's side thy father, though thy right
Be now in powerful hands, that will not part
Easily from possession won with arms.
Judaea now and all the Promised Land,
Reduced a province under Roman yoke,
Obeys Tiberius, nor is always ruled

160   With temperate sway: oft have they violated
        The Temple, oft the Law, with foul affronts,
        Abominations rather, as did once
        Antiochus. And think'st thou to regain
        Thy right by sitting still, or thus retiring?
        So did not Machabeus. He indeed
        Retired unto the Desert, but with arms;
        And o'er a mighty king so oft prevailed
        That by strong hand his family obtained,
        Though priests, the crown, and David's throne usurped,
170   With Modin and her suburbs once content.
        If kingdom move thee not, let move thee zeal
        And duty—zeal and duty are not slow,
        But on Occasion's forelock watchful wait:
        They themselves rather are occasion best—
        Zeal of thy Father's house, duty to free
        Thy country from her heathen servitude.
        So shalt thou best fulfil, best verify,
        The Prophets old, who sung thy endless reign—
        The happier reign the sooner it begins.
180   Rein then; what canst thou better do the while?"
        To whom our Saviour answer thus returned:—
        "All things are best fulfilled in their due time;
        And time there is for all things, Truth hath said.
        If of my reign Prophetic Writ hath told
        That it shall never end, so, when begin
        The Father in his purpose hath decreed—
        He in whose hand all times and seasons rowl.
        What if he hath decreed that I shall first
        Be tried in humble state, and things adverse,
190   By tribulations, injuries, insults,
        Contempts, and scorns, and snares, and violence,
        Suffering, abstaining, quietly expecting
        Without distrust or doubt, that He may know

What I can suffer, how obey? Who best
Can suffer best can do, best reign who first
Well hath obeyed—just trial ere I merit
My exaltation without change or end.
But what concerns it thee when I begin
My everlasting Kingdom? Why art thou
200   Solicitous? What moves thy inquisition?
Know'st thou not that my rising is thy fall,
And my promotion will be thy destruction?"
To whom the Tempter, inly racked, replied:—
"Let that come when it comes. All hope is lost
Of my reception into grace; what worse?
For where no hope is left is left no fear.
If there be worse, the expectation more
Of worse torments me than the feeling can.
I would be at the worst; worst is my port,
210   My harbour, and my ultimate repose,
The end I would attain, my final good.
My error was my error, and my crime
My crime; whatever, for itself condemned,
And will alike be punished, whether thou
Reign or reign not—though to that gentle brow
Willingly I could fly, and hope thy reign,
From that placid aspect and meek regard,
Rather than aggravate my evil state,
Would stand between me and thy Father's ire
220   (Whose ire I dread more than the fire of Hell)
A shelter and a kind of shading cool
Interposition, as a summer's cloud.
If I, then, to the worst that can be haste,
Why move thy feet so slow to what is best?
Happiest, both to thyself and all the world,
That thou, who worthiest art, shouldst be their King!
Perhaps thou linger'st in deep thoughts detained

Of the enterprise so hazardous and high!
No wonder; for, though in thee be united
230   What of perfection can in Man be found,
Or human nature can receive, consider
Thy life hath yet been private, most part spent
At home, scarce viewed the Galilean towns,
And once a year Jerusalem, few days'
Short sojourn; and what thence couldst thou observe?
The world thou hast not seen, much less her glory,
Empires, and monarchs, and their radiant courts—
Best school of best experience, quickest in sight
In all things that to greatest actions lead.
240   The wisest, unexperienced, will be ever
Timorous, and loth, with novice modesty
(As he who, seeking asses, found a kingdom)
Irresolute, unhardy, unadventrous.
But I will bring thee where thou soon shalt quit
Those rudiments, and see before thine eyes
The monarchies of the Earth, their pomp and state—
Sufficient introduction to inform
Thee, of thyself so apt, in regal arts,
And regal mysteries; that thou may'st know
250   How best their opposition to withstand."
With that (such power was given him then), he took
The Son of God up to a mountain high.
It was a mountain at whose verdant feet
A spacious plain outstretched in circuit wide
Lay pleasant; from his side two rivers flowed,
The one winding, the other straight, and left between
Fair champaign, with less rivers interveined,
Then meeting joined their tribute to the sea.
Fertil of corn the glebe, of oil, and wine;
260   With herds the pasture thronged, with flocks the hills;
Huge cities and high-towered, that well might seem

The seats of mightiest monarchs; and so large
The prospect was that here and there was room
For barren desert, fountainless and dry.
To this high mountain-top the Tempter brought
Our Saviour, and new train of words began:—
"Well have we speeded, and o'er hill and dale,
Forest, and field, and flood, temples and towers,
Cut shorter many a league. Here thou behold'st
270   Assyria, and her empire's ancient bounds,
Araxes and the Caspian lake; thence on
As far as Indus east, Euphrates west,
And oft beyond; to south the Persian bay,
And, inaccessible, the Arabian drouth:
Here, Nineveh, of length within her wall
Several days' journey, built by Ninus old,
Of that first golden monarchy the seat,
And seat of Salmanassar, whose success
Israel in long captivity still mourns;
280   There Babylon, the wonder of all tongues,
As ancient, but rebuilt by him who twice
Judah and all thy father David's house
Led captive, and Jerusalem laid waste,
Till Cyrus set them free; Persepolis,
His city, there thou seest, and Bactra there;
Ecbatana her structure vast there shews,
And Hecatompylos her hunderd gates;
There Susa by Choaspes, amber stream,
The drink of none but kings; of later fame,
290   Built by Emathian or by Parthian hands,
The great Seleucia, Nisibis, and there
Artaxata, Teredon, Ctesiphon,
Turning with easy eye, thou may'st behold.
All these the Parthian (now some ages past
By great Arsaces led, who founded first

That empire) under his dominion holds,
From the luxurious kings of Antioch won.
And just in time thou com'st to have a view
Of his great power; for now the Parthian king
300   In Ctesiphon hath gathered all his host
Against the Scythian, whose incursions wild
Have wasted Sogdiana; to her aid
He marches now in haste. See, though from far,
His thousands, in what martial equipage
They issue forth, steel bows and shafts their arms,
Of equal dread in flight or in pursuit—
All horsemen, in which fight they most excel;
See how in warlike muster they appear,
In rhombs, and wedges, and half-moons, and wings."
310   He looked, and saw what numbers numberless
The city gates outpoured, light-armed troops
In coats of mail and military pride.
In mail their horses clad, yet fleet and strong,
Prauncing their riders bore, the flower and choice
Of many provinces from bound to bound—
From Arachosia, from Candaor east,
And Margiana, to the Hyrcanian cliffs
Of Caucasus, and dark Iberian dales;
From Atropatia, and the neighbouring plains
320   Of Adiabene, Media, and the south
Of Susiana, to Balsara's haven.
He saw them in their forms of battle ranged,
How quick they wheeled, and flying behind them shot
Sharp sleet of arrowy showers against the face
Of their pursuers, and overcame by flight;
The field all iron cast a gleaming brown.
Nor wanted clouds of foot, nor, on each horn,
Cuirassiers all in steel for standing fight,
Chariots, or elephants indorsed with towers

330   Of archers; nor of labouring pioners
        A multitude, with spades and axes armed,
        To lay hills plain, fell woods, or valleys fill,
        Or where plain was raise hill, or overlay
        With bridges rivers proud, as with a yoke:
        Mules after these, camels and dromedaries,
        And waggons fraught with utensils of war.
        Such forces met not, nor so wide a camp,
        When Agrican, with all his northern powers,
        Besieged Albracea, as romances tell,
340   The city of Gallaphrone, from thence to win
        The fairest of her sex, Angelica,
        His daughter, sought by many prowest knights,
        Both Paynim and the peers of Charlemane.
        Such and so numerous was their chivalry;
        At sight whereof the Fiend yet more presumed,
        And to our Saviour thus his words renewed:—
        "That thou may'st know I seek not to engage
        Thy virtue, and not every way secure
        On no slight grounds thy safety, hear and mark
350   To what end I have brought thee hither, and shew
        All this fair sight. Thy kingdom, though foretold
        By Prophet or by Angel, unless thou
        Endeavour, as thy father David did,
        Thou never shalt obtain: prediction still
        In all things, and all men, supposes means;
        Without means used, what it predicts revokes.
        But say thou wert possessed of David's throne
        By free consent of all, none opposite,
        Samaritan or Jew; how couldst thou hope
360   Long to enjoy it quiet and secure
        Between two such enclosing enemies,
        Roman and Parthian? Therefore one of these
        Thou must make sure thy own: the Parthian first,

By my advice, as nearer, and of late
Found able by invasion to annoy
Thy country, and captive lead away her kings,
Antigonus and old Hyrcanus, bound,
Maugre the Roman. It shall be my task
To render thee the Parthian at dispose,
370   Choose which thou wilt, by conquest or by league.
By him thou shalt regain, without him not,
That which alone can truly reinstall thee
In David's royal seat, his true successor—
Deliverance of thy brethren, those Ten Tribes
Whose offspring in his territory yet serve
In Habor, and among the Medes dispersed:
The sons of Jacob, two of Joseph, lost
Thus long from Israel, serving, as of old
Their fathers in the land of Egypt served,
380   This offer sets before thee to deliver.
These if from servitude thou shalt restore
To their inheritance, then, nor till then,
Thou on the throne of David in full glory,
From Egypt to Euphrates and beyond,
Shalt reign, and Rome or Caesar not need fear."
To whom our Saviour answered thus, unmoved:—
"Much ostentation vain of fleshly arm
And fragile arms, much instrument of war,
Long in preparing, soon to nothing brought,
390   Before mine eyes thou hast set, and in my ear
Vented much policy, and projects deep
Of enemies, of aids, battles, and leagues,
Plausible to the world, to me worth naught.
Means I must use, thou say'st; prediction else
Will unpredict, and fail me of the throne!
My time, I told thee (and that time for thee
Were better farthest off), is not yet come.

When that comes, think not thou to find me slack
On my part aught endeavouring, or to need
400   Thy politic maxims, or that cumbersome
Luggage of war there shewn me—argument
Of human weakness rather than of strength.
My brethren, as thou call'st them, those Ten Tribes,
I must deliver, if I mean to reign
David's true heir, and his full sceptre sway
To just extent over all Israel's sons!
But whence to thee this zeal? Where was it then
For Israel, or for David, or his throne,
When thou stood'st up his tempter to the pride
410   Of numbering Israel—which cost the lives
of threescore and ten thousand Israelites
By three days' pestilence? Such was thy zeal
To Israel then, the same that now to me.
As for those captive tribes, themselves were they
Who wrought their own captivity, fell off
From God to worship calves, the deities
Of Egypt, Baal next and Ashtaroth,
And all the idolatries of heathen round,
Besides their other worse than heathenish crimes;
420   Nor in the land of their captivity
Humbled themselves, or penitent besought
The God of their forefathers, but so died
Impenitent, and left a race behind
Like to themselves, distinguishable scarce
From Gentiles, but by circumcision vain,
And God with idols in their worship joined.
Should I of these the liberty regard,
Who, freed, as to their ancient patrimony,
Unhumbled, unrepentant, unreformed,
430   Headlong would follow, and to their gods perhaps
Of Bethel and of Dan? No; let them serve

Their enemies who serve idols with God.
Yet He at length, time to himself best known,
Remembering Abraham, by some wondrous call
May bring them back, repentant and sincere,
And at their passing cleave the Assyrian flood,
While to their native land with joy they haste,
As the Red Sea and Jordan once he cleft,
When to the Promised Land their fathers passed.
440   To his due time and providence I leave them."
So spake Israel's true King, and to the Fiend
Made answer meet, that made void all his wiles.
So fares it when with truth falsehood contends.

BOOK IV

Perplexed and troubled at his bad success
The Tempter stood, nor had what to reply,
Discovered in his fraud, thrown from his hope
So oft, and the persuasive rhetoric
That sleeked his tongue, and won so much on Eve,
So little here, nay lost. But Eve was Eve;
This far his over-match, who, self-deceived
And rash, beforehand had no better weighed
The strength he was to cope with, or his own.
But—as a man who had been matchless held
In cunning, over-reached where least he thought,
To salve his credit, and for very spite,
Still will be tempting him who foils him still,
And never cease, though to his shame the more;
Or as a swarm of flies in vintage-time,
About the wine-press where sweet must is poured,
Beat off, returns as oft with humming sound;
Or surging waves against a solid rock,
Though all to shivers dashed, the assault renew,
(Vain battery!) and in froth or bubbles end—
So Satan, whom repulse upon repulse
Met ever, and to shameful silence brought,
Yet gives not o'er, though desperate of success,
And his vain importunity pursues.

10

20

He brought our Saviour to the western side
Of that high mountain, whence he might behold
Another plain, long, but in breadth not wide,
Washed by the southern sea, and on the north
To equal length backed with a ridge of hills
30   That screened the fruits of the earth and seats of men
From cold Septentrion blasts; thence in the midst
Divided by a river, off whose banks
On each side an Imperial City stood,
With towers and temples proudly elevate
On seven small hills, with palaces adorned,
Porches and theatres, baths, aqueducts,
Statues and trophies, and triumphal arcs,
Gardens and groves, presented to his eyes
Above the highth of mountains interposed—
40   By what strange parallax, or optic skill
Of vision, multiplied through air, or glass
Of telescope, were curious to enquire.
And now the Tempter thus his silence broke:—
"The city which thou seest no other deem
Than great and glorious Rome, Queen of the Earth
So far renowned, and with the spoils enriched
Of nations. There the Capitol thou seest,
Above the rest lifting his stately head
On the Tarpeian rock, her citadel
50   Impregnable; and there Mount Palatine,
The imperial palace, compass huge, and high
The structure, skill of noblest architects,
With gilded battlements, conspicuous far,
Turrets, and terraces, and glittering spires.
Many a fair edifice besides, more like
Houses of gods—so well I have disposed
My aerie microscope—thou may'st behold,
Outside and inside both, pillars and roofs

Carved work, the hand of famed artificers

60   In cedar, marble, ivory, or gold.
           Thence to the gates cast round thine eye, and see
           What conflux issuing forth, or entering in:
           Praetors, proconsuls to their provinces
           Hasting, or on return, in robes of state;
           Lictors and rods, the ensigns of their power;
           Legions and cohorts, turms of horse and wings;
           Or embassies from regions far remote,
           In various habits, on the Appian road,
           Or on the AEmilian—some from farthest south,
70   Syene, and where the shadow both way falls,
           Meroe, Nilotic isle, and, more to west,
           The realm of Bocchus to the Blackmoor sea;
           From the Asian kings (and Parthian among these),
           From India and the Golden Chersoness,
           And utmost Indian isle Taprobane,
           Dusk faces with white silken turbants wreathed;
           From Gallia, Gades, and the British west;
           Germans, and Scythians, and Sarmatians north
           Beyond Danubius to the Tauric pool.
80   All nations now to Rome obedience pay—
           To Rome's great Emperor, whose wide domain,
           In ample territory, wealth and power,
           Civility of manners, arts and arms,
           And long renown, thou justly may'st prefer
           Before the Parthian. These two thrones except,
           The rest are barbarous, and scarce worth the sight,
           Shared among petty kings too far removed;
           These having shewn thee, I have shewn thee all
           The kingdoms of the world, and all their glory.
90   This Emperor hath no son, and now is old,
           Old and lascivious, and from Rome retired
           To Capreae, an island small but strong

392

On the Campanian shore, with purpose there
His horrid lusts in private to enjoy;
Committing to a wicked favourite
All public cares, and yet of him suspicious;
Hated of all, and hating. With what ease,
Endued with regal virtues as thou art,
Appearing, and beginning noble deeds,
100   Might'st thou expel this monster from his throne,
Now made a sty, and, in his place ascending,
A victor-people free from servile yoke!
And with my help thou may'st; to me the power
Is given, and by that right I give it thee.
Aim, therefore, at no less than all the world;
Aim at the highest; without the highest attained,
Will be for thee no sitting, or not long,
On David's throne, be prophesied what will."
To whom the Son of God, unmoved, replied:—
110   "Nor doth this grandeur and majestic shew
Of luxury, though called magnificence,
More than of arms before, allure mine eye,
Much less my mind; though thou should'st add to tell
Their sumptuous gluttonies, and gorgeous feasts
On citron tables or Atlantic stone
(For I have also heard, perhaps have read),
Their wines of Setia, Cales, and Falerne,
Chios and Crete, and how they quaff in gold,
Crystal, and myrrhine cups, imbossed with gems
120   And studs of pearl—to me should'st tell, who thirst
And hunger still. Then embassies thou shew'st
From nations far and nigh! What honour that,
But tedious waste of time, to sit and hear
So many hollow compliments and lies,
Outlandish flatteries? Then proceed'st to talk
Of the Emperor, how easily subdued,

How gloriously. I shall, thou say'st, expel
A brutish monster: what if I withal
Expel a Devil who first made him such?
130   Let his tormentor, Conscience, find him out;
For him I was not sent, nor yet to free
That people, victor once, now vile and base,
Deservedly made vassal—who, once just,
Frugal, and mild, and temperate, conquered well,
But govern ill the nations under yoke,
Peeling their provinces, exhausted all
By lust and rapine; first ambitious grown
Of triumph, that insulting vanity;
Then cruel, by their sports to blood inured
140   Of fighting beasts, and men to beasts exposed;
Luxurious by their wealth, and greedier still,
And from the daily Scene effeminate.
What wise and valiant man would seek to free
These, thus degenerate, by themselves enslaved,
Or could of inward slaves make outward free?
Know, therefore, when my season comes to sit
On David's throne, it shall be like a tree
Spreading and overshadowing all the earth,
Or as a stone that shall to pieces dash
150   All monarchies besides throughout the world;
And of my Kingdom there shall be no end.
Means there shall be to this; but what the means
Is not for thee to know, nor me to tell."
To whom the Tempter, impudent, replied:—
"I see all offers made by me how slight
Thou valuest, because offered, and reject'st.
Nothing will please the difficult and nice,
Or nothing more than still to contradict.
On the other side know also thou that I

160   On what I offer set as high esteem,
Nor what I part with mean to give for naught,
All these, which in a moment thou behold'st,
The kingdoms of the world, to thee I give
(For, given to me, I give to whom I please),
No trifle; yet with this reserve, not else—
On this condition, if thou wilt fall down,
And worship me as thy superior Lord
(Easily done), and hold them all of me;
For what can less so great a gift deserve?"

170   Whom thus our Saviour answered with disdain:—
"I never liked thy talk, thy offers less;
Now both abhor, since thou hast dared to utter
The abominable terms, impious condition.
But I endure the time, till which expired
Thou hast permission on me. It is written,
The first of all commandments, 'Thou shalt worship
The Lord thy God, and only Him shalt serve.'
And dar'st thou to the Son of God propound
To worship thee, accursed? now more accursed

180   For this attempt, bolder than that on Eve,
And more blasphemous; which expect to rue.
The kingdoms of the world to thee were given!
Permitted rather, and by thee usurped;
Other donation none thou canst produce.
If given, by whom but by the King of kings,
God over all supreme? If given to thee,
By thee how fairly is the Giver now
Repaid! But gratitude in thee is lost
Long since. Wert thou so void of fear or shame

190   As offer them to me, the Son of God—
To me my own, on such abhorred pact,
That I fall down and worship thee as God?
Get thee behind me! Plain thou now appear'st

That Evil One, Satan for ever damned."
To whom the Fiend, with fear abashed, replied:—
"Be not so sore offended, Son of God—
Though Sons of God both Angels are and Men—
If I, to try whether in higher sort
Than these thou bear'st that title, have proposed
200 What both from Men and Angels I receive,
Tetrarchs of Fire, Air, Flood, and on the Earth
Nations besides from all the quartered winds—
God of this World invoked, and World beneath.
Who then thou art, whose coming is foretold
To me most fatal, me it most concerns.
The trial hath indamaged thee no way,
Rather more honour left and more esteem;
Me naught advantaged, missing what I aimed.
Therefore let pass, as they are transitory,
210 The kingdoms of this world; I shall no more
Advise thee; gain them as thou canst, or not.
And thou thyself seem'st otherwise inclined
Than to a worldly crown, addicted more
To contemplation and profound dispute;
As by that early action may be judged,
When, slipping from thy mother's eye, thou went'st
Alone into the Temple, there wast found
Among the gravest Rabbies, disputant
On points and questions fitting Moses' chair,
220 Teaching, not taught. The childhood shews the man,
As morning shews the day. Be famous, then,
By wisdom; as thy empire must extend,
So let extend thy mind o'er all the world
In knowledge; all things in it comprehend.
All knowledge is not couched in Moses' law,
The Pentateuch, or what the Prophets wrote;
The Gentiles also know, and write, and teach

To admiration, led by Nature's light;
And with the Gentiles much thou must converse,
230   Ruling them by persuasion, as thou mean'st.
Without their learning, how wilt thou with them,
Or they with thee, hold conversation meet?
How wilt thou reason with them, how refute
Their idolisms, traditions, paradoxes?
Error by his own arms is best evinced.
Look once more, ere we leave this specular mount,
Westward, much nearer by south-west; behold
Where on the AEgean shore a city stands,
Built nobly, pure the air and light the soil—
240   Athens, the eye of Greece, mother of arts
And Eloquence, native to famous wits
Or hospitable, in her sweet recess,
City or suburban, studious walks and shades.
See there the olive-grove of Academe,
Plato's retirement, where the Attic bird
Trills her thick-warbled notes the summer long;
There, flowery hill, Hymettus, with the sound
Of bees' industrious murmur, oft invites
To studious musing; there Ilissus rowls
250   His whispering stream. Within the walls then view
The schools of ancient sages—his who bred
Great Alexander to subdue the world,
Lyceum there; and painted Stoa next.
There thou shalt hear and learn the secret power
Of harmony, in tones and numbers hit
By voice or hand, and various-measured verse,
AEolian charms and Dorian lyric odes,
And his who gave them breath, but higher sung,
Blind Melesigenes, thence Homer called,
260   Whose poem Phoebus challenged for his own.
Thence what the lofty grave Tragedians taught

In chorus or iambic, teachers best
Of moral prudence, with delight received
In brief sententious precepts, while they treat
Of fate, and chance, and change in human life,
High actions and high passions best describing.
Thence to the famous Orators repair,
Those ancient whose resistless eloquence
Wielded at will that fierce democraty,
270 Shook the Arsenal, and fulmined over Greece
To Macedon and Artaxerxes' throne.
To sage Philosophy next lend thine ear,
From heaven descended to the low-roofed house
Of Socrates—see there his tenement—
Whom, well inspired, the Oracle pronounced
Wisest of men; from whose mouth issued forth
Mellifluous streams, that watered all the schools
Of Academics old and new, with those
Surnamed Peripatetics, and the sect
280 Epicurean, and the Stoic severe.
These here revolve, or, as thou likest, at home,
Till time mature thee to a kingdom's weight;
These rules will render thee a king complete
Within thyself, much more with empire joined."
To whom our Saviour sagely thus replied:—
"Think not but that I know these things; or, think
I know them not, not therefore am I short
Of knowing what I ought. He who receives
Light from above, from the Fountain of Light,
290 No other doctrine needs, though granted true;
But these are false, or little else but dreams,
Conjectures, fancies, built on nothing firm.
The first and wisest of them all professed
To know this only, that he nothing knew;
The next to fabling fell and smooth conceits;

398

A third sort doubted all things, though plain sense;
Others in virtue placed felicity,
But virtue joined with riches and long life;
In corporal pleasure he, and careless ease;
300   The Stoic last in philosophic pride,
By him called virtue, and his virtuous man,
Wise, perfect in himself, and all possessing,
Equal to God, oft shames not to prefer,
As fearing God nor man, contemning all
Wealth, pleasure, pain or torment, death and life—
Which, when he lists, he leaves, or boasts he can;
For all his tedious talk is but vain boast,
Or subtle shifts conviction to evade.
Alas! what can they teach, and not mislead,
310   Ignorant of themselves, of God much more,
And how the World began, and how Man fell,
Degraded by himself, on grace depending?
Much of the Soul they talk, but all awry;
And in themselves seek virtue; and to themselves
All glory arrogate, to God give none;
Rather accuse him under usual names,
Fortune and Fate, as one regardless quite
Of mortal things. Who, therefore, seeks in these
True wisdom finds her not, or, by delusion
320   Far worse, her false resemblance only meets,
An empty cloud. However, many books,
Wise men have said, are wearisome; who reads
Incessantly, and to his reading brings not
A spirit and judgment equal or superior,
(And what he brings what needs he elsewhere seek?)
Uncertain and unsettled still remains,
Deep-versed in books and shallow in himself,
Crude or intoxicate, collecting toys
And trifles for choice matters, worth a sponge,

330   As children gathering pebbles on the shore.
Or, if I would delight my private hours
With music or with poem, where so soon
As in our native language can I find
That solace? All our Law and Story strewed
With hymns, our Psalms with artful terms inscribed,
Our Hebrew songs and harps, in Babylon
That pleased so well our victor's ear, declare
That rather Greece from us these arts derived—
Ill imitated while they loudest sing
340   The vices of their deities, and their own,
In fable, hymn, or song, so personating
Their gods ridiculous, and themselves past shame.
Remove their swelling epithetes, thick-laid
As varnish on a harlot's cheek, the rest,
Thin-sown with aught of profit or delight,
Will far be found unworthy to compare
With Sion's songs, to all true tastes excelling,
Where God is praised aright and godlike men,
The Holiest of Holies and his Saints
350   (Such are from God inspired, not such from thee);
Unless where moral virtue is expressed
By light of Nature, not in all quite lost.
Their orators thou then extoll'st as those
The top of eloquence—statists indeed,
And lovers of their country, as may seem;
But herein to our Prophets far beneath,
As men divinely taught, and better teaching
The solid rules of civil government,
In their majestic, unaffected style,
360   Than all the oratory of Greece and Rome.
In them is plainest taught, and easiest learnt,
What makes a nation happy, and keeps it so,
What ruins kingdoms, and lays cities flat;

These only, with our Law, best form a king."
So spake the Son of God; but Satan, now
Quite at a loss (for all his darts were spent),
Thus to our Saviour, with stern brow, replied:—
"Since neither wealth nor honour, arms nor arts,
Kingdom nor empire, pleases thee, nor aught
370   By me proposed in life contemplative
Or active, tended on by glory or fame,
What dost thou in this world? The Wilderness
For thee is fittest place: I found thee there,
And thither will return thee. Yet remember
What I foretell thee; soon thou shalt have cause
To wish thou never hadst rejected, thus
Nicely or cautiously, my offered aid,
Which would have set thee in short time with ease
On David's throne, or throne of all the world,
380   Now at full age, fulness of time, thy season,
When prophecies of thee are best fulfilled.
Now, contrary—if I read aught in heaven,
Or heaven write aught of fate—by what the stars
Voluminous, or single characters
In their conjunction met, give me to spell,
Sorrows and labours, opposition, hate,
Attends thee; scorns, reproaches, injuries,
Violence and stripes, and, lastly, cruel death.
A kingdom they portend thee, but what kingdom,
390   Real or allegoric, I discern not;
Nor when: eternal sure—as without end,
Without beginning; for no date prefixed
Directs me in the starry rubric set."
So saying, he took (for still he knew his power
Not yet expired), and to the Wilderness
Brought back, the Son of God, and left him there,
Feigning to disappear. Darkness now rose,

As daylight sunk, and brought in louring Night,
Her shadowy offspring, unsubstantial both,
Privation mere of light and absent day.
Our Saviour, meek, and with untroubled mind
After hisaerie jaunt, though hurried sore,
Hungry and cold, betook him to his rest,
Wherever, under some concourse of shades,
Whose branching arms thick intertwined might shield
From dews and damps of night his sheltered head;
But, sheltered, slept in vain; for at his head
The Tempter watched, and soon with ugly dreams
Disturbed his sleep. And either tropic now
'Gan thunder, and both ends of heaven; the clouds
From many a horrid rift abortive poured
Fierce rain with lightning mixed, water with fire,
In ruin reconciled; nor slept the winds
Within their stony caves, but rushed abroad
From the four hinges of the world, and fell
On the vexed wilderness, whose tallest pines,
Though rooted deep as high, and sturdiest oaks,
Bowed their stiff necks, loaden with stormy blasts,
Or torn up sheer. Ill wast thou shrouded then,
O patient Son of God, yet only stood'st
Unshaken! Nor yet staid the terror there:
Infernal ghosts and hellish furies round
Environed thee; some howled, some yelled, some shrieked,
Some bent at thee their fiery darts, while thou
Sat'st unappalled in calm and sinless peace.
Thus passed the night so foul, till Morning fair
Came forth with pilgrim steps, in amice grey,
Who with her radiant finger stilled the roar
Of thunder, chased the clouds, and laid the winds,
And griesly spectres, which the Fiend had raised
To tempt the Son of God with terrors dire.

And now the sun with more effectual beams
Had cheered the face of earth, and dried the wet
From drooping plant, or dropping tree; the birds,
Who all things now behold more fresh and green,
After a night of storm so ruinous,
Cleared up their choicest notes in bush and spray,
To gratulate the sweet return of morn.
Nor yet, amidst this joy and brightest morn,
440   Was absent, after all his mischief done,
The Prince of Darkness; glad would also seem
Of this fair change, and to our Saviour came;
Yet with no new device (they all were spent),
Rather by this his last affront resolved,
Desperate of better course, to vent his rage
And mad despite to be so oft repelled.
Him walking on a sunny hill he found,
Backed on the north and west by a thick wood;
Out of the wood he starts in wonted shape,
450   And in a careless mood thus to him said:—
"Fair morning yet betides thee, Son of God,
After a dismal night. I heard the wrack,
As earth and sky would mingle; but myself
Was distant; and these flaws, though mortals fear them,
As dangerous to the pillared frame of Heaven,
Or to the Earth's dark basis underneath,
Are to the main as inconsiderable
And harmless, if not wholesome, as a sneeze
To man's less universe, and soon are gone.
460   Yet, as being ofttimes noxious where they light
On man, beast, plant, wasteful and turbulent,
Like turbulencies in the affairs of men,
Over whose heads they roar, and seem to point,
They oft fore-signify and threaten ill.
This tempest at this desert most was bent;

Of men at thee, for only thou here dwell'st.
Did I not tell thee, if thou didst reject
The perfect season offered with my aid
To win thy destined seat, but wilt prolong
470   All to the push of fate, pursue thy way
Of gaining David's throne no man knows when
(For both the when and how is nowhere told),
Thou shalt be what thou art ordained, no doubt;
For Angels have proclaimed it, but concealing
The time and means? Each act is rightliest done
Not when it must, but when it may be best.
If thou observe not this, be sure to find
What I foretold thee—many a hard assay
Of dangers, and adversities, and pains,
480   Ere thou of Israel's sceptre get fast hold;
Whereof this ominous night that closed thee round,
So many terrors, voices, prodigies,
May warn thee, as a sure foregoing sign."
So talked he, while the Son of God went on,
And staid not, but in brief him answered thus:—
"Me worse than wet thou find'st not; other harm
Those terrors which thou speak'st of did me none.
I never feared they could, though noising loud
And threatening nigh: what they can do as signs
490   Betokening or ill-boding I contemn
As false portents, not sent from God, but thee;
Who, knowing I shall reign past thy preventing,
Obtrud'st thy offered aid, that I, accepting,
At least might seem to hold all power of thee,
Ambitious Spirit! and would'st be thought my God;
And storm'st, refused, thinking to terrify
Me to thy will! Desist (thou art discerned,
And toil'st in vain), nor me in vain molest."
To whom the Fiend, now swoln with rage, replied:—
500   "Then hear, O Son of David, virgin-born!

For Son of God to me is yet in doubt.
Of the Messiah I have heard foretold
By all the Prophets; of thy birth, at length
Announced by Gabriel, with the first I knew,
And of the angelic song in Bethlehem field,
On thy birth-night, that sung thee Saviour born.
From that time seldom have I ceased to eye
Thy infancy, thy childhood, and thy youth,
Thy manhood last, though yet in private bred;

510 Till, at the ford of Jordan, whither all
Flocked to the Baptist, I among the rest
(Though not to be baptized), by voice from Heaven
Heard thee pronounced the Son of God beloved.
Thenceforth I thought thee worth my nearer view
And narrower scrutiny, that I might learn
In what degree or meaning thou art called
The Son of God, which bears no single sense.
The Son of God I also am, or was;
And, if I was, I am; relation stands:

520 All men are Sons of God; yet thee I thought
In some respect far higher so declared.
Therefore I watched thy footsteps from that hour,
And followed thee still on to this waste wild,
Where, by all best conjectures, I collect
Thou art to be my fatal enemy.
Good reason, then, if I beforehand seek
To understand my adversary, who
And what he is; his wisdom, power, intent;
By parle or composition, truce or league,

530 To win him, or win from him what I can.
And opportunity I here have had
To try thee, sift thee, and confess have found thee
Proof against all temptation, as a rock
Of adamant and as a centre, firm
To the utmost of mere man both wise and good,

Not more; for honours, riches, kingdoms, glory,
Have been before contemned, and may again.
Therefore, to know what more thou art than man,
Worth naming the Son of God by voice from Heaven,
540   Another method I must now begin."
So saying, he caught him up, and, without wing
Of hippogrif, bore through the air sublime,
Over the wilderness and o'er the plain,
Till underneath them fair Jerusalem,
The Holy City, lifted high her towers,
And higher yet the glorious Temple reared
Her pile, far off appearing like a mount
Of alablaster, topt with golden spires:
There, on the highest pinnacle, he set
550   The Son of God, and added thus in scorn:—
"There stand, if thou wilt stand; to stand upright
Will ask thee skill. I to thy Father's house
Have brought thee, and highest placed: highest is best.
Now shew thy progeny; if not to stand,
Cast thyself down. Safely, if Son of God;
For it is written, 'He will give command
Concerning thee to his Angels; in their hands
They shall uplift thee, lest at any time
Thou chance to dash thy foot against a stone.'"
560   To whom thus Jesus: "Also it is written,
'Tempt not the Lord thy God.'" He said, and stood;
But Satan, smitten with amazement, fell.
As when Earth's son, Antaeus (to compare
Small things with greatest), in Irassa strove
With Jove's Alcides, and, oft foiled, still rose,
Receiving from his mother Earth new strength,
Fresh from his fall, and fiercer grapple joined,
Throttled at length in the air expired and fell,
So, after many a foil, the Tempter proud,
570   Renewing fresh assaults, amidst his pride